Like soaring gu   girl
Pierrette hovered h   of
an island. "Follow n   rill
voice. She tilted he

Pierrette knew where she was—the kingdom known
as the Fortunate Isles, pulled from the realm of time's
passage by the sorcerer-king Minho more than two
thousand years before, when the empire of the Cretan
Bull was buried in flaming ash and flowing lava. Her
hard-working seagull's heart lightened. *Ma*'s task could
not be too terrible: Minho was handsome and charming. "Marry me!" he had begged her twice before. "Rule
with me, and never grow old."

They glided down on silent wings. She glimpsed a
crowd in the outer court, all kneeling. Before them
stood a man with the head of a great horned bull. The
Bull of Minos, the high priest.

Now the taurine man emerged in the smaller courtyard, letting the bronze door swing shut behind him.
He tossed his white robe aside with a relieved sigh, and
lifted the hollow horned head from his shoulders.

Minho. Pierrette's seagull heart altered its rhythm.
An anxious rustle of *Ma*'s feathers warned her not to
reveal herself. "Come," said the goddess.

Pierrette opened deep blue, altogether human eyes,
and saw the cool shadows of beech branches reflected
in the sacred pool.

"Will you remember everything you have seen?"
asked the goddess, again a crone in worn, frayed wool.
"You must remember, because your task is to find that
place, and that man. You must set foot on Minho's soil
in the real world, and you in the flesh. Find the Isles
and their king, and then . . ."

"Yes? And then?"

"Then," said the goddess, "you must destroy his kingdom and he must die."

BAEN BOOKS BY L. WARREN DOUGLAS

Simply Human

The Sacred Pool
The Veil of Years
The Isle Beyond Time

THE ISLE
BEYOND TIME

L. WARREN DOUGLAS

THE ISLE BEYOND TIME

This is a work of fiction. All the characters and events portrayed in this book are fictional, and any resemblance to real people or incidents is purely coincidental.

A Baen Books Original

Baen Publishing Enterprises
P.O. Box 1403
Riverdale, NY 10471
www.baen.com

ISBN: 0-7434-3598-2

Cover art by Dominic Harman

First printing, March 2003

Distributed by Simon & Schuster
1230 Avenue of the Americas
New York, NY 10020

Production by Windhaven Press, Auburn, NH
Printed in the United States of America

TABLE OF CONTENTS

Part One—Dusk 1

Prologue 3
Chapter 1—The Goddess Commands 5
Chapter 2—The Scholar Demands 13
Chapter 3—An Old Ghost Importunes 21

Part Two—Darkness 39
Chapter 4—A Journey Begins 41
Chapter 5—Beggars and Sacred Whores 49
Chapter 6—Of Bishops and Priests 59
Chapter 7—The Pagan Tale 77
Chapter 8—A Christian Tale 83
Chapter 9—The Last Tale 93
Chapter 10—An Anomalous Vision 107
Chapter 11—Darkness from the Land 115
Chapter 12—A Close Call 121
Chapter 13—The Burning City 129
Chapter 14—Strange Houses 137
Chapter 15—Lovi's Confusion 143
Chapter 16—Moridunnon 149
Chapter 17—A Deadly Companion 169
Chapter 18—The Boatman 179
Chapter 19—The Isle of the Dead 193
Chapter 20—The Storm-wracked Sea 213
Chapter 21—An Improbable Encounter 223
Chapter 22—Gesocribate 239
Chapter 23—Lovi's Choices 249

Part Three—Dawn 265
    Chapter 24—The Long Voyage Ends 267
    Chapter 25—An Inauspicious Welcome 277
    Chapter 26—The Sorceror-King 285
    Chapter 27—An Imperfect Vision 319
    Chapter 28—Black Metal and Bronze 329
    Chapter 29—An Attraction of Opposites 341
    Chapter 30—The Not-So-Fortunate Isles 351
    Chapter 31—The Ancient Child 367

Part Four—A New Day 375
    Chapter 32—The Fall of the Kingdom 377
    Chapter 33—The Way Home 409

Epilogue 425
Afterword 427

Acknowledgments

Dave Feintuch, for reading and criticizing an early manuscript and making suggestions. Leo Frankowski, for scathing criticism of the last chapters, as I had written them, and for thus saving the climax of the trilogy, and saving Pierrette from unbearable guilt.

Alain Bonifaci and Nathalie Bernard, Hotel Cardinal, 24 Rue Cardinale, Aix-en-Provence, France, *pour une chambre jolie et confortable, et un gai "bonjour" chaque matin.* And Alain, for the *tarasque.*

The French people for the preservation of so many antiquities among which we may, on certain magical occasions, part the Veil of Years.

Sue, as always, for everything. Celeste Anne and Emma Sue, of course, just for being warm and furry.

Dedication

For Sue E. Folkringa, my wife, my friend and companion on all the trails and byways of Provence, and wherever else the endless quest may lead us.

Part One ∽ Dusk

Prologue

The land is vast and ancient, and has many faces. Once it was Gaul, center of the Celtic lands that stretched from Anatolia to Hibernia, linked by a common ancestry, a single speech, and by the machinations of its scholarly caste, the *druidae*.

Already, in the days of Our Lord, it had fragmented. Gauls spoke Latin, Gaels Celtic, and Galatians Greek. They all worshipped gods with different names. Only when they accepted Christianity was there a new commonality within the Celtic realm.

Now, eight centuries later, northern Gaul is called Francia, and is ruled by a coarse Germanic king. East is Burgundia, west the Occitain lands, and here is Provence, my own sunny country. All exist beneath the Frankish mantle.

But names and kingdoms are deceptive; beneath the differences beats an ancient heart, and the rhythmically surging blood of the land is not Germanic alone, but Roman, Greek, Phoenician, and Celtic. Here and there are currents of an earlier strain, too, a small dark-haired people sprung from the earth itself, from dirt, rock, and the waters of the sacred pools.

This is a tale of a woman of that old blood, a devotee of *Ma*, the most ancient goddess of mountain springs and forest pools, from whose name come words for breast, for female horse, and for mother. It is the tale of the last priestess of the most ancient faith, whom the unenlightened call a sorceress.

Otho, Bishop of Nemausus
The Sorceress's Tale

Chapter 1 ∾ The Goddess Commands

Old skinny fingers stirred the dark water of the mossy pool. Old eyes peered into the dancing, sparkling ripples at a scene from the Christians' Hell: towers of iron loomed above a dead sea, their tops blazing with oily, stinking light. Strung like unseemly garlands from one shadowy edifice to another, fading only with distance, were harsh, unblinking stars.

Black smoke billowed like a greasy cremation, staining the slate-gray sky. No sun cast shadows upon the lifeless land.

"The Black Time comes," the hag intoned, and then: "From least beginnings forward creeps the dark, and reaches backward from the world's demise; the Wheel of Time is broken—naught forfends." She spat upon the water, and the ugly vision faded. Again, the sacred pool was clear and cold, fresh from the depths of the earth.

Stark hills protected the moist, green sanctuary on three sides, so the drying winds slipped by overhead. Such places were rare in Provence, where tiny-leaved scrub oaks, gnarled olives, and coastal pines prevailed. They were magical places, providing what the broader land did not: sweet water and shady refuge.

The goddess *Ma* arose gracefully, for all her great age, and brushed dry beech leaves from her patched homespun skirt. She paced impatiently from mossy boulder to great gray-trunked beech, from rough-barked maple to lissome sapling, covering in half an hour the length and breadth of her holy grove. "Where is that girl?"

The old woman paced and muttered. Even when a slight, dark-haired girl ascended the steep path from the abandoned Roman fountain, *Ma's* complaints did not lessen; the girl Pierrette was not really *there*—not yet.

Ma watched her settle in a soft hollow upholstered with crinkly leaves, beneath a sapling no thicker than her slender calf. Yan Oors, an aging Celtic demigod, had planted the tree, when Pierrette was only five. Yan believed the tree was the girl's mother, magically transformed by a spell gone awry.

Pierrette crumbled blue-and-yellow flowers in her palm, then picked a small red-brown mushroom. She ate flowers and fungus at once, grimaced, then washed the bitter taste away with a cupped handful of springwater. She lay down, closing her eyes, waiting for sensation to fade from her hands and feet: waiting to fly . . .

❖   ❖   ❖

On magpie's wings she fluttered down among the branches, beneath the speckling leaf shadows, and alit beside the old woman. Her iridescent green, black, and white feathers blurred, and became a black wool skirt, a white chemise, and a watery green silk sash. Now a clear jewel veined with red and blue, a Gaulish priestess's "serpent's egg," hung from a string at her waist, glowing with ruddy, internal light, like embers or the eye of a demon.

"Where have you been?" snapped *Ma*. "I have a task for you."

Goddesses' wishes and human ones seldom jibed, and Pierrette had no reason to welcome such words. She wrapped her arms around herself, feeling a sudden chill.

"You won't like it at all," *Ma* said, confirming the girl's silent unease.

"Show me," Pierrette said. "Let me make up my own mind."

The goddess knelt by the pool's edge, and Pierrette lowered herself to the mossy verge. *Ma* roiled the water, and again an image formed beneath the ripples . . .

Like soaring gulls, goddess and girl hovered high above the black, jutting crags of an island, a truncated volcanic cone awash in waves. It was a great ring many miles in extent, and leaden swells broke against it. Lashing winds swept away a froth of white spume.

"Follow me," *Ma* commanded in a gull's shrill voice. She tilted her wings and dropped swiftly toward the scarps and across . . . into a world unsuspected from outside. Ring after ring of concentric islands lay within a serene, deep blue lagoon, remnants of eruptions and explosions millennia past. Verdant forests clothed the inner slopes of the immense caldera. A patchwork of green, gold, and russet fields covered the islands like the plaid of a fine Gaulish cloak. Houses of imported marble lay scattered like handsful of dice across cultivated land and pasture, linked by the threads of roads and lanes.

Pierrette knew where she was—the kingdom known as the Fortunate Isles, pulled from the realm of time's passage by the sorcerer-king Minho more than two thousand years before, when the empire of the Cretan Bull was buried in flaming ash and flowing lava.

Her hard-working seagull's heart lightened. *Ma's* task could not be too terrible: Minho was handsome and charming. Though she had never seen him in the flesh, she was in love with him. "Marry me!" he had begged her twice before. "Rule with me, and never grow old." She remembered herself seated on a throne next to Minho's own. She was laughing, calling upon Taranis, god of thunderstorms, to roil the waters of Minho's placid sea, commanding winds to shake his pear and olive trees, which bore fruit regardless of season. From her fingertips sparked lightning bolts that rose to dance among the swelling clouds . . . She had been only five, when she had that vision. It had not really happened—yet.

At fourteen, testing her expanding skill at magic, she visited Minho again, arriving on a vessel made of clouds, clothing herself in mist and vapor, moonbeams and the green and gold of spring irises. That time, she begged the king to free her mentor, the mage Anselm, from the spell that held him trapped in his keep atop the cliffs of the Eagle's beak. Again, Minho had offered her his kingdom, and again, she refused—but his stolen kiss had remained on her virgin lips. Too distraught to recreate her vehicle from the clouds and mists, she had fled on familiar magpie's wings.

Now, eager to see Minho again, she swept over the central island, a flat-topped cone, toward the swelling black-and-vermilion columns of his palace.

"Wait!" screeched *Ma*, winging in front of her. "Don't alert the king of our presence."

"But I want to see him . . ."

"You will. But he must not see you. I brought you here to refresh your memory, not to make sheep's eyes with him. Come. We'll land on the parapet of the inner courtyard."

Puzzled and disappointed, Pierrette acquiesced. They glided down on silent wings, onto the painted tiles. Below, a fountain bubbled and splashed, its ripples blurring the shapes on the pool's bottom— sleek dolphins and sinuous octopi portrayed in obsidian, jasper, and cobalt glass.

She had glimpsed a crowd in the outer court, colorfully dressed merchants, plain farmers, and white-robed temple acolytes all kneeling, their foreheads against the smooth cobbled pavement. Before them stood a man with the head of a great horned bull. Its eyes were rubies set in ivory, the horns leafed in gold, and from its nostrils gushed the smoke of sweet incense. Minos-tauros. The Bull of Minos, the high priest.

Now the taurine man emerged in the smaller,

more intimate courtyard, letting the bronze door
swing shut behind him. He tossed his white robe
aside with a relieved sigh, and lifted the hollow
horned head from his shoulders.

Minho. His hair was glossy black, oiled and
curled in the Cretan style of an ancient age. He
was clad only in a black kilt, cut longer in back
than in front. When he stretched, athlete's muscles
rippled beneath bronzed skin. He eased himself
onto a heap of cushions set beside the splashing
water, his forehead beaded with sweat from the
heat inside the bull's-head mask. He wiped drop-
lets from his raptorial nose, and let tired eyelids
droop over dark, warm, penetrating eyes.

Pierrette's seagull heart altered its rhythm. An
anxious rustle of *Ma*'s feathers warned her not to
reveal herself.

"Come," said the goddess. She leaped into the
air and coasted away from the wall, so the sound
of flapping wings would not disturb the king's slum-
ber.

Pierrette opened deep blue, altogether-human
eyes, and saw the cool shadows of beech branches
reflected in the sacred pool.

"Will you remember everything you have seen?"
asked the goddess, again a crone in worn, frayed
wool.

"How could I forget?"

"People remember what they think serves them,
and forget the rest. You must remember, because
your task is to find that place, and that man."

"I can find him anytime. We've just been there."

"That was a vision. Here you are flesh—human,

not an ephemeral gull. You must go there not on magical wings, but on your own feet. You must find the Theran king, and then . . ."

"I don't know how to reach the Fortunate Isles, except through the Otherworld, where we are now. Where we always meet."

"You may seek them however you wish—but when you set foot on Minho's soil, it must be in the real world, and you in the flesh. That is your task. Find the Isles and their king, and then . . ."

"Yes? And then?"

"Then," said the goddess, "you must destroy his kingdom, and he must die."

Chapter 2 ∾ The Scholar Demands

Below lay Citharista, once a Roman port. Now, centuries after Rome's fall, it was a crumbling fishing village. On the far side jutted Eagle Cape, three rounded scarps that, from the sea, resembled a raptor's head. High atop the crest, the walls of the so-called "Saracen fort" were silhouetted against the bright, blue afternoon sky. Saracens had not built the fort; the *magus* Anselm had lived there since Caligula's reign.

Pierrette had no eye for scenery. Kill Minho? The vision of herself on a throne beside the king had sustained her since her lonely, half-orphaned childhood. When she learned everything about magic, when the threat of the Black Time was ended, she would wed the handsome king. Kill him? She could sooner slay her toothless father. And the goddess had given her no idea how she was to accomplish the task, anyway. How was she, hardly out of childhood, a sorceress more at home with theory (after eons of study, of course) than with the actual practices of spells, to kill so mighty a sorceror? Angrily, she spat strong words . . . and a brushy oak beside the path shrivelled, and dropped its leaves, all brown and dry where a moment before they had been green. Then, relenting, she uttered a softer spell, but did not wait to see its results. Had anyone been following her, a few hundred paces or so behind, they might have seen the first tiny green buds appear above the scars where leaf stems had been. Or maybe not. What people saw wasn't always real, despite their eyes, and what they didn't see was sometimes no less an illusion.

Pierrette stumbled past the overgrown Roman fountain, through rocky pastures, and out into the valley, passing ancient olive trees without seeing them, without waving at the men and women in the fields or nodding to the soldier standing watch at Citharista's rotting gate.

She passed her father's house, and only drew herself up sharply in front of the wine shop. Two finely saddled horses were hitched there, and two laden mules. What rich strangers had arrived? She caught a glimpse of a blond head of hair: a tall Frankish boy was checking one mule's lashings. It was the scholar ibn Saul's apprentice, Lovi.

Pierrette backed away. The mysterious ibn Saul, who voyaged extensively and wrote of his travels, was drinking wine with Anselm and her father, Gilles. Neither the scholar nor his apprentice had seen Pierrette except disguised as a boy; even now, almost sixteen, she could still pass for a boy of twelve. Perhaps a small spell made people look less closely than otherwise.

She slipped away to her father's house, where she kept odds and ends of clothing. She did not want to reveal her true self to them. Once Lovi, though believing her male, had been attracted to her, and had distanced himself from his uncomfortable desires by accusing her of being Anselm's catamite, not his apprentice. That rankled still, and it was all the same to her if Lovi were to continue to suffer the barbs both of desire and of confusion about his own nature.

The back room of the small, two-room dwelling was windowless and dark. Pierrette could have lit the lamp—a wick of twisted lint in a shallow bowl of oil—with a flick of her fingers. Her firelighting spell was the first she had ever learned, and she didn't even have to murmur the proper incantation for it to work. But magic, even small magic, was unreliable. The thrust of her studies with Anselm had been to codify the complex rules that underlay its unpredictability. What she now knew was that a spell written in one era, in one language, might have different results in other times and tongues. She had learned that ranges of high hills, rivers, and even great stone roads separate the realms of different magics. No spells worked at all in the highest places, or afloat—except on the open sea—or on a Roman road. But in the Camargue, the delta of River Rhodanus, a magical place where dry land graded imperceptibly into a sea of reeds and then open water, where the water was neither entirely fresh nor salt, and ocean creatures rubbed shoulders with upland fish from the streams, her small firemaking spell had once started a conflagration.

Spells, like geometric theorems, owed their utility to the validity of their axioms—those unprovable, irreducible assumptions that underlay them. When people's beliefs changed, so did those assumptions, and so did spells' results. Pierrette no longer uttered such dangerous words casually. She took the time instead to allow her eyes to adjust to the gloom. . . .

When she stepped from the house, it was as a shabby boy with dirty bare toes, worn *bracae*—short trousers—and tunic, and a conical leather hat. The hat concealed long, black hair bound in a tight bun. Townsfolk who passed glanced at Piers with only ordinary interest.

At the tavern, that changed. Lovi was seated with the three older men, a disparate grouping. His eyes bored into her. He was, thought Piers, quite attractive. Perhaps her opinion showed, for his scowl deepened.

Muhammad abd' Ullah ibn Saul was tall, and as skinny as a post. Gold threads gleamed at the hem and sleeves of his tunic, watery silk lined his dark travelling cloak, and his hair was concealed within a tightly wound cloth fixed with an emerald-encrusted fibula. His beard was curled and oiled.

Gilles, Pierrette's father, back from a morning at sea, wore only a ragged kilt, and reeked of fish, salt, and seaweed. His few teeth were yellowed or brown.

Anselm's white hair and bushy beard, threaded with black, were only slightly darker than his robe, a shapeless drape worn in the Roman style long out of fashion.

Gilles addressed his child appropriately: "I was looking for you, Piers. You weren't in the olive grove."

"I was out walking," she replied noncommittally. It would not do for ibn Saul to hear of the sacred pool: he would want to see it, and then perhaps to write of what he saw—what he did not see. He would not write of the goddess, or of visions in the water, but only of moss, trees, and cool air, and if he wrote it, there would be no more goddess, and no more visions, for the written words of a disbeliever were a spell of their own, that destroyed magic before the ink dried on the page.

"I'm glad you're here, boy," said Anselm, seamlessly continuing Gilles's deception. "My friend Muhammad has a proposition that might interest you." His voice was easy, but Pierrette read tension in the lines around his eyes.

"I am planning an expedition in search of a land unvisited for centuries," the scholar said. "Anselm claims you have read every history written, and might know where I should begin. The place consists of islands, and your father assures me that you're handy aboard a boat. Will you accompany me?" As always, ibn Saul treated her as a colleague, an equal, and not an unbearded boy—much to Lovi's discontent.

Anselm's unease made her cautious. "I'm interested enough to listen," she said. "Does this place have a name?"

"The Hibernian Brendan called it 'The Fortunate Isles.'"

Pierrette paled. Minho's kingdom. First *Ma*, now the geographer. Could that be coincidence? Twice before, she had felt compelled to follow a course of action when events pushed her from behind and pulled her ahead, giving her no choice. Each time, she had resisted, but in the end had done what was required of her when things went from irritating to unpleasant to intolerable.

If she helped ibn Saul to find the Fortunate Isles, Minho would be ill served: he would be forever wrapped in the geographer's scroll. Did the goddess mean for her to "kill" the sorcerer-king by exposing him to the unbeliever's eyes?

She must be cautious, and not reveal anything. "Aren't they near the mouth of the River Baetis, where Tartessos stood before it sank into the morass?"

"They *were* once there," said ibn Saul. "They were also among the southern Kyklades in an earlier age still—and they disappeared in the great upheaval that destroyed the Sea People, the Atalantans ruled by Minos the Bull."

"I've heard of that," Pierrette said, searching for neutral ground. "The Hebrews recorded the islands' convulsion as a pillar of fire by night, and smoke by day. But volcanoes are natural events, even ones that blanket whole kingdoms in ash. I wouldn't have thought you interested in chasing disappearing islands."

"The plagues that preceded your pillars of smoke and fire were real enough, as was the recession of the sea, and its resurgence in a great wave that destroyed Pharaoh's army. The walls of cities still stand beneath the sea off Crete, and on the island's other side, the wharves are miles inland. The whole island tilted. The Greek Theseus was only able to conquer Knossos and slay the bull-king because there was nothing left with which to defend the kingdom. All was buried in ash. Those things are real."

"Of course they are," she agreed, "but they can be explained as natural results of a great cataclysm. Nothing in the histories indicates that the so-called 'Fortunate Isles' still exist, or that Brendan was not mistaken."

"There are too many tales," countered ibn Saul. "The Isles were seen near Tartessos, beyond the Pillars of Herakles, and at the mouth of the Gold River in furthest Africa. Each time and place, the lands nearby flourished, and great civilizations arose there. There must be some truth to the tales. I intend to find out what it is."

Pierrette made a skeptical moue. "And where are those civilizations today? Gone, destroyed and forgotten. And if the islands can move from one sea to another, how do you propose to find them? Where are they now?"

"You can help answer that."

"Master, have you gone mad? Ibn Saul is the last person in the world you want to find your homeland!" Pierrette and Anselm were alone on the steep trail to his keep, even now looming up at the top of the crumbling red marl scarp called the Eagle's Beak. Dry but salty sea breezes swept the sweat from their brows as soon as it formed, and caused the graceful umbrella pines shadowing the path to sigh and rustle.

"He's my friend! He'll help me to go home at last."

"He'll destroy your 'home' as if it never existed—in truth, it will never *have* existed."

Anselm claimed to have come from the Fortunate Isles at Minho's bidding, his task to subvert the nascent Christian faith by suborning its leaders. Now, hundreds of years later, his failure was obvious: churches stood in every town, shrines at every crossroad, and the old gods and goddesses were only worshipped by a secretive few. But Anselm's magic had kept him alive, and he had taught Pierrette what he knew.

If ibn Saul destroyed Minho's kingdom with his skepticism, then the destruction of Thera—Atalanta—would indeed have been only a volcanic explosion, and Anselm would never have existed. Then what of his apprentice? Would she be a village girl without gift or talent, pregnant with her second or third child?

The goddess's motivation became clear: if Minho died *before* the scholar could translate the wonders of his magical kingdom into something prosaic and ordinary, his legend and magic would live on. Ibn Saul could not find what no longer existed—but which *had* existed. That was why she had to kill the king.

"Oh, come!" said her master. "Things can't be that bad."

"You're probably right," she lied.

Chapter 3 ∿ An Old Ghost Importunes

While Lovi and ibn Saul enjoyed the late afternoon and evening in Citharista, Pierrette buried herself among Anselm's scrolls. She was not concerned that the scholar would grow impatient waiting for her answer, because the sun that painted the blue tiles of her master's library stood always at high noon. Within the influence of the sorcerer's magic, time lay bound, always the same clear, early spring day on which the spell had first been cast, centuries before. She could study books, maps, and scrolls for a year or a decade between ibn Saul's one sip of wine and the next. The spell was a trivial application of the greater one that Minho used to keep his island kingdom forever peaceful and green, and himself eternally young and virile.

Anselm, less skilled than his erstwhile master, could not maintain the appearance of black-haired youth, even here within his keep, unless he concentrated on it. But he did not grow older here, nor did she, and, if she stayed here for a decade, she would not have to take up the goddess's burden, because outside not a single hour would pass. But that only put the day of reckoning off. It solved nothing. Kill Minho? She might prefer to die herself.

Pierrette was not looking for clues to the present location of the mysterious island kingdom. She knew where it had been last year, and she doubted Minho had moved it since . . .

Tracing a route on the map unrolled on her table, she envisioned herself cushioned upon a westward-drifting cloud, observing vast forests passing by below. The river Sequana was a thread of silver. Soon flat, forested land gave way to the rough, dark hills of Armorica, where a Celtic Breton king still ruled and hairy Vikings howled at the borders. Ahead, great Ocean was a vast plate of tarnished silver.

Not for the first time, Pierrette wondered what lay on its far side. The world was known to be a great sphere, and Eratosthenes of Cyrene had calculated that its circumference was six times the breadth of the known world, from Hibernia to the Indus. Were there whole continents to be discovered beyond the horizon?

The edge of the land was beneath her finger now—spines of brown, barren rock reaching like two westward-groping fingers. Between were the wave-washed ruins of a city. In a century or two, they would be gone, pounded to sand by the heaving, frothing surf, the racing tides.

Pierrette shook her head to clear it. Had she

slept, or merely daydreamed? Her head had been
resting on the map, and there, beneath her finger,
was the city whose ruins she had seen: Ys, the
northernmost outpost of Phoenicia, abandoned
when Carthage's empire fell to Scipio Africanus—
the latest of those great civilizations now turned
to dust.

Her fingers traced a westward course from Ys
across the Bay of Trespasses, past the terrible tidal
race that had claimed a thousand ships. There,
beyond the tip of land's extended finger, was Sena,
the island of the dead. There *druidae* had borne
the bodies of heroes, and there nine *Gallicenae*,
sacred virgins, once sang over long rows of druids' graves.

Did the maidens still sing? The druids were long
gone; they had trusted their religion and philosophy only to the memories of men, knowing full well
the dangers of writing them down. It took nineteen years to memorize even the basics, and when
the druids had been hunted first by Caesar's
Romans, then by Christians, there had been no time
to learn. Now the last graduates of the druidic
schools were dead.

Perhaps the *Gallicenae* were gone, and Sena was
uninhabited even by ghosts. Or else they lingered
like poor Yan Oors, John of the Bears, his ferocious
companions faded to shadows with glowing eyes,
his staff—iron forged from a fallen star—now dull
and rusty.

Her finger continued westward to the very edge
of the parchment, and then beyond. *"There,"*
Pierrette whispered. "There, beyond the
edge . . . the Fortunate Isles."

Did she want to find the Fortunate Isles, in person? That was like asking if she wanted to marry a handsome man, to be rich and powerful, sit on an ivory throne and use the great forces of nature as toys, to amuse herself. Hadn't she wanted that all along? Wasn't that the culmination of all her years of study in this timeless place—to learn the postulates and theorems of magic, the knowledge that would make her a true sorceress? And wasn't Minho the last of the ancient sorcerers, the world-shapers, who remembered what magic had once been, and what it might—again—become?

Ma had to be wrong—there had to be another way to preserve the legend of the Fortunate Isles. Only half in this universe, and half in another, could not Minho just complete the separation—if his kingdom existed entirely in that other world, it would disappear from this one. Wouldn't that encompass its "destruction" in every sense that mattered?

But, she mused uncomfortably, if she were queen of such a kingdom, she would not be able to come back here, would she? She would have to give up everything. Minho's library would surely be better than Anselm's, and would have ancient sources from the dawn of time, books that had been burned at Alexandria and were now lost. But it would not have . . . Anselm. And it would not be a short hour's walk from sunny Citharista's docks, where her father's fishing boat waited, or from the ancient olive grove where she had spent so many seasons with Gilles and her sister Marie, pruning and harvesting . . .

She was suddenly overwhelmed with visions of

all that she would lose if she took that course. Never to visit Marie in her peaceful convent in Massalia, a short day's sail to the west? Never again to lie dozing in the dappled sunlight, the cool, moist shadows of the sacred grove? Never to visit again the sprite Guihen in the high woods, or ponder the contorted white stones of the hill country that people said were the bleached bones of dragons slain long ago?

There had to be another way—a way to save Minho's kingdom, to fulfill her vision, and yet not to have to give up everything else. But to find out, she had to do as *Ma* commanded—go there, in this world, not in vision alone. And that would not be easy. Armorica was far away, and she did not think she could get there alone. That meant ibn Saul, and Lovi—but the risk to Minho and his kingdom was great, if she acquiesced to that. She wasn't ready to say "yes" to the scholar. Not yet.

When villagers came to beg infusions, concoctions, or magical aid from the *magus* Anselm, they rang the small silver bell in the niche by the portal. Then the mage or his apprentice came down the long stairway and let them in. Villagers did not knock. Above all, they did not beat upon the door, as with a great hammer, until the walls within seemed to tremble, and dust motes danced in time with the blows.

"Yan Oors!" she exclaimed as the door swung open. The gaunt face was like old leather, riven with crevices that held every shadow. His clothing was black and dirty brown: a wooly tunic and a kilt overlain with *pteruges*, brass-trimmed leather straps like Roman soldiers had once worn. His hands and feet were gnarly as old cypress roots, and thick with black hair. His teeth were very big, very yellow, with gaps between them.

How far the ancient ones had fallen! Once Yan had been a brave boy who had slain giants and dragons, and had married a grateful chatelaine, becoming himself a king—or so the tales said. Once, long before that, Gauls had called him "Father of Animals," and had worshipped him as a forest god—or so said *Ma*, the goddess. But his last worshippers were long dead and he clung to existence only by virtue of the beliefs of ignorant villagers who feared the thumping of his iron staff in the night. Yan Oors had been around since she was a tiny child, chiding her when she was stubborn, comforting her when she was sad or afraid. He, too, was of this universe—at least most of the time—and would be lost to her if . . .

"Hello, little witch," he rumbled. "Are you going to let me in?"

"Why . . . of course. But you've never come inside before. What has changed?"

"Nothing has. And that is why I'm here. You have maps, don't you? I need to see them."

"Maps? What are you looking for—and why?"

"You once brought me back from the brink of dissolution, and you taught me to stalk the night, to make frightening noises with my staff, and to moan like a *fantôme*, a Gaulish ghost. People heard me—and they believed, and because of that I still live. But my bears are still wraiths without substance. Nothing I have done has changed that. I want to go back where I first found them, long ago, and catch two newborn cubs of their lineage, for their souls to inhabit."

"Will that work?"

"If the cubs are young enough—before their mother licks them, and their proper souls come. And if a sorceress is there to murmur just the right words, at the right moment."

"A sorceress? You want me to go with you?" He nodded gravely. She said neither yes nor no. "Come in." She led him up the dark stairway, to a landing where a great door stood ajar. The library. The walls were lined with books, scrolls, codices, and stacks of papyrus, vellum, even the new "paper" made with lint. "There are many maps here," she said. "How will you know where to start looking?"

"Here," said Yan Oors. She turned. He was not looking at the shelves, but at the table—at the map she had left there. His big finger traced a path down the river Liger to its mouth, then north past a big island, to a cape that jutted westward into the endless sea. "That is where my bears come from," he said. "That is where we'll go." And there, off the end of that point, lay Sena Island, the isle of the dead, and beyond that, hidden behind veils of fog, mist, and confusion also lay . . . the Fortunate Isles.

"As long as you're here," Anselm remarked to Yan Oors, "I could use your strong back."

Yan was indeed very strong. He wielded his iron staff (forged in the heat of the Mother's breath from metal fallen from the sky) as if it were a splinter of pine. "What is it this time? Have you found a fulcrum on which I can place my staff, to move the earth itself?" That was an old joke between old friends.

"Hmmph. You may not be far off. Perhaps the earth has moved. Help me hoist my pendulum, and we shall see. The new rope it is suspended from has stretched." Yan and Pierrette followed him down several flights of stairs. At the bottom of the many-storied stairwell was a bed of sand edged with black stone. At dead center was a great stone ball, once suspended from a beam far above, but now resting in the sand.

"Why did you lead me down here, Mage?" asked Yan. "I'm not going to lift that stone while you retie the rope, and the mechanism to tighten it is way up there."

"Oh, yes—silly of me. Well, let's go up, then."

At the top of the stairwell a great, round oak beam rested in hornbeam cradles. Pierrette surveyed the beam, the holes around its circumference where it projected beyond the cradles, and the notches where counterweighted bronze dogs lodged, keeping the rope that wound around the beam from unwinding. The holes looked exactly sized to fit the diameter of Yan Oors' iron staff— but that was surely a coincidence.

Yan, when so instructed, stuck one end of the staff in a hole, so it rested at an angle more than halfway to the vertical, and then put his weight on the opposite end. The beam turned, the dogs clacked into new notches, and the rope tightened. "Good!" said Anselm. "Now again." Yan Oors repositioned his staff, and pulled, grunting. That time, the beam turned more slowly, and the bronze dogs clacked only thrice. "Not far enough," the mage said. "The pendulum must rise clear of the sand."

"Are you sure you've calculated everything correctly?" asked the gaunt man. "Have you allowed for the weight of the stone and the length of the lever?"

"The beam's radius is one span," Anselm mused, "and the exposed portion of your staff, plus one radius, is . . ." His hand fluttered along the staff, measuring increments the distance between his outstretched little finger and his thumb . . . "Eight spans, or a little more. I'm sure the stone is no heavier than eight of you."

"There is only one of me," said Yan Oors.

"Yes, but . . ."

"Yan," said Pierrette, "put all your weight on your staff, then I'll put my foot in your scabbard-sling and add my weight to yours. If that doesn't work, we must find a longer lever." That is what they did.

"The stone is free!" exclaimed the mage. "Now, I must see if my suspicions are correct—if some fundamental constant is not."

"Is not what?" asked Yan.

"Is not constant, of course. If it has—as I suspect—changed, then it cannot be, can it? By definition, 'constant' means . . ."

"I know what it means. But just what inconstant constant are you speaking of?"

"I'll show you." He scurried down the stairs, his sandals clattering on the worn stone treads. Not for the first time, Pierrette wondered how they could be worn, in a place where people did not age, where the sun never rose or set, but was always at high noon. For that matter, if time were a "constant," why had the rope stretched, and not retained its "youthful" tension? But that was only one of many unanswered questions that had waited a long time, and would have to wait longer. She followed Yan Oors down, at his leisurely pace.

When they arrived, Anselm had raked the sand smooth, and had stretched several strings across it, secured to little wooden pegs stuck in holes in the basin's perimeter. Referring frequently to a scroll stretched out on the floor, he made marks in the sand where the cords intersected. This process took an hour—if there had been hours, within his ensorcelled keep. *If there is no time,* Pierrette mused, *then how can I be bored by its slow passage?* But at last, Anselm removed the strings.

"This is the Saxon Island, once Britannia," he said, pointing, "and here is Hibernia, there Armorica. See?" Pierrette saw, and wondered at the coincidence—that Anselm had duplicated a portion of the same map, there in the sand, that she and Yan Oors had pored over in the library.

"There"—he stuck a peg in the sand—"is the great stone circle in Saxon-land, and there"— another peg—"the lesser one. Here are similar stone rings in Hibernia, and here, another one in Armorica. Now observe." He pulled the pendulum to the edge of the stone bed. It made a mark, a line, as it moved. Pierrette deduced that there was a stylus of sorts at the bottom of it. "Smooth that out," Anselm commanded. "Careful! Don't erase anything else."

Pierrette watched Anselm align the center of the pendulum with the mark inscribed on one of the perimeter stones. For the first time she noticed several other marks that she had taken to be merely scratches. Anselm released the pendulum. "Now we wait," he said, "while it draws its patterns. Let's go on the terrace and sip wine. Is there any of that chewy bread left, Pierrette?"

The terrace was on the keep's roof, a story above the mechanism that raised the pendulum. From that height, she paused to watch the stylus drawing its curved lines in the sand.

Much later, well fed on bread, olives, and delicious fatty sausages spiced with pepper and thyme, they again descended. The pendulum, slowed by the stylus dragging in the sand, now hung motionless near the center of the bed. "See!" exclaimed Anselm. "It is not exactly over the center, as it should be. And the lines it has scribed are awry!"

"How can you tell?" growled Yan Oors. "It's only a pretty pattern in the sand."

"Once some of these lines would have intersected where I stuck those pegs in the sand. Now they are all shifted westward, and the pendulum has stopped somewhere at sea, south of the Saxon land, not over the great stone circle. And here"—he indicated a line of pegs trending north and south, on the Armorican shore—"there are great lines of stones that once matched perfectly with lines of power in the earth, but now do not."

"What lines of power are those?" asked Yan.

"The lines the pendulum has drawn—or rather, the lines in the earth that the pendulum's lines represent, on the map in the sand." There ensued a discussion of mystical lines that bound the entire earth in a web of immaterial forces, lines whose intersections marked places of great power. "They are like fulcrum points," Anselm said, "where the effect of even the weakest spell is magnified many-fold."

Pierrette had never dreamed that the fluctuating nature of magic could be as symmetrical and elegant as those lines in the sand and their intersections. But something about them did not make sense to her. "I have often watched my serpent's egg sway on its chain, and it has never described such patterns. It only swings back and forth."

"Your bauble is not heavy enough," explained the mage, "and its chain is not long enough, and besides, you did not swing it here, inside my keep, where time marches to a different pace. Outside, a similar pendulum would take a full year to come to rest, and the pattern it drew would be entirely different."

Pierrette's head swirled. A year? And here, what? Two hours? A few thousand heartbeats. But though her beating heart marked time here, as it did outside, it measured nothing relevant, because outside not a single heartbeat would have occurred. No mind could encompass the contradictions. But then, if everything made complete sense, and could be explained, there could be no magic, and the dead world of the Black Time, shown to her in the reflections of the goddess's pool, would come to be. That brought her back to a new dilemma: one strong intersection of many lines in the sand was right where the pendulum had come to rest—offshore of the last point of land, beyond Sena, where lay . . . the Fortunate Isles.

First *Ma*, then ibn Saul, then Yan Oors—and

now this. It could not be coincidence. She was not going to be able to avoid the trap. She must go there. But kill Minho? Kill the one she was promised to? No goddesses, scholars, or scary old ghosts with iron staffs could make her do that. There had to be another way.

"So all of those alignments of great stones once marked such lines of power in the earth?" asked Pierrette, after Yan Oors had departed. "And the stone circles were where several lines intersected?"

"That is how it used to be. Where possible, roads followed the lines, and even minor crossroads were concentrations of magic—expressed, of course, as shrines to this god or that." Pierrette reflected that all roads, all crossroads, had magical influence, but that a road built of stone slabs, like the Roman ones, nullified spells instead. There were obviously two separate principles at work: a trail made by human feet, that followed the course of a mysterious line of power, partook of that influence, but a road expressly constructed according to the lay of the land was subject to a different rule. She called that rule the "Law of Locks," though it applied as well to water wheels, windmills—that is, to any complex fabrication of human hands, including roads. Near such constructions, no magic worked at all.

So what did this shifting of lines mean? Was the magical nature of the entire earth rebelling against the imposition of stone roads, of mills, of doors with locks, of man-made and mechanical contrivances?

The Black Time—or so she had long suspected—was in part the result of such building: wherever the land was bound in such a reticulation of artifices, no magic worked. When men built roads, mills, canals, and cities, they augmented the natural barriers to magic, like rivers and watershed ridges, a restrictive network like the cords that bound a bale of wool.

Of course, the Black Time's coming was not driven by a single cause. When scholars like the voyager ibn Saul wrote down their prosaic "explanations" of why ancient rites and spells seemed to work, their writings, published and copied and distributed widely, were also counterspells, and destroyed a little more of the magic that had once been.

The great religions had similar effect: when the priests first named ancient gods evil, that created an anti-god they called Satan, who drew sustenance from ancient, banished spirits. Named as evil, Moloch was eaten, and Satan acquired his fiery breath; he ingested Pan and the satyrs, and his feet became cloven hooves, his legs covered in shaggy fur. When the priests named snake-legged Taranis Satan's avatar, the Devil grew a serpent's tail; when the horned Father of Animals was eaten, Satan assumed his horns.

When at last all the gods and spirits were named Evil and were consumed, then would Satan stand alone and complete. When all the magics were bound in a net of stone roads, every waterfall enslaved in a mill-race to labor turning a great wheel, every spell "explained" in a scholar's rational counterspell, then would the Black Time indeed loom near.

Even common folk contributed their share:

when a child died, and bereaved parents no longer railed at unkind fate, at the will of the sometimes-cruel gods, but called it Evil, then Satan claimed the death, and all such deaths, for himself. Where would it end? Would the Black Time only arrive when house fires, backaches, and children's sneezes and sniffles were no longer merely devastating, uncomfortable, or inconvenient, but . . . Evil? Pierrette forced herself not to think of that. Her concern was—or should be— more immediate: "Can we transpose the new lines your pendulum has drawn onto a tracing of this map? It might be useful, on my coming journey."

"Oh—then you are going?"

"Do I really have any choice?"

Pierrette traced the original map onto thin-scraped vellum, carefully labeling features of terrain, rivers, and towns. Then, again using strings stretched between the marked points on the sand basin's rim, she transferred the curving, intersecting lines in the sand onto her chart.

"Look at that!" exclaimed Anselm when he examined her work. "See those four lines that intersect just below the mountainous spine of the land of Armorica? How strange. An old friend used to live near there. I wonder if he still does?"

"Master, you haven't left the vicinity of your keep in seven or eight centuries. Your friend is surely long gone."

"Oh no—Moridunnon was a sorcerer of no mean skill. I once believed him an old god in mortal garb, so clever was he. Besides, whenever he fell asleep, he did not wake for years, even decades—and while he slept, he did not age. Will you stop there, and see him? I'll write a letter of introduction and . . ."

"Master ibn Saul has planned a more southerly itinerary for us, I think. We will follow River Rhodanus, then cross to the headwaters of the Liger, and thence downstream to the sea, where we will take ship to search for . . . your homeland."

"Surely a little excursion will not delay you much. And see? Not far from the mouth of the Liger, an earth-line marks the way. You'll have no trouble following it. I'll square it with the scholar."

"You'll do your old friend—Moridunnon?—no favor, introducing him to the skeptical ibn Saul."

"Then you go, while he makes arrangements for a ship. You'll have a week or so."

"Write the letter to Moridunnon, master. If I can deliver it, I will."

"Oh—there's something else. For you. Now where did I put it?"

"For me? What is it?"

"Your mother left it for you—or, rather, she gave it to you, when you were little, and you brought it here . . ."

"I did? I don't remember."

"Of course not. I put a spell on it. Ah! Here it is!" He pulled a tiny object from between several scrolls. "Your mother's pouch."

Suddenly, Pierrette did remember. She remembered a winding line of torches on the long trail from Citharista to the Eagle's Beak, and the terrible humming notes, sounding to a child like a dragon on the prowl, that was the Christian chant of Elen's pursuers. Elen: Pierrette's mother, a simple masc, a country-bred witch of the old Ligurian blood. She was the *gens'* scapegoat for a failed harvest, a drought . . . for whatever sins festered in them, which they would not acknowledge.

She remembered Elen shedding the spell she had hidden behind until Pierrette and Marie appeared on the trail ahead of the mob, and she remembered being taken in her mother's arms for a brief, desperate moment. "Go now!" Elen had commanded them, handing Pierrette a little leather pouch. It held something small, hard, and heavy. "Go to Anselm's keep. There, that way!" Those were the last words Pierrette's mother ever said to her.

A shadow hovered in front of Pierrette's face. She took the pouch from Anselm. Her eyes were blurred with the tears she had never before shed. Marie had wept when it was clear that their mother was gone, but not Pierrette. Little Pierrette instead made a secret vow, that she would learn all that her mother knew, and more. She would be not just a masc, but a sorceress—and then, she would have her revenge on the murderers. Only after that would she weep.

Now she understood that she would never fulfill that vow. The townspeople had created their own revenge: they walked always in the shadow of their guilt, dreading the day they would die, for Father Otho had not absolved them from their great sin. Would he do so if on their deathbeds they asked? Who knew? No, she desired no revenge, and now, remembering, she allowed the tears to course down her cheeks.

She tugged at the leather drawstring. A seam broke, and a single dark object fell in her lap. It was a ring. Her mother's ring. She held up her left hand and spread her fingers, blinking away tears, gauging where to put the ring . . .

"No! Look at it but, don't put it on!" said Anselm with great urgency. She looked. It was dark, heavy, and . . . and cold. An iron ring? There was no rust, but it could be no other metal. Now that her eyes were clear, she saw the pattern cast into it—the entwined loops and whorls of a Gallic knot, like a cord that had no beginning or end. A knot that could not be unraveled.

"What am I supposed to do with it?" she asked.

"You're a sorceress. You tell me. I just thought now was a good time for you to have it, since you're going away." He cleared his throat noisily, to conceal his sudden emotion. "I'm going to take a nap on the terrace. Don't forget to copy those maps, before you go. You may need them. Take a handful of gold coins from the jar in the anteroom. Fill your pouch. And don't go without saying good-bye." He departed abruptly, stumbling on the door sill because his own eyes were far from clear.

Part Two ∾ Darkness

Pierrette's Journal

To resolve the dilemma the goddess has given me, I must understand the nature of Minho's spell. I have always assumed that it is a special application of the principal I know as *Mondradd in Mon*, because genuine sorcery is only possible in the Otherworld, and even small magics part the veil between worlds to some elemental degree. Thus an essential, often silent, postulate of all spells is that *Mondradd in Mon* is always valid: that the Otherworld exists and can be entered.

Principles like the Conservation of Good and Evil denote a perpetual balance of underlying forces yet undefined, perhaps undefinable, and lesser ones like the Law of Locks suggest that the imposition of rational human design upon the natural world thickens the veil or obscures it.

However—by the very nature of the quest *Ma* has laid upon me—I must assume that the Fortunate Isles exist not in the Otherworld, but in this one. How can that be, if they are not subject to the rules of mundane existence? Immortality is not a natural state nor, if I read history aright, is the persistence of a nation, tribe, or way of life in perpetuity.

If I were to experiment with my master Anselm's lesser application of Minho's spell, the solution would surely surface, but I dare not risk it. Anselm's existence—

like Yan Oors's, Guihen's, and that of every nameless and shadowy spirit of rock, forest, and watercourse—depends upon people's belief in it. That is also a premise, an underlying axiom that I dare not tinker with.

If I had an eon for study, I would know what I had to do, but even here, within Anselm's ensorcelled walls, the pressure upon me to act does not abate, as Yan Oors and the lines drawn by the pendulum have demonstrated. I can only hope that as I get nearer the focus of Minho's magic—that is to say, the great intersection of lines drawn in Anselm's sandbox—the relationship between all the spells and principles will become evident, and I will not be forced to choose between my lifelong mistress and my lifelong dreams.

Chapter 4 ∾ A Journey Begins

Pierrette could hardly slither through the small opening beneath the wooden stairs that led to her father's house. When she had been little, she had spent many hours in the dim space the hole led to, between the broad floorboards of the house and the sloping, irregular bedrock beneath. There, she had experimented with the powders and potions her dead masc mother no longer needed—her mother's dying legacy to her youngest child.

Pierrette had not been in that secret place of late, but now . . . if she were to leave Citharista, there was one thing, one terrible, dangerous object, that she did not dare leave behind. Wiggling a small stone loose from the house foundation, she reached behind it, and withdrew a shiny bauble on a string. It was a globule of fused glass, mostly clear, but veined with red and blue, the patterns not painted on its surface but weaving through the clear crystal like a fisherman's net, tangled in the water.

The reticulations of that net held no fish, but something deadlier than a shark. The warmth of her hand, or the anxious tenor of her thoughts, set the droplet aglow, an orange light like the flame of a cheap, fatty candle. It illuminated her tense features. "Is that you, little masc?" The harsh, scraping voice was inaudible to the mice huddling in their shredded leaf nest in the corner, and to the old ladder snake (so called for the pattern on its back) that preyed on them. Only Pierrette heard it, and answered the speaker.

"Who else, Cunotar? Did you hope it was some innocent you could charm into breaking my 'serpent's egg' and freeing you to devastate this world and time as you strived to do to your own?"

"Why do you disturb me? You aren't seeking pleasant conversation, I warrant, though you must be bored with your trivial life, and surely crave conversation with someone wiser than yourself."

"Wiser? You've been locked in that egg for eight centuries. Events have passed you by, and the world outside is like nothing you remember. You have nothing worthwhile to say."

"But you're here. That's cause for hope, isn't it?"

"I've come for you only because I dare not leave such evil unguarded. I—we—are going on a trip."

"How lovely! Will you let me see what ruin you and your kind have made of the countryside, or must I ride in the darkness and sweat between your breasts?"

Ruin, indeed. For the most part sunny Provence was a lovely place, and people didn't give much thought to ghosts, demons, or creatures of darkness. It had not always been so. In Cunotar's day, druids like him had ruled with terror, commanding a legion of *fantômes*, dead Celtic warriors who served because the druids owned their heads, and kept them preserved in cedar oil.

But Pierrette did not like to think of that. Long ago, the druids' plans had been foiled, the heads burned and the *fantôme* souls freed, and only Cunotar was left to remember. Struggling with Pierrette, she had tricked him into falling on his own sword, and Pierrette's bauble, a goddess's gift, had been his only refuge: confinement forever, or death. Carefully wrapping the "serpent's egg" in cloth, she crept out through the opening into the bright, clear Provençal sunshine.

She carried her meager belongings to the stable behind her father's house. In her guise as the boy Piers, she always travelled lightly burdened; her donkey, Gustave, was as stubborn as a root, as skeptical as the scholar in ibn Saul, and bore his wicker panniers with less and less grace, the heavier they were loaded. "But we've been through a lot together, old ass," she said. "I wouldn't dream of going anywhere without you."

One of Gustave's panniers contained oats to supplement his grazing, and to bribe him with. The other contained Pierrette's own things: pens, ink, and a leather-bound sheaf of blank paper for her journal, a pouch of coins and the Celtic "serpent's egg" that held the trapped soul of Cunotar. So much for his hopes of seeing her world. The less he knew of it the better.

She packed a pale blue dress of ancient Gaulish

cut, a tan leather belt with gold *phalerae* mounted on it, engraved disks whose patterns changed when one looked at them, from snakes to a maiden's long hair, to leaves and branches . . . She rolled those in a tight bundle in her white wool *sagus*, her cloak; together those comprised her "official" wardrobe.

She tossed a wheel of cheese in the pannier along with several fat loaves of bread, two dried, salted fish, and a flask of oil from her father's olive grove. She made sure the pannier's clasps were tight, proof against Gustave's mobile lips and strong teeth.

"Are you ready, Yan Oors?" she asked. No one answered her. John of the Bears would not be seen unless he wanted to be, and he most definitely did not want Muhammad abd' Ullah ibn Saul to see him. Even worse would be if he *did* want to be seen, and the scholar could not see him—would he cease to exist on the spot, in a withering blast of the scholar's disbelief? But outside, something metallic clanked against the cobbles, as if someone's horse had stamped an iron-shod hoof.

Ibn Saul did not travel lightly. Two horses were hitched to heavily laden carts; three others, saddled and bridled, stood with their reins tied to posts. There were three unsaddled remounts as well. A glossy black mule stood by them, lightly burdened with the scholar's carefully packed and padded instruments—devices, he said for measuring the earth, the sky, and everything in between. Pierrette shuddered when she thought about that.

Pierrette's father Gilles came to see them off. So did the village priest, Father Otho. She wished she had some token of her father's, to carry with

her. Whether things went right or wrong on the
upcoming voyage, it was not likely she would return
here, or see Gilles again. She would be dead,
destroyed along with Minho's kingdom (in the
unlikely event that she succeeded with the goddess's
task) or lost in distant enchantment or, as in her
childhood visions, sitting on a gold-and-ivory throne,
far away. But Gilles was poor, and had nothing to
give her, and would not have thought to do that
anyway. She carried Gilles's heritage in her blood,
and that would have to be enough.

But Father Otho? He had been her first teacher,
and had (unknowingly, of course) prepared her for
her apprenticeship with Anselm, by teaching her
Greek and Latin, and by stimulating her small mind
to feats of thinking. Perhaps she uttered those
thoughts aloud, or perhaps Otho needed no such
urging. "Take this," that priest said, holding up
something small and glittery. It was a cross on a
delicate Celtic gold chain, and she knew at once
that it was something ancient. "It was my mother's,
and her mother's before that," the priest said, his
eyes downcast as if embarrassed. Pierrette had
known Father Otho all her life. He had consoled
her when her mother died. He had helped drive
a demon from her sister Marie, now a nun in
Massalia. But . . .

"Father Otho, that is a cross, and I have never
been baptized."

"It won't harm you, child. It's not magical—only
a token. Take it. Wear it—for me." Frankish kings
in the north might issue Christian edicts against
pagan practices, but here in the dry, remote
southlands, where broken Roman gods still pushed

marble arms and heads from the soil, an uneasy
tolerance reined. And besides, if rumor was true,
Otho had known—and loved—her mother Elen
before he took vows, and she married Gilles. He
would not willingly do Pierrette harm.

Did she dare? He said it was not magical, but
what did he know? Christians had made baptismal
fonts of ancient sacred pools, and the goddesses
that had inhabited them fled, or were now worshipped as Christian saints. Priests chopped down
ancient sacred trees, and built chapels of the wood.
They placed little shrines and crucifixes at every
crossroads—which had always been sacred to the
ancient spirits. Only the pool of *Ma* was left,
because nobody knew of it except Pierrette. Once
she had feared that Christianity was consuming all
the magic in the world, and that it was almost gone.
When it was gone, she feared, the Black Time *Ma*
spoke of would come. Now she was not so sure,
because the world was much more complicated than
that, but still . . .

She sighed, and lifted the chain over her head.
It nestled between her small, tightly bound breasts,
and she did not even feel it there. She didn't feel
any different either.

Travelling, in an age when Roman hostels had
crumbled, when Roman roads were overgrown
with veritable trees pushing up between their great
paving slabs, was not undertaken lightly. But if one
were rich—as was Muhammad abd' Ullah ibn
Saul—it was not uncomfortable or terribly risky.
The carts carried tents, folding cots and soft
featherbeds, pots, pans, and jars of spices. Ibn

Saul and Lovi went armed with long swords and lances.

Because Pierrette wanted to maintain her disguise as the boy Piers, she made her own camp a bit apart from the others. The role came easily to her because she had been raised as a boy, in *bracae* and tunic, her hair cut short. An inheritance dispute over her father's lack of a male heir, long since settled, had been the initial reason for the deception, but now it was a convenience: girls could not travel as freely as boys, and were subject to the importunities of male lust. Besides the necessity for privacy for her female functions, her secluded bed allowed a secret visitor once dusk had fallen. . . .

"He is like an uneasy draft," said the gaunt one, squatting, leaning on his iron staff. "He himself is preposterous—neither Jew nor Moor, or perhaps both. Why should I fear his chill gaze?"

"Ambiguity suits him—not knowing what he is, neither Christians, Moslems, nor Jews inconvenience him in his travels. I, too, find such deception . . . convenient."

"It seems unfair. If my bears were real, not ghosts, I'd give him such a scare he'd have to accept me."

"If he decided you were a clever peasant with trained animals, and wrote of you in that light, you would be trapped in that guise, because the written word is a terrible, powerful spell. You must continue to avoid his attention. Have you given thought to how you'll do that, when we board ship in Massalia?"

"I'll think of a way," said Yan Oors.

Chapter 5 ∾ Beggars and Sacred Whores

Massalia: the great city, five centuries old when the first Roman legions set foot in Provence, showed her years. She lay nestled in a bowl of mountains that had protected the Greek colony from marauding Celts and Ligures, and from the Gaulish Salyens against whom she had once enlisted Rome's aid (and lost her freedom because of it). After that, the fine Greek temples on the north hill overlooking her pretty harbor were joined by Roman ones, and by an amphitheater cut into the native rock. Now the temple pillars were eroded by dust blown out of Africa and by mad Mistral winds that swept down River Rhodanus's long valley, and the amphitheater was frequented mostly by whores and their customers.

South of the harbor sprawled the red tile roofs of Saint Victor's Abbey, where lay the bones of Lazarus, first Christian bishop of the Roman city, who had not proved immortal though he had been raised from the grave by the Christ's own hand.

Great chains linked fortresses north and south of the harbor mouth, and kept raiding Moorish galleys at bay. Massalian ships traded with the Moslem world, in Sicilia, Iberia, and Africa, but the focus of prosperity in what was coming to be called "Francia" was northward now, around Parisia on the Sequana River, and in the cities of Germania. Thus the cloak Massalia spread across the land was frayed at the edges, and moth-eaten with vacant lots. Shoddy edifices built of stones thrice-used were shabby patches on the ancient, faded fabric.

Ibn Saul had a house north of the *forum*, the great market square. Though during an ordinary visit to the town the market was a much-anticipated destination, that afternoon Pierrette intended to visit the convent overseen by the Mother Sophia Maria, within whose walls her sister Maria lived, and prayed, and sang . . .

The three travellers parted outside the Roman gate, agreeing to meet at dawn by the wharves. Pierrette's route was south along a causeway, over a weedy creek and canebrake, past the rope-makers long, cobbled workplace. Oily scum floated on patches of open water, reeking of feces, bad meat, and moldy rope fibers. Spoiled food floated amid broken pots and household trash. The causeway was like a bridge over a very minor hell, and she hurried along it.

On Saint Victor's side of the harbor, the streets were unpaved, thankfully dry in this season, and she picked her way between fresh-thrown deposits of night soil and garbage. Those odors contrasted in a confusing manner with the delicious aroma of roasting lamb from one doorway, of rising bread from another, of fresh, crushed rosemary and hot olive oil . . .

Gustave snorted, and she whirled around. The young thief howled, and clutched his bitten hand. Pierrette grabbed the cord that held up his ragged kilt. "I didn't take anything. Let me go!" he shrilled, his voice girlish, manhood years away.

"Thanks to Gustave, you didn't," she replied. His choice was to run—and lose his only article of clothing, or to wait and perhaps be beaten. She could see the options as they passed over his dirty, mobile face.

"What do you think I have in that pannier?" she asked. "Gold? Silk from the East?"

"Cheese! I smelled it." His boyish skinniness took on new meaning: his black hair was tinged with the red brown not of sun bleaching, but of malnutrition. His belly was swollen and round not with excess, but with bloat.

"There is bread and oil, too, and salted mullet, red as sunset. But I have nothing to drink with it. Is there a fountain nearby?" The old city across the harbor was still supplied by a decrepit Roman aqueduct, but its lead pipes and channels did not extend here.

His eyes went wide with distrust. Had this older boy implied he might actually share his bounty? Again, expressive eyes signaled his warring impulses—but he could not be much hungrier that he was, and he did not wish to lose his ragged kilt. . . . "There's a well. It's not too salty to drink," he said.

"Then let's go there," Pierrette said. "I have a cup we can use." Wisely, she did not let go of the tag end of his makeshift belt.

Seated on the stone rim of the well, they ate. A half dozen skinny children crept near—and with a sigh, Pierrette motioned them to sit, and divided fully half her provisions with them. Now she herself would go hungry sooner, unless she could replace them from the market. When it was evident that no more food was forthcoming, the urchins slipped away without thanks.

Pierrette remained, remembering: long ago—had she been seven or nine?—she and her sister had approached the priest Otho with a moral dilemma. The town's Burgundian castellan, nominally Christian, but also a wearer of the horns of his own tribe's ancient forest god, was attracted to Marie. He offered to save her betrothed, Bertrand, from the burden of shedding virgin blood on Marie's wedding night. The custom—warrior-shamans were proof against the dire evils of blood—was common among Burgundian and Gaulish folk, though among Christians the blood of Christ had rendered such fears moot, at best. But the Burgundian had been sincere, if overanxious, and Marie had been—secretly—attracted to him as well. Pierrette had almost dragged her sister to the priest—who was no help at all. He took two jars of oil, each half-empty, half-full, and named one good, and one evil. He poured oil from one into the other and then back, and shuffled the jars until neither girl knew which one was which, or how much oil was in either. "Where is the good?" he asked. "Where the evil?" What had he meant? At that time, Pierrette

blamed him for caring more for his own security—
the castellan could insist upon a new priest, and
might get one. Later she decided that good intents,
evil means, and conflicting religions (neither of
them like her own simple Ligure faith in the
Mother) were inextricably entwined.

And now this: the evil of hunger in this rich, taw-
dry city, and of her own hunger, somewhere on the
road ahead. The needs of one, the needs of many.
Adult practicalities versus the rumbling bellies of
children. The city might have a thousand urchins,
and many would be indelibly blighted by starva-
tion, their minds dulled and their bodies withered.
But at least they had sunshine, and water not too
salty to drink. If the terrible Black Time that *Ma*
saw in her roiled waters came, and there was
nothing living on the land, only souls enslaved in
humming metal boxes, without eyes to see or hearts
to ache, or bellies to feel the pangs of
hunger . . . then where was the real evil? And if
Minho's magical kingdom, where all were good and
everything was beautiful, was destroyed—then was
its destruction not evil? Which jar held goodness,
and which evil—and how much was in each jar?

Pierrette removed her hat and shook out her hair
before approaching the convent gate, where taci-
turn Sister Agathe answered her ringing. The air
was redolent with the scents of exotic herbs whose
neat, tiny patches quilted the colonnaded cloister.
It was one of Pierrette's favorite places, a placid
island in the bustling, stinking sea of the city. She
settled onto a stone bench to wait Mother Sophia's
convenience.

"Welcome, child," the abbess said when she

swept into the courtyard, her arms outstretched. Once again, Pierrette was a small, motherless child, starved for such warm, feminine affection. They embraced, then Mother Sophia stood back, hands on Pierrette's shoulders. "You've grown again!" she exclaimed. "You'll soon be as tall as Marie."

"Will I be able to see her, Mother?"

"You mean, 'Is she in trouble again?' don't you?" Marie had a mischievous streak, and thus often incurred penances that kept her occupied when Pierrette visited. "She is not—and that worries me."

Pierrette laughed. "That worries me too! In this world, a surfeit of goodness is more suspect than the evils we have come to expect."

Mother Sophia gave her a queer glance. "Philosophy, child? What strange paths do your thoughts tread?"

Pierrette sighed. She recounted her sharing with the urchins. "And here," said the abbess, "where we pray and worship God, we are well fed. Some women come here to fill their bellies, and consider roughened knees and tedious routine a small price to pay. Their first year, we don't even question their true conviction." She shook her head. "And then there's Marie—here not for the food, but for the prayer, her life itself a penance—who still plays pranks on naive newcomers, and winks at the bishop during mass." She shrugged. "Share her pallet tonight," the abbess said, "and if she has no mischief to recount to you, her sister, I will really begin to worry. . . ."

Pierrette dined with the abbess, and when dusk crept up the walls, Mother Sophia suggested they have light. Pierrette glanced at the bell-cord that would summon someone with a lamp, but: "Would you once again allow me to see by . . . a different light?"

Pierrette could not refuse her. So quietly that none but she herself could hear it, she voiced ancient words . . . and this time, no flame perched atop her finger. Instead, from a shadowy object on the far wall issued a pure, white light, that suffused the room and left no shadow undispelled.

"Saint Mary's light," gasped the abbess, her face a theater-mask of rapture as she gazed upon the rude old crucifix that was its source. "Thank you, child, for this blessing."

Pierrette was not so sure of that. For her, the different effect of her firemaking spell, in this Christian place, demonstrated how mutable—and ultimately how vulnerable—was all magic. Here, in Christian Massalia, in the shadow of Saint Victor's great abbey, the premises underpinning the spell's words were Christian ones, and allowed not fire, but this pure, holy light. Elsewhere, where neither the innocent pagan relics of Citharista nor Christian purity prevailed, the spell produced a red and oily glow, funereal flames as of flesh burning atop a pyre.

But here it was white and Christian, and the dear woman's smile was all the payment Pierrette could make for the hospitality she was receiving.

Moonlight cast a distorted image of Marie's barred window across the patchy gray blanket they shared that night. Neither sister was as prone to giggling as she had been as a child, and they gave the nuns in neighboring cells nothing to curl their pious lips about. Marie seemed as jolly as usual, especially when she recounted her personal mission—only recently allowed by Mother Sophia's superiors—among the whores in the old amphitheater, where the dramas were all small, each one with a cast of two.

"You should have seen the poor girl's face," said Marie, grinning, her teeth aglitter with moonlight. "She made sixteen coppers that night—and she slept with seven men. And the little slut was proud of herself! Sixteen coppers! So I showed her . . . this." Cool moonlight seemed almost magically to warm, to turn as golden as noonday and as green as springtime, transformed when it reflected from the ruddy precious metal and the luscious emeralds of the dangling necklace.

"Marie! Where did you get that?"

"From a customer—my own last customer, I think—when I was earning my living in the amphitheater. I retrieved it from its hiding place, a chink in the wall."

Pierrette could not suppress her shudder. She didn't want to remember that. She wanted to remember her big sister as a girl, and as a nun—and nothing between. But Marie had not forgotten.

"I told her if all she could make was a few coppers, she was in the wrong profession, and that despite my own success, I had given it up to . . . to become God's whore."

"Marie!" Pierrette, though herself pagan, was scandalized.

"Oh, don't be stupid! After all I've done, how

could I ever call myself a 'bride of Christ,' or wear
his ring? And besides, it worked. The little wench
is here, on her knees, not her back."

"So which jar is half-empty," Pierrette mused
quietly, "and which one half-full?"

"What?"

"What Father Otho said, when the castellan
Reikhard gave you his medallion, with the horned
god on it, and you . . ."

"Oh, that. I always thought he meant the
Church couldn't help me get out of that, and to
accept my . . . fate. And since the Church wouldn't
intervene . . ."

"You rejected it. And a demon took you. We took
you to Saintes-Marie-by-the-Sea, where it was
exorcised, and . . ."

"Not all of it was—or I'd be a perfect little nun,
and wouldn't even think of strolling around in that
brothel, talking with whores."

"And you wouldn't impress any stupid little girls
with your emeralds, either—or convince them to
come here, instead."

"I suppose not. Go to sleep now. You can sleep
in, but I have to be up long before dawn."

"I wouldn't worry about Marie, Mother,"
Pierrette told the abbess in the morning. She did
not explain further.

Chapter 6 ∾ Of Bishops and Priests

Ibn Saul had hired a galley—a long, low vessel with twelve oars, a triangular sail, and Moorish lines. Its shallow draft would allow it to stay close to shore, and to navigate the silty *Fossae Marianae*, the Roman canal to Arelate, that bypassed the lagoons of Rhodanus's delta.

Pierrette was content to sit far forward with her donkey, away from the sour, sweaty aroma of the rowers and the clack of the *episkopo's* little drum, keeping time. The long, sandy coast was low and undistinguished, and the monotony gave her mind free rein for pondering. After nine hours at sea, the long sandspit at Rhodanus's greater mouth was off the port side, the creamy rocks of the Estaque mountains far aft; she was bored, and the sun's glare, low over the bow, made looking ahead painful.

She turned around, and settled against the rail.

What was Lovi doing? Just ahead of the mast, he had slipped out of his long-sleeved Frankish shirt, and was lying down on the deck. How strange. As if there wasn't enough heat and sunlight, without deliberately exposing oneself to it. And his skin was so pale. Pretty, though. Creamy, with tinges of gold and pink. Most skin was olive-toned, or dark and leathery from the fierce Mediterranean sun. Lovi's looked soft as a baby's, and the fine curls of hair on his chest were yellow-gold. Pierrette's fingers tingled, almost as if she had uttered her small fire-making spell—but the golden tendrils she imagined her fingers running through were not flames.

She shook her head to clear it of such imagery. Sorcery—so *Ma* insisted—required she remain virgin, and those were not a virgin's thoughts. Unfortunately for her composure, she was not as innocent as virginity might imply.

Her mind ranged northward, beyond the low coast, gray with tamarisk and sand willows. There lay the Crau plain, the Plain of Stones. There, in a long-ago age, born hence by the great, dangerous spell called *Mondradd in Mon*, she had made love with the Greek explorer Alkides. There, she had learned that what the gods commanded and what they intended were not always the same. "Virgin" meant many things, but what it came down to, parsed and analyzed to the final degree, was one single forbidden act. And even that was not universally true. For want of clear evidence otherwise, every girl who had not borne a child was considered a virgin.

Again, she shook her head, almost sending her leather hat flying. That would not do! Such thoughts about the lovely blond boy were dangerous. She did not intend to endure the discomforts of tight-bound hair and breasts, the heavy chafing of men's clothing, only to give herself away with hot-eyed glances. Already, Lovi was looking her way, as if he had sensed her intensity.

He sat up abruptly, an arm across his chest like a girl startled while bathing. Quickly, he turned away from her gaze, and pulled his tunic over his head. His skin, she saw, had turned quite pink, not entirely from sunburn. She barely suppressed a low chuckle. Poor Lovi. What horrible things he thought about her—about Piers.

Shortly later, the galley glided up against a stone wharf, having attained the *Fossae Marianae* in near-record time. Galleys were not subject to the vagaries of wind, and did not tack back and forth like sailing craft. The sun had not quite set, and they had been at sea less than twelve hours.

That night they slept at an inn—Lovi and ibn Saul in a wide bed, and Piers, pleading a touch of claustrophobia after the open sea, on the stone balcony. Only when the others were long asleep did she feel a calloused hand on her shoulder. "Yan Oors! Where were you? How did you get here?" she whispered.

"I rowed," he said, a grin crinkling his dark face. "It wasn't much fun."

"But how?"

"Last night I followed the scholar to the docks, and listened while he haggled with the galley's master. Then I followed a crewman home, and when he drifted off to sleep . . ."

"Then what?"

"He dreamed dark creatures of the deep, tugging on his oar, pulling him overboard. What a wondrous dream he had, called to account before the king of the watery realm, who had octopus arms, and fish swimming in and out of his nostrils!"

"You're cruel! That poor man! What then?"

"This morning his bench was empty. I sat down in his place, and took his oar. The master even paid me. See?" The tiny silver bit was dwarfed in his huge hand. "He says he'll exchange this for a shiny obol if I stay on as far as Arelate, at the end of the canal."

"Where did you learn to row, to keep time with the others?"

"I don't remember. Perhaps I sailed with the Venetii, buying tin from the Cassiterides, or maybe I guided Pytheas the Massilian there, hundreds of years ago. It's all very vague to me now." His deep voice was tinged with regret.

"I'm sorry. But you're here. You remembered enough, and you're here now. I'm glad for that."

"Me too, little witch. And so are my bears." He gestured over the stone balustrade. Did the shadows conceal ghostly ursine shapes? Was that flicker of greenish light an eye—a bear's eye—or only a cat stalking small prey?

Enormous salt pans crowded the approach to the canal—dikes separating shallow ponds where seawater evaporated. Many ponds were blood-red with tiny salt-loving organisms. The galley progressed up the weedy waterway under oars: why should its master pay good coin to rent oxen who could not walk as fast as his crew could row—and the only crewman who was getting paid extra for this leg of the journey was the craggy fellow at the third starboard oar.

Even now that Pierrette knew Yan Oors was aboard, she could not distinguish him from the other broad backs on the benches, without going aft to look in every face on her return to the bow. She chafed at the tedium of this phase of the voyage. On her left, never far from the canal, were the weedy, shifting channels of the river, the vast reed sea of the Camargue, and on her right just beyond the towpath was the Plain of Stones, just as flat, radiating heat.

Bored, she wished Lovi would repeat his odd pastime. Ibn Saul had explained that northerners who never got enough sun in their native lands often did that, and called it "sunbathing." At least, the scholar had commented, Lovi had sense to limit his exposure to the hours before dusk, when the sun was not too fierce. "I've seen northern galley slaves burn and blister so badly they died," he said, "and after all the effort I've spent training that boy . . ."

Cattle grazed a broad expanse of open ground from the rude stone wharf to the monstrous structure that towered over even the broken Roman aqueduct. "What is that?" asked Pierrette.

Lovi smiled condescendingly. "That," he said, "is the town of Arles, once called Arelate. What did you think it was?"

"I know what it *was*," she snapped. "It was a Roman arena, before all the arches were blocked up with stones and mortar, and those four square towers were built. If that is the city of Arelate, I am ashamed how far we descendants of Roma have fallen."

"Don't be too critical," said ibn Saul. "This city has been ill used by just about everyone—the Visigoths were not so very bad, but the Moors breached the old walls, and burned most everything outside of them. When the Franks took the city back, they burned most of what was inside the walls. Now the survivors live in the only completely defensible place left. There are probably two hundred houses inside the amphitheater, and two churches that I know of. I think it would take a bigger and better army than Franks, Moors, or Burgundians could produce to overwhelm it without a long siege."

"I want to go inside," said Pierrette. The theater in Massalia was a brothel, while this was a town. Whatever ambiance, whatever tenuous connection with the Roman past might have existed in Massalia's stone warren, the misery, greed, and passions of the present overwhelmed them. Pierrette thought it might be the same here, but such monuments of the past sometimes provided glimpses of what had once been, as if the Veil of Years were worn thin there.

"Are you sure? It's crowded, dark, and dangerous. I have sent a boy from the wharf to announce me to Arrianus, a bishop, who is reputed to be of a scholarly bent. Otherwise I would not go in myself."

They entered the fortified town through the west gate, a Roman portal now surrounded by one of those ugly foursquare towers. Flaring torches illuminated patches of smoke-stained wall, and Pierrette had the impression of vast, dark spaces beyond. This had once been the outer concourse of the amphitheater. She tried to imagine it with graceful arches open to the sunlight, clean-swept and crowded with Romans in togas, with red-and-bronze-clad soldiers managing the traffic—but the exercise was doomed to fail, because everything was too dark, too ugly, and once beyond the gate itself, the air was still and foul, the Roman tile flooring lost beneath the humped fill and rubble of centuries, and the once-noble corridor was crowded with mostly roofless enclosures, which she realized were dwellings.

"This way," said ibn Saul, working his way leftward, pushing through a clot of dull-clad denizens of this awful place, who had gathered beneath a guttering torch. They ascended a worn stone stairway, Roman stone that emerged from Visigothic, Saracen, and Frankish dirt as if pushing up through it. Pierrette followed, lured by the faintest glimmer of clear natural light from an archway ahead.

That light came cascading down a stairway, which they ascended. At the top was another arcade, just as crowded as the one below, but some of its inward-facing arches were still open. Pierrette drew a welcome breath of air that did not taste as if it had already passed in and out of hundreds of pairs of lungs. From below, smoke trickled upward from a hundred hearths: the entire floor of the amphitheater was crowded with stone, timber, and plaster houses, amid a maze of tiny streets hardly wide enough for two skinny people to pass.

To her relief, the scholar led her upward, not down into that chaos. She suddenly appreciated poor run-down Citharista. It had not known prosperity since Rome fell, and though half its ancient buildings had collapsed and not been rebuilt, at least its streets were still Roman-wide, and its Roman cobbles were still unburied. But Arelate had remained a prosperous town, a hub for northbound travelers, the seat of an archbishop and a Burgundian kinglet (who wisely spent his days elsewhere, traveling about his realm).

The bishop's house, and his church, were built atop the uppermost tier of stone seats, their leveled floors cannibalized from the Roman stone of the uppermost arcade. A cool, moist breeze eddied through the anteroom. The bishop himself ushered them into a white-plastered hall with scenes from the lives of saints, and a long table set with silver candlesticks, goblets, and a tall pitcher bedewed with moisture. "Please sit," he urged. "I've recently read your treatise on the progress of Mother Church among the savage Wends," he said to ibn Saul, ignoring Pierrette entirely. "I must hear all about your voyage among them."

Pierrette sat quietly, and both men forgot that the boy Piers was even there. Although four goblets had been set out, Bishop Arrianus poured wine only for himself and the scholar, and Pierrette was not so thirsty she was willing to disturb either of them.

Ibn Saul obviously wanted to speak of his present voyage northward, but the bishop had interests of his own. "You wrote that the entire mission among the Wends is comprised of men of the *ordo vagorum*, itinerant priests unaccountable to authority higher than their own questionable consciences. Is it entirely so? We have nothing but trouble from such wanderers in these parts. They come, drink our sacramental wine to quench unquenchable thirsts, regale us with tales that are surely lies, and then most quickly heed some inner call that leads them onto the roads again, when the novelty of their welcome wears off, and the topic of labor and toil arises. In fact we have one such here now, a self-proclaimed Father Gregorius, who claims to have voyaged with the Norsemen who infest the lands above Armorica."

Ibn Saul snatched at that straw. "Ah! Armorica! How opportune it is that you should speak of it. I have long suspected that those hairy Viking barbarians—more savage, some say, even than Wends—must know the place we seek . . ." He described the rumors and tales of a mysterious pagan kingdom, a relic of ancient days, that was reputed to lie somewhere in those very waters the Norsemen claimed as their private sea. "Is this Gregorius nearby? I would like to question him . . ."

"Better still—as his welcome here has worn thin, and his tales have grown stale, I'll provide him with whatever impetus he needs to move on, and a letter—to whom it may concern—that I will give not to him, but to you. If he serves you well in your quest, you may choose to pass it on to him— I'll tell him that. He won't refuse to accompany you as a guide and perhaps as a . . . spiritual counselor." He said that with raised eyebrows as if someone with the odd name of Muhammad abd' Ullah ibn Saul might not welcome such a one, but the scholar smiled and nodded. "If he is truly 'Father' Gregorius, he will know the sacraments, will he not? I hope that is so, not only for myself, but for my Frankish apprentice, Lovi, who is most devout, and whose moods become quite black when he is denied confession, when we voyage far from Christian lands."

"Lovi? That is Louis in our local patois. Is he perhaps related to the Frankish kings?"

"You mean the descendants of Chlodowechus, called Clovis? I doubt it."

"As do I. But isn't it strange how such an odd and savage name, Chlodowechus, that sounds like someone choking, can be transmuted by time and Christian influence into the mellifluous 'Lovi' or 'Louis?'"

At that moment Pierrette, though she had no wine to choke on, made a sound that sounded very much like "Chlodowechus." The bishop then noticed her presence. "Here, boy. I've forgotten you. Have some wine. Are you ill?"

"I'm sorry, *Episkopos* Arrianus," ibn Saul interjected. "This is Piers, who is, though young, a scholar in his own right, who has read many ancient works not only in Latin, but in Greek and Hebrew, and in the dead tongue of the Phoenicians as well. I am thinking he choked not on an absence of wine, but on something you may have said. Piers? Is that so?"

Pierrette nodded. "When you spoke of the transmutation of 'Chlodowechus' to 'Clovis' to 'Louis,' and attributed the improvement in the sound of it to the blessing of the Church, I was reminded of my own observations of how Christianity has claimed much else that was pagan, and made it its own. I was further reminded of Saint Augustine's own advice, in that regard, and that of the Holy Father Gregorius, whose ideas paralleled his."

The bishop was wholly captivated now—and Pierrette had shaped her words just so that her own pagan estate would not likely come up. She had never lied outright even to devout Christians, and did not want to. "Yes?" said Bishop Arrianus, leaning forward until his prominent nose almost rested on the gleaming rim of his goblet.

"It is not enough to say that Christianity mellows what was once pagan," Pierrette said. "It is closer to truth to say that the very realities of the pagan world have been reshaped by it. Christian influence reaches not only forward into lands where no vagrant priest has trod, and into a future no one has visited—it reaches back through time itself, and changes pagan gods into Christian saints."

"How can that be? You speak rhetorically, of course—nothing can change the past. What has been written cannot be erased."

"Is that so? When Pope Gregory suggested that the wood from holy pagan oaks be hewn and split, and Christian shrines built where they stood, and when pagan folks had no choice but to come and worship before a cross made from that once-holy tree, didn't Gaulish Esus, the carpenter-god, become Jesus, still a carpenter, still a god?"

"But no! You tread on fearsome ground, boy! There is no connection between the one Jesus and the other!" The pronunciation of the two names was so very similar—"Ay-soos" and "Hay-soos," that the bishop had missed Pierrette's slight aspiration of the one name and not the other. "I have never even heard of a Gaulish 'Jesus.'"

"That is exactly my point," Pierrette said firmly. She leaned back and took a leisurely sip of wine. "You must accept my assurance that the Celtic 'Esus' once existed—at least in the minds of his worshippers—because the texts in which his name is written are not here, and I cannot show them to you. Accept that, and the rest becomes evident: Esus once was, but is no longer. Jesus once was not, but now is. The very past in which pagan Esus existed is no longer: now the roots of the Christian tree are deeper in the heart of this land than were those of the pagans, and Esus, in truth, never was."

"You play with the meanings of words!" Arrianus spat. "You flirt with terrible heresy!"

"Where is the heresy? I have said that—in this world we live in—there is and was only one Jesus, ever."

"But you just said there was once another . . ."

"The very fact of his existence has been erased, not just memory of him. He does not exist, and because of the strength of the Church, he never did. And he is not the only one! Shall I name other names?"

"I am afraid to ask them."

Pierrette's dark eyes held the bishop's with their intensity. "In the north, in Armorica, Britannia, and Hibernia, there was once a goddess whose name has changed just as Chlodowechus's has. She was the Mother Goddess, whose flesh was the soil itself, whose bones were the rocks beneath it, and whose flowing breasts were the sacred pools and springs that well hot and cold from dark, buried places. Do you know her name?"

The cleric could not look away. He wanted to. He wanted to flee from this terrible boy who knew of such things—but he was in his own house, that shared a common wall with his church, which was consecrated ground. He could not flee.

"Her name was Brigantu. That was the name of a tribe as well, a warlike tribe whose name comes down to us as 'brigand.' Today the goddess does not exist—but my friend Ferdiad, an Irish singer and teller of tales, whose people have been Christian for many centuries, says that Saint Bridget is the patron saint of his land—and has always been so. . . . If you need still another name, to be convinced, there is Mary Magdalen, patron saint of this land . . ."

"Stop! Please! No more! Magister ibn Saul, who is this frightening child you have brought here? I am afraid for my very soul, here in my own home."

"Then you should be grateful. When we fear for our souls or our mortal bodies, we consider our actions carefully. And I have listened to what Piers has said. As I understand it, he claims that the strength of the Church is such that when a pagan deity falls before it, there can be no true apostasy. As a priest of God you should rejoice."

"No apostasy? But there is. Everywhere, in the villages, in the countryside, folk fall into error so easily, and throw offerings into pools and springs, or holes in the ground."

"No *true* apostasy, I said—for if the deities they importune do not exist, and indeed never did exist—then where do their prayers go? Who is there to hear them, but the One God?"

Bishop Arrianus nodded grudging agreement, then turned the conversation in a direction more immediately useful to the scholar—the state of the countryside of the Rhodanus Valley, and the portage road to the headwaters of the Liger. The bishop gave them names of churchmen they could call on for hospitality on their way, and promised to have a packet of letters, in the morning, for them to deliver for him. Still uneasy with the boy Piers's revelations, he was quite obviously happy to have an excuse, the letters, to bid them farewell.

"Shall we sleep on the boat?" ibn Saul asked, wrinkling his great nose as they descended into the darkness of the erstwhile amphitheater. "I can't imagine any inn here that would smell better than the garbage in the canal."

With several hours of daylight left, ibn Saul arranged for the galley to be towed to the river itself—the canal ended at Arelate—and they spent the night moored offshore, free from the stinks of the town and the risk of sneak thieves in the night.

"Isn't the next town Tarascon?" asked Pierrette when they were under way in the early hours, with the bishop's letters and the hedge-priest Father Gregorius aboard. Ibn Saul nodded.

Then Father Gregorius spoke (he had until then been sullenly resentful about his premature ejection from the comforts of the bishop's house, and about ibn Saul's jovial refusal to part with the letter of recommendation at their very first port of call).

"Of course we will be stopping there, won't we?" he asked.

"I hadn't planned to," said the scholar. "According to the galleymaster's calculation, it may be less than a full day's row, against this sluggish current. We may be well beyond Tarascon by nightfall. Why?"

"Tarascon is a very holy place," said the priest, avoiding the scholar's eye. His gaze slid away upstream like a slippery fish. "Saint Martha lived there, and slayed a ferocious river monster, a great beast called a 'Tarasque.'"

Pierrette laughed out loud, and Gregorius turned angry eyes upon her. "You don't believe it?"

"Of course I do," she replied. "I know better than anyone that the stories of the saints here in Provence are true. I myself saw them where they came ashore, in the little town that grew up on that spot. I have been in the church there, built over the graves of Mary Salome and Mary Jacoba, sisters of the mother of Jesus. I was only laughing because Magister ibn Saul, the bishop Arrianus, and I, had quite a discussion of names and tales, and how they change."

"You are mocking me," said Gregorius. "The saints came many hundreds of years ago, and you are still a boy."

"I don't mean that I was *there* then," Pierrette replied, "or not exactly. Indeed I saw the Saints— all eight of them: Mary Magdalen, her sister Martha, their brother Lazarus, Cedonius who was blind and was healed by Jesus, Saint Maximinus, Sainte Sarah, whom some say was the elder Marys' Egyptian servant—but I saw them in a vision granted me by a very holy old woman. And another time, I spoke with one of the two old sisters, and with Sarah, in their cottage on the very spot where the church stands today."

"Oh," said Gregorius flatly. "Visions."

"You don't believe in visions, Father? Then what of burning bushes, and blinding lights on the road to Damascus, and . . ."

"I didn't say that!" Only now did he realize what a formidable opponent the slender boy in the conical leather hat could be. Did he perhaps fear that he might be unmasked as a fraud? But no rule stated that a vagabond priest had to be educated, though many, the bishop might have said, were far too erudite for their own—and the Church's—good.

"Tell us why you laughed," said ibn Saul. "What about Tarascon, or river monsters, bears on our own conversation with the bishop?"

"To answer that, I must tell not one, but three tales, and it is almost noon. Let us eat, and then nap through the heat of the day, and I'll tell the first of them tonight, around the evening fire, when we have moored the galley.

Pierrette napped, as did ibn Saul, but Gregorius did not, nor Lovi. The priest recited poetry in fine, classical Latin, and the apprentice was obviously enraptured. From what Pierrette heard, they were not stolid Christian verse, but romantic tales of faraway places, of adventures, treasure-seekers, and seventh sons. Were they the same tales with which he had captivated the bishop's clerks and scribes?

As luck and River Rhodanus's currents would have it, they had not reached Tarascon by the time the sun dropped below the trees on the river's west bank. They drew up along a sandy spit downstream of a summer island—so called because it did not exist in winter or spring, when the water was high. Though no trees grew on it, several dead ones had snagged on its upstream end, and there was plenty of wood for a cheerful fire, where crew and passengers alike settled when their stomachs were full.

Chapter 7 ∾ The Pagan Tale

"This is how it was in the most ancient time," said Pierrette. "The people called Gauls or Celts came out of the east riding war chariots, wearing arms made of iron, which was a new metal then, and was cheap, if one knew the secret of drawing it from red, yellow, and black rocks, which were everywhere. Because it was cheap, every man was well armed, and was a warrior, so Gaulish iron overwhelmed bronze, and took this land from the small, dark Ligures who had cherished it from the very beginning. That is why, to this very day, some old granny-women who dabble in herbs and potions will not touch cold iron.

"The Gauls' main gods were Taranis, who was the sky, Teutatis, father of the *teuta*, the tribe, who was a war god, black as iron, red as blood, and lastly Danu, the river. Danu was really goddess of another river, far away, but wherever Gauls conquered, they brought her, and gave every great river her name.

That is why so many great streams bear it, as does this one: Rhodo-danu, the 'rosy river,' perhaps so called for the red salt pans that are her painted mouth.

"But the Gauls did not conquer the Ligures easily. The small folk resisted, and killed them when they ventured from the high ground and open-sky places, and the gods of the land fought them also. *Ma*, whose belly was the soil, whose bones were the rocks, whose breasts were springs and holy pools, whose veins were rivers and streams, did not accept the usurper-goddess Danu, and she kept many dark ones safe in her swamps and low places.

"The Gauls called upon Taranis, whose legs were snakes, and upon Danu, herself winding across the land like a serpent. Danu promised to mate with Taranis if he rid her of the flukes and worms—the humans—that infested her. So Taranis lay with her, and in time she gave birth to a beast with a serpent's body, but with legs to stride on land, with a great maw filled with teeth sharp as lightning bolts, and as bright. The beast's name was Taran-asco, which meant 'in Taranis' stead,' and it went where the Gauls feared to go, into the swamps and low places, where it lived upon the bodies of the small folk.

"Only iron could harm it, and the dark people had no iron, only bronze, and little of that. They had nowhere further to flee, so many of them died. When Taran-asco came upon a village, it consumed young and old, women and babes, and this was an abomination even to the Gauls, especially Teutatis, who was of honest blood that tasted of iron.

"Nor did Taran-asco limit his hunger to the little people. When he found Gauls on the river in wooden boats, he consumed them as well, and when women with bright gold hair came down to the river to wash clothing upon the stones, he ate them also, and no people were happy in the land.

"But one old woman of the original people remembered how *Ma* had ruled the land kindly, and had given freely of her flesh, her blood, and her milk, and that woman wondered what had happened to her. On a night with no moon, she sent her youngest daughter up the rocky riverbank near the present church, where there was a cave, and inside it a spring sacred to *Ma*. As she approached the cave, a Gaul woman, herself virginal, little more than a child, espied her, but gave no alarm. Instead, both girls descended together into the earth.

"What transpired there is not remembered, but that next morning the goddess *Ma* emerged from her cave, and went down to the river. She waded in until the waters swirled about her knees, and created a great disturbance. The monster Taran-asco came to see what food had come his way, and saw her there.

"What a great battle ensued! Oh, what splashing, what roiling of mud. Riverbank reeds soon festooned the highest trees, and river water fell like rain many miles away. Great willows were uprooted and flung aside. Taranis looked down, but saw nothing through all the water, mud, reeds, and trees. Teutatis also watched and wondered, but dared not come near. Danu screamed in agony as the battle rended her. She writhed in her bed of silt and rocks, and begged relief. Then *Ma* emerged from the water, clutching Taran-asco in her arms of stone and soil, and all the gods saw her.

"'What shall I do with this beast that consumes yours and mine alike?' she asked them.

"'Kill it!' pleaded Danu, 'for it has rended me.'

"'Kill it!' demanded Teutatis, 'for it has eaten of my flesh.'

"Only Taranis did not speak, because it was his offspring, and had not harmed him, though it had created discord among his peers. So *Ma* knew she should not kill it.

"'I will take it with me,' she said to Taranis. 'Once each year, send me one virgin of Gaulish blood and one of Ligure, and they will bring it forth for you.'

"To Teutatis, she said, 'My folk and yours lie beneath my mantle now, and in death are at peace with one another. Let it be so also in life.' Teutatis nodded, and it was so.

"To Danu, she said, 'You sleep in my bed, and it disturbs me not. Let it remain so.' Then she departed, and was seen no more above the earth and beneath the sky.

"She sent the two maidens forth, and in good time each gave birth to a child. The golden-haired Gaul's son was dark as a Ligure, but tall, and the Ligure girl's daughter was small and delicate, but golden and pale—and so it has been ever since, that the people of the land are one, dark and light, earth and sky, and it is no surprise when dark parents create a golden child, or yellow-haired people a dark one.

"For many generations thereafter, young women went beneath the earth and brought forth the beast

Taran-asco for his father Taranis to see, and people remembered what had transpired, and gave every god its due."

Pierrette sighed, and then was silent, and so were the others. There was only the crackling of the fire, the lap of the waters, and the distant soughing of a breeze in the trees on the far shore.

Then Gregorius spoke. "That is a pagan tale, unfit for Christian ears." Several low voices murmured, though whether in agreement or protest was unclear, for even in Provence, long a Christian land, the old roots burrowed deep, and spread wide, and Pierrette had not been exactly truthful with the bishop, because much of what she had told him was her own fear of what was happening, and the final changes had not yet occurred.

The tale had taken time to tell, and though young Piers had promised them three stories, everyone knew the rest would have to wait, because they had heard the hoarseness in her voice. They could see that the fat moon was already high overhead, and was purest silver, and they knew that dawn would not come at a later hour just because they had not gotten a full measure of sleep.

Chapter 8 ~ A Christian Tale

As chance would have it, Tarascon lay just around a long bend in the river from their island camp, and they passed below its low, unimpressive walls close to the west bank, rowing briskly. Pierrette kept an eye on the vagrant priest Gregorius the while, observing the wistful look on his face, the way his eyes seemed to measure the wide brown expanse of river between him and the town, and the tiny shake of his head when he at last decided he had no hope of jumping from the galley rail and wading ashore.

"We must keep an eye on him," she told ibn Saul later. "Letter or no letter, I think he'll debark at the first stop where he thinks there may be a welcome for him."

Ibn Saul agreed. "I'll have the galleymaster keep to the west bank—for some reason, most towns and villages are on the east, along this stretch."

"The west has always been less tame—and was

never rebuilt after the Saracen conquests. A vagrant priest will find no hospitable, comfortable abbey refuge there."

That day Lovi again stretched out on the warm deck, shirtless, and Pierrette again admired his lithe, golden form. Strangely (she only noticed it because she kept a wary eye on the priest most of the time) Gregorius also seemed entranced by the sight, and during the hour Lovi lay in the sun, his eyes did not stray once, longingly, to the tree-shrouded east bank.

They made good time, and camped late, and there was no opportunity for Pierrette to tell a second tale. Next day they passed the mouth of the Druentia River, and knew that Avennio was just ahead. It was the most important town on the river save Lugdunum itself, which lay many days north. Because, like Nemausus further to the west, the city had willingly joined with the Saracens—who, though not Christian, were at least civilized—against the Franks, the Frankish ruler Charles the Hammer had allowed Avennio to be most cruelly sacked. Its key position at the confluence of two great rivers had aided its recovery but, like Arelate, it was said to be a shadow of its former self.

Much to Gregorius's disappointment, just as the city's walls came into view on the right, the galley slipped behind an island into the left, or western, channel. Lovi, who had been spending much time with the priest, put a sympathetic hand on his knee. "Perhaps at Lugdunum, near where we must leave this galley and proceed overland, you will have your chance," he said. The stories

Gregorius had told the Frankish boy of his life among the Norsemen were not much like those he had told to entertain Bishop Arrianus and his household. In truth, he had been a slave, treated cruelly, and had not converted one Norseman to the Christian faith. Lovi completely sympathized with his need to escape, to avoid being taken back into a land they controlled. Lovi alone had seen the scars on Gregorius's neck and shoulders, from the iron collar the Vikings had put on him. They were usually hidden beneath his clerical robes.

Gregorius put his own hands over Lovi's. "Without your sympathy, I should go mad," he murmured. "You are my one bright candle on this dark voyage."

That night, when the galley's complement settled by a cheery fire, and Pierrette prepared to tell her second tale, the two of them sat at some distance from the fire, and warded off the damp chill by huddling together under the priest's warm *sagus,* his woolen greatcloak.

"This is the story of Saint Martha," said Pierrette, "who came ashore with Magdalen, Lazarus, and the elder Marys, having been put to sea by the Jews of Palestine in a ship without oars or sail.

"When the Saints parted, there by the sea, Jesus' elder aunties remained, too old for the hardships of the road. Their servant Sarah, whom some say was Egyptian, remained with them. Magdalen went to Lugdunum, where she converted many in that city to the new religion, which as yet had no name. Lazarus became *episkopos*, overseer, to the believers in Massalia, and survived the purges of the emperor

Nero, but was beheaded during the persecutions of Domitian. Maximinus went to Aquae Sextiae, and some say Cedonius accompanied him.

"When the sisters Magdalen and Martha neared Tarascon, they heard of a river-monster, a *tarasque*, which overturned every boat that tried to pass the town. 'Wait here,' said Martha, ever the practical one. 'I'll take the shore road ahead, and make sure it is safe for you.'

"She arrived at nightfall outside the gates of Tarascon, and the watchman bade her hurry inside, because the night belonged to the monster. 'The night, like the day, belongs only to God,' said Martha, 'just as do all creatures that walk, crawl, or fly beneath the sun and moon.'

"'Which god is that?' asked the townsfolk. 'We have prayed to all of them—to Roman Jupiter—*Deus Pater*, the Father—and to Gaulish Belisama, the Mother, and still the *tarasque* consumes us at will. If your god is able to help us, we will build him a temple greater than any others in the city.'

"'My God is the only God,' said Martha, and at that moment understood why she had been driven here, by contrary winds, in a boat without oar or sail. 'He can tame the *tarasque*, just as he made a lion lie down with a lamb without consuming it. But because he is the only God, you must tear down all other temples, and build from their stones and timbers a single church, consecrated to him alone.

"The *maior* of Tarascon and his counselors agree that if Martha brought the *tarasque* to the town gate with a chain about its neck, they would do as she bade them, and would henceforth worship only her God and his Son, and his Spirit—which appealed to their Gaulish natures, for which all things came in threes.

"Saint Martha asked for an axe, and a woodsman to wield it for her. She asked for a smith with a small forge, an anvil, and tongs and hammer as well. The *maior* sent both men forth, though they were reluctant, because they were very afraid.

"Nearby was a great oak tree which had so many nails in its trunk that the bark was entirely hidden. It was a tradition that every carpenter who passed that tree, sacred to Esus, their patron god, should sacrifice a nail to him, or themselves be hanged from the tree. She ordered the woodsman to cut down the great oak, and to split from its trunk two beams, and to fashion from them a cross. Because the town gate was shut, and because it was night, and the woodsman was more afraid of the *tarasque* than of Esus, he obeyed. When that task was done, Martha allowed him to scurry back to the gate, and to safety.

"She commanded the smith to gather all the nails that had fallen from the tree, and to pull those that remained in the wood, and to forge from them a great iron collar and a length of chain. That he did, and quickly, so that he also might be allowed to return to the safety of the town walls.

"Martha stayed outside, and picked up the cross and the chain. She carried them down to the river, and there began to sing. Far out in the dark water, something heard her singing, and it came to investigate. It was the *tarasque*. It came, but it did not slay her. Her song captivated it, because she sang of how all things on earth, beneath it, and in its waters, were God's creatures: even *tarasques*.

"The creature (for she had convinced it that it was so, a creation of God) allowed her to place the collar about its neck, and permitted her to lead it to the gate of the town. When the townsfolk looked down from their wall, they saw the wooden cross, and beneath it the *tarasque*, enchained, and the saint standing with her hand on the beast's head.

"They opened the gate, although it was night, and the people came forth, and danced around the long, scaly beast. When dawn's first glow appeared in the east, they picked up the chain, and led the monster through all the streets, even the narrowest ones, and Saint Martha went with them, carrying the wooden cross, thus consecrating all the streets and alleys to God, to Jesus Christ, and to the Holy Spirit.

"Then Martha went back down the river to where her sister awaited her, and sent Magdalen on her way, to her own mission in Lugdunum, and her own fate. Martha stayed in Tarascon, and oversaw the destruction of all the pagan temples and shrines, and the building of God's church. Perhaps she stayed on there, or perhaps when she had taught the folk all she knew of God and Jesus, she went on, for there are other stories, in other towns."

Pierrette sighed and stretched, because it had been a long tale. The fire had died to embers, because no one had wanted to disturb her while she spoke. Then everyone rose, one by one, and made their beds for the night. Only two remained where they were, already far from the fire, already wrapped in a single cloak as if they had slept through her telling . . .

✧   ✧   ✧

Lovi in truth had not heard much of the story. At first, he had listened because he was entranced by the boy Piers's sweet voice, which moved him in a way he could not explain, but that generated uncomfortable feelings. From the first time he had met Piers, he had felt that attraction, and it had generated an anguish of self-doubt, because he should not have felt such things about another boy. Because he did feel them, he had treated Piers with disdain, short of outright insult but calculated to maintain a safe barrier between himself and the necessity of admitting his unnatural attraction.

But now he sat warm beneath Father Gregorius's cloak, and the priest's strong, heavy arm lay over his shoulders, and he felt an entirely different, but equally discomfiting emotion. That arm now pulled him close against the warmth of Gregorius's ribs and thigh, and did so with a force not of physical strength, but of unquestionable authority, as if Lovi were not himself a thinking being, a person, but an object that Gregorius owned, as he owned the cloak itself. Lovi, rather than resisting as was his first impulse, allowed himself to be held. At that moment, that crux, that surrender of autonomy, he felt a great sense of well-being, as if a decision had been made that greatly simplified his complex feelings about himself, and filled him at the same time with anxious excitement. . . .

As Piers's sweet voice murmured on, Lovi lost track of the story, because Father Gregorius's other hand was moving beneath their shared cloak, in a manner that implied not an intrusion, but an exploration of that domain Lovi had ceded to him.

Lovi himself felt as if he were made of soft wax, that Gregorius might move and shape as he willed.

As if they were still on the galley, moving to the surge of waves beneath its hull, Lovi rocked to the insistent rhythm of his own need, the beat of his own drumming heart, the commands of his ship's master. On plowed that immaterial galley through the black, shining, rolling seas behind Lovi's tight-closed eyes, until the darkness gave way to a great shining, as if the moon had risen from horizon to zenith in one great bound, and now covered him in its silvery light. In that eternal moment of rolling waves he sank, broached by the seas and overwhelmed, into the darkness of the deep—into exhausted sleep. When Pierrette had finished her tale, when the others arose to make their beds, Lovi slept on.

Another day passed, and another. They progressed upstream past the mouths of several influent streams, which had heretofore contributed to Rhodanus's breadth and flow. Their own path of water became correspondingly narrower, its current swifter, and their pace slower, even though the rowers' efforts were undiminished.

On several occasions, Pierrette observed brief interchanges between father Gregorius and Lovi, when Lovi's eyes seemed to follow the priest's movement. Each time, Gregorius seemed to sense that gaze, and he turned, smiling, then wagged a finger from side to side as if enjoining the boy to patience—to what end she did not know. She also observed that Father Gregorius's own eyes no longer strayed to the shore whenever they passed a village or town, and one day she mentioned both things to ibn Saul, who chuckled indulgently, and explained.

"They have become lovers," the scholar said, "though I would never have thought it, because the Franks abhor such affairs between men. It does not displease me—though I admit to some small jealousy, having admired Lovi myself—because now our guide through the Norsemen's territory is bound to us in a way no iron chain around his neck could do." Pierrette knew of such things, but had never observed such a relationship, and for many days she was unable to explain why ibn Saul's revelation distressed her. Not until the day before they were to leave River Rhodanus and journey overland to the westward-flowing Liger did she understand.

It was a lovely day, weeks since she had told her second tale. She had not yet told the third one as promised because, with the increased current, the oarsmen were too tired to stay awake once they had eaten. For the first time in all those weeks, Lovi cast off his tunic and *bracae,* and clad only in a cloth about his loins, sunned himself on the warm deck.

She observed Gregorius's expression of smug possessiveness, and how Lovi stretched and preened for him—and also saw that Gregorius was not the only one watching. For a long moment, the helmsman's eyes drifted from his course, and several oarsmen missed their strokes. The vessel was only bought back on course with much effort and cursing by overseer and galleymaster.

The master approached ibn Saul shortly later, and extracted a promise that the scholar would no longer allow his apprentice to flaunt himself so, in circumstances where even men who preferred women had been deprived long enough to find him attractive, pale and golden as he was. Then Pierrette realized that her distress was simple to explain: it was jealousy. It was not fair that the lovely Lovi, whom she had coveted almost since they were both children, should be possessed and enjoyed by the sneaky, unscrupulous Gregorius, and not by her.

It was resentment, too, that her chosen course had forced her to deny her desire for him because she had been afraid she could not have resisted, had he urged her with all the intensity of his youth and vigor, to surrender herself completely.

It was anger, because she had allowed Lovi to see the pain in her eyes when she looked at him, and he had smiled as prettily as any tart in the amphitheater in Massalia, and shook his head as if to say, "You had your chance, and you didn't take it. Too bad. Too late."

It was sadness and loss, because she sensed that, by becoming Gregorius's lover, Lovi had crossed some great divide, placing himself beyond her reach forever, and though she had not wanted to surrender to her own desire, she did not want to accept that such fulfillment was no longer considerable at all.

Chapter 9 ∾ The Last Tale

Just below Lugdunum they disembarked at a wharf half stone, half rotted timbers, on the western bank. Had they entered the city itself, on the east bank, said the galleymaster, there would have been tolls to be paid on vessel, crew, and passengers. By taking the west shore road north to the portage, only the scholar's party and its goods would be so taxed.

Because many other boatmen routinely evaded the city tolls in like manner, there were ox-drawn wagons for hire at the wharf. Ibn Saul paid off the galleymaster and immediately began haggling with the wagoneers. Because a nasty, northerly wind had sprung up, a precursor of the mad Mistral that drove men insane in winter, few more laden boats would put in until springtime. That, and their relatively scant luggage, resulted in an almost immediate bargain. Within hours, everything was loaded, and they were under way.

What, Pierrette wondered, had become of Yan Oors? He had not visited her for several nights. Was he following them, afoot? Many local people trudged the portage road, some with great sacks or bundles, others with staffs not unlike Yan's in appearance. Was he one of them, in sight, but unseen? She hoped so.

The road followed the river for several miles, during which Lugdunum was visible on the far side. Red tile roofs jutted above its cream-and-yellow walls, and Pierrette caught tantalizing glimpses of columned temples or public buildings of the Roman age—Lugdunum, where emperors had resided at times, where Magdalen had preached. But her path lay elsewhere. Regretfully, Pierrette tugged Gustave along, and turned her head away from the city.

Already, a certain awkwardness had arisen in their small company. Before, there had been others with them, oarsmen, shipmaster, and overseer, to fill out sociable moments, but now there were only four—the scholar, Lovi, Pierrette, and the hedge-priest Gregorius. Ibn Saul rode with the caravan owner on the first wagon, Lovi and the priest followed in the second, and Pierrette, by her own choice, strode well ahead of them and their dust, with Gustave. The road, though rough in spots, was deeply rutted and easy to follow. Later, when bones and buttocks had endured all they could of the jolting ox-drawn wagons, ibn Saul joined her.

That night, and the two that followed, all four of them fell onto their makeshift bedding as soon as they had eaten. On the fourth night—their last before they reached the Liger, and hopefully found a boat for hire—they were becoming enured to land travel, and after they had supped, ibn Saul reminded Pierrette that there was yet one tale untold.

Tarascon seemed far away, and events pertaining to it hardly relevant now. Even the countryside was different, foreign, and strange. Fields were green, not yellow or brown. The colors of stone were more intense, as if less bleached by the sun. Trees and brush were less dark, as if the land enjoyed a perennial springtime. Even the lilt of nearby voices was different, quicker, as if everyone were impatient all the time. When someone agree with you, they said "Oy" instead of "Oc."

For want of other ways to pass the time between supper and sleep that night, she agreed to tell the tale. "This third story about the monster of Tarascon," she began, "commences much as did the second. The saints arrived at Saintes-Marie-by-the-Sea, and there parted from one another. Martha and Magdalen followed River Rhodanus northward, and in time arrived at Tarascon, which was not a happy place.

"Remember that much of Gaul had at that time been subject to Roma for only a century or so, and had never been completely pacified. From time to time the threat of rebellion arose, which the Romans dealt with in four ways. First, they maintained a garrison at Arelate, a full legion, and stationed cohorts in other towns. Second, they reorganized key towns like Tarascon, on the river, as *coloniae*, with streets laid out like Egyptian

chessboards, with arenas and amphitheaters, hippodromes, *fora*, and temples for the Roman gods.
Thirdly, because there were not enough men in
Roma to man all the garrisons in all the lands the
empire governed, Roma recruited Numidians in
Africa, and sent them to the eastern cities. They
recruited Gauls in these parts, and shipped them
to Africa, Egypt, or Greece. That way, legionaries
were never sympathetic to local causes, and did not
ally themselves with conquered peoples against the
interests of Roma.

"Thus the legion at Arelate was comprised of
Egyptians—officers who spoke Greek, and common
men who spoke a dialect related to that of the Jews
of Palestine. Now Greek, Latin, and Gaulish are
similar tongues, and it is not difficult for a speaker
of one to learn the others. But the Egyptian com-
moners could not easily learn any of them. When
an Egyptian legionary shopped in the forum at
Arelate, he could only point and shout for what he
wanted. Thus there was little communication
between legionaries and the people they controlled,
and there were many misunderstandings. No love
was lost between them.

"Remember, Rome maintained her dominion in
four ways. This is the fourth: legionaries, from the
time of Marius on, served twenty years, and when
their time was done, they were promised ten or
twenty acres of farmland, and a mule of their own.
Many such retired soldiers were given land near
coloniae like Tarascon, but such land did not appear
like magic, nor was it hewn from virgin forest.
When Rome conquered, she divided the estates of
noble Gauls, taking a portion for herself. Such state

lands were often left in Gaulish hands for a generation or more, and when the time came for them to give it up, they did not do so with good grace. They resented the Egyptian legionaries, and because they had no common language, they could not discover that, as farmers, they had more in common with each other than either did with Roman officials and tax collectors.

"Thus when Gaul and Egyptian met at a crossroads or a well—both sacred places to Gauls—there were often fights, because the Egyptians did not know how to behave there. And when Egyptians averted their eyes in passing, it was a mark of respect, but Gauls considered them sneaky, because they would not look a man in the eye. Because the legionaries had no wives, they looked covetously at Gaulish women, not knowing which ones were married, and which not. Gaulish fathers and husbands took offense, and sometimes sneaked up on Egyptian farms by night, and killed the farmers.

"That was the situation Saint Martha found when she arrived. 'You go on to Lugdunum,' she told Magdalen. 'I see that my mission is to be here.'

"Now Martha spoke with the Gauls of Tarascon in Latin, because most educated people knew a bit of the Roman language. She told them of her God, and his Son, and said that those who believed and worshipped them were like brothers and sisters who sometimes quarreled, but in the end were reconciled, and shared the house and land of the Father in peace.

"'Go tell that to the legionaries,' said the Gauls. 'It is they who covet our women and defile our sacred places.'

" 'To the one God and his Son, the whole world is a sacred place,' said Martha, 'but I will speak with them also, and tell them the Word.'

"So she trudged the roads from one farm to the next, Gaulish and Egyptian alike, and gave the farmers the same message: that in the House of the one true God, they were all one family. To the Gauls she said, 'Come to the basilica in Arelate, where the bankers, scribes, and moneylenders preside, and I will tell you more.' To the Egyptians she said the same, for the basilica was neutral ground for both peoples."

"Wait!" objected Gregorius loudly, breaking everyone's rapture. "If Gauls and the Egyptians had no common speech, how did the Saint address both of them?"

"Did I not say that the Jews of Palestine spoke a language much like Egyptian, and was not Martha a Jew? And was not Sarah, left behind by the sea, also Egyptian? Had not Martha spoken with her often enough, during those long weeks at sea, to learn where Jewish Aramaic and Egyptian were different, and where they were the same? Saint Martha stayed in Tarascon because she knew she was the bridge between the Gauls and the colonists, or rather, the Christian faith was."

Gregorius snorted. "You led us into your trap, didn't you?" Ibn Saul, annoyed that the mood of the tale was now broken, scowled at the priest. Lovi put a restraining hand on his lover's knee.

"We are all tired," said Pierrette. "If you wish, we can continue this another night. Now I'm going to lay my bed." She stood, then made her way from the fire to the place she had tethered Gustave, beneath a pine tree where the ground was cushioned with fallen needles.

At the far end of the portage was a village, a cluster of stone-and-timber houses without walls or a gate. The Liger was narrow there, and ibn Saul was concerned that it might not be navigable. "Those long, narrow boats seem just right for such a stream," said Pierrette who, a fisherman's daughter, knew more of boats then the others did. "I suspect they drift with the current, which is quite fast, and use those long poles to fend from the banks."

So it was. A single boat could not bear the four of them, their baggage, and Gustave the donkey, so ibn Saul was forced to hire two. The scholar and his treasured instruments, Pierrette, and the donkey went in the first boat, and the others in the second, with the rest of their goods. One poleman on the trailing boat was very tall. He seemed to wield his long, heavy pole with great ease, as if it weighed nothing at all. Was that Yan Oors? If it were, how had he managed to get his position there? The boatmen were clannish, and Pierrette thought they were all from the same village. How could a stranger fit in among them?

The valley through which they threaded that first day, and several that followed, was heavily forested. Willows, elders, and cedars crowded the banks and leaned out over the water. If there were villages or tilled fields beyond, they could not be seen from the water or the occasional beaches that formed on the insides of bends in the stream.

To Pierrette, it seemed as though every bend

they rounded took them deeper into a darkening land. Strangely, it was not exactly unfamiliar. Ordinarily, within the limited scope of most people's travel, someone might observe changes in the life surrounding himself as he climbed from deep, watered valley to wind-swept plain, and to scoured ridge-top. Rich greens gave way to dark shades, broad leaves to narrow, then to hard, prickly vegetation that even goats spurned. Now Pierrette observed such changes on a grander scale, because the entire northern country was as moist as a sheltered Provençal valley, and the trees and bushes were everywhere those she had seen only in two places—the sheltering northern face of the Sainte Baume range, and the tiny vale that concealed that pool sacred to *Ma*, the ancient goddess who had sent her on this voyage. Great beeches stood like gray, smooth sentinels where springs splashed down the banks, and delicate maples cloaked the hills. Oaks with leaves as large as her hand grew tall as pines, and spread their heavy branches wide.

But she was not comfortable with the familiarity. Here, though everything was lush, there was no sense of refuge in the verdure. Instead, with every footstep she took ashore, she felt as though the detritus beneath her soles was soft and rotten, and if she kicked over a clod it would smell not of rich humus, but of something dead and corrupt. But she kept such impressions to herself, and even though she felt uneasy, when night fell she still made her bed at some distance from the others.

❖   ❖   ❖

"Hello, little witch," said the deep, soft voice.

"Yan! I thought it was you, wielding that pole. But how . . ."

"Such a stick weighs nothing at all," he said. "It was no trouble for me to demonstrate my ability to wield it—and besides, I am related on my mother's side to one of the boatman's god-fathers."

"You are?"

"Well . . . Everyone has an uncle who married someone from the next village, or went off to seek his fortune in the city, or . . ."

"Whatever ruses you used, I'm glad you're still with us. I have been worried. There is something dark, something ugly, about this land. Have you felt it?"

"I have. Sleeping in the woods at night, away from the rest of you, I have . . . seen things."

"What?"

"Dark things, mostly quite small, hiding when the moon is out, then scurrying westward when clouds cover it, as if its meager light is more than they can bear."

"But what do they look like? Are they beasts? Do they scurry on four legs, or six, or two? Have they fur, or scales?"

"I see only shadows, not what makes them, and shadows are distorted shapes without either fur or scales. I know only that the sight of them makes my blood clot in my veins."

"You said they were going westward. Is it always so? How can that be?"

"Whatever their goal, it is the same direction we will be taking once this river completes its great bend to the west. I hope it's not the same place we're going."

How could it be so? mused Pierrette. Her own path led beyond the furthest point of land, beyond the last known island. Could the shadowy things cross over water? And why? When Minho had voiced the great spell that saved his kingdom from fiery destruction, he had left behind everything that was not sweet and good. If the shadows were ugly or evil, what would they want there?

But Yan Oors knew no more than she did. Perhaps as time and miles passed, things would become clearer.

When the Liger began its long turn from north to west at last, Pierrette's discomfort lessened for a while—or perhaps she only became enured to it. Other streams joined the river, and where one broad tributary entered it, the combined flows widened it considerably. "The next town is Noviodonnum," said the owner of their boats. "That is as far as I will go. I can pick up a cargo of wool, and perhaps a chest or two of tin from the mines across the sea. You'll travel more comfortably, anyway, on the broad-bottomed craft that ply these slow waters."

"We are in the heart of the Franks' domain now," ibn Saul told his companions privately. "I think it wise to continue our policy of avoiding all encounters of an official nature. I have thus far not taken advantage of any of the names good Bishop Arrianus gave me, and I do not intend to do otherwise now, though there is an abbey in Noviodonnum. Just a mile beyond that town, I have been told, at the confluence with a minor river, is a traders' entrepôt. We will go ashore there."

The entrepôt, above a bank where haphazard planks and pilings constituted a wharf, was a collection of staved hovels roofed with bark. There they ran into a snag: a Viking ship had been seen at Fleury only a fortnight before, and no boatmen would fare downstream. Several broad boats were drawn entirely up on shore, as if for a long wait.

At a loss how to proceed, they made camp in a sheltered spot well away from the muddy, stinking streets and midden heap. For the first time since their portage, the donkey Gustave earned his oats, dragging their luggage thence on a rudely made sledge.

After a frugal meal, a gruel of greens and grain flavored with the last of the salted fish, ibn Saul suggested that Pierrette finish the third tale of Saint Martha.

"There isn't much to tell," she said. "Martha brought Gauls and Egyptian legionnaires together in the basilica, and taught them what she knew, repeating everything she said in both Latin and Aramaic, or perhaps Egyptian. The basilica was home to administrative offices and a trading floor. It was technically the emperor's personal property, but Martha told them that while they occupied it together for a purpose not the emperor's, but God's, it was His house, and His peace was upon it. Seeing how easy it was to rub shoulders with those they had hitherto considered enemies, both Gauls and legionaries paid close attention to her words, and some were even converted right on the spot.

"As time went on, weeks and then months, others joined them, impressed how well the new Christians got along with each other, despite their barriers of language and customs. Also, once they had agreed to coexist peacefully with the Gauls, many of the legionaries revealed just how much Latin they actually knew, after twenty years in Roman service. Now that they no longer felt clannish and excluded, they were willing to use it more, to speak with their neighbors."

Then Pierrette fell silent. When Gregorius realized she was finished, he protested. "That's all? But what of the *tarasque*, the river monster?"

"Oh, that. Did I forget to say? When the Legion had first come to Egypt, it was as conquerors, under the emperor Augustus, who gave them a new emblem to commemorate their victory—one of the great crocodiles of the Nile, with an iron collar and chain at its neck. The 'monster' Martha 'subdued' was not the beast itself, but the legion whose emblem it was."

"So the third tale is really the second one, and vice versa," reflected ibn Saul. "Or rather, the pagan tale and the historic one combined in the memories of people to become the middle tale, the one that they 'remember' today."

"You could say that," Pierrette replied equitably, "but I'm not sure of it. Perhaps each story is true, in its own fashion."

"Perhaps so. There may be historic and etymological fragments in the earliest one, and this last one is reasonable enough, as an explanation—but the second tale? It is an allegory, as you have shown."

Pierrette knew she was not going to get the scholar to see what she saw: that the first two tales reflected the realities of their respective times, and carried underlying lessons or meanings that shaped the perceptions of teller and listener alike, while the third was flat and without value except for men like ibn Saul, for whom a loose end was an irritant, not an invitation.

Chapter 10 ∿ An Anomalous Vision

"I wonder how much one of those boats would cost?" Pierrette mused. The riverboats were heavy and broad of beam, with great log keels. Each had stations for four oars or six, a long steering oar aft, and carried two poles forward that could be used to fend off or propel or, lashed, would form a kind of bipedal mast to carry a triangular sail. Of course, such a sail would be of little use going downstream, she reflected, because it could not be set to catch winds from abeam, only following breezes, and there would be few easterly winds on the Liger once its course turned westward toward the sea.

"Could the four of us manage one, without a skilled master and extra hands?" asked ibn Saul.

As Pierrette pondered that, she saw, standing in the shadow of a large oak tree, a tall figure in a broad hat, leaning on a dark, thick staff—and she modified the words she had been about to say.

"With two oars in the water, and two men ahead to watch for rocks and snags and to wield poles to fend us off them, and with a fourth man at the steering oar, it should be possible," she said. "We would need only to propel our craft a bit faster than the river current when we needed steering way. Most of that time, we could just drift."

"That is one more person than we now have," said ibn Saul, "but I will see what can be arranged." He got to his feet, and strode purposefully to where the boatmen lazed by their craft. The negotiations were heated—Pierrette could hear them from their camp—but the riverboat owners were backcountry people with few of the negotiating skills that the scholar had mastered in his dealings with Greeks, Moslems, Byzantines, and the barbarians of Raetia and Pannonia, on the fringes of the Frankish domain.

"It was not the cheapest of the boats," he said later, showing it to Pierrette, "but it shows signs of recent repairs, and perhaps it will not fall apart beneath our feet. And, too, I have found a stout fellow, braver than the rest, who will wield a pole for us. He is some distant relation to our former boatman, but he's not a regular crewman, and has business of his own downriver.

Pierrette was glad she had specified their needs just as she had, when she had spotted Yan Oors beneath the oak tree's shadow. But it was dangerous for the gaunt one to be there, even in disguise. She almost hoped the one ibn Saul had hired would be someone else, but there, beside the boat, leaning on his staff, was Yan Oors.

By noon, their dunnage was stored amidships,

and they pushed off. They were able to keep to the midriver channel with little effort, and to ease their heavy craft into the swiftest flow at the outside of each bend, avoiding the sandy shallows that formed at the tightest parts of the turns. Yan Oors and the husky priest worked the bow poles, and because the gaunt fellow responded only with grunts and monosyllables, Gregorius soon tired of trying to draw him out. Lovi and ibn Saul each stood at an oar, and Pierrette at the helm. There was not much work for any of them, because the current bore them swiftly, but once in a while Pierrette called for oars, so she could steer them into the proper channel to avoid some impediment in the stream ahead.

"Tomorrow," ibn Saul grumbled, "I will stand forward and lean on a pole. You, priest, can row."

Fleury Abbey, famed as the seat of Theodulf, a Visigothic bishop, lay in ash and ruin, but it was not empty. The Vikings had leveled the town that had grown up around it, and had put Theodulf's villa, a few miles distant, to the torch, but now walls rose where none had been before. They were of wood, not stone, and they enclosed only a fraction of the original town, but they had twice withstood the Northmen's assaults.

"If this place is to your liking," Lovi whispered to his paramour, "you must part from this company."

"And will you also?" replied Gregorius, shaking his head. "Even were this place not a ruin, I would not leave you. I have told your master the true nature of my sojourn among the Norsemen, which he accepted most philosophically. Now, having seen the evidence before us of their true nature, he may be less eager to try to bargain with them, and I may be allowed to remain safely obscure."

"You could go back the way we came."

"Alone? Even if you came with me, it is a long row upstream, and I have no coin of my own for a boat or for sustenance. No, I will stay on. Perhaps, if there is substance to ibn Saul's Fortunate Isles, we will find refuge there."

They did not linger at Fleury. The city of Cenabum was less than a day's drifting downstream, and Cenabum had withstood Attila the Hun, and would not fall to mere Vikings, who were surely lesser warriors than had been the Scourge of God. There, in this city, the records and documents of six hundred years—of Romans, Visigoths, and Franks—remained intact. There, if anywhere, ibn Saul might find accounts of merchants who had encountered those mysterious Isles he sought, or who had at least sighted their high, black crags from afar, rising from a mist that confused them and confounded their strivings to draw nearer.

The great gates of the city were closed for the night when they arrived. Seeing the flicker and glow of campfires on the far shore, beneath the ruins of a fort at the head of the stone bridge across the Liger, they rowed over. They set up camp amid other travellers, and shared a fire with a wool merchant, because they were too late to gather wood for one of their own.

Pierrette felt uneasy there. The tumbled building stones were stained not only with soot, but also with blood. Was it the blood of Gallic defenders, or of the Vikings who had destroyed the fort? She felt faint, and her head swirled with strange imagery: she perceived ghostly images of men wearing strange armor that was neither Roman nor Gaulish, Visigothic nor Frankish. Was this a vision of a battle recently fought, and could those be Norsemen? But no, beneath those helmets were smooth-shaven or well-trimmed faces, and hair finely brushed and coiffed. Who, then, were they? She was dizzy, as if she had eaten mushrooms and nightshade, and was about to enter the Otherworld, but she had eaten neither, and had not uttered a spell.

Men both on foot and on horses swirled around her, as if she were not there. Somehow, none jostled her, as if she was made of mist, or they were. High overhead loomed walls that she had not seen when they had crossed the river. There had not even been enough rubble on the shore to account for such walls.

This, then, was no vision of the past, but of something that had never been. But according to everything Pierrette had learned, that was impossible! In the most ancient ages, Time had been a wheel that turned, bearing the observer inexorably into the future. Spells allowed powerful magicians to resist the turning of the wheel, to return to earlier times, merely by staying where they were. But no spell existed that gave even the greatest of them wings to fly faster than the turning wheel, and thus to visit, or even to envision, what lay ahead.

But Time was a Wheel, its rim a circle, and any point could be reached by staying in one place while the wheel turned and, beyond the furthest past, lay . . . the future. Thus spells like *Mondradd in Mon* had allowed the future to be seen.

But the Wheel of Time was broken, long ago. The sorcerer whose spell had broken it was long forgotten, but the devastation remained. In the most remote past lay eons of empty desolation, that could not be crossed, because it consumed all magic, all brightness, all life. And in the future lay . . . the Black Time, equally desolate, equally dead, where loomed only the dull husks of towering machines in which all the magic and wonder of the world were trapped.

Pierrette was afraid. If what she was seeing could not be, then was this a delusion? If so . . . was everything? Either this was the future, passing before her eyes like mist, or it was insanity. If the great walls of the fortress she could see had fallen in the past, the tumbled stones would remain. If those walls had not yet been built, then she was seeing the future, and that could not be.

A battle horn brayed. On Pierrette's left, scores of men lifted tall, spindly ladders, and flung them against the walls. She heard a high, clear voice urging men to climb. She turned, and for the first time noticed the owner of that voice—a figure astride a war-horse, armed and armored, bearing a pennant and wearing no helm. Despite the armor, that commander of men was no bigger than Pierrette, and she was convinced it was not a man but . . . a girl. A girl, leading men to war, urging them to scale the fortress's walls?

For a moment, Pierrette felt relieved. This vision must be the past, because only ancient Scythians or Gauls had allowed their queens to bear arms, to lead them in battle. But no, never had Gauls worn armor like that, and the girl-general's words were almost recognizable, a melange of Latin and another tongue, perhaps Frankish.

Dust swirled around Pierrette, but she could not feel its grit, nor smell it. The dust, like the horses, soldiers, and walls, was in some Otherworld she could see, but not touch or feel. Again, she heard that clear voice, but this time it ended abruptly in a cry of pain and dismay—and the bold rider fell backwards from her mount, a thick bolt protruding high on her chest, by her shoulder.

Pierrette felt herself moved—not walking, but drifting, as if she were dust borne on air churned by rearing horses and running men. Nearer she came, until she hovered over the wounded commander, and heard her begging someone to break off the arrow and push it through her flesh.

"You will bleed to death, Jehanne," protested a gruff soldier, his words coarsely accented and strange.

"If God wills it, I will not," said the maid—for indeed she was a girl. But who was she? And where, or when, was this?

Pierrette watched the soldier remove the arrow. The girl arose shakily, a crumpled cloth bound over her wound. Two men helped her mount her horse. A third handed her the banner she had dropped, and from the ranks arose a cry: "For God, Francia, and Jehanne la Pucelle!" The assault on the walls gathered new force, and even as Pierrette watched, a banner like the one that girl bore rose atop the wall, and black smoke arose from fires within . . .

Chapter 11 ∿ Darkness from the Land

Pierrette got to her feet, shaken, but saw around her only the fallen stones of a lesser fortress, grown over with woodbine. There, beyond, was ibn Saul's canvas pavilion and their fat boat, and across the river the Roman walls of the city of Cenabum, which the Franks called Orleans.

"Are you well, little witch?" asked Yan Oors, who had come upon her when she was still lost in her vision.

"Oh, Yan. I'm glad you're here. You've known me since I was a small child. Tell me now: have I been mad all this time, thinking I'd deciphered the nature of magics—those of the past that work no more, and those pitiful few spells of the present that have not been destroyed by the great religions, or by the likes of Master ibn Saul?"

"If you are mad, then I am a figment of your madness—and I consider myself real. I suppose you could be imagining that I am speaking to you, but could *I*? I think you must assume that what you perceive is real, and then freely infer everything that stems from that assumption."

Pierrette nodded. "I must, mustn't I? But then I must throw out other principles I have depended on, because . . . Oh, how can I do that?"

"Explain it to me. Even if I don't understand, sometimes explaining things makes them clearer for the explainer."

"I'll try. A vision came upon me here, though I uttered no spell to call it forth. It was an overwhelming seeing, a terrible scene of a battle that may someday be." She described everything she remembered of the vision. Then: "You see? If I saw the future, then I must discard the assumption that the Wheel of Time is broken, or else that those few spells that allow their worker to travel upon the Wheel, in mind or in body, all point into the past, and never the future."

"If the sprite Guihen were here, he might have another conclusion," said Yan Oors. "You once used the spell called '*Mondradd in Mon*' to go back to an age where he was a youth, and there prophesied a future he could not see, but which you knew would come to pass. In that past, you knew the future—and did you not conclude that all oracles must be as you were then: minds from future times, prophets in ours, able to 'see' our future because it was really their own present?"

"But I am not from a future time. I am from . . . now."

"Yet you neither strode upon that future ground on your own feet, nor viewed it from the eyes of a magpie, as you have done before. You yourself said you drifted like dust on the wind, bodiless. Perhaps you were but a dream in another mind, and thus you circumvented the rules you have gleaned from other experiences."

"That is not elegant, Yan Oors. It presupposes someone in some far future, to whom the events I witnessed are in the past. It presupposes that the spell *Mondradd in Mon*, or something like it, is known, will still be known, and . . . it is all too perplexing."

"Then let it be so, for now. You did not begin your seeking, as a little girl, with full understanding—are you perhaps growing impatient at the 'old age' of eighteen?"

"I am not yet eighteen, and you know it!" she said, chuckling, realizing the truth of what he said.

"Then wait until your birthday, at least, to worry that you are mad, just because you do not understand everything."

"I will," she promised. Her girlish smile endured a moment longer, then faded. "What of the dark shapes you saw, all travelling westward? Have you seen more of them?"

"I have been sleeping on the boat, guarding it. I think that like magic, unnatural things do not easily abide moving water. But even now, standing ashore, I sense them without seeing them. They are still about."

"I wonder what they could be?" Pierrette mused. In truth, she was not sure she wanted to know.

Early the next morning the scholar ibn Saul left the camp. About noon, he returned from the city

of Cenabum, wearing a sour face. "All the city's
archives are now buried in secret places, walled in
with old stones, to hide them should the Vikings
ever breach the walls. There is nothing for us
there." He barked commands at Lovi, Gregorius,
and Yan Oors, who dismantled his tent and stowed
it aboard the boat. By mid-afternoon, they were
many miles downstream.

At Sodobrium they spent one night in the
shadow of a stone church. "We're lucky this place
is unburned," said Lovi. "Perhaps these brothers
are more holy than those of Fleury, and have thus
been spared the Vikings' scourge." The priests and
monks were eager for news, and plied the party
with fine wines surely intended for sacramental use,
which Pierrette did not think was especially pious
of them. Eating little from their table, she excused
herself early and went in search of Yan Oors, who
refused to tread Christian sanctified ground.

Outside, in the little street of half-timbered
houses surrounding the church, she saw for herself what the gaunt one had described: a shadow,
like a stain upon the dirt street, but no object stood
between it and the waning sunlight. It was a
shadow, but it hovered above the dirt, as if stuck
in it, and straining to be free. Pierrette drew back
from a whiff of corruption like old blood spilled,
or a dead rat. The shadow was intent upon its own
struggle. In absolute silence, it writhed and twisted,
now connected to the ground only by a tenuous
thread.

Her thoughts receded to another place, another
church, where she had seen something all too

similar: her sister Marie lay on a stretcher of cloaks and poles, struggling in the grip of the demon that possessed her. Around her huddled Father Otho, Sister Agathe, Anselm, her father Gilles, the castellan Reikhard, and Marah, Queen of the Gypsies. The same low, westerly sun sent tenuous fingers of golden light among the church's columns, light that was absorbed by the darkness emerging from Marie's mouth, her ears, her very pores, darkness that strained against the ligature of virgin's hair that constrained it, that drew it forth . . . Marie's demon had fought to remain within her, while this smoky apparition strained to break free—but otherwise they were all too similar, and Pierrette trembled now with the fear and revulsion she had felt then.

With a soundless gasp, the shadow broke free. It spun around as if seeking its bearings, then scurried off, hugging the walls of houses, tracing the niches of doorways like the shadow of a bird flying down the street—yet there was no bird.

Then it was gone, leaving behind only a sense of its avid craving, it's mindless urge for . . . for whatever it craved. It had gone west, like the ones Yan Oors described. West, into the setting sun. But why? And had it been a demon? It had been so small, so . . . unformed. Marie's demon had assumed one shape, then another, in its struggle: it had fought Reikhard as an ancient warrior, confronted Anselm as an eagle, battered Gilles like a storm at sea. No, what Pierrette had just seen was no powerful demon, shaped by the evil in men, and in Marie herself. It was tiny and weak, shapeless and mindless, but . . . it was still evil. Of that much Pierrette was sure.

She made her way to the boat, where Yan Oors stood solitary watch. "I saw that of which you spoke," she said, leaning on the wale. "It broke free of a foul stain in the dirt, as if it had taken form there. It went westward just as you said." Yan Oors nodded, having nothing to add. "Why westward?" Pierrette asked, not expecting an answer. "What evil draws them? What are they seeking? The Norsemen come from the west. They pillage, rape, and burn. Are the apparitions only seeking their like? Are they formless demons, newborn in filth and corruption, seeking amenable hosts? If so, then are the Norsemen who plague this country truly infested with evil?"

"I suppose any explanation will do," rumbled the gaunt one, "for want of a better."

"What else could they seek?" asked Pierrette. "What other evil lies in the west?"

"We are going that way also," Yan replied. "When we get there—wherever 'there' is—perhaps we will see for ourselves."

"I'm going to stay on the boat with you for now," Pierrette said. "Perhaps if you let out the lines, so the flowing river is all around us, I will be able to sleep."

"I never sleep. I will watch over you," Yan Oors said, leaning on his rusty iron staff, brown as old wood.

Chapter 12 ～ A Close Call

Sodobrium to Turones was a day on the river. Turones, city of miracles, where Saint Martin had brought Christianity hundreds of years before, was the goal of pilgrims from as far as Rome itself. Its shrines and streets had witnessed the saint's appearance long after he was in his grave. In Turones, a Bishop Gregorius had written a history of the Frankish kings for the edification of those Merovingian louts, now themselves long in their graves.

Now the great city stood surrounded by a wall half wood, half stone quarried from its own ruins. *Here*, Pierrette saw a broken column carved by Roman hands and tools, now embedded in the city wall. *There*, she saw laborers sliding another great stone on sapling rails. It had once been part of an arch in the cathedral whose charred walls stood bleak and useless. Turones, city of miracles, was now a city of ashes and ruins, from which dark, shapeless shadows arose and set off westward, ever westward, seeking what hideous goal no one knew.

The ashes were no longer fresh. The blood in the streets was old and black. But still, Pierrette sensed the dark entities that rose from the ferment of ashen lye, old blood, and human tears. She did not see them, but they were there. Even Lovi and Gregorius treaded lightly in those ruined streets. Only ibn Saul, impervious in his disbelief in such things, strode unheedfully to the bishop's temporary quarters, an unburned house that had belonged to a cloth merchant slain by Norsemen two years before.

"Oh, no," said the bishop, "the archbishop has moved away. What records and books remained unburned, he took with him for safekeeping. You'll find nothing here but ashes."

Disappointed but unsurprised, the small company returned to their boat, intending to camp downstream where the water's flow had diluted the stink of mud, ash, offal, and sewage that washed down from Turones, city of miracles.

On an island in the river stood an ancient shrine, miraculously unharmed. "The Vikings have destroyed everything else," muttered ibn Saul. "Why not this also?"

Pierrette examined the stone monolith, a dark column set on a white marble base of Roman design. "The whole story is here," she said. "See the pictures?" She pointed.

"That appears to be a saint standing in a boat."

"For a while, it was. But look how someone has battered the cross, and has scratched lines at the boat's prow and elsewhere."

"What meaning do you attach to that?"

"First, the bishop's miter and cross were added, perhaps when the original pagan stone was elevated on its Roman base. The carvings' styles differ. Before the figure was a Christian saint, he was a pagan river-god. Now the Vikings have freed him by hammering away his cross, scratching horns on his hat, and adding a serpent's head to the boat's prow. Now this is a pagan shrine once again."

"The way you say it, I almost think you believe that there are gods and saints, all vulnerable to the whims of their worshippers."

"They are vulnerable, aren't they? The stone attests to that. As for what I believe, I am only one person, and my convictions do not affect the world very much."

Pierrette liked the little island, and wished they could linger there. The day was bright and sunny, the shade of old, gnarled willows was cool, and whether by some magic of the once-again-pagan shrine or of the river, there were no slinking shadows, no ominous mists. But ibn Saul wished to press on. "We have many days' travel before this river debouches in the sea. Besides, the shores are flatter here, the banks are broad beaches with no place to hide our boat. I don't wish to linger."

"And this is the favored season for Norsemen," added Gregorius, now constantly on edge. Whenever his arms were not required at the oars, he sat in the bow, afraid that Yan Oors and Pierrette, who had never been owned by a Viking, might be less alert than he, who had, and might delay for the space of a dozen vital heartbeats before crying alarm. He urged that if any large boat were spotted, they ground their own craft and flee inland, leaving their baggage to occupy potential pursuers.

"Leave my instruments?" objected ibn Saul. "Leave my notes and commentaries? Never!" Every night, the scholar unpacked his devices and took sightings of certain stars, then made cryptic notes in a wood-covered codex. If clouds covered the stars, he took an ornate brass bowl, its rim inscribed with symbols, and filled it with water, then floated a skinny splinter of black rock on it, resting on a flat disc of pine wood. However cagey he was not to let the others see exactly what he did, Pierrette had a fair idea: the bronze tool with its sliding arc and movable arrow measured elevation above the horizon, and when sighted on the pole star, indicated how far north they were. The stone in the bowl was a lodestone, of which the ancient Sea Kings had known. It always pointed north. When she mentioned it to Lovi, he said that Gregorius had seen Vikings use something similar, though he had never gotten close enough to see if it was exactly the same.

"Your chest is not large, Master ibn Saul," she said. "Were you to repack its contents in my donkey's panniers, they would be ready on an instant's notice." He resisted her suggestion at first, because the chest's clever internal partitions kept everything secure and in order, but when the river broadened further and hiding places could no longer be found, he at last acquiesced. Now Pierrette's own belongings were rolled in her Gallic greatcloak, and the scholar's tools rested in Gustave's panniers.

❖   ❖   ❖

Where the river Meduana entered the Liger, they saw columns of smoke rising somewhere upstream, and rowed quickly past. "That is the town of Juliomagus," said Gregorius, "and that smoke is not from bakers firing up the bread ovens."

Just then a shout echoed across the water, and Pierrette saw a dozen men scrambling to drag a long, narrow boat into the water. "Vikings!" squalled Gregorius. The quick efficiency of the boatmen assured the party that they were not fishermen or traders—already the craft was afloat, and oars were in the water. Round shields painted in garish colors hung from pegs at the sheer rail, and helmets gleamed—iron, gold, and polished bronze. "Row!" shouted ibn Saul. Lovi and Gregorius scrambled to unship their oars. Pierrette grasped the steering oar's shaft and ibn Saul went forward where Yan Oors already had his pole over the side. With each tremendous push—he had room for several long strides aft before he had to lift the pole and reset it—the heavy craft seemed to surge ahead, and Pierrette felt her own oar become alive; the boat responded to her slightest push or pull. But despite their best efforts, the Vikings, with six oars in the water, each pulled by a strong, fit warrior, gained rapidly on them. When Pierrette looked back, she saw the gleam of their helmets, the bright paint of their round shields, the glimmer of spearheads, broadaxes, and unsheathed swords.

"Ashore!" Gregorius yelled at her. "Steer us ashore!" Instead, Pierrette pulled sharply on her oar, sending the craft further from the near bank into the middle of the river.

"Go back," shouted ibn Saul from the bow.

"We're too deep, and the poles cannot reach bottom."

Ignoring him, Pierrette steered sharply across the river's course, into the muddy brown ribbon where the Meduana's current had not yet lost itself in the main stream. Propelled only by Lovi and Gregorius at the oars, the boat lost steering way. Pierrette had to pull her oar over sharply to make the boat turn at all. A spear splashed in the water beside her. Another thumped against the sternpost, but it did not stick. The Vikings were so close she could see beads of sweat on the brow of the big man in the prow of their skinny boat.

Ahead was a bend northward, where both currents swirled against a steep, eroded bank. Pierrette forced the ungainly craft toward it. She felt the boat tremble as the swift water took it. Gregorius and Lovi's efforts at the oars hardly seemed to matter; the steering oar lay limp in the water, but when Pierrette looked up at the willows along the bank, only an oar's length away, their branches were rushing past so quickly she had no time to distinguish leaves or limbs. A quick glance back show that the northmen's boat no longer gained on them—in fact, the rowers had raised their oars. They had avoided the confluence of the waters, where green met brown, and now they swung completely around. She heard the Viking helmsman's cries and watched oars splash into the water, then pull in time with the chant. The distance between the two craft widened quickly now.

In moments, the Vikings were out of sight as the heavy boat rounded the bend, moving swiftly, only a scant few fathoms from the south bank. When they were sure that the pursuit had ended, ibn Saul asked Pierrette to explain what she had done, and why the Vikings had broken off. "I steered us to the outside of the approaching bend," she said. "Our pursuers thought to cut across the inside, overcoming the slower current there with their superior force of oars, but the combined power of the two streams and the river's rush to continue in a straight course despite the shape of the bed that constrains it gave us the lead. Perhaps, too, the heavy sediments of the Meduana, all accumulating where the current was slowest, made their keel drag and their oars foul. Besides, every mile they chased us downstream, they would have had to row back against the current, in the heat of the day. Perhaps, also, they realized that our craft rides high in the water, even with five aboard, and thus could not be loaded with rich plunder."

"Next time, I won't question your decisions at the helm," said the scholar.

Chapter 13 ~ The Burning City

They went ashore before dusk, when a mist on the river shortened visibility downstream. "Were we to encounter Norsemen, we would not see them until it were too late to escape as we did today," ibn Saul said. Pierrette did not remind him of the special conditions—the confluence of two streams and the bend beyond—which had made their escape possible.

When Pierrette, as was her custom, went off to her isolated bed, she observed the last glow of sunset reflected on the water downstream. But no—the sun was long set. What she had observed was . . . fire. Somewhere, not far, raged a great conflagration. She roused ibn Saul, and when his eyes had adjusted, far from the campfire's light, he too saw the glow reflected on the water. "It is a city burning," he said. "It can be nothing other than an attack by Norsemen—and judging by the extent of the flames, they must be inside the walls, for no buildings but great abbeys and churches would provide fuel for such a blaze. We are trapped between Norsemen upstream and down."

Pierrette observed that the fire's reflection was now redder still, and had there been more than a sliver of moonlight, she would not see it at all. "We must get aboard our boat now," she said. "By dawn, we'll have no chance but to take to the woods. Afloat, keeping to the south bank, we may be able to slip by the Norsemen, whose eyes will be dazzled by the light of the burning city for some time still."

Lovi and Gregorius muffled their oars' shafts with woolen cloth. Only Yan Oors took up a pole, because only he could wield one with strength and dexterity enough to keep it from clunking against the boat's side.

This stretch of the river had many islands, and it was not easy to decide which channel to take at any divide in the stream. Every one would be narrower than the full river, and any might, in this season, peter out in reeds or skim so shallowly over a sandbar that they could not remain afloat. Any might narrow so much that a watchman ashore might not only see them, but also cast a spear at them, with deadly result.

Generally choosing the southernmost channels, they drifted downstream, as silent as a log, huddling low unless required to steer, pole, or row. The red stain of firelight spread across the water. Now a column of spark-littered darkness blotted out the stars downstream. Ahead loomed a greater blackness. "It's a bridge," whispered ibn Saul from the bow. "There is a great arched bridge spanning the entire river." Soon they could all see it. Each arch straddled a thirty-foot channel and stood easily that high above it. Pierrette counted four such spans— there might have been more—and steered for the leftmost, furthest from the burning light. Crenellated walls loomed high—forts commanding both ends of the bridge. The water's surface was no longer smooth, but riffled as if sharp rocks lay just beneath it.

A hoarse shout echoed across the water, and Pierrette saw movement on the bridge ahead—but it was too late to turn aside. The accelerating current had them in its grip, and they could only plunge ahead. "Row!" Pierrette cried out. "Row as hard as you can!"

Lovi and Gregorius put their backs and arms to it. The boat groaned and grumbled as it slid over a submerged rock, but hardly slowed. Now several voices shouted from ahead and above. Something splashed alongside—a thrown cobble. They would pass close by the south abutment, directly beneath the fort's wall. That wall wobbled: the Vikings, loath to throw away good spears in the water, were rocking a crenel, a great mass of stone whose mortar had perhaps been loosened by fire. It teetered ominously as several men wrestled with it.

"Row! Row!" she shouted. She felt the boat's surge as Yan Oors's pole found purchase in the channel bed, and they glided beneath the bridge . . . A black lump tumbled downward, and fell with a huge splash, just aft. Pierrette's steering oar leaped from her hands, splintered and broken, and the wave from the fallen masonry inundated her.

When she wiped her eyes, the bridge was behind. But their troubles were not over. The shouting had roused others, ashore where the dark hulls of uncountable long, narrow vessels were drawn up side by side. Dozens of men swarmed over the boats, and struggled to pull them free of the bank. Pierrette heard the rattle and thump of a score of heavy oars being run out, and then the clap of a tambour, establishing the stroke.

There were no islands to hide among, only the broad, open river. The bridge was now a mile behind, the fire-glow from the town imperceptible. Only the distant, rhythmic drumming indicated they were still being pursued. The splintered shaft of the steering oar dragged in its lashings. Water gleamed and swirled around the baggage amidships. Gustave the donkey snorted uneasily as it chilled his fetlocks. . . .

"We're sinking!" Pierrette cried. "Gregorius, pull harder. Lovi! Slack your oar." She could no longer steer from the helm, but it might still be possible to attain the low, reed-brushed shore. Ibn Saul grabbed their soil-bucket and bailed madly. It might slow their sinking by some imperceptible degree. It could not hurt to try.

Reeds squealed alongside and impeded the oars. Yan Oors continued to push them ahead, finding purchase for his pole somewhere beneath the riverbottom muck. Isolated reeds became clumps and hummocks, and they glided among them. Then, with a soft lurch, they came to a halt. The boat's wales were almost awash, and their baggage bumped and floated about. "Take what you can carry," Pierrette hissed. She helped Master ibn Saul

sling Gustave's panniers and then dived beneath the
murk to fasten his belly strap. Gustave, for once,
did not suck in breath to keep the strap loose, but
allowed her to draw it tight on the first try.

The rap of the Viking coxwain's tambour maintained the oarsmen's strokes. The only other sound
was the faint swish of water as they slipped out
of the boat, and pushed waist-deep through the
reeds. Yan Oors took the lead, probing with his
iron staff for a solid path. Angry cries arose
behind—the Norsemen had found their empty
boat. They heard the sounds of breaking wood—
their baggage being broken open, or the boat
being stove in, eliminating any hope of returning,
repairing it, and continuing to the sea, now only
a scant ten miles further on.

"It's just as well," said ibn Saul, good-natured
because he had managed to save his precious
instruments, and had had the foresight to wrap his
codices in oiled cloth and leather. "Considering the
state of the towns along the river, I doubt the
Norsemen left any villages near its mouth
unscathed, or any oceangoing boats uncaptured.
When we find dry ground, we must head north into
the forest. If my sightings of last night's stars were
correct, we may find succor there with your master Anselm's old friend, the Magister Moridunnon."

Pierrette was both excited and uneasy about that
prospect. Of course ibn Saul did not know everything about Moridunnon—that he was, or had been,
a most powerful druid, a sorcerer and a *guatatros*,
a speaker with the ancient Gaulish gods. He did
not know, as did Pierrette, that Moridunnon was
almost as old as Anselm himself was, and had been

an adviser to kings now centuries in their moldy graves. What he did not know, he could not write about. It was imperative that, if they did locate the ancient sorcerer, Pierrette should speak to him first, and warn him not to reveal himself to ibn Saul.

"We should wend a bit westward as we go north," she said. "I'm sure we'll have an easier time of it."

"Why so?" asked the scholar. "This forest country all looks much the same to me."

"Anselm said the best route was directly north of the Liger's mouth. We are near enough to that."

"I'll determine our position tomorrow, at noon. Then we shall see."

Pierrette knew enough of the scholar's methods to know that his instruments could only determine which way was north, and how far north they were. Only the ancient Sea Kings of Thera had known how to measure westering, and thus to make maps as accurate as the one she kept safe and dry, rolled up in her meager bundle of clothing.

They soon found high ground, and followed a sluggish stream until they attained a grassy clearing. There they made simple beds and wrapped themselves in whatever clothing they had managed to bring away with them. Pierrette's woolen *sagus* was almost as warm wet as dry, and she would sleep well, as would Lovi and Gregorius, who shared the priest's cloak. Yan Oors went off by himself— perhaps, indeed, he did not sleep. But Pierrette could not sleep, listening to the sound of ibn Saul's chattering teeth. He had not salvaged a cloak from the boat, and his once-fine raiment gave little comfort in the damp chill of the night. Pierrette got up, wrapped her own cloak around his shoulders, then snapped dry twigs from low pine branches to start a fire.

"I hope you have tinder," said the scholar. "Mine was ruined, and my flint seems to be missing as well."

"The inner bark on these twigs is powdery dry," she replied. "I think it will suffice." She laid her small handful of twigs like a tiny round hut, and surrounded it with larger ones, then spanned those with others, close together over the tinder heap but with enough space between for flames to have a free path upward. Then, placing herself between the unlit fire and the scholar, she whispered her spell.

The glow at her fingertips was no clear, Christian light, nor was it the warm, yellow glow she expected; it was sultry and red, a dull, angry flicker. Uneasily, she touched her fingertip to the tinder. To her relief, the flames that arose as the dry twigs ignited were entirely ordinary.

"That was quick," said ibn Saul, when she stepped aside so he could warm himself at the now-cheery blaze. Pierrette was not cheerful. The fire itself was ordinary, but the initial spark had not been so, and she now knew that in this place, this devastated land, no magic would work the way she might expect. The oily red flame was not a comfort, but a warning: do not trust the spirits of these trees, brooding shadows, murky streams and pools, because you do not know them, nor they you. Do not utter ancient words heedlessly, because they may mean something different here, something red and angry, something deadly, something . . . evil.

The scholar was completely unaware of what

Pierrette sensed. "Now I again believe we may survive to reach Moridunnon," he said before he fell asleep. "For a while, I feared I would die before morning." Pierrette let him keep her cloak. She did not expect to sleep that night, and the fire, despite its sinister source, was warm and bright.

Chapter 14 ∾ Strange Houses

The next day brought them to a divide, and to a stream that flowed northward. With the remainder of their luggage heaped atop Gustave's panniers, they made good time.

At noon, when the sun was near the height of its arc, ibn Saul unwrapped his instruments and a codex containing long columns of numbers. They were written in a variant of the Arabic numerals that facilitated calculations that would have stymied the most proficient Roman mathematician of yore. The scholar stuck a stick in the ground, angled northward, and at the exact moment its shadow was shortest, used his movable arc and arrow to determine the sun's height. "We are only three or four days short of our goal, even if we find no decent road," he announced. But they had salvaged only a small wheel of soggy cheese and a single fat sausage from the supplies on the boat, and those were soon gone. They would need food, and soon, if they were to continue.

They camped on a ridge overlooking a broad valley, where a sizable stream snaked and twisted. Surely, it led west to the sea, but no one suggested they try to acquire a boat. Broad enough to float on, the stream was navigable for Norsemen as well. A bit left of their planned descent rose columns of smoke—the trickles of hearth fires, not the billows of burning buildings. Despite their rumbling stomachs, they decided it would be wise to wait until morning to approach the community. It was not close enough for them to arrive before darkness.

They slept comfortably enough, at the edge of the woods, but Pierrette's sleep was frequently interrupted by uneasy awakenings, as if dark, unseen things scampered over her bedclothes, heading always westward.

The village stood astraddle a low-water ford. Its houses, mostly one- and two-story, were of heavy timber and mud brick—both available in good supply nearby. Much of the timberwork looked new, yellow instead of gray. The arrival of five strangers created not the outcry they would have expected, but only a sullen, wary caution. A boy herding a flock of geese deftly goaded his charges into the underbrush, and moments later Pierrette saw him slinking along the bank toward the town's only street. Thus forewarned, three white-haired men came forth, gripping an assortment of rusty weapons—a Gallic longsword with a chip in its blade, a boar-spear with a bronze crosspiece a foot from its point, and a short, broad gladius that, from its rust and its style, might have belonged to some Roman ancestor, many centuries before.

Lovi and ibn Saul kept their own superior weapons sheathed, and Yan Oors leaned on his staff as if it were only what it seemed: a none-too-well-fashioned walking stick. Pierrette, least threatening of their band, stepped ahead of the others. She explained how they had come to be afoot, without baggage or food.

"We also have experienced Viking wrath," said the village magistrate, who bore the Roman name Sempronius. "Our town once perched on a bluff overlooking the sea, at the mouth of this stream. They burned it, and took most of our young men and women as slaves. We are all that's left. If you want to stay, you will be welcome."

"We can't do that. But will you sell us food for our journey, and cloaks or blankets, if you can spare them?"

Sempronius agreed to discuss it. He motioned Pierrette and ibn Saul forward—the rest must stand where they were. He led them into the first house, to a table of rough wood, with splintery benches not yet worn smooth. He produced a pitcher and clay cups, into which he poured a clear, golden wine.

"This is fine, strange stuff," ibn Saul said after his first sip. "What grape produces it?"

Sempronius laughed. "The red grape of the forest—this is apple wine. Our vineyards lie overgrown with weeds, too far away from here to tend, but even the sourest apples, properly bruised and crushed, yield a sweet nectar." When the bargaining was done, the scholar resolved, several skins of apple wine would be included with their new supplies.

"What is that strange little hole in the wall?" asked Pierrette. "I saw similar ones on other houses here."

Sempronius's gaze turned cautious. "Indeed you must be new to this country. That is a spirit hole." Reluctantly, when ibn Saul pressed him, he explained that when an evil dream plagued someone, the hole provided escape for whatever had caused it, when the victim awakened and cried out in fear or misery. "Without the spirit holes, our houses would become infested with nightmares, and we would have to sleep on the roofs or in trees to escape them." He was reluctant to say more, sensing that the scholar considered him foolishly superstitious, and Pierrette had no opportunity to question him privately.

"What odd beliefs country folk evolve in their isolation," mused ibn Saul, when they were again under way, following a stream that, so they were told, led upward to the mountainous spine of the land, to Broceliande, the great forest of ancient trees no man had cut, even in the time of the Romans. "Spirit holes, indeed."

Pierrette did not respond to his scoffing, but when she later found herself walking next to Yan Oors, ahead of the others, she asked if he had noticed the holes. "Nightmares indeed. I saw several holes," he responded. "And all were in the west walls. Some houses had several of them. I presume that those houses had several rooms, and one such hole for each chamber." He had noticed something else that Pierrette had not: the village street trended north and south, instead of along the river, as might have been expected, unless there was a definite road going north from the ford, which there was not. "I think that when they built that new village, they laid it out with those 'spirit holes' in mind—so no western wall would abut another house, or even another room."

"We haven't seen any other towns here," Pierrette said, "but none of the ones we passed through before were like that. I wonder if it is an old custom in these parts, or . . ."

"Or if the shadows that well up from spilled blood and offal, and creep always westward, are more recent, and only a new village might be built like this, to allow them passage?"

Pierrette formed a mental image of just such an apparition, trapped in a house with no hole, bumbling mindlessly along its westernmost wall seeking an exit, but without the intelligence even of a rat, which would know enough to retrace its steps and find freedom. "If we pass through another town, one not thrown up by refugees from the Norsemen, and it is not so arranged, we will know that such westward-creeping shades were not known of old. But we will be no closer to knowing why they creep and bumble always to the west, or what drives them, or what they seek." Yan Oors agreed that was so.

But the gaunt man had something else on his mind. "I have spoken with the scholar," he said, hesitantly. "I have told him that . . . that I must go my own way, from here on."

"You mean . . . you're leaving me? But you said your destination was the same as mine!"

"Near enough, it is. But you are now going to visit this old magician, who lives north of here—if indeed he still lives. I will take a more direct route, and if I find a sow bear that is big with cubs, I'll come and fetch you—and you alone. Besides, though he has accepted me uncritically, and I have tried not to give him anything to write about, I have been pressing my luck. Later or anon, I might find myself moved to do something . . . magical . . . and he would feel obliged to explain it away."

"I don't want you to go."

"I must. When I have my cubs, I will be whole again."

Pierrette considered that a mistake. "This is a vast land. How will you find me? And if I am not there when the cubs are born . . ."

"You will follow the earth-lines. I will be able to find you, and when I do, we'll travel more quickly than we have up to now, bumbling through the bushes at your donkey's pace."

Pierrette did not agree, but what could she say? That his haste seemed precipitate and ill-planned? Any plans she might have had were shattered when the boat sank, many leagues from her own destination.

Yan Oors took his leave without further words. He had no baggage, only his staff and pouch, and he faded into the dark woods as if he had never been. That night, feeling quite abandoned, Pierrette cried herself to sleep.

Chapter 15 ∾ Lovi's Confusion

There were always clear paths leading northward, and easy, shallow fords at every stream. Always, they found themselves walking in sunshine during the dew-spattered early hours, then in the shade of huge overarching trees in the heat of the day. The few villages they happened on were clean and prosperous, mostly new ones built by refugees from the Viking terror that surged and ebbed in the valleys of the navigable rivers. In some, every room had a small hole at ground level but, increasingly as they bore northward, floors were of puncheon planks set on joists above the ground, and open beneath.

"It's because of the dampness," villagers explained. "Breezes sweep under the floors, as does runoff from the rains." Other things also passed beneath those dry floors, unheeded, or at least unmentioned.

The going proved easy. Ibn Saul was generous with his purse's contents, and everyone now had a good cloak and a full stomach after every meal. The local bread, made with flour so deep a purple that it was called "black wheat," was as hefty in the belly as an equal portion of lean meat, and just as sustaining. The new apple wines were effervescent and never cloying, and their cart was always well laden with redolent cheeses. There was no oil to be obtained at any price, but a taste for butter made from cow's milk was not hard to acquire.

One afternoon, as they walked silently on cushions of fallen needles beneath tall, sighing pines, Pierrette found herself in step with Gregorius. The others were strung out well ahead. "At last," he said, "I can speak with you alone." Pierrette did not know what he might have to say to her. She cocked her head attentively. "I think Lovi and the scholar are both blind," he said. "But you see them, don't you? The big, silent fellow did too, didn't he?"

"See what, Father Gregorius?"

"The creeping things! I've seen you cringe when one crossed your path. Are they ghosts, or demons?"

"I know little more than you do," Pierrette replied. "If they are ghosts, they are not spirits of people who have died, for they do not linger near graves or scenes of death. If they are demons, they exhibit no desire for human bodies or minds to infest. As for where they originate . . ."

"In the last village but one—the settlement with the priest and his little wooden church—I saw one emerge from a man's mouth."

"Tell me."

"Surely you were there. Remember the carpenter with the black tooth?"

"Of course. The blacksmith pulled the tooth with his smallest tongs, and then the priest gave him a paste of sawdust from the new altar, mixed with holy water, to ease his pain."

"And it worked! I saw his face ease, and his moans soon ceased. I also saw the blackness emerge from his mouth like smoke. But unlike smoke, it did not dissipate. It slithered down his bloody chin and chest, and then it fled . . . that way."

"Westward. Yes, it would have done that. But there is something missing. What else do you remember? What did the village priest say?"

"Why, only the usual . . . he bade the pain be gone, and . . ."

"What words, exactly, did he utter?"

"I think he said 'Let this dust and water drive out all that is evil.'"

"There you have it. The equation."

"I don't understand."

"I suppose not. Mathematics is not as easy to learn as are bawdy songs, or tall tales of life among the Vikings, is it?"

"You insult me. I learned my sums. What you said was a non sequitur. We were not talking of mathematics."

"In a sense we were. Consider that 'one plus one' is half of a proper equation. What is in the other balance pan of the scale—and what separates the two?"

"One plus one equals two. That is elementary."

"Then 'two' rests in the other pan, doesn't it? And the word 'equals' represents the scale itself."

"I see that. But what does it have to do with—"

"Before the priest uttered his spell, the carpenter's pain was one thing. Afterward, it became something else. The priest did not say outright 'Pain equals evil,' but that is what he implied—and you saw what happened."

"The pain left him. The twice-holy stuff drove it from him, but his words were not a spell, they were—"

"The spell came first. Water and sawdust could not put pain to rout. But once defined as 'good,' the magic paste was hostile to 'evil.' Don't you see that now?"

"I do not."

Pierrette sighed. "For the priest's paste to work, he had first to transform pain—which is of itself useful when it warns of injury, else how would we know to bandage a wound, or pull a bad tooth?— into 'evil,' which could be driven off by what he called 'good.' That transformation was the spell. The rest followed from it, a logical necessity."

She saw that Gregorius was not able to grasp her distinction. She sighed again. "As for why such shadows travel always westward, I do not know."

"There is another matter I wish to address," said Gregorius, uneasily.

"What is that?"

"Lovi. He still loves you."

"What?" She stumbled, though the trail was smooth.

"It's true," he said. "I am only a poor substitute for what he truly desires."

"But that can't be! I am not . . ."

"Not attracted to others of your sex? I am—

personally—grateful for that, else this journey would be a torment for me, because Lovi would be yours."

That was not what Pierrette had almost said: "But I am not a boy at all." Instead, she merely asked, "What do you want from me?"

"I don't know, exactly. But we two have become quite close. Had it not been so, I would surely have left this company while we were still in hospitable country. I consider our relationship no casual thing, but still, your shadow looms over us. I wish you could find some way to turn his thoughts away."

"I think I have an idea," she replied, "but now is not the time for it. When we reach the coast, and have found a ship, perhaps we can discuss it again."

"I do not wish to wait so long, but if I must, I will endure."

Shortly thereafter, the terrain became rougher, their trail not much more difficult, but narrower as it threaded between black, craggy outcrops. Gregorius moved ahead of her. Pierrette had much to think about, and was glad to be alone. Her contemplated "solution" to the problem of Lovi was a simple one: she would reveal herself as a woman, not a boy, and Lovi would know that his infatuation was baseless, its object unattainable. But she did not want to do that yet—and not until she herself was well on the way to the Fortunate Isles, alone, prepared to throw ibn Saul off her trail, or more likely her wake.

The matter for contemplation was the small, evil shadows, and their unexplained migrations. Was it a coincidence that the lines of power within the earth, like the one whose course they now traced, had also shifted westward? She thought of the shadows as the lingering aftermath of all ugly events—spilled blood and death, pain transmuted by spells like the village priest's, and occasions perhaps less trivial, and more. Had the displacement of the entire earth-pattern caused them to uproot themselves and to migrate west in search of some new balance of good and evil?

But if that trend were as she feared, with more things being defined as evil and fewer as good, then there could be no new balance, for the scales would hold evil's rock in one pan, and goodness's pebble in the other. In that case, were the small evils only tumbling effortlessly down some unseen slope toward a great gathering of unthinkable horror—and were she and her companions rushing willy-nilly into its midst?

The lure of Minho's sunny kingdom warred in her heart with that ugly speculation, and her conflict was made worse by the commission the goddess had given her: to destroy the sorcerer-king, and thus his kingdom.

Chapter 16 ∾ Moridunnon

As the day wore on, Pierrette and Gustave found themselves well out ahead of the others, and when she came upon a tiny meadow sheltered by sun-warmed boulders, with a lightning-felled tree that promised dry wood for a cheery fire, she stopped and gathered branches, then knelt to light the smallest ones. She laid her pouch, with her flints for firemaking, on a flat stone. She would not use them.

She had not dared employ her firemaking spell when the others were near, being unsure how it might manifest itself, but now was the perfect chance. She needed to know if the last time had been a fluke of some local magic, or something entirely more sinister. Bending low, with her arm outstretched toward the tinder and twigs, she subvocalized the words. . . .

At first she thought the spell had not worked at all. No sparks flew from her fingertip to the charred linen tinder. No small flames licked the heaped twigs and shavings. No trickle of smoke arose. Her shadow fell across only the inert makings of an unlit fire. Her shadow . . . Pierrette jerked upright: her shadow, where no shadow should have fallen. The sun was low and west, not overhead.

She did not dare turn and look for the source of the light that fell on her back and shoulders. The edge of her shadow was haloed with dull crimson as if it smoldered like tinder, but without smoke. Slowly, cautiously, she arose. . . .

The greasy red glow was not sunlight from the west. It emanated from all the places no sunlight fell: from the dark clefts of the dead tree, from the shadowy patch where a boulder's east face masked the feathery grass, from every lightless cranny that ordinarily went unnoticed, because eyes slid over such darknesses, where there was nothing for them to see.

But now there was . . . something. The bloody light emanated from everything that was unlit, and cast shadows of its own making, shadows of shadows that everywhere smoldered at the edges, a hideous, heatless glow. And someone was watching her! She could feel it. Her eyes darted this way and that . . . and then fixed upon her pouch. Its drawstring was loose, and there, on the flat rock, lay her serpent's egg—and Cunotar.

"What is this place?" She heard his harsh voice in her head, not with her ears. "This is not our sunny land, girl." How odd—he sounded almost . . . afraid?

"I should think you'd feel right at home. Shall I break my egg, and let you loose here?" Of course she would not do that. Cunotar was not only a druid and a sorcerer, but a warrior of renown, and at the moment of his confinement, he still had his sword . . .

"Thank you, but no. I am free of the Nameless One in here. I do not wish to enter his service again. But if you're not careful . . . he'll have you instead."

Despite her terror, Pierrette was still capable of speech. "I am amazed. Didn't he eat your soul, and aren't you his slave?"

"My soul is my own, and I prefer it that way. Besides, have you forgotten? I received my death wound, thanks to you. Out there, I would again bleed, and would die. Even this limited kind of life is better than death—for now."

"Only for now? Is there anything at all you'd deem worth dying for? I can't imagine what it would be."

"Nor I; but should it come to me, you'll be the first to know. Now put me back in your pouch before . . . someone . . . discovers me. This ugly light . . ."

Pierrette did as he asked. She pulled the drawstring tight, but still the sick, red light persisted. Wherever it fell on her, Pierrette felt dirty. Her skin looked gray and drained, every pore a pock of corruption, every downy hair a moldy tendril crawling with unseen lice. She did not dare breathe, for fear of sucking in something unspeakable. . . .

"Ah! There you are!" Ibn Saul's voice washed over her like a cleansing breeze. "What a lovely spot. Shelter, firewood, and soft grass for our bedding." The unnatural shadows shredded and dissipated with the clean, cold force of his scholarly disbelief in such things. Suddenly the little meadow was again awash in ordinary sunlight, and Pierrette's usual shadow stretched eastward across the wavy grass.

"Did you lose your flint, boy?" asked the scholar. "I see you've laid tinder."

"I . . . I had a cramp in my calf, so I stood to relieve it. I'll light the fire now." Pierrette reached for her pouch, and the flint she kept there that she would use now, and from now on, to light fires. She squatted, turning so ibn Saul would not see her bleak expression. Now she knew. Indeed the nature of this dark, forested land was qualitatively different. If the tiny fire-spell evoked such horridness, then what of her other spells, so laboriously learned? If she whispered words to give her soul magpie's wings, would she flutter instead on black, leathery appendages, chittering and squeaking between tiny sharp teeth, her face become not a graceful beak but wrinkled and flat, her eyes filled with the red glow of smoldering evil?

She hardly dared contemplate what might result from a greater spell, like *Mondradd in Mon*, which thinned the veil between this world and another—because what other world would there be? Would she find herself plunging headlong into the Christians' Hell, or into the Black Time itself? Would she wrench the world itself out of its proper course, shredding the lines of power that bound it as a maddened porpoise shredded a fishing net?

But then, what of Cunotar? Were his words true? Was he indeed free of the Eater of Gods (and of mortal souls, also) within the refuge of her egg?

Was he thus a free agent? Then at least something good had come from her foolish attempt to use magic in this forbidding land. He had certainly sounded less hateful and bitter than ever before.

She struck sparks into the charred cloth, and blew on the tiny red pinhole of combustion that formed, then fed hair-fine shavings to it . . . and the flame that sprang up was yellow and fresh, the puff of smoke white and clean. Once several split twigs as thick as her thumb were burning cheerily, she laid dry branches atop them, carefully, so they did not crush out the flames or smother them. Then she stood, but there was no liveliness to her motion. Her shoulders sagged like a crone's, and she felt old, as if there was no life ahead of her, only the shadowy blackness, the red funeral pyre, the gray ashes, forever.

If she had been able to choose her own path, at that moment, she would have turned back. What use, after all, was a sorceress who dared not utter a spell? What use was a terrified girl who must cleave by the scholar, because his obliviousness to the things she feared was her only protection against them?

"We must be almost upon Moridunnon's stronghold, now," said ibn Saul, while packing his instruments following his daily sightings the following noonday.

"Well then," said Lovi, disgustedly, "where is it?"

They had combed the countryside for any sign of habitation. Ibn Saul sent each of them up separate hills to search for telltale columns of smoke, whether from a palace or a village, for a glimpse of any man-made construction, whether a shining roof of golden tiles or the mossy terra-cotta of a half-collapsed Roman villa. No one had seen a trickle of smoke or as much as a patch of yellow thatch protruding from the endless expanse of greenery.

"I don't understand," said the scholar. "My calculations indicate it should be right here." He stamped his foot for emphasis, or as if the earth itself were stubbornly to blame, concealing Moridunnon's residence behind some copse, crag, or bank of fog, like that which now began to condense about them. "Exactly right here," he said, and Pierrette reflected that his calculations had been remarkably accurate, but not . . . quite . . . precise enough. Her own, made after sightings from three separate hilltops, with the advantage of her map that showed the exact intersection of the earth-line they had followed with another that trended east and west, placed the exact spot a few hundred paces to the west. . . .

She could barely see the slope of the hill, now, the curiously round, steep hill overgrown with tall, ancient oaks and gnarly beeches whose roots penetrated to a depth that only hundreds upon hundreds of years of growth could explain.

While the others made camp and sought dry wood for a fire—not a hopeful task, in this moist forest—she slipped away and began to climb that slope, soon emerging above the blanket of fog that thickened below. This was the place—this mound, where the two lines of power intersected. This was the palace of the mage Moridunnon. Only there was no palace, just great old trees.

If she had dared, Pierrette might have whispered a spell to clear away illusions and thus verify what she believed, that even now, Moridunnon or one of his unseen minions was watching her, waiting to see what she was going to do. But she did nothing, except to brush some small creature's droppings from a fallen log, and to sit upon it. She would not speak magical words here, in this terrible land, where even the most innocent spells evoked sickly shadows of shadows, edged in greasy red flame. Eventually, she was sure, someone . . . something . . . would tire of her sitting on its roof, as it were, and might invite her inside.

Dusk was still hours away. Here, above the damp and chill of the foggy forest, she was quite comfortable. Perhaps—as she realized later—too comfortable, because before too long, her eyelids began to droop, and . . .

She sprang to her feet. What had she heard? Was it a muffled thump, and a wordless expostulation, as if someone had tripped on a root? Was it the jingling of tiny bells? Below and all around, the fog lay undisturbed, except—there! A deer! It was a deer, come to browse above the fog, its antlers shiny even in the dull light of the sunless day. But no deer's horns would gleam so, this time of year. They would be no more than little nubbins covered in velvety skin.

It was no deer. It was not Cernunnos, the horned god either, but a man, an old man, dressed in skins and tatters, wearing atop his head a wooly cap from which protruded a pair of lopsided branching horns. His yellow-gray hair and beard were a tangle of burrs, seeds, and twigs. A young pigeon hawk, a merlin, perched on his shoulder.

Pierrette giggled. She could not help it. The old fellow was standing on one leg like a stork, with one arm outstretched, and one eye tightly shut. He teetered there, just at the edge of the fog, only kept upright by means of a staff whose upper end branched and rebranched, a staff that jangled with the tinny notes of little bells, attached like flowers at the end of each bare twig.

"Oh, stop that!" she said, unthinkingly waving a hand to brush away the spell he was casting at her, the *keo-dru-videcta*, the magic fog. "You can't get rid of me that easily." Only then did she realize she had indeed countered magic with magic—without unseemly result. "Are you Moridunnon?"

"Am I great? Am I strong?" He looked down at himself in deprecation. He was skinny and ragged.

"Are you *mor'h*? Are you *dunnos*?" she threw his own back at him. *Mor'h-i-dunnos* meant "great and strong."

"Is this place a fortress by the sea?" he asked. "Mor" could also mean "sea," and a "dunnum" was a fortress.

"Put your foot down, and open your other eye," Pierrette demanded. "Perhaps you will see for yourself and stop asking silly questions. You are Moridunnon, the great sorcerer, and I am sitting on the roof of your palace—or perhaps on a terrace. I cannot tell, for all these trees."

"Moridunnon," he said, rolling the syllables around in his mouth as if they were acorns. "Moridunnon. Hereabouts, they call me 'Myrddin,' and they have forgotten what my name means. Who are you, girl, that you remember?"

Pierrette was momentarily taken aback—she was, as always, dressed as a boy. The old man's sight was not, then, as weak as his beady little eyes pretended. It was better than Lovi's, Gregorius's, or the observant ibn Saul's.

"I am Pierrette of Citharista, apprentice to Ansulim of the Fortunate Isles." She used Anselm's Minoan name, not the one people at home knew him by.

"Ansulim? Anselm? But that was years ago! Ages ago. Surely he has had the grace to grow old and die, by now?"

"You haven't. Why should he?"

"Indeed? Anselm lives? How remarkable. Come! I must hear more of this. Come."

"Where?" Pierrette looked around. The woods were as old and as thick as ever.

"Here!" She peered where he tapped his jingling staff, between great twisted roots, and saw a dark opening lined with mossy rocks. "We'll use the back door."

"Down there? It looks dark and wet."

"Do you believe everything you see? Apprentice, indeed! Hasn't Anselm taught you anything?"

Stung by his scorn, she lowered herself into the hole in the ground. Probing with her feet, she discerned what felt like a step, then another. It was a stairway. The hole became a tunnel, a corridor leading downward. She heard the old man's tread behind her, and was—slightly—reassured. But then she heard what he was mumbling, and the blood in her veins turned to ice. . . .

"*Mondradd in Mon*," he intoned. "*Borabd orá perdó*." The ancient words flowed, never repeating themselves, yet always almost the same.

"No!" she exclaimed. "You mustn't say that! It's dangerous here, where . . ."

"Where what? How else can I invite you in, if I don't open the door? What's wrong with you, anyway?" He proceeded to utter the rest of the spell. "*Merdrabd or vern*," he croaked, "*Arfaht ará camdó*." A door indeed opened, a door to . . . the Otherworld. It was a portal that had never twice opened, for Pierrette, into the same place, or even the same time. What would it open upon now?

She had no choice. She stepped ahead, and heard his footsteps, sounding much firmer now, behind her. Ahead, a rectangular line of warm, yellow light limned what she believed was a door. "Don't just stand there," Moridunnon rumbled. "Push it open." A chill coursed up her spine, then down her ribs. That was not the voice of a crotchety old man. She felt herself pushed from behind, and the door swung easily, silently aside when she lurched against it.

The light of a thousand sweet wax candles washed over her, from every side, and from above, where clear, crystalline glass balls hung from gold-and-electrum chandeliers, magnifying each candle's light twofold. Rich paneling of polished yew rose from a floor of white marble veined with gold, and overhead, beyond the dazzle, she discerned a tracery of dark, carved beams. The air was thick with the aroma of beeswax and honey, with just a trace of something richer . . . "Ah, yes!" said Moridunnon, sniffing. "Dinner. Come. A cup of chill Etruscan wine on the balcony, first, though. This way."

She stared at him. Moridunnon was no longer old. He was . . . ageless. His hair was not dirty gray, but purest white, combed loosely back, and held there by a gold chaplet with little branching horns of silver. His rags and skins were now a soft, thick cloak, a Celtic weave of crisscrossed maroon and black, with a collar of fur like the mane of a Roman lion, but white as ermine. His beard was neat and short, his mustaches trimmed above his lip, his eyebrows no longer bushy but arched, the left one slightly pointed as he raised it, as if asking her approval of what she saw. His young pigeon hawk spread its wings gracefully on his shoulder.

"Why are you surprised?" he asked in a firm, mellow voice. "You obviously knew the spell *Mondradd in Mon*, when I voiced it. You must know what door it opens."

"The door to the past," she replied softly. "The portal to the Otherworld and the broken Wheel of Time. But this is a new thing to me. You are no longer old, but I . . . I am yet as I was."

He shook his head sadly. "My appearance results from a separate spell entirely. It is a trifle, a vanity, that you might see me as I . . . as I remember myself, when I was indeed *Mor'h-i-dunum*."

"My master Anselm," she said pensively, "has never looked as young as you."

"He is older than I, by a thousand years or so. Even Minho's magic can't change that."

"Minho? Do you know him also? Tell me—where are his Fortunate Isles? I must find them, and . . ."

"Of course. I'll show you where they are. But

first wine, and then a slab of that fine venison even now turning above the fire . . ."

She followed his lead. He pushed through a doorway she could have sworn was the one that they had entered by, which led up a staircase that felt just like the one she had recently ascended, but was well lit and dry, and the upper steps were flooded with light that could only be a clear, sunny day.

The wide bronze-railed balcony was not Anselm's sunny terrace overlooking the azure Mediterranean Sea, but it could have been. The magic that held the sun overhead at perpetual midday was surely the same, but the scenery was not. The dark forest that stretched from horizon to horizon, broken by stony gray ridges, looked much as it would in a later time, but east and west of her vantage point was a roadway paved with great, flat, square-hewn stones. Half were red, and half black, like a Gaulish cloak. At regular intervals the road broadened and two lanes diverged around square, white stone monuments. A column and a polished bronze sphere surmounted every eighth stone block. With distance, the smaller stones faded, but Pierrette was able to count twelve bronze-crowned columns before they were entirely too small to see.

Each small stone marked a *stadion*, she was sure, and thus the pylons were one mile apart—whether by Greek or Roman measure, or some other, she did not know, but all were much the same—one thousand soldier's marching paces to the mile were much the same, whatever the race of the soldier himself. Thus the horizon was thirteen, maybe fourteen miles distant. And beyond it . . . "Where does the great road lead?" she asked her host, her voice hushed with awe.

"You asked about Minho. That is the road to Ys—or, in your era, which is still many centuries away, I might say, 'the road to the Bay of Sins, and the Isle of the Dead.'"

"In my era? Then . . . *when* are we?" Pierrette's face twisted in wry confusion, for two reasons, and the overt question expressed only one. The other was a matter of language. "When are we?" was an awkward construction in any language, because none had evolved to express such a displacement in time as the spell *Mondradd in Mon* implied. In what language had she and the mage been speaking? Had they been conversing in Latin or Gaulish? She was fluent in several, able to shift easily between them. She awaited Moridunnon's next words.

"This is the Roman year 120," he said. "In a few years Pytheas of Massilia will voyage north, seeking the Cassiterides, the Tin Islands, and will discover the mysterious 'Ultima Thule,' somewhere north of here." Now she had it. He was speaking Greek. But before, when he mentioned "Ys," had he spoken in Punic? And had she responded in Latin? It was all quite confusing. It lent the whole experience a dreamlike air, but she did not feel as credulous as she would have in a dream, where dogs could become bears in an eyeblink, and even the most abrupt shifts in perceived reality went unquestioned.

She forced her attention back to the current reality. "The legend of Ys survives in my era," she said reflectively. "The dearth of observable ruins, according to some scholars, can be explained by the failure of its great seawall, and the winter storms that swept every trace of the city away out to sea. But surely, some trace of that great road, with its marching lines of pylons, must remain." She could not seek the Fortunate Isles here, in this Otherworld, within the spell *Mondradd in Mon*, but if in her own age there were still milestones, however weathered and worn, however hidden by tangles and thickets . . .

"Did you stumble across any, in the forest, while seeking me?" He raised his eyebrow. "No? I thought not. Perhaps, being of fine white marble, they have all been long since turned into Roman statues, their inscriptions chiseled away with the rest of the chips."

"You don't know for sure, Master Moridunnon? Weren't you watching when the columns were hauled down?"

He snorted—an old man's expression, incongruous because, except for his white hair, he was looking younger every time her glance fell across his face. "I was not always the homebody I was . . . I will be . . . in your time. A scant three centuries ago (or rather, six or seven hundred years from now, for no tongue has proper tenses for what we mages do with time, does it?) I will voyage across the channel north of here, to Old Britannia, and will meddle in the succession of their kings."

"You mean Artorius, don't you—the one with the famous sword?"

"Is that old tale still circulating? Yes, that was I. At least I think so." He wrinkled his brow, as if puzzled. "The tales change, and sometimes I seem to remember events one way, sometimes another."

Pierrette understood that, at least. All the old gods and heroes changed, with the tales people told, the legends they created. But she did not explain that to Moridunnon. She was here on his terms, not her own, and she resented that, being a sorceress in her own right. She was not accustomed to being whisked willy-nilly along the rim of the broken Wheel of Time by a spell she had not uttered herself. She would hold her counsel and retain whatever slight advantage that conferred.

"You said your name—in my era—was Myrddin, not Moridunnon. The Franks have yet another name for you . . ."

"Bah! They are savages! Pretentious savages at that, with courtly cloaks over their woolly shoulders. In Frankish 'Myrddin' means 'shitty,' so they call me 'Pigeonhawk' instead. That's what 'Merlin' means. And ever since, I've been stuck with this damned bird."

Pierrette giggled. "'Merlin' is better than 'shitty,' I think. What if they had called you 'eagle' or 'vulture?'" Thus legends changed. The old sorcerer was lucky the Franks had changed his name, or he might have been doomed to spend an eternity steaming and reeking, a man-sized heap of . . .

"What's so funny?" he snapped.

"I'm sorry. My thoughts wandered. I was smelling something . . ."

"The venison, of course! Come. Let's eat." That was not what she had been thinking of, but . . .

He led her to a room paneled with rich waxed

nutwood, hung with blue-and-scarlet tapestries. A low table held platters of steaming meat, plates of neatly sliced fruit, a plank of golden, broiled fish, and a dozen bowls with olives and dates, and with cherries steeped in honey wine. The two low benches with fluffy cushions indicated they would feast Roman-style, reclining. But where were the servants who had laid this rich repast?

"They are as ephemeral as the dragons that guard my fountains out there," said Moridunnon, waving casually at the room's single window. Pierrette glanced out, and saw a great courtyard where water splashed from one clear pool to the next. One, two, three . . . were those the waters of youth, of invincibility, and of death? One pool looked much like another, and the water flowed between them, so it could not have had different qualities from one pool to the next—could it?

At Moridunnon's insistence, she chose a bench, and they lay head to head, she leaning on her left elbow, he on his right. She ate lightly, a sliver of crisp venison from the edge of the roast, a sip of clear wine, an olive that tasted of warm Mediterranean sunshine. When she raised her eyes from her chosen morsel of the moment, she saw that the mage's eyes were deepest blue, like Lovi's. She had not noticed that before. In the oblique light from the window, his hair looked gold, not white.

Between one sip of wine and the next, she wondered where his beard and mustaches had gone, but it was only a passing thought, and did not rouse her from the pleasant languor that suffused her. He looks like Lovi, she thought. Somehow, that seemed exactly as it should be.

A brief thought furrowed her brow: Gregorius. But the imaginary flutter of his clerical garment did not linger. She was here, and so was Lovi. There was no one else. He rose and pushed back the table, as if it weighed nothing at all. He let his white cotton tunic fall to the floor. Sunlight reflecting from the gleaming marble turned the fine hairs on his chest to gold. She raised her head, and ran slender fingers through them. Her breath came quickly, in little pants, and her head felt light and empty.

Where had her tunic gone? Lovi drew her to her feet, and caught her small breasts in his hands, his expression amazed, as if he had not expected them to be there at all. . . .

What else might he not expect? she wondered briefly when he knelt and loosened the cord around her waist. She could not see his expression, but his fingers seemed unsurprised. Wave after wave of warmth coursed through her, spiced with prickly sparks as if she were made of wool, and he were stroking her. His body rippled with smooth muscles as he guided her back against the bench, and swept her feet from the floor with one arm, raising her knees, pinning her shoulder with the other arm . . .

At some great distance, as if outside the window, she heard the harsh, cackling laugh of a magpie, and for a moment her eyes widened, and she saw . . . Moridunnon. The mage hunched over her with twigs and brambles in his beard, his eyes alight with an oily red glow, rimmed with shadows of shadows and swirling darkness that crawled across his wrinkled face . . .

She screeched, and flung herself sideways in a

flutter of green, azure, black, and white feathers. Madly flapping her magpie wings, she careened toward the refuge of the window's welcoming light. Wings beating, she struggled upward through air thick as honey, fleeing the brown, long-winged form that rose below her like a shadow freed from the ground and flying into the air.

The magpie wheeled and the merlin followed, its talons spread for the kill. Magpie writhed and twisted in midair, and felt the brush of merlin-claws against its wings. Magpie, tiring, recited in its small mind strange words that magpie throat could not utter: "*Mondradd in Mon, bora . . .*" and it fluttered to the moss atop the great mound, among the roots of the sentinel beech trees.

Far off, above the obscuring branches and leaves, she heard a hawk's shrill cry. She was cold. Her garments lay scattered on top of the yellow, fallen leaves. Quickly she gathered them and dressed, glancing anxiously upward. "I'm not up there," said an old, cracked voice. She gasped, and stiffened, but the old man in his patchwork of skins, his lopsided antlers, made no move toward her. "Fear not," he said, quite sadly. "The moment is past. The magic is gone, and I am old and impotent. Your maidenhood is safe—from me."

She felt almost sorry for him. She felt almost sorry for herself. Lovi: illusion or not, the scene had been lovely, the lust heady and compelling, their mutual desire entirely real. But now he was old and drained, and she was again neutered by her guise, a boy almost too young to have felt such pangs.

"Was it magic?" she asked. "I mean, was it all illusion? The feast, the fountains, the Punic road?"

"It seemed real to me," said Moridunnon. "It always does."

As ever, the distinction between reality and illusion was vanishingly small. Something perceived was something real, unless substantial and tangible evidence precluded it. Thus there was no way to establish that the Phoenician road to Ys, with its milestone columns and brazen orbs, had not once existed. There was equally, short of finding a broken bronze sphere, green with age, or a chunk of a marble pylon still inscribed with Punic words, no way to confirm its erstwhile reality.

Pierrette glanced at her fingernails, looking for some trace of a fine golden hair plucked from her lover's chest in a moment of abandon, but she saw only ordinary dirt under them.

"You aren't going to find what you want," he said softly. "The Fortunate Isles, I mean."

"Maybe not, but I'm still going to try. I have to."

"That's not what I meant. You won't find anything different there than you might have had here, with me."

"You aren't Minho. This mound is not a magical kingdom. If I find the Fortunate Isles in the real world, by sailing there, not by using a spell . . ."

"I'm telling you, things won't be as they seem, even if they're 'real.' You won't like it."

"I have to find out for myself. I have had visions of the Fortunate Isles, of Minho, since I was little. He wants to marry me."

"That may be, but are you sure you'll want to marry him?"

"I do. I always wanted that."

"Have it your way. Just remember, you can always turn back. I'll still be here, waiting for you."

His sad demeanor moved her. He reminded her of her own master, Anselm, who was as old, or older, and who was often sad. Anselm too—despite his age—had felt lustful toward her at times, though it had never gone so far. As a lonely and motherless child, she had sometimes crawled into his bed, and the avuncular emotions he had felt when she had been no more sexual than a warm kitten always overrode the ones he felt later, when she began to mature.

She stood on tiptoe and kissed Moridunnon's leathery, wrinkled cheek. Then she ran down the steep slope into the fog, which roiled and swirled with the speed of her passage. Soon, ahead, she saw the red-and-yellow glow of the campfire, and the moving shadows of her companions, not yet settled around the fire.

Chapter 17 ∾ A Deadly Companion

What, she wondered as they trudged now entirely westward along the new earth-line known only to her, had the encounter with Moridunnon been about, really? She would have taken it at face value had it not been for a small detail: when she had first recognized that she was making love with Moridunnon, not Lovi, she had seen the embrous glow in his eyes, the dying coals of an unfed fire. She had seen it again, just before she left him. And she had seen that tragic light in other eyes as well: the stag god men called Cernunnos, which in Gaulish meant "The Horned One," had possessed just such a light, after the Dark One had taken him. The same light had shined in the eyes of the demon that invested her sister Marie. Pierrette knew what it meant. When the Christian missionaries declared an old god, who was neither entirely good nor evil, to be only an avatar of their own chief demon, whom they called Satan, and who had no goodness at all, then the old one was doomed. He was consumed, and Satan, eater of gods, grew stronger.

There was a principal at work. Pierrette called it "The Law of Conservation of Good and Evil." Simply put, most things were neither good nor evil, they were neutral. It took a powerful spell to tease a thing apart, to separate its components, to polarize them against each other. But it could be done, and once separated, each could be separately consumed. Nothing was lost, nothing gained: consumed by Satan, the evil portion did not disappear, and the good, wherever it had fled, still existed . . . somewhere. But nothing remained as it had been, either. She imagined the Christian spells parsing the mystic places, the springs, the caves, the crossroads, blessing the sparkling waters, cursing the darkness and shadows, locking up what they called Good in fonts and reliquaries and leaving the rest to be consumed by . . . another.

Moridunnon. Had a Christian bishop in Turones or Cenabum (perhaps Saint Martin himself? Who could say?) heard country folk telling of the old mage, and named him evil, and thus doomed him? But he had not seemed evil to Pierrette. Crotchety, deceptive, manipulative, lustful, indeed—but was that evil? She considered it only human, and forgivable, but then, she was not Christian. In her experience, most Christians lived in a world all black and white, and left little undefined.

Only the telltale fire banked behind Moridunnon's beady eyes had warned her. The conclusion was inescapable that the Eater of

Gods had gained subtlety since her last encounter with him, and she could no longer count on anything being what it seemed, when even Cunotar the warrior druid sounded thoughtful, and even . . . kindly.

Did he know what her assigned goal was? Had his—Moridunnon's—attempted seduction been intended to stop her? The loss of her maidenhood, the goddess had assured her countless times, would render her ordinary, unable to work even the smallest spell. And it had been a close call, because her longtime infatuation with Lovi, silly and girlish as it was, had been exacerbated by his absolute unattainability in the real world, unless she became a boy, which she could not. It had almost worked.

She caught a whiff of something foul, something dead. She saw movement out of the corner of her eye. There. A dead rabbit hung from a trapper's snare, forgotten. A haze of shadows surrounded it, shifting and pulsing. The darkness moved and stretched as if trying to pull itself free of the maggoty corpse. Pierrette glanced back along the trail. She could hear Lovi and Gregorius, but they were still some distance behind. She continued to stare.

At last, the nebulous blot broke free, and as soon as it touched the ground, it slithered away along the faint trail—westward, of course.

The following morning, ibn Saul and Lovi climbed a rocky escarpment north of the camp, where the scholar could orient himself using his lodestone, and would then sketch a rough

impression of everything he could see. Pierrette
considered his efforts at mapmaking crude, but
after all, she had the advantage of having read the
lost treatises of the ancient Sea Kings, and had
seen their maps of lands the rest of the world had
forgotten.

At times like this, she slipped away, usually in
an opposite direction, hoping for, though never
expecting, Yan Oors. She always carried a rude willow basket, because whether wood, moor, meadow,
or mountainside, she could usually find something
useful to bring back to camp. Today, she found a
patch of berries, and filled her basket while waiting, hoping for company. This time she was not disappointed. But Yan Oors did not usually make so
much noise, so she slipped behind a tree until she
was sure it really was him. Walking beside him,
doing most of the twig crunching and leaf thrashing,
was . . . a bear. It was a big bear, brownish-black,
with summer clumps and tatters of loose fur dangling from its belly and flanks.

Pierrette did not understand. What was Yan
Oors doing with a big, male bear? His long, big-
knuckled fingers trailed between the shaggy
creature's shoulders. Since he seemed to have it
under control, she stepped out from behind her
tree. "There you are!" said Yan Oors jovially. "How
do you like my bear?"

"I . . . have I misunderstood? We spoke only of
cubs, and this is definitely not a . . ."

"This is much better. This bear will take up the
spirits of my poor faded companions, and I will
not have to wait for cubs to grow up." The bear
seemed to glower at Pierrette, its head lower than

its shoulders, its eyes red-rimmed. It seemed almost to challenge her.

"Are you sure? We aren't anywhere near the end of the cape you showed me on the map. Shouldn't you be patient for a while longer?"

Yan Oors frowned. From the bear came a deep rumble. "You see?" said Yan. "He feels as strongly about it as I do. So will you, when you get acquainted with him."

"I'm sure I will," she lied. "I was only momentarily taken aback by the change in plans. You know how I hate surprises. Now come. I have picked a big basketful of berries. I'll share them with both of you." Yan seemed so happy. Why couldn't she share in his elation?

"How nice," said Yan. "Come, bear." The animal seemed reluctant to follow. As Pierrette led the way to where she had left her basket, she seemed to feel the creature's angry eyes boring into the back of her neck. Why had Yan changed his mind? Something felt terribly, terribly wrong.

They sat around the berry basket as if it were a hearth, and Yan scooped handsful of the fruit into his mouth. When she offered some to the bear, the creature turned its snout away disdainfully. "He likes meat better," Yan said mushily, his mouth full. "I've been trapping rabbits for him."

"It must have been one of your snares I found yesterday," Pierrette said. "There was a rabbit in it, but it was half rotten."

"He seems to like them best that way," said Yan, gesturing at the bear with his thumb. "But only to a point. Sometimes, he turns his nose up at the very ripest ones."

Pierrette now understood what Yan did not: what the bear craved was not dead meat, but something else, something that was present in the dead rabbits for a while, but eventually escaped. Slowly, as if only shifting away from a twig poking her behind, she edged to one side, where the gaunt man had leaned his iron staff against a sapling crotch. She stood, and made as if to stretch, then in one quick motion grasped the staff.

The cold, brown iron stuck to her hands, a coldness that burned, that sucked the heat and life from her fingers, her palms, and her wrists. Quickly, before her arms became leaden and could not move, before the greedy iron's craving reached her heart and stilled it forever, she swung his staff in a sweeping roundhouse arc, at the dark, dirty snout of Yan's companion.

The staff's butt landed solidly across the bear's tender nose, making a dull sound. For Pierrette, it was as if she had struck a boulder. The shock of the blow travelled up the staff and up her arms. She cried out in pain as she dropped it—as it released her.

The bear roared, and rose up on its hind legs, its great front paws held forward, exposing long, yellowed claws. It staggered toward Pierrette, who backed away. The staff lay forgotten on the ground between them. "Here now! Here!" cried Yan Oors, his eyes shifting rapidly between Pierrette and the bear. "Stop that!" To Pierrette he said, "Why did you do that? He's angry now."

Catching her heel, Pierrette stumbled and fell backwards. The bear advanced, then loomed over her, and drew back one enormous paw to strike.

Thump! Pierrette didn't know what made the sound, but the creature's roar became a high-pitched squeal. She rolled sideways, and it came down on all fours, raking up great gobbets of soil with its claws.

Thump! Again the beast squealed, twisting around to get at the source of the blows that rained down on it: Yan Oors, who had recovered his staff. "Stop that now! Pierrette's my friend! She's sorry she hit you." The bear, as if it had understood, glanced her way, snarled scornfully, and advanced upon Yan. "Hey! You're my friend! Lie down now!" The bear rumbled ominously, and spread its forelegs as it rose to envelop him in a crushing hug.

Man and bear went down in a tangled heap. Pierrette feared Yan would be overwhelmed, disemboweled, but his cries sounded more indignant than agonized. Then he wrested himself free. "Pierrette was right," he exclaimed. "You're not my bear!" He swung his staff over his head, and brought it down on the bear's head once, twice, and the creature sank to its belly, still snarling, its huge, stained teeth bared. Yan shook his head sadly. "You never were mine, were you? You wanted Pierrette!" He raised his staff one last time, and brought it down with such force that leaves on nearby trees rustled. *Thump!* That time, the sound was wet and soggy, and Pierrette heard the crackling of broken bone. The bear now lay still.

She saw that her friend's face, dirty from the tussle on the ground, was streaked with muddy tears. She put an arm around his waist. "I'm sorry," she said.

"It's not your fault," said Yan Oors. "You saw. You

knew something was wrong. I only saw what I wished. It was all a trick. He only wanted me in order to get at you, didn't he?"

"I don't know. He wanted what you gave him."

"Not my love," Yan said. "Only the rabbits, I suppose."

"The rabbits and . . ." She pointed. From the bear's nostrils and ears, from beneath its stubby tail, and from its bloody death-wound were emerging dozens of dark shapes, like greasy smoke. There was no struggle, as if to break free of the corruption that spawned them, only silent emergence, and then the swift, smooth slide as each one departed . . . to the west. "Those are what it wanted from you."

The big fellow's skin was gray, as he watched the procession of shadows. It went on for quite some time, but at last there seemed to be no more. "I had forgotten about those," he said.

"I suspect you forgot many things, while it had you in thrall. Perhaps now some of them will come back."

"I was a fool! I wanted a bear so much . . ."

"Don't feel too badly. I, too, was almost taken, because I wanted something that I could not have. We must both be on our guards, from now on. There is still much that I don't understand in this horrid land, but I know that the Eater of Gods is here, and he grows ever more clever."

She sighed. "Tomorrow, or the next day, we may glimpse the sea. There you may find proper bear cubs, and I may find . . . answers. Now come. The others will be back in camp soon, and we must get you cleaned up. You have no injuries?"

Yan assured her that he did not, except for one that could not be seen, and that would not yield to poultices or healing herbs.

Chapter 18 ～ The Boatman

Pierrette dreaded every step westward now. Yan Oors was safe, for the time, and she herself would not easily be fooled again. Ibn Saul remained safe within the armor of his disbelief in all things supernatural. But Lovi and Gregorius? They were both vulnerable innocents, especially Lovi. The next attack might well be directed through one of them. She would have to be more suspicious of her friends than of any enemies she might encounter.

Enemies? There was only one enemy, whatever guise he chose. But why did he want to stop her? That didn't make sense, did it? If the Fortunate Isles held nothing that was evil, and if ibn Saul's skepticism could destroy them, then why wouldn't the Eater of Gods want her—and the scholar—to find them?

She shivered. Moridunnon had not tried to stop ibn Saul, only Pierrette. And Yan Oors, enthralled, had not approached the camp and the others, only her.

They trudged over rolling hills where cleared fields and pastures usurped all but the forested slopes. Weeds and thistles grew high everywhere, because no ground had been tilled for at least a year. Had the farmers all fled to the forests to escape the Viking depredations, or had they fled something else?

It was all too confusing. She attempted to set forth what she knew, suspected, and feared. First, *Ma* wanted her to destroy Minho and his magical realm—in this world— so it would remain a potent force in another, in the world of myth and legend, where it would remain an elusive paradise always just beyond the next wave, a goad and a goal for explorers like ibn Saul, but forever unattainable. In that scenario, the Fortunate Isles could not be destroyed by skeptics who would make them prosaic, because they would no longer exist—but the fact that they had existed once would no longer be subject to the test.

On the surface of things, it seemed that the Eater of Gods opposed *Ma*'s wishes, that he wanted Pierrette to fail, and ibn Saul to succeed. But could he really want the Isles to become ordinary and unmagical? What kind of victory was that? Only if the Isles became not merely neutral, but evil would he . . . her blood turned to icewater. Gregorius. A priest, even a priest whose profession was merely a convenience, who never spoke of God, was still a priest. If he attained Minho's kingdom, could Gregorius become a fire-eating reformer who would denounce Minho as an evil magus and declare his realm the devil's work? Was that what the Eater of Gods wanted—not ibn Saul, but Gregorius?

She shook her head. She could not even imagine the vagrant priest becoming suddenly sincere and genuinely religious. And that was what it would take. There must be another answer, but she could not even make a guess what it was.

It was a lucky day. From a high ridge, they caught their first glimmer of the sea, the merest speck of pale silver between two gray, distant hills. Shortly thereafter, they came upon a wide Roman road, surfaced with well-packed gravel that made the going easy.

Lovi found a horseshoe that was hardly rusty at all. Most peasants believed horseshoes brought luck, but Pierrette knew they did not. They were lucky because they were valuable—for the price of a horseshoe, a farmer could buy an ox or a donkey. Only *milites* or *equites*, rich and noble soldiers, rode shod horses, and only the Frankish king's couriers were too much in a hurry to stop and search for a shoe that had been thrown, so horseshoes were rare, too. Luck came first, then horseshoes.

She didn't know if Lovi believed them lucky, but she doubted he would have pranced around so if he had found a silver quarter-mark, which was worth more, and which was much easier to carry.

They crested the last hill. There, with a red-gold path drawn by the setting sun, was the sea. Just on their right was a deep bay whose south shore they had unknowingly paralleled for some time. Pierrette stared into its waters, trying to see past the surface glimmers and waves, because beneath that very bay were supposed to lie the ruins of Ys, a great Phoenician city that had been destroyed when a king's daughter foolishly gave the keys to its seawall floodgates to her lover—who opened them during a storm.

Now Ys was gone, but the reason it had been sited there remained: Raz Point, named for the terrible tidal race that had smashed a thousand ships against the rocks. The point was like the skeletal spine of a dragon lying with its tail out to sea, as if it were biting a great chunk out of the shore. It was a ragged line of brown-and-black crags, sharp and forbidding, draped in hardy salt-loving vines that grabbed at ankles as if they hated for anyone to tread upon them.

Beyond the point, individual crags jutted from the sea, black, spiky, hammered by the waves, becoming smaller with distance and in fact. Further still, white flecks marked the dragon's submerged "tail," rocks revealed only in the troughs of the swells.

The scene was more forbidding than anything Pierrette had imagined, or seen in incorporeal vision, and was made unique by one detail: the seas piled up on the north faces of the sea-crags, because the ocean was not only swelling and surging, but was rushing from the north, as if it were indeed Oceanos, the world-girdling river of the ancients, and was in springtime spate. South of each crag lay a deep, smooth hole in the water, a frighteningly deep pit unfilled by the rushing sea, and beyond that, the turbulent ocean rose up in a crest like the white plumes of an egret in mating finery, a long, bubbling trail that stretched like the wake of a great ship.

It was the tidal race, the great bore, driven by the moon and sun, that swept ships up like wood chips and dashed them on the rocks. It was the tidal bore, even more than the great seawall, that had girded ancient Ys, for only the Phoenicians had learned the tides' secrets, and knew how to use the deadly rush to propel their ships in and out of the Bay of Sins, instead of onto the rocks.

Pierrette looked further, straining her eyes. There, beyond the furthest rock, the last white riffle, was a low, gray shape: Sena, the Isle of the Dead, the last solid ground, beyond which Oceanos went on . . . forever? Sena, where the nine *Gallicenae*, priestesses or goddesses, ruled over the graveyards all of all the generations of druid dead.

"Do you see them?" Ibn Saul's voice startled Pierrette.

"See what, Master ibn Saul?"

"The Fortunate Isles, of course. Young eyes see further than old ones. If there is land out there, beyond Sena . . ."

I see nothing, master." And would I tell you, if I did? Not likely. She resented his intrusion. Alone, might her "young eyes" have penetrated the mists on the far horizon, and seen the tops of crags whose bases were below the curving edge of the world, which were the rim of the immense caldera that enclosed Minho's kingdom?

She sighed. "I see no way across that maelstrom, master, and I fear the Phoenicians' secret ways are lost."

"You're probably right. At any rate, the village at the head of the bay has no boats drawn up on shore, and may be deserted. I fear we have a long

hike ahead of us, to Gesocribate, where we may
be able to hire a vessel—if the Vikings have not
burned the town."

Gesocribate was easily a week's walk away, north
across the spine of Armorica, and Pierrette did not
easily contemplate that. As luck would have it, she
did not have to, for long. Soon after the four of
them had turned their steps eastward, they began
to hear a faint, high, shrill sound, as if many voices
were crying out. It was an eerie, atonal ululation
that grated on ears attuned to meter and melody.

"*Fantômes*," gasped Lovi, gripping his horseshoe
tightly.

"Bah!" growled ibn Saul. "It is merely a funeral
dirge. Look over there—the procession." Pierrette
followed the line of his outstretched arm. There,
indeed, was a line of people whose path would
intersect their own shortly.

"I don't see a casket or a body," said Lovi.

"Use what powers of observation you can mus-
ter," replied the scholar. "Observe, for example, the
big man at the rear, who is carrying two long poles.
Observe also that two women lead the procession.
Further note that their skirts are darker below the
knee. Perhaps you will conclude, as I have, that
the wrapped corpse of a man, not a woman, already
has been disposed of in a cave or crypt at water's
edge."

"How can you tell, master?"

"The women's skirts are wet, dolt, because they
have waded into the water. The sling-poles are not
carried for the pleasure of it. They once supported
a body—but no longer. One woman is old, the other
young, and they lead the procession, thus they are

mother and wife, or wife and daughter, to the deceased. All that should be obvious. Now let us step lively, or you'll have to run to catch up with them."

The villagers, from the settlement at the head of the bay where had stood ancient Ys, had indeed rid themselves of the body of the women's husband and son, but they had not interred it. In a rough Gaulish dialect that only Pierrette could understand at all, they told her of a sea cave at tide's edge, of the "*magus*" who carried the bodies of Old Believers to their final rest on the Isle of the Dead.

"Was your husband a druid?" Pierrette asked the old woman, after noting that there was no Christian priest with the funeral party.

"He was the last of his lineage. Henceforth, the boatman will have no more passengers."

When Pierrette asked—prompted by ibn Saul in Greek, which none of the others could understand—she was told that the trail to the old mage's cave was easy to follow, and with only one body in his boat, he might be willing to take them all to the island as well. "Don't climb down there tonight. Make your camp here, where there is wood for a fire, and trees to shelter you from the wind. He will not depart until tomorrow, on the making tide."

That night Yan Oors took Pierrette aside. "I am not going with you, tomorrow," he said. "I am going to search for my bear cubs."

"Oh, Yan—be careful. Remember the last time."

"I will. But it is not yet the season for cubs.

They're not born until late, when the weather turns cold. I'll just hunt for a likely sow, whose belly is getting big, and follow her when she seeks her winter nest. Then, when you return . . ."

"I don't think we'll be gone that long. Cubs won't be weaned until summer, will they?"

"The sea is unpredictable. And this island you're going to—what if it's the one you seek? Who can tell how long you'll want to linger there?"

"Ibn Saul thinks it might be the place, but I doubt it. It is flat, and Minho's kingdom is craggy. Besides, the *Gallicenae* of Sena are druid priestesses, not Minoan. I think we'll be back in a day or so."

She would have been wise to have heeded Yan Oors's doubts. The sea is indeed unpredictable, as are the many lands whose shores it laps.

That night she dreamed of Minho of the Isles. It was not (she reflected later) a true vision, because she had spoken no spell, and it had none of the immediacy, the tactile reality, that she had come to expect in a genuine seeing.

"Wake up, Pierrette," she heard. The voice was muffled and indistinct. "Wake up! Where are you?"

Where was she? How ridiculous. If someone was telling her to awaken, then he knew she was asleep, and if he knew that, he must be able to see her. She opened her eyes. There were Lovi and Gregorius, a single shapeless shadow under a cloak, and there, near the smoldering fire, ibn Saul. She heard his snores. "Yan Oors?" she whispered. "Have you come back?"

"Look up," the voice soughed like a wind through

pine trees—but there was no wind, and no pines. The moon was quite bright, for all the veil of haze that drifted across its face, and she saw nothing out of the ordinary.

"There! Didn't you see me? Look again."

Again? At what? She could feel eyes upon her, but all she had seen when she looked up had been . . . the moon.

"Yes! The moon! Can't you see my face?"

There was always a face in the full moon, but it was a goddess's face, and the voice she heard was not womanly at all. "Who are you?" she whispered.

"I can't say my name aloud. I have purloined the goddess's eyes for this glimpse of you. It's not as easy as it once was. The world changes, and I do not. We move apart . . ."

"Minho?"

"Hush! No names. Are you coming? I sense you aren't far away."

"I don't know where you are, or where your kingdom is. Not exactly. How will I find it?"

"I will give you a map."

"How? When?"

"Follow the stars. Come soon, before I drift beyond all mortals' ken. Leave your companions behind. There must be no Christian priests and no scholarly wizards with you, or I'll give you no map to show you the way—and bring no iron, either! Send your ugly bodyguard with his metal staff away to find his bears. Do you understand?"

"Yan Oors is already gone, and I have no intention of bringing the others with me. Where is the map? You said you'd give me one."

There was no answer. A cloud drifted across the

moon, and everything became quite dark. It didn't make sense. She had no map and the stars only told where she was, not where another place might be. Pierrette laid her head on her arm, and slept again.

Wishful thinking, she decided, by the gray light of morning. I wish I did have a map. I wish I were close to my destination, but though Sena is reputed to be a mystical place, it will not turn out to be the Fortunate Isles.

"I'm not sure this is wise," Lovi muttered as they scrambled downward over sharp, black crags. Already, the morning sun was high, and they had not yet reached the bottom of the cliff. "Even if the old *magus* really exists, and has a boat that can weather the tidal race, and knows its currents, how do they get the bodies down to him? They can't carry them down this so-called trail. Even your fractious donkey is having a hard time of it."

"Are you cultivating your master's skepticism, Lovi?" said Pierrette, softly, so only he could hear. "Somehow yours does not sound properly academic—more as though you're afraid. And didn't you notice the pile of timbers and the ropes atop the last promontory we passed? I suspect they rig some kind of hoist. After all, unlike us, most people have no reason to *talk* with the boatman."

"I don't think there is a boatman. I think they just dump the dead people for the tides to carry away. I think I already smell them."

Pierrette laughed aloud. "That's seaweed. I can tell you never lived by the shore. I think it smells nice, like home."

Lovi opened his mouth to reply, but the sight that met his eyes just then, as his feet touched the slippery rock beach, took his words away. There in the side of the cliff was the dark mouth of a wave-cut cave, its entrance awash, and from it jutted the gray, salt-bleached prow of a boat. Standing next to it, with his bare legs knee-deep in swirling water, was the boatman.

He was old, his skin white and blotchy as if it had been soaked for years in saltwater. Pierrette, for whom the phrase "old mage" or "magus" evoked an image of Anselm, or at worst, Moridunnon, was shocked and repelled. He stank of fish long dead. His hair and beard were not really white or gray, or even yellow from the smoke of peat fires, but slightly greenish, like sun-bleached seaweed.

Ibn Saul addressed him as he if he met people just as revolting every day. The shiny Byzantine solidus that gleamed between the scholar's thumb and forefinger was surely as heavy as any dozen lesser gold coins people might ordinarily leave in the mouths of their dead loved ones. The old boatman never took his eyes off the coin while ibn Saul explained what they wanted.

"The Isle of the Dead, eh? Oh, yes, I can get you there. Hee hee hee." His voice was rough and raspy, like ballast-stones being dragged over a cobble pavement. "But you don't look very dead to me. Are you going to die soon? That would make it easier, you know. The witches frown upon live people arriving on their doorstep. Lately, they haven't been happy to see anyone at all."

"Witches, old man? Surely you can't mean the

Gallicenae? The druidesses? I'm sure those are just an old tale."

"Some of them are old, all right. They were old when I was just a sprout, and that was no few years ago. They haven't changed a bit since then, either."

"That's some kind of trick. One old hag looks much like another, anyway."

"That may be so, but don't you think I recognize my own granny? She's the one got me this job, collecting the stiffs for them."

"What do they do with them?"

"I never asked. I don't want to know."

The scholar shrugged. "When can we leave? It took half the morning to get here, and the island must be ten miles away . . ."

"Tide's coming in. When my boat floats free . . . don't worry. The sea is smoother after dark, and I'll have you there by midnight."

"Midnight? You mean we'll be sailing at night? In that treacherous channel?"

The old fellow laughed raucously. "Don't worry. You'll be safe with me. Nobody's ever died on my boat."

"How many live people have you transported?" snapped the scholar.

"Why . . . now that you mention that . . ."

"Don't tell me! We're the first!"

"Not exactly. Last fellow was a Hibernian priest, like that husky one over there." His thumb jabbed in Gregorius's direction.

"I'm not Hibernian!" Gregorius protested. Hibernians were mostly hairy savages, and those who were not, were churchmen. Gregorius remembered a monastery outside Lutetia Parisiorum run by an Irishman. The cagey fellow had seen through his pious masquerade almost immediately, and he had not been able to get away without a fortnight of heavy toil, far too much prayer, and not a sip of wine the whole time.

"Never said so," the boatman replied. "Said he was a priest, like you are, judging by your haircut. Was going to say, he was almost dead when he arrived here, but I kept him alive, and when he went overboard, he was still kicking."

"You threw him overboard? You murdered him!" said Ibn Saul.

"Did not. Said he *went* overboard. Can't beach a boat on the Isle of the Dead. Have to wade ashore, because the old hags don't want black wigglers on their island."

"Snakes?" queried ibn Saul. Pierrette glanced at Gregorius, who raised an eyebrow. They both knew what the "black wigglers" were.

"Call them what you will. The hags don't like them. They pile up on the shore, until the next storm blows them away, but they won't cross water. Had you descended to the sea at the end of the point, you would have had to wade through them, so thick they are there."

"I'm no naturalist. Snakes don't interest me— unless they force me to get my feet wet." Ibn Saul glanced at the boat, still resting aslant on keel and strake. "Why can't we drag your boat farther into the water, and leave sooner?"

"Why, I suppose you can. Never thought of it. Most of my passengers wouldn't dream of helping out." Again, he laughed. It was, thought Pierrette, going to be a long trip, if he had a store of such witticisms. "Tie your beast up there in the bow," he said. "You can't leave him here, because he'll drown if the tide's especially high—and besides, I don't like donkey meat." His laugh was already wearing on Pierrette.

The five of them got the boat into the rising water. The old man tossed a hefty sack aboard, next to the linen-wrapped corpse. He then ordered Lovi and Gregorius to take up the oars, and indicated where ibn Saul and Pierrette should sit, to maintain the craft's trim. Pierrette's critical eye found nothing in his preparations to be concerned with. He laid out the short mast and sprit neatly. The sail was tied to them using cloth grommets, with knots that would release with a quick tug, even if the strips got wet. He waited until just the right moment, a rising swell that lifted the keel free of the cave floor, then shouted, "Row, now!" The boat slid out of the cave, into the sunlit water of the Bay of Sins.

Chapter 19 ∽ The Isle of the Dead

Pierrette had not realized how much she had missed the sea, how much a part of her it was—even this rough, dark water, with no trace of Mediterranean azure. It felt wonderful. She wanted to sing, as she and her father had always done when the wind was fair and the rigging hummed, when the boat's prow cleaved the salty waves like a sharp knife. The crisp breeze blew away the malaise she had felt ever since leaving Rhodanus Flumen and embarking on the Liger. She had, she realized, become so enured to the malevolent aura of the land that she had ceased to notice it, just as she ceased to notice the aroma of ripe fish that clung to her father's boat, after an hour or so asea.

She scanned the horizon. Somewhere out there was Minho's land. She had gotten this far. Now she had to figure out how she could separate herself from the others. Ibn Saul wanted to hire a ship to find the Isles, but all she would need was a boat like this one, rigged for single-handed sailing, a keg of drinking water, and . . .

"Out oars!" cawed the boat's master. "Wind won't help us now, until we're past those rocks." A quick tug, and the sail and sprit rattled down. Without being told, Pierrette gathered the crumpled cloth, keeping it clear of the water sloshing beneath the sole planks. The old man nodded thoughtfully, appreciatively, but said nothing.

By the time they had pulled clear of the looming rocks, where the water now heaped in its rush to follow the unseen moon, the wind had died. "No matter," the boatman said cheerily. "From now until dusk, the tide is our friend." And just as he said, the swift waters swept them along, entirely without sense of motion, around the south end of the distant island. The sea became still. Again, the boatman ordered the oars into the water, and the creak and clunk of leather-muffled wood accompanied the last leg of their journey.

Sena. The beach was low and flat, the water now smooth. The sun was just setting. "Midnight?" grumbled ibn Saul, realizing that the boatman had been toying with him. "What else was he lying about? Getting thrown overboard?"

"Not exactly that, master," said Pierrette. "See how flat the island is—no hills, nothing taller than those scruffy trees. The beach slopes so slightly that we'll be aground on it before we're within forty paces of the shore. You . . . all of us . . . are going to have wet feet soon."

She was wrong, through no fault of her own. The sounds a boat makes, rowing through quiet water, can be heard at a distance, and soon the flicker of a torch could be seen in the gathering dusk ashore. Its bearer was heavily robed and cowled, face concealed in shadow. "Boatman, anchor your craft," said a woman's voice, smooth and mature, not a hag's croak at all. "You"—she pointed right at Pierrette—"come with me. The rest of you must remain between high storm tide and low. Someone will come for the body of our brother Kermat."

"How did she know the corpse's name?" Lovi's whispered question went unanswered. "And why did she pick Piers to go ashore, and not us?"

"They have their ways," said the boatman.

"This is intolerable!" fumed ibn Saul. "I must accompany Piers. Who paid for this trip? Am I to miss everything?"

"Unless you're invited, you'd better shut up," said the boatman. "They get nasty when they're mad."

"Piers!" shouted ibn Saul. "Make sure you demand they invite me ashore."

Pierrette climbed over the rail. The water was only ankle deep, the boat solidly aground. She waded to the torchbearer, who nodded somberly and said only, "Follow me." Pierrette obeyed. Her guide strode purposefully through the almost-total darkness, as if every turning of the path, every root crossing it, were well known to her. The flatness of the island helped. Pierrette noted no ascent as they moved inland. The island, she realized, was as low as it looked from afar, with not a single hill or crag. When the winter storms came, did the waves wash over its entirety? Did such annual baths in brine explain the scruffy nature of the trees and bushes, the apparent lack of clearings that might be construed as cultivated plots?

Ahead were shadows darker than their surroundings. They resolved themselves into buildings, all dark, with one exception. The warm light of oil lamps spilled from a single wide doorway at ground level. Moving shadows showed that the chamber was already occupied. "Come," said the cowled one. "The Nine have gathered, and await you."

The Nine? The *Gallicenae*? Pierrette did not know what to expect—the nine red-haired Gallic goddesses of legend, with the voices of sirens, who lured unwary sailors onto the reefs and shoals, or nine old, embittered priestesses of a dying or dead cult? She kept her eyes upon the illuminated doorway as she approached, so the light would not blind her when she stepped through it.

Back at the shore, the boat now lay fully on its keel and the turn of its bilge, its mast angled lamely. It had not been at all difficult for the donkey Gustave to chew through the leather lead that secured him in the bow. He had enjoyed the salty taste, much like sea purslane. He had not been fed since the previous morning and, as no one but Pierrette ever did so, he had no reason—if indeed donkeys had reason or reasons—to believe that would change. Only a little distance away were bushes and scrubby trees that would provide succulent browsing. Besides, there was an annoying itch between his shoulders, as if his pelt was crusted with mud or salty seaweed, and there was no room to roll about to rid himself of it.

Cautiously, he ascended the sloping planks, and

stepped over the rail into the water. Just as his hind hooves were aswirl to the fetlocks, Lovi noticed him. "Hey! Where do you think you're going?" he cried. He lunged for the trailing tether, but it was wet with saliva, and slid through his fingers.

He was about to vault over the rail after Gustave, but ibn Saul restrained him. "He'll follow Piers," the scholar said. "We've been bidden to remain aboard, and I don't wish to test the limited hospitality we've been offered. The cowled woman made no mention of donkeys, though."

"What's that on his back?" asked Gregorius.

"I don't see anything," Lovi replied. By then, Gustave was already ashore, making for the shadows of the low trees.

The Nine stood in a half circle, all robed and cowled, and the light from the sconces along the walls did not—quite—illuminate their faces. "Welcome, daughter of our Mother," said one. Pierrette thought the voice came from the most central figure, but she could not be sure. Nonetheless, she addressed that one. "Thank you . . . sister." What else call someone who had addressed her so? Someone who was not fooled by her boy's clothing.

"We have watched you for some time," said a voice—another one, somewhere to the left. "We have awaited you."

Watched her? Awaited her? "I don't understand. What am I to you? And how have you watched me?"

"You may be our last hope," said someone near the left, "though we do not know what you must do, because the Isles you seek are not open to our sight. Whether you obey the goddess, or your own heart . . ."

"How do you know about that? I haven't told anyone . . ."

"We have seen you here and there—at Rhodanus's mouth, as a child, and in Aquae Sextiae Calvinorum, when it was only a Roman camp, and most recently, in the palace of Moridunnon."

"The Otherworld!"

"Of course. In the land-beyond, glimpsed in a crystal serpent's egg, in a bronze mirror, or the still waters of a pool . . . Twice now, you have saved us from the darkness that gathers, that would over-whelm us."

What did she mean? Pierrette did not have time to ask, when another spoke: "The black spirits gather together ashore—water holds them back, but some have gotten here, once upon a floating log, another time hidden in a fisherman's craft. Each time, one of us died."

But Pierrette still counted nine: four to the right, four left, and the first one who had spoken, in the middle. One of the cowled figures must have noticed her eyes moving from one side to the other, counting. "Let's not toy with our guest, sisters," said the one on the far left. "She has not come all this way to see the show we put on for ordinary visitors." With that, she tossed back her cowl, and revealed . . . nothing. She had no face, no head, and no hair. "I was the first to die." The words came from the proper place, but Pierrette saw only a shapeless robe hanging as if upon something solid, but unseen.

"Then is this the Otherworld? I was not aware that I had passed through to it."

"Who can tell?" said another, removing her cowl to reveal an ageless face, smooth, but not young, framed by pale hair neither gray nor blond. "Here we exist between the lands of man and the boundless sea, between the spirits of the air and the unfathomable deep. Here, the dead speak, and we the living, often as not, are silent."

Her bitter tone prompted Pierrette's next question: "It has not always been so, has it? Can you say what is behind the change?" The answer to that question had come to her even as she voiced it, but did these women, living or dead, know what it was?

They did not. The rightmost, who had red hair and an old woman's sharp bones, but the smooth, freckled skin of a girl, shook her head. "It came slowly, as mortals measure things. A generation, a single lifetime, no more. Though our ancient records hint that the changes began slowly, they have only now gathered enough momentum to be readily observed."

"What do you know of . . . of the Fortunate Isles?" That question might seem a non sequitur but, as Pierrette came only now to realize, it pointed toward an answer to another question, one so formidable she might not dare ask it.

"They are a myth," said red-hair. "There is no evidence for their existence."

"But didn't you—one of you—just say . . ."

"I said that they aren't open to our sight. I say now there is no evidence. I did not say, first, 'They exist,' and then 'They don't.' My speaking is exact, but your hearing wants refining."

Pierrette might have chuckled, had the setting

been less serious. Evidence. She sounded just like ibn Saul, or like Anselm, criticizing his pupil's methodology, urging always that she examine her assumptions, lest error creep in unannounced. "They are said to lie not far from here, behind a bank of fog," she pressed, "or just below the horizon. Surely you have had visitors—storm-driven or shipwrecked—who made claim to having set foot on them, or to have seen them from afar."

Another woman laughed sourly. "Many that have come *here* believed they had arrived *there*," she said, tossing back blond braids from a face far too severe for such a girlish coiffure. "We give them a day and a night in the Otherworld, and send them on thinking they've glimpsed their heart's desire, and found it wanting."

Pierrette thought of Moridunnon and his eva-nescent realm, and believed she understood: once having been deceived, and having seen as well the bleak reality, such men would depart with divided hearts, believing that the Fortunate Isles existed only within the spells of the druidesses, not in the harsh world of storm-driven ships with ice on the rigging and cold filth slopping back and forth below the decks.

She sighed. "I must return to my companions," she said. "Soon the tide will turn, and our boat will again be afloat."

"But no—stay. We have not yet shown you our realm. Who knows: when you are done with your seeking, when you become disillusioned with the world outside, you may wish to return here—once you see what we offer you."

"I've seen enough. Will you show me towering

mountains on this flat island? I've seen your houses, where the ground floors are unoccupied because the storm waters wash over them. I've seen your salt-loving scrub forests. Will you show me tall maples and beeches, and springs gushing sweet water?" She turned her back on the Nine.

But where the broad portal had been was now a wall of unbroken stone. Pierrette voiced a spell for the clearing of a deception, but the unwavering wall remained. She whirled around angrily. "Am I a prisoner?"

"You are a guest. Now come. The way in is not always the way out. Besides, we are not the only ones who live here, and many others clamor to meet you. You must speak with them, if only a few words on your way back to your boat." She gestured at a bronze-bound door that now stood open, where no door had been. It was a small, low doorway, but as Pierrette approached it, it seemed to expand, and by the time she passed through into clear, cool moonlight, it was as grand as a city gate.

Moonlight shone on dew-polished cobbles, on fine bronze balconies and roofs of silver slate. Pears hung rich and ripe like golden teardrops from lush branches tied against polished marble walls.

The donkey Gustave had lost his mistress's trail at the doorway to the well-lit building, which stank of smoke, lamp oil, and people. A fringe of sweet, soft grass grew where street cobbles met walls, and he followed it around the building, nibbling as he went, occasionally reaching back over his shoulders to nip at the uncomfortable clinging sensation that still plagued him, which now seemed to be centered on the back of his neck, where he could not reach it.

Though it was night, there were people in the street—men in calf-length togas, women wearing blue skirts and crimson shawls. Gold glittered everywhere—the horned or flared torques around men's necks, the women's necklaces and armbands, and upon one man's head, great golden antlers that seemed to spring from his skull, for he wore no leather cap to support them.

"Come," said her guide. "This way." The street opened on a broad market square, whose centerpiece was an artesian fountain, raised three steps above the cobbles, where a dozen men and women, perhaps a score, sat, stood, or squatted in animated discussion. As they approached, heads turned and conversations ceased, but not before Pierrette had heard snatches of what they were saying.

"Your premise is flawed, Cadmos," a scholarly elder said, shaking his head. "You assume the synchronicity of the Great Year with Lugh's waxing and waning, when in fact the shadows on his face appear every eleven years, not nineteen." Pierrette wanted to push into the discussion, to interject that the Minoans had claimed the sun was a sphere, and sunspots appeared at regular times in its eleven-year rotation.

Nearby, two women sat face-to-face, and Pierrette overheard one say, "The elements are indeed four, but fire is only a shadow of true light. Combustion requires matter to burn, while the sun does not, so . . ." Pierrette wanted to add that combustion also required air, and thus that fire could not really be considered elemental at all.

And from the fountain's lip, where a man dangled long, ringed fingers in the moon-silvered water: "Attribute the theorem not to the Greek Pythagoras, but to Diviacos, who was his teacher, and to the generations of mages who laid out the great stone circles. What the Greeks learned of philosophy and numbers, they learned from us Gauls."

Pierrette's head spun. All around the fountain, people were discussing not gossip and scandal, as might the people of Citharista or Massalia, but deep concepts of natural science, of philosophy, of cosmology and history . . .

She yearned to say to young Cadmos's tutor that he must not forget that the cycle of sunspots also ruled the patterns of storms, and painted those great curtains of colored lights that explorers ever since Pytheas had seen above the northernmost seas. She wanted to mention to the man with his hand in the water that the concept of transmigration of souls, that the Pythagoreans had adopted, also sprang from druidic thought, and reached its culmination in the far East, where Brahmin scholars sat in similar converse, themselves descendants of the earliest druids before the great migrations of all those who spoke Aryan tongues. She wanted to discuss the four elements with the seated women, and to add her own observation that they distinguished themselves also as fluid and not-fluid, and that only earth was inherently stable, and . . .

"Who are these people?" she whispered. Not since the time of Socrates had such colloquia, such gatherings of obviously brilliant minds, occurred in one place.

"They are refugees from the turmoil of the world beyond, where the ignorant and superstitious would scorn and persecute them for seeking to understand the universe and everything in it. Here, among them, you may find the answers you seek."

Pierrette almost trembled like a high-strung horse in the starting lineup of a race. Someone on her left was holding forth on the geography of the land beyond the Indus. She wanted to nose in on that conversation, to compare what he was saying with her memories of Anselm's ancient maps and travelogues.

Most of her life had been spent within the loneliness of her own head. Conversations and lessons with Anselm, though they expanded her intellectual horizons, were only brief excursions outside that confinement. With her father Gilles, she discussed fishing or olive groves, subjects he knew well. With Claudia the baker she might speak of yeasts and flours, with Father Otho of the scriptures. With ibn Saul she might study the geographies of far places, and the customs of the savage Wends. But put all of them in one room, and they could speak together only of commonplace things.

Her own interests spanned the breadth of what could be learned, theirs only what they already knew, and she herself was the only element they had in common. But this: " . . . the Isles of the Blessed are no mere rumor," said a burly man wearing the course plaids of the far islands beyond Britannia. "There are monks who inhabit an island

far to the west of my own, who traffic regularly
with them, and Norsemen gather black grapes
there, and dry them for trade with the fur hunt-
ers of the sunless north."

"The Blessed Isles?" interjected Pierrette, pushing forward into the small group gathered around
the islander. "If those monks traffic regularly with
them, they must be able to find them consistently,
and not get lost in the trackless sea."

"Ah! The newcomer. We heard murmurings of
your arrival. But you are so young! That seems
unfair. So handsome a youth, so pretty a girl—you
are a girl, aren't you, despite your baggy panta-
loons?"

What was unfair about it? "I am. But please
continue—you were speaking of . . ."

"Ah, yes, that mysterious, elusive land. It is said
the Norsemen have a magical stone that always
points to it. They have only to sail according to the
stone . . ."

"A lodestone. I know of such things. But they
point only approximately north, and a captain must
judge the degree of deflection his course must take,
to bring him to a particular destination."

"Is that so?" He turned to the others. "You see?
It is possible to learn something new. I told you
so." Pierrette thought that statement a truism, but
several others nodded, grudgingly, as if they had
hitherto truly disputed it. But why? Unless everything was already known—and even among such
a gathering of knowledgeable heads as this, that
could not be so. There were always new experiences, fresh experiments, and unseen horizons—
weren't there?

"The Blessed Isles," she prompted.

"Some equate them with Ultima Thule," reflected a bearded fellow dressed as a Greek, in a short kilt like those Pierrette had seen on the vermilion-and-black vases that adorned Anselm's sitting rooms. "There is no other explanation for what Pytheas describes . . ."

Pierrette listened, and when she could, attempted to steer the rambling discussion back to the specific location of the Blessed Isles, which had to be the very place she sought. She glanced frequently up at the moon, concerned that she might linger too long, that the boat with her companions aboard would float free and she would be stuck here, but the moon had hardly moved from high overhead. There was still time.

But though the islander was right (it was of course possible to learn new things) the course of such learning was often tedious, and never more so than now, when Pierrette wanted not only to find out how to locate Minho's Isles, but how she was going to get back to the boat as well.

Despite her efforts to guide the speakers in fruitful directions, each one went off on tangents of his own. It was really little different than listening to her father and his friends in the wine shop. Glancing around herself surreptitiously, she decided that this town was of no great extent, without walls or gates at the ends of the four streets that converged on the fountain. When it was time to go, she would have only to sidle away from this gathering and make her way along the southerly avenue, and she should emerge within sight of the sea and the stranded boat. There was no sign of the woman

who had led her here. Getting away should pose
no problem, so . . .

Gustave had picked up his mistress's scent at the
rear of the building, having nibbled his way around
it. He set off at a walk, his nose low to the cobbles.
There were few scents to distract him—the aroma
of storm-washed salt and a faint reek of carrion,
not strong enough to make him uneasy. As far as
his nose was concerned, this city was entirely
unoccupied, though his eyes reported the presence
of numerous people conversing on street corners
and in the moonlight. They were not entirely real,
as far as he was concerned.

Being a donkey, having experienced all the
vicissitudes that might plague a lowly beast of burden, Gustave had a low opinion of people in general, who seldom carried bowls of tasty oats with
them, but often bore sharp sticks and resented his
innocent nibbling in their dooryard herb patches
or upon the espaliered pear trees against their
garden walls. Thus he kept to the shadows, even
though he was not convinced that the people he
avoided were really there. For a person, perhaps,
seeing was believing, but for him, smelling came
closer to the truth.

The topic had shifted while Pierrette was considering other things. "There have been many such
cataclysms," said a tall woman whose pleated cotton gown and smooth, dark hair reminded Pierrette
of the Egyptian paintings on the inner walls of ibn
Saul's house in Massalia. "Several Roman towns
were destroyed when Vesuvius became angry, and

the great mountain of Sicilia is never entirely quiet. Such things are surely entirely natural phenomena."

"The Fortunate Isles are said to have been born in such an eruption," Pierrette interjected.

The sleek woman seemed annoyed at her interruption. "Nothing but a Phoenix could survive such burning heat," she said flatly.

"Ah, yes—the Phoenix," said a man dressed entirely in a patchwork of furs, with a necklace of huge teeth around his neck. "Did you know that not only the Phoenix, but 'Centaurs' as well, all originated among my own Scythian people?"

"Again, I say, those are mythical things, not seen in nature," the Egyptian snapped.

"Not so, not so," said the furry one. "The myths arose to explain the actuality. The centaurs were really horsemen, observed and described by peoples who had never seen men astride animals. The Phoenix was the 'magic' of flint and steel, observed by ignorant folk who could not make fire, but had to keep it always burning, or lose it."

"Bah! We are not discussing how nature's clarity becomes twisted by ignorance. Tell that to the druid Boromanos over there. He and his friends are interested in that kind of nonsense."

Pierrette, who was very interested in the evolution of myths, and the changing realities they seemed to represent, wanted to draw the man Boromanos aside, but she got no chance. A brass bell was ringing somewhere down the street. "Dawn comes!" someone cried mournfully. "Dawn, and the hours pass. It is time. It is time."

Everywhere the babble of animated voices that had been a constant underlying music, like the rushing of a nearby brook, ceased abruptly. "What's going on?" Pierrette asked the Egyptian woman.

"Dawn comes," she said, as if that were explanation enough. She walked away. Everywhere, others were doing likewise. The fountain square emptied rapidly as people strode briskly down the streets and into the close-packed buildings. Pierrette looked this way and that. She was alone in the plaza.

Dawn? But because the moon was almost full, and was still high overhead, morning must be hours away. Or was it? She glanced upward, but now clouds scudded overhead in the darkness, and she saw no moon or stars at all. She felt a hand on her arm. "Come," said her red-haired hostess. "It is time for rest."

"Rest? If it is almost dawn, then I must go. The tide is turning. I am not going to sleep all day and get left behind!"

"Come. You must. At nightfall, everyone will be back, and you will find the answers to all your questions." She intensified the pressure of her grip on Pierrette's arm. Pierrette tried to pull away—but could not.

"Let me go!"

"Come."

"No!" Pierrette writhed and twisted, but could not break that grip. She felt herself being pulled along the cobbled pavement, back the way she had come—eastward, where the silhouettes of roofs were dark against the sky's dim, gray light. There was enough light, already, for her to see her shadow.

Somewhere, not far off, she heard a donkey's braying, a strange, foreign sound here, where—she suddenly realized—there had been no sounds at all but human ones. A donkey—and it was not just any donkey—it was Gustave. Her donkey. He almost never bellowed like that unless he was angry or afraid.

"Come! Hurry!" her captor urged.

"Gustave! Gustave! Come here!" Pierrette saw him emerge in the square. He shook himself as if he were wet. "Here!" she yelled—just before a hand clamped itself over her mouth. But the *Gallicena* was too late. Hooves clattered on cobbles. Gustave galloped toward her. Even as she struggled to break free, her mind raced. She had seen something, when Gustave had shaken himself—something dark and formless that the beast had flung aside.

Gustave scented his mistress's distress, which had greater impact upon him than merely seeing her struggling with the dark, scentless non-person. Donkeys were not noted for loyalty or noble behavior but, more often than not, when Pierrette called him to her, she rewarded him with some tidbit or another. He gave one good shake that at last dislodged the annoyance between his shoulder blades, that prickled like a burr in his pelt against his tender skin. For the first time, he saw what it was, as it humped and slid over the cobbles toward Pierrette: one of those tasteless, scentless creatures that had startled him a few times, until he learned to ignore their constant, slithering passage. Then, as now, they were irrelevant—to a donkey.

Pierrette also saw it. This time, the shadowy apparition was not moving westward, unless her sense of direction was entirely awry, but directly toward her. She threw her head from side to side to dislodge the hand over her mouth and, abruptly, she was free.

"No! Get away!" screamed red-hair. Her erstwhile captor was backing down the narrow street, her features contorted with horror and revulsion. Several heartbeats elapsed, between Pierrette's realization that she was no longer captive and her understanding that it was not she herself but the shadow-thing that the redheaded one feared.

The *Gallicena*'s fear undid her—backing away, her heel caught on an overlarge cobble. She fell— and the shadow scrambled over her. She screamed, and her desperate fingers attempted to push it away, but shadows have no substance, and it slipped past, and momentarily it covered her face.

Had she not screamed, then, would it have pushed past her closed lips? Unobstructed, the formless darkness entered her open mouth, and . . . and was gone.

The woman now struggled silently, her red hair flaming in the gray light of impending sunrise. She clawed at her face. Then her long fingers—fingers as strong as a man's—clutched at her own neck, as if she were strangling herself. But no—she was engaged in one last desperate attempt to stop the invasion of her innermost being by closing off the shadow's route of entry. She failed. She convulsed, silently, then lay still, her garments collapsing like an empty sack that held nothing but . . . bones.

A few wisps of flame-red hair lay in contrast to the dark material of her garment, but the face that now glared up at Pierrette had no eyes, only shadowed, empty sockets. Teeth gleamed without lips to cover them. Then those last stray tresses grayed, crumbled, and were gone.

Gustave, who expected neither threat nor reward from dry old bones, now placidly tugged at a stubby thistle, his lips pulled back from his teeth to avoid its barbs, teeth larger and yellower than those in the bare skull that grinned up at Pierrette.

Somewhere nearby, several voices raised a high, keening wail. They knew, didn't they? The next night, at moonrise, would there be one more cowled and faceless figure within the lamplit room?

Pierrette shuddered. She grasped Gustave's trailing tether, and made her way down the empty street, past one doorway after another, set in walls that seemed to shrink as she progressed southward, until the last ones she passed were hardly more than chest high, their dew-spangled tile roofs low enough for her to trail her fingers along the eaves, coming away wet as tears, but not at all salty.

Chapter 20 ∾ The Storm-wracked Sea

Reluctantly, Pierrette gave her companions an account of what had transpired ashore. Gregorius seemed to believe her implicitly. Ibn Saul, true to his nature, was able to explain everything. "They drugged you," he decided. "Perhaps it was an herb in the lamp oil, whose fumes rendered you credulous. And the 'invisible woman' is an old charlatan's trick—had you been in the right state of mind, you might have seen the eyes of a much shorter person peering out from the 'empty' robe whose cowl was held up with smoked wicker." Pierrette was glad the scholar was only speculating. Had he been there himself, he would surely have seen just such peering eyes, and events would have taken a decidedly different course.

"The 'city' whose streets you walked was indeed a place of the dead," ibn Saul continued, "a necropolis whose burial chambers are elevated above the winter storm tides that sweep this low island. You yourself said they were only chest high, when you left there, with the potion's effect wearing off."

"What of the wise scholars?" asked Pierrette. "What explains such a gathering of profound thinkers, on that barren, unlikely island?"

Ibn Saul laughed indulgently. "When I sit down with Anselm, Father Otho, and your father Gilles in Citharista's tavern, a few glasses of wine render even Gilles's talk of fish and olives profound. I find myself reflecting upon his wisdom, and comparing it to Hesiod—earthy, pithy stuff, but quite wise, for all that."

Was it possible? Could she have been deceived so completely? She felt as though she teetered on a precipice, like the narrow ridge-top trail that led to Anselm's keep, where a misstep to either side would plunge her hundreds of feet onto the wave-washed rocks below. If the *Gallicenae* and the dead scholars were illusion, then what was everything else? When she met with the goddess *Ma* at the pool, she always ate one of the tiny red-and-white mushrooms first. When she flew on a magpie's wings her hands and feet were numb from the effect of the blue-and-yellow flowers she had ingested. Were such visits, such flights, no more than drug-induced hallucinations? Was the goddess herself a delusion?

She tried to think of a single instance where she had done something in the Otherworld that had incontrovertibly affected the "real" world that she shared with other people. She examined every instance for a single proof, a solid example—and she found not one.

❖   ❖   ❖

The sun had come up by the time she reached
the boat, and the keel was already free of the
strand. Soon they were miles away from the island.
Stretched flat and sheeted close against the rail,
the sail drummed on the mast. Pierrette glanced
toward the sun, then toward the low, gray land
astern, puzzled. The boatman gripped the tiller with
a tenacity that would surely exhaust him in short
order. Of course, no sailing vessel ever went directly
from its starting point to its destination. More often
than not, the shortest course was a long series of
zigzags, first on one tack, then another, using not
only wind but also current and tide, or fighting
against them.

"Is something wrong?" she asked. "Shouldn't you
slack the sail?"

He gestured westward with a toss of his head,
and with his eyes. "See those clouds? If we're not
clear of the island when they reach us, we'll be
driven ashore—on the rocks, not on a nice beach."

"Why not sail down the wind—northeasterly—
into the Bay of Sins?"

"The bones of a thousand ships lie on the bottom there—and the bones of the captains who tried
to do that. It's the tides." The tides. The treacherous tidal race had reversed its direction, or would
shortly do so. "If we missed the rocks and shoals,
we'd end up . . . who knows where? We have to be
well south of the point, for the tide to carry us
northward into shelter."

"Will we make it?"

"I don't think so." Just then, the wind shifted
ever so slightly—or the tidal current, pushing

against the keel, moved the boat—and the sail was taken aback with a resounding thump. The vessel heeled suddenly, precariously, to the other side. Cold salt water poured over the rail.

The boatman saved them by letting the tiller have its way, so they fell off the wind. Ibn Saul, no stranger to boats, tossed the wooden slop-bucket to Lovi. "Bail!" he shouted.

Pierrette eyed the boatman, who shook his head and released the sheet. "Haul the sail down," he said. "We'll be better off using it as a tarpaulin." Pierrette, who alone of the passengers knew which ropes to release, and in which order, dropped the sail, and began unthreading it from the sprit without being told.

Gregorius and ibn Saul, at her direction, spread the ungainly sail from the bow aft, covering three-quarters of the open boat. The donkey Gustave viewed the cloth roof, now draped overhead, with his usual skeptical roll of the eyes, but to Pierrette's relief he did not protest or panic. Perhaps (such being the depth of his cynical nature, as she imagined it), he considered himself doomed already, and was resigned to it. She showed the others how to tie the sail down at the rail by bunching the material over a knotted cord and tying it there with strips torn from their clothing, then securing it to the boat with a loop between rib and rail.

The boatman, ignoring the useless tiller, held their empty water keg in the bilge until it was half full, pushed the end of the sheet rope into the bunghole, then drove the plug in tightly. He then scrambled forward over the spread sail and tossed the barrel overboard at the bow, securing the loose end of the rope.

"What did he do that for?" asked Lovi.

"It's a sea anchor. With luck, it will keep our bow into the wind when the squall hits. With a bit more luck, if the tide carries us northward faster than the wind blows us east, we'll clear the point. With a bit more luck . . ."

"Enough!" snapped ibn Saul. "What must we do now?"

The boatman pointed forward at the darkness under the makeshift tarpaulin. "Take the bucket with you, and try not to knock it over when you have filled it with your last several meals."

He then turned to Pierrette. "You too."

She shook her head, and pointedly looped a bight of a mooring line through the braided sash that held up her trousers, and secured it beneath a limber, a notch in one of the boat's ribs that allowed water in the bilge to flow freely back and forth. The boatman nodded, and then did the same for himself. They might drown, but they would do so with the boat, not washed overboard to die alone in the storm-tossed sea.

The wall of black clouds, reaching from the crests of the waves halfway up the sky, was almost upon them. The Isle of the Dead was somewhere within them, already lashed by the rain and waves the wind drove across that low land. As the first gusts struck the boat, it turned obediently into them, pivoting on the cord attached to the half-sunken keg.

Pierrette's glances darted between the cloud-wall and the shore astern: their lives depended now on the relative forces that commanded their frail nut-shell of a boat. Try as she might, she could not discern their motion relative to the mainland shore, to the deadly rocks of Raz Point. Though the boat pointed west, the tidal race was driving them north, the wind pushing them east. If the wind were the stronger, they would be pounded and shattered on the rocks. If the tide prevailed, there was a chance they would get past them—if, of course, they were not driven broadside against one of the hundreds of jagged black crags that jutted from the water, the spine of the dragon she had seen from the headland so long ago that it seemed like another life entirely.

The wind and rain struck them like a volley of rocks from the slings of an army, and Pierrette could see nothing, could hardly keep her eyes open enough to squint. She might as well have gone below with the others, for all the benefit her vantage gave her now, but being under cover in a small boat in a heavy sea was enough to make even the most seasoned sailor terribly ill, so she squinted and shivered, but did not have to add vomiting to her discomfort.

She had no sense of direction, except that she believed the wind was still coming out of the west. The horizon was no farther away than the crest of each approaching wave. Those crests were higher than any but the worst storm-driven billows of the Mediterranean, because this ocean was no bowl surrounded by land, and the storms that marched across it had an endless expanse in which to build up strength, to pile wave atop wave until . . .

How far did the ocean extend? Did it stretch

all the way around the world until it reached some shore on the far side of India, where even Alexander had never gone? Despite her misery and the peril of rocks she would never see before they smashed the boat and killed her, she could not stop wondering. Were there many islands in that great sea, far beyond Minho's elusive land? Were they so isolated, so foreign, that even their magics would be incomprehensible to her? If so, were they immune to the malaise of the Black Time that would someday extinguish the last vestiges of magic from her own world?

Conversation was impossible while the storm beat about her, lashing her face with wind-flung spray, but thinking was still possible, and Pierrette had much to think about. Had the nine *Gallicenae* and all the people she had spoken with been an illusion? She now accepted that ibn Saul had been at least partly right—the town had been a necropolis, indeed, and its inhabitants dead. That was what the one man had meant, that it was unfair she was pretty—he had considered it unfair that someone so pretty was also dead. She was not, of course, but he was, he and the rest of them, and he had assumed that she was like them.

That they were dead also explained the debate about the impossibility of learning anything new—not that everything in the world had been learned, but that only the living *could* learn. The dead, of course, were . . . dead.

Then, there was the Scythian. Scythians, as a people, had been gone for centuries. He must have died a long time ago. She wondered how he had gotten so far from his homeland by the Euxine Sea.

But the *Gallicenae* remained unexplained. Were they all dead? Then how could they "die?" Was it possible to be deader than other dead? Of course bodies died, but did souls? Was that what had happened to the two—now three—who had encountered the slinking shadows? Pierrette was reminded of the Gallic belief in the triune nature of man—body, soul, and *fantôme*, or ghost, all united only in the living. Was the "death" she had witnessed the destruction of a *fantôme*, or of a soul? That question was unanswerable and she dismissed it.

But the final question, the one whose answer she feared, still loomed in her thoughts. If what she suspected was true, then neither the goddess *Ma*, Minho, nor the Eater of Gods, really understood what was happening, or why.

Somehow she slept, or perhaps merely sank into unconsciousness because of the cold, the hammering wind. She awoke to a terrible stink and to the sound of someone cursing: it was Lovi, who had emerged with the bucket.

"Not there, you fool!" growled the boatman. "Throw it over the lee side! And don't lose the bucket. That's it. Now rinse it. As soon as we get the sail rigged again, you can use it to bail."

The sail? Through salt-encrusted eyes, Pierrette saw that the boat rocked on a short, choppy sea. The sun was cloud-free, only a hand's breath above the horizon, in what must be the west. The rope leading out to the bobbing water keg was slack. Wisps of fog floated just over the water.

"Where are we?" she asked.

"I can only say where we are not," replied the boatman. "We are not on the rocks. Neither are we ashore. There is no land in sight, and unless the wind shifted and combined with the current to drive us far to the north and west, there should be."

"There must be land over there," Pierrette reflected, indicating a flight of distant seabirds.

"I think so too. That's where we'll head, when we get under way."

With Pierrette's help, he got the sail up in short order, and they were soon about on a broad reach that would get them to where the seabirds wheeled overhead, without changing tacks. "It's a skerry," the boatman granted when the wave-washed rocks came in view. "It's no proper island at all, but we'll find nothing better now, because the fog is thickening. At least we can moor there. It's better than drifting onto other rocks we won't be able to see.

Pierrette was the first one ashore. "The storm must have swept right over this place," she said. Everything was wet, and tasted salty. She had hoped for a puddle of rainwater, or even raindrops on leaves that she could lick, but her thirst went unsatisfied. There was no fresh water. Even Gustave, expert forager that he was, found nothing he would deign to consume. Pierrette sat on a rounded boulder, sucking on a bit of gravel to allay her craving for something to drink. Was this where it would end, here on this scattering of rocks between high tide and low, between empty sky and fog-wrapped sea?

Chapter 21 ∾ An Improbable Encounter

A shout echoed off the rocks. Ibn Saul had climbed the tallest one he could find, and had set up his instruments, hoping to gain some clue as to their whereabouts. Now he was jumping up and down, and pointing. "A ship! People!"

Pierrette and Lovi scrambled up beside him. When Gregorius joined them, he put an instant damper on their elation. "That," he said, "is a Viking vessel."

"But there's no dragon-head at the prow," Lovi protested. And the boat was not long and skinny, like the ones they had seen drawn up on the Liger's banks.

"That's because it is a *knorr*, a workaday vessel, not a *drakkar*, which is a warship. But a Norseman is a Norseman, whatever deck he treads."

"But who are those men wearing brown robes?" asked Lovi. "Isn't that a cross hanging from the tall one's neck? They must be Christians, but they are far too well dressed to be slaves."

"Those are Thuleans," said the boatman, just joining them on the high rock. "They are Christian Norsemen from a remote island, who trade widely. They are only distantly related to the Danes, Jutes, and Frisians who raid and pillage."

"Christians? Traders? Then surely we can get some water from them," said Lovi.

"And what would you trade for it?" said an unfamiliar voice behind them and below. They spun around as one, almost knocking each other off the rock. The brown-robed man, they realized by the contents of his basket, had been collecting mussels. Hearing ibn Saul's shouts, he had come to investigate.

"I have never heard of Christian Vikings," said Gregorius. "You don't look like a Viking at all, with your dark hair. You look more like a Hibernian."

The fellow laughed. "*They* are Christian Vikings," he said, "and yes, I am Hibernian. I am a priest, and they are my flock—just as I assume these people are yours." Gregorius had long since abandoned his priestly garments, but he still maintained his tonsure—the Roman cut, which was only a bald patch at the crown of his head. The brown-robed one affected the "Celtic" tonsure, his head entirely shaved forward of a line from one ear over the top of his head to the other ear. It was, Pierrette reflected, actually a druidic tonsure, out of favor in all but the most remote Christian lands. The transition from pagan druid (or Pythagorean philosopher) in the Celtic lands had been almost seamless, as had that of Brigantia to

Saint Brigid, and Madron, the goddess, to Mary, Mother of Jesus.

"Perhaps I am mistaken," the Irish priest said, taking Gregorius's silence for negation. "Still, come down to our camp and be welcome. You look like people who have a tale to tell—a fair trade for ale and steamed mussels—or water, if you really prefer it."

The "Thuleans" had made the most of their makeshift camp amid the rocks, stacking many small stones between the larger ones as a windbreak, over which they had spread a large square sail. A cheery fire blazed in front of the shelter. Its fuel was great chunks of hewn wood—the ribs and planks of a wrecked vessel half-buried beneath washed-up seaweed and gravel.

Some of the Norsemen spoke rough Latin, some only their own guttural language, so everything that was said, when the newcomers were settled by their fire, had to be translated either by the priest or by Gregorius. Ibn Saul was first to begin the evening's entertainment, detailing their journey from the warm Mediterranean shore. That took quite a while, and when he finished, a big Norsemen stood up. "The Fortunate Isles? My Uncle Snorri was there once. They lie a long way south and west of here. Their ruler lives at the top of a man-made mountain, in a red, yellow, and black house from which he surveys his domain. One of their gods lives in a very deep well, and four times a year the king puts on a robe of songbirds' feathers, and delivers a virgin bride to him. And the gold! Even the meanest peasant has a gold ring for his nose! Snorri came home with enough to outfit six ships for a voyage back there again."

"Where is he now? I must speak with him," said ibn Saul.

The Norsemen laughed. "If you can find him, tell him to come home sometime. He left again when I was just a sprat. He'll be an old man now, cosseted by a dozen young wives down south . . . unless there's a tunny nuzzling his bare bones, somewhere on the bottom of the sea."

Ibn Saul sank into apathetic silence, now believing that his goal was immeasurably far away, and that even if he knew the way, as had Snorri, he would have a hard time getting there, and a harder time still returning home alive. But Pierrette was not so sure. A black, red, and yellow house? Minho's palace had black-and-vermilion columns, and she supposed the limestone of its walls might seem yellow, but nothing else sounded like the Fortunate Isles she knew—or thought she did.

Gold? Of course. Minho was rich. But sacrificial virgins? Not unless the story about Theseus was literally true and the Athenian youths sent to the Minoan capital had been sacrifices, not hostages. No, the Norseman's Fortunate Isles were not hers, but let ibn Saul go on thinking so. When it was time for her to go her own way, that might make things easier. One of the brown-robed men—there were three of them, and only one ordained priest—rose. "Friend Egil's uncle may have found the Fortunate Isles," he said, "but there may be more than one such place. My ancestor Brendanos visited a place called Hy Brasil, west and south. It bore little resemblance to what Snorri found, but that was a long time ago—over three hundred years—and things change, so it may be the same place.

"At any rate, schooled in the druidic arts and Christian scholarship, knowledgeable, as all Hibernians are, in the ways of the sea and the guidance of the stars, Brendanos and fourteen other monks set out to find a place called 'The Isle of the Saints.' The first island they found, after long weeks at sea, had nothing but goats and sheep, but they were able to reprovision their boat and fill their water skins. At Easter time they discovered another island, little more than a smooth rock, which sank beneath them as soon as they lit a fire for a cooked meal. Ha! It was no rock, but a whale—a very annoyed whale indeed. They survived their immersion, and regained their boat without further mishap, and soon found a third island, where dwelt a solitary monk who had gone mad, and who claimed he was Judas Iscariot, exiled for his great sin. Eventually Brendanos became the first man to discover our own home island, which he called Thule, after a legendary kingdom in the far north.

"That voyage took seven years. Returning home to Hibernia, Brendanos lingered for many years, before setting out to sea again, though some of the others took their families to Thule. But at last Brendanos, having become rich, outfitted a fine oak ship with trade goods and a crew of sixty men. After visiting his people on Thule, he sailed west, and during the fourth moon after Christmas, encountered an island entirely of ice, in the shape of an arched doorway. It must have been a wandering island, because no one ever saw it again.

"The first land southwest of the ice island was home to great beasts with cat's heads and tusks bigger than an old boar's. The crew killed some, because they had eaten their last pigs, then prevailed on Brendanos to sail more southerly, in hopes of finding warmer seas and more hospitable lands. Indeed, in the weeks that followed, the sea became warm enough to swim in, and the air itself smelled of spices and honey. On one small island, seeing smoke, they found an elderly monk, a hermit, exiled from a colony of Hibernians to the west. He gave them directions, and that is how Brendanos found the Fortunate Isles."

The tale-teller paused, grinned, and held out his horn cup for more ale. Several Viking sailors hooted and urged him on, but he waited until his cup had been filled, then downed it in two great quaffs. "The land next encountered, eight days to the west, was ripe with fruits and flowers, and when they found the monks' colony, they were feted like returning sons, and their ship was restocked with everything the land could offer. The monks told of a lovely city inland from their colony, whose king lived on top of a mountain, though they said nothing of gods living in wells, or of feathered cloaks. If the people of that city were rich in gold, no one ever said so— nor would they, if they were smart, and wanted to get as much of that as they could, for themselves.

"Brendanos and his men sat out afoot, for there were no horses in that land, and they hiked northward. They searched for forty days, and though they found villages aplenty, there was no city, and when they encountered a river too wide and deep to cross, they turned back.

"Brendanos returned home by sailing directly east, on strong winds that bore him almost to his own doorstep, and his next voyage was in a different direction—to Rome, with a letter from Festinus, bishop of the Fortunate Isles, and from there he went to the Holy Land . . ."

The tale continued, but Pierrette lost interest. She pondered everything she had heard. The two accounts, different as they were, did not discourage her. Neither place was her destination, but both mysterious lands contributed to the legend, and thus served what she believed was the goddess's end. Not only that, the stories implied that should the earth prove as vast as Eratosthenes of Cyrene had calculated, the unexplored portion was not all just trackless ocean, but included islands, perhaps whole continents, untouched by the malaise that threatened the known land—the Black Time.

How that could be was not clear. Had such undiscovered lands always existed, or did they somehow—spontaneously—appear, just over the horizon, off the bows of the first ship to sail toward them, or just over the next hill but one from the intrepid explorer by land?

So lost was she in thought that when the tale-telling was over and the gathering divided itself into multiple centers of conversation, she alone remained uninvolved, until the big Norsemen—Egil—sat next to her and proffered a wooden tankard slopping with fresh-drawn ale. "Are you morose?" he asked. "Ale is the cure for horizon-struck eyes." One of the two untonsured Irishmen also sat. Close up, Pierrette saw that he was still a boy, no older than she purported to be.

"You speak Gaulish?"

"It's near enough to the Hibernians' tongue," Egil replied, "and my family has long traded in Brittany."

Brittany? Oh, yes—that was what immigrants from old Britannia called Armorica, "Little Britain."

"Traded? Not raided?"

"Is every Roman an emperor? Is every Hibernian a priest? It only seems so."

"Tell me about your island—Thule? I had not heard of that, except in the most ancient accounts of Pytheas's explorations, over a thousand years ago."

"I doubt it is the same place. My island was only discovered a lifetime ago, by Hibernian monks fleeing the fleshpots of their own green land. For want of a congregation to listen to their preaching, they induced my father and others of like mind to settle there. Until then, there was nothing but smoking mountains and thornbushes—and the ice bed that covers all the central lands."

"It sounds like a formidable place."

"Formidable indeed, but kind as well. In winter we bathe in hot water that springs from the rocks, and in the long days of summer, the sun hardly sets before it rises again, and crops grow so fast we harvest the near end of a field before we've planted the far."

Pierrette recognized hyperbole when she heard it. She laughed. "Are you recruiting settlers to farm your ice fields? How many such crops can they take in a year?"

"Well—that is a difficulty. The summer days are long, but the summer itself . . . three months from snow to snow." He grinned. "But think of this—

all winter we need do nothing but lie around our houses and drink ale."

"How lucky for you—or is that simply because in winter the sun sets soon after it rises, and it is too dark and cold to go outside?"

"You're a clever one! You saw right through me. Drink more ale. I am not defeated yet. I'll sell you a patch of ice and a bag of gravel to seed it with, before the night is over."

Pierrette sipped from the mug. The ale was clear and crisp, and rather than dulling her senses like cloying wine, it seemed to sharpen them. Attempting to calculate how far north the storm had blown them, she studied the stars overhead—and one star in particular, that stood slightly over halfway up the northern sky. She also asked many questions about Egil's island home, until she was truly convinced it was not what she sought.

The ale passed through her rapidly, and at her body's urging she excused herself, to go among the rocks. But the Irish boy said, "I'll join you," in that offhand yet sociable manner boys affected about such things.

"Actually," Pierrette replied, "I think I need a bit of a walk to clear my head. But please don't leave—either of you. I'll be back shortly." Such bodily functions had always been the greatest threat to her disguise, traveling in a party of men who would stop and pee wherever they were. She had cultivated the air of being a very shy young boy, and that had seemed to suffice—and she had learned great control over her bladder as well.

She found a suitably private spot. When she arose from her task, she was disoriented for a moment. Which way was the camp? She glanced at the sky, seeking the pole star, but did not immediately spot it. When she did . . . was it just a tiny bit higher in the sky than she expected it? She then knew what her next question for Egil would be.

When she returned, the big man sat alone. The boy did not come back, with fresh tankards of ale, for quite some time. "If I were standing in that field you want to sell me, with my sack of gravel in hand, how high overhead would that star be?" She pointed.

He smiled. "Why should it be higher or lower?"

"I think that if your summers are only a month or two long, and your winter days but an hour or two, that star must stand almost overhead, and all the heavens whirl around it."

The Norseman's eyes narrowed. "You look like a boy, but what are you? A shaman? A shapechanger? A reader of minds?"

It was Pierrette's turn to laugh. "I am a student of a wise master—and could I have come all the way from the warm southland without noticing that the guide star appeared slightly higher in the sky at the end of each week's travel?"

"You aren't going to tell that to every sailor you run across, are you? It would be very bad for trade, if the master of every leaky southern washtub could read the stars aright, and find his way around the northern waters without getting lost."

"I won't tell anyone. I have no wish for the far places of the world to lose their mystery. But the scholar ibn Saul also knows the stars, and what he knows, so do all those he writes to."

"Then I should kill him before he leaves this place."

Pierrette realized her mistake too late. She rushed to repair it. "It would do you no good. What he knows, the others already know also. And besides, aren't you a Christian? Murder is no light burden to take with you on your final journey."

Egil sighed. "I suppose you're right. Even if his relatives never heard of his death, and made no complaint, our priest would see me banished. Everyone takes murder seriously, these days."

"Don't look so glum. Of all the scholars I know, ibn Saul is the only one who puts his knowledge to practical use. His correspondents are content for him to travel cold seas and wet, and to read of his exploits from the comfort of their sunny terraces."

He nodded. "Still, it is a sad thing, that all the mysteries have a way of becoming common knowledge, and the furthest lands become as well known as one's own garden plot."

"What you say is truer than you can imagine," said Pierrette, "and only a little while ago I would have commiserated with you, but now I have come to suspect that for every new shore we explore, a newer one appears somewhere beyond it, and we will never find the end of everything."

"You are deep, whether you are really a boy or are an old shaman in disguise. But I am not. My head is heavy with new thoughts and ale, and we must depart at first light." He arose with a popping of knees and a rasp of salt-stiffened clothing.

All the time Egil and Pierrette had conversed, the young Hibernian had remained silent. Now alone with Pierrette, he spoke. "My father knows of the islands you seek," he said. "He once described them to me, exactly as your scholar said: a rim of black rock, broken by several channels, and within, circle upon circle of other channels, with great wharves. In the exact center of that maze is a black peak, flat-topped, upon which stands a palace or a fane, whose columns are red and black."

Pierrette's heart thudded noisily in her chest. Her breath caught in her throat. The boy truly described Minho's land—concentric circles, the cones of successive volcanic eruptions, the outer ones breached by channels that led inward to the central, newest cone, on whose leveled top stood the sorcerer-king's residence. "What . . . what else did he say?"

"He was not allowed to stray from the wharf when he docked, but he was paid well for his cargo—furs from the Norsemen's mountains and a chest full of amber." The boy reached within his clothing, and drew out a small object that gleamed warmly in the fire's light. "He was paid with gold. This was the smallest morsel, which he gave to me." He held it out to Pierrette. Her hand trembled as she took the gleaming object from him.

It was a cylinder of gold the size of Pierrette's thumb, sharply incised.

Rolling it across her palm, she envisioned the pattern it would make, pressed into a wax tablet or soft clay: the entwined figures of a dolphin and an octopus. A chill coursed up her ribs. For the very first time, she held an object that had definitely come from the Fortunate Isles, not in Otherworldly hands, but here, in the ordinary world. She had seen similar seals in Minho's library, which was very much like her master Anselm's, but larger—the original, after which Anselm's was modeled. "It is indeed the land I seek," Pierrette whispered. "Why are you showing this to me?"

His young, soft face turned red and he whispered, "When you left us to pee, I followed you. I . . . I saw you. You aren't a boy at all."

Pierrette's mind raced. If her own party discovered they were travelling with a girl, a woman, she did not fear they would suddenly become strangers bent on bedding her—especially not Lovi or Gregorius. But the Norsemen, with the thin Christian finish the Irish priest had painted on their rude, Viking natures, were a different case. "Why didn't you tell Egil?"

"There is more to my father's tale," he said. "All the rest of the gold was shaped into chains, like necklaces. Only the piece you hold was different. When Father gave it to me, he told me what the ruler of that kingdom had said: 'There will come a virgin girl, seeking my kingdom. This I have foreseen. She will dress as a boy, but her eyes will be as old as your grandmother's. This is for her. If you trade it for cattle, they will bloat and die. If you trade it for furs, they will stink and become slimy. A boat purchased with this, however sound, will fall apart when least you expect it. But who does as I bid will live a hundred years, and have forty grandchildren.'"

Minho! He knew! This was the sign he had promised, and it had been held in his own hand, in this world. He had foreseen this very meeting, on this remote skerry, out of sight of land. "Why did your father give it to you?"

"What good is gold you can't spend? Father was

already wealthier than was good for his soul. When Egil's Norsemen discovered our island and its little community of monks and Christian families, father gave the rest of the gold as peace gifts, impressing them with the generosity of our God to sailors on the cold sea. Only that small morsel of gold remained ungiven—until now."

Pierrette rolled the little cylinder back and forth. Dolphin and octopus. Octopus and dolphin. The dolphin's eye glistened as if it were faceted, as if it were a tiny star.

"It was true, what the king said. I am indeed the one this is intended for. But I have nothing to give in return."

"You need give me nothing. I will have my reward. There is a girl, at home . . . I have hopes that she will be the grandmother of my forty grandchildren."

"But he gave it to your father, not you."

"I considered that, and asked Father to repeat the words. '*Who does as I bid*,' he said. Not 'if *you* do as I bid.' I think he foresaw that I, not my father, would be the one to give it to you."

Pierrette also believed that. Later, when she slept for the hour or two that remained before dawn, she dreamed of a white room with paintings of blue dolphins and octopi on its walls, and a bed heaped with pure white furs. The breeze on her naked skin was balmy, not cold, and sunlight's captured heat radiated from the dark floor tiles. She glanced down at herself, wondering placidly where she was, and where her clothes had gone, but she could not see her own body. When she lifted a hand to her face, the magnificent coral and gold of the sunset streamed right through her invisible fingers. "That is because you are not really here, yet," said a resonant, masculine, tenor voice. "Come. Hurry. It is the end of an age, and I have waited a thousand years for you."

She awoke with the little cylinder still clutched in her hand. The impression of the octopus and the starry-eyed dolphin was pressed into the palm of her hand, and did not fade until they were once again at sea, in their own small boat, with their water keg full.

Chapter 22 ∾ Gesocribate

Much to Pierrette's regret, ibn Saul had reached the same conclusion she had: the stories told around the Thuleans' fire were fascinating, and they assured him that explorers would not run out of new places to discover, in his lifetime—but the places they described were not the Fortunate Isles.

"These are not a month's sail to the south or far away to the west. They are here." His fist thumped against the sheer rail. "They are not far at all—and I will find them." Gesocribate was their destination now. Consulting with the Vikings, ibn Saul and their boatman determined that the storm winds had driven them about twenty-seven miles north of Sena and a bit west as well. From the green, moss-covered rocks of the skerry, by fresh morning light, they had gazed northwest. Only five miles distant loomed a large island, which the boatman recognized. They could just make out the rocky mainland coast by squinting eastward into the sun's brightness.

With a steady breeze just abaft the beam, they sailed crisply on a course opposite the one they had willy-nilly arrived on. When the last of the treacherous rocks and shoals between the island and the mainland were behind them, they turned east and north with the wind astern, on a port tack. Gesocribate lay on the north shore of a bay ten miles long whose entrance was only a mile wide. When they cleared that gullet, Pierrette saw a vast expanse of smooth water dotted with brown, yellow, and tan sails, and fringed with fat, green fields. Surely, Vikings had entered the bay, despite the Roman fortifications on both sides of the gullet, whose catapults and stone-throwing slings were still manned, but though they might have burned farmhouses and stolen sheep, the city itself seemed untouched.

Grass grew in the cracks between the Roman wharf stones, worn by centuries of barefoot sailors, grooved by wagon wheels, polished by the crates, bales, boxes, and barrels that had been pushed across them. Gesocribate was not the busy place it once had been, when Roman ships had swept Venetii and, later, Saxon, pirates from the sea, but there were ships in port—and ibn Saul headed for them as soon as his feet touched stone.

Pierrette tagged along with him. It was too much to hope that the masters of those vessels—she counted seven she deemed worthy of being called ships, not boats—would one and all refuse his commission. She would have to delay her own search.

Her hand crept to her pouch, where nestled the gold cylinder seal, among her other treasures—

Father Otho's cross, her mother's ring, and the crystal bauble veined with red and blue. The seal was her key to Minho's kingdom. She had not dared study it in the presence of others, but she was sure that the dolphin's tiny eye was a star—and the stars would be her guides. But for now, she would have to remain with the others, and do what she could to keep the scholar from finding the Fortunate Isles.

Ibn Saul paid for a room over a wharfside wine shop—or cider shop, if truth were told. They dined on black wheat pancakes wrapped around vegetables, bits of meat, and chopped eggs—a delectable change from rough forest fare and meager meals afloat. Her stomach full, her head slightly fuzzy with drink, Pierrette looked forward to a night in a bed—even one shared with ibn Saul, Lovi, and Gregorius.

But though she lay long abed, sleep did not come. She lay thinking about one thing, then another. Was Yan Oors well? Had he found a likely she-bear? How would she find him, when it was time for the bear to drop her cubs? And ibn Saul's next exploration: only one shipmaster had been willing to consider his charter offer, and Pierrette did not like the look of him. His eyes were too close together, for one thing, but more to the point, the caulked seams of *Shore Bird*'s hull were green and oozing, and her standing rigging had not been tarred in a long time. It was frayed and brown, not glossy black. If a man cut corners with ship maintenance, how reliable could he be in other ways?

Also, she had seen one of the small, evil shadows emerging from a heap of dung; when it slithered away, it had gone slightly south of west, and she wondered what that meant. Had the noisome things' destination somehow changed, or did her own position, now many miles north of the Liger's mouth, make the difference? If so, if a mere fifty miles of northing had such an effect, then the shadows' destination, or the point at which their paths would all converge, was not far away at all.

She visualized a map of the coastline, and guessed that their destination must lie no more than a hundred miles offshore. That was, of course, further than any but a shipmaster desperate for money would go, but it was not as far as Viking Egil's warm paradise on the far side of the world. She now suspected she knew where the shadow's destination was, and it confirmed the hypothesis she had formed, but as yet she had too little evidence, and could not act upon it.

Lying awake and silent, she must have seemed asleep to Gregorius, when he slipped out of the bed. At first, she assumed he would seek the chamberpot, but when she heard him quietly rummaging in their baggage, she squinted in his direction. She heard the faint clink of coins. The priest had ibn Saul's purse! Then she knew what was afoot. Gregorius was sneaking away. Pierrette saw him take a single Byzantine solidus from the purse, then put the sack back where he had found it. At least he did not intend to rob ibn Saul of everything. With his small bundle of possessions, he slipped out the door.

Pierrette dashed to the small balcony and scrambled to the ground. Guessing which way Gregorius would go, she rushed ahead to the wharf, and hid herself behind a large cask. She saw the swath of light spread across the cobbles when he emerged from the inn. "Gregorius!" she whispered as he neared her position.

He sucked in breath, and halted. "Leave me alone!" he whispered. "I don't want to fight with you."

"I can't stop you. And I saw that you only took one coin for your passage, when you could have taken the whole purse. But why? Why leave us now?"

"The *Merry Dancer*'s destination is Burdigala! From there, I'll be almost home—in a country where no evil shadows creep, where the sun is warm, and olives and peaches grow, and . . ."

"What about Lovi?"

His face wrinkled in anguish. "He would never leave his master. I've hinted at it, but his mind is completely closed. Love is one thing, but he has a vision of himself as a famous explorer someday. I didn't dare ask him outright. He might have betrayed my intentions to ibn Saul—out of his love for me, and his wish to have both of his desires."

The priest shook his head sadly. "As I've said before, I am only a substitute for his true desire— which is you. As long as you are near, he won't willingly go elsewhere. I know this." He smiled ruefully. "Will you comfort him, when I'm gone?"

"I can't do that. Not as you mean it. I've told you that before. Will you really leave, if I assure you of it yet again?"

Gregorius sighed. "I must. I'm no more an explorer than I am a cleric at heart. I'm a singer and a tale-teller." His gaze became sharp. "Are you going to betray me?"

"For Lovi's sake, I might. But no. I'm going back to the inn. And you must hurry. I can hear the creak of a sail being hoisted, and the tide has turned. With this offshore breeze, your ship won't wait long for you. Good-bye, and good voyaging."

He turned away and rushed off down the wharf, where a large ship, mainsail aback against the mast, was straining against her mooring lines astem and astern.

When Lovi and ibn Saul awakened, there arose the ruckus Pierrette had dreaded. The scholar raged and ran down the wharf, shaking his fist at the empty water. By then, Pierrette guessed, the vessel must be breasting the narrows with a following breeze, with her sails bellied full and sheets straining. By mid-morning, when the offshore winds died in the face of the prevailing westerly one, she would swing southward on a beam reach and struggle past Raz Point, and would have no further fear of land so close off her lee rail. "Good luck," she murmured.

Another uproar ensued when ibn Saul discovered the missing solidus, but that died quickly. "It's less than I'd spend, feeding him, if he stayed." That was, of course, not really true. One solidus would feed all of them for some time, and pay for wine and cider as well.

Lovi could not yet accept that Gregorius was gone: had Piers actually seen him board the ship? Might he have jumped back off before it left the wharf? Lovi's hurt and anger seemed directed not at Gregorius, but at her. Pierrette was relieved when ibn Saul put them to work loading baggage onto *Shore Bird*'s dingy deck.

Shore Bird was an inauspicious name for a ship that was going to sail straight out into the unmapped sea, where no land was known to be. Further, she seemed weak in the spars, like a sandpiper or a phalarope indeed, not a sturdy duck or a graceful tern. Pierrette decided to keep a close eye on ship, master, and crew.

They pushed off at mid-morning on the last of the tide. Pierrette waved at their erstwhile boatman, who did not intend to sail back to the Bay of Sins. "There'll be no more business for me, and I hate fishing," he had said. "Here, at least, I can ferry people across the narrows, or onto ships at anchor in the roads."

"But you are the last person who knows the secrets of navigating the tidal race."

"So what? There is no longer any reason to. There, I was a relic of an old tradition as dead as those who inhabit Sena's necropolis. Here, I am a sailor among other sailors, and do not have to live in a musty cave."

Pierrette eyed him curiously. He had cut his hair and beard, and no longer looked old. His hair was now merely gray, not mottled as with green algae. It was as if he had shed a certain physical resemblance to the sea-spirits along with his former occupation, and now was as other men. She judged that his decision was a wise one.

Shore Bird struggled through the narrows with half-filled sails, because the early offshore breeze was now almost gone. There had been a brief altercation between ibn Saul and the shipmaster, Kermorgan, when Pierrette led Gustave to the down-slanting gangplank. "Another passenger! You did not mention this. There is no room for four more feet on my deck."

"That is Gustave," said ibn Saul. "He is not a passenger any more than my sacks are. You saw him there on the wharf when you asked what goods and chattels we would bring aboard. And at any rate, you agreed to take four of us, and now we are three."

"I will allow it. But keep him from underfoot—and don't expect to split an extra, fourth, ration among the three of you."

The Fortunate Isles had to lie beyond the last islands and skerries—or so ibn Saul had calculated. That meant there was no direct course to them, because the usual winds were westerly, and square-sailed *Shore Bird* could not come closer to the wind's eye than a beam reach. For every mile of westering they made against those seasonal winds, they would have to sail ten or twenty north or south, slowly gaining distance from the black, rocky lee shore of Armorica.

Pierrette stayed in the bow with Gustave most of the time, among the chicken cages, grain barrels, and caged pigs that provided their sustenance. On their second morning at sea, she observed Lovi standing at the rail, dangling a dark object over the water below. It was his "lucky" horseshoe. "You aren't going to throw it away, are you?" she asked softly.

"What do you care?" he snapped. "It hasn't brought me luck, has it?"

"Who can tell? Without it, where might we be now?" She didn't think "luck" worked like that, but

Lovi had been so happy to find the horseshoe, and she felt quite sorry for him now. "Besides, you can never tell what may happen if you throw something of value into the sea."

"Oh? Is that another of your stories?"

"It is. If it will cheer you up, I'll tell you."

Just for a moment, Lovi seemed to brighten. "Is it a changing tale, like the ones about the Tarasque? One with several beginnings or endings?"

"Wait and see. Tonight? You must promise not to throw away your horseshoe."

He nodded, grinning crookedly. "Who knows— perhaps this is not an ending, but the beginning of a new kind of luck for me."

If Lovi had been like other men, she might have considered comforting him in a physical way, at least with a hug and a chaste kiss—had she not been wearing the tunic, *bracae*, and conical hat of a peasant boy. "Perhaps so," she replied, not meeting his eyes. "It's too bad you aren't attracted to girls. You wouldn't have a hard time finding an affectionate companion, then. I've seen the way they look at you, in every town."

He sighed. "Once, that might have been," he said sadly. "I didn't choose to be what I am. It just happened that way. Perhaps if I had fallen in love with a girl, before . . . but no. I suspect my nature was different from the beginning."

"Perhaps so," she replied.

"What about you?" he asked—now peering intently at her. "Now that I think upon it, I've never seen you yearning after girls, either."

"I . . ." Pierrette was nonplused. "I've been too busy. I try not to think about such things."

"I think you're lying. I think you are attracted to men also. I think . . . you are attracted to me." He put his hand on hers, atop the ship's rail. She snatched it away.

"No! I mean, you don't understand me at all." Of course she was attracted to him, but it was Pierrette who was attracted, not her alter ego Piers. "Besides, my . . . my mentor . . . has forbidden me such things. The consequences would be dire."

"Aha! He would not have forbidden you such a thing unless he knew you leaned in that direction already. You do find me desirable, don't you?"

This was not going well at all. Lovi had assumed that the "mentor" in question was Anselm, as she wished him to do, but he had made more of it than she expected, and had gotten all too close to her true feelings—but not her true nature. "What you want can never happen," she said, not looking at him. "It is absolutely out of the question. It is impossible. You must accept that."

"I don't believe you. I'm not going to give up. We'll be at sea for many weeks, and I'm not going away. Sooner or later, you'll come to me." He turned away and strode aft with as firm a step as if he had been ashore, not on a slanting deck, wallowing in a contrary sea.

Chapter 23 ∾ Lovi's Choices

Once, after a week at sea, the lookout spotted a concentration of clouds on the horizon east of their position. "That's them!" cried ibn Saul. "No rain or storm has passed over us, so they cannot be storm clouds. They are the kind that form where a tall obstacle disturbs the passage of the sea winds—an object like . . . an island, like mountains." He scrambled aloft with amazing agility for one his age, and despite his long scholar's robe.

An hour later, back on deck, he was dejected. "I saw nothing. Change course in the direction where the lookout saw them. By morning, they'll be clearly visible."

They were not. Such tantalizing glimpses occurred several times—unnatural clouds, or flocks of seabirds riding updrafts that could only form in the presence of land. But when they sailed toward them, clouds dissipated, birds drifted away, and there was the only the endless sea.

Ibn Saul made scratchings on a vellum skin, noting their position, as best he could determine it, at the time of each sighting, and from his notes he determined that their elusive destination had to lie in one particular, very limited area of the sea.

Brandishing his vellum, he attempted to explain his reasoning to the captain, Kermorgan, but the seaman was highly skeptical of lines, notes, and numbers.

"Our destination lies a hundred leagues south and west of the Ar Men rocks," ibn Saul insisted.

Shore Bird's master was adamant: "There is nothing there! We've been at sea for three weeks now, and have only once seen land. Our water is almost gone, and what's left of our food reeks. The last chicken's neck was wrung yesterday. We must put in at Gesocribate again."

"Just one last try!" Ibn Saul sounded desperate— as well he might. Thus far the voyage had been entirely unproductive. As if some malign god did not wish them to succeed, they sometimes found themselves far north or south of where ibn Saul calculated their course would take them, after a day or two of cloudy skies. When the skies were clear however, there was no such confusion. Pierrette had thus concluded that the scholar's lodestone` had ceased to function properly: when they sailed by the stars, ibn Saul was able to determine which way to sail, by the pole star, and to estimate their latitude, but using the lodestone they went astray, as if it no longer pointed north at all.

Still, on two occasions, from different directions, they had spotted isolated clouds on the horizon, clouds that did not change position, as if they were anchored in place. Such clouds had only one explanation: the presence of a land mass high enough to disrupt the smooth flow of the oceanic winds—the presence, in short, of a mountain in the sea.

Now, even without exact knowledge of their longitude, ibn Saul was sure that the Fortunate Isles lay . . . "There! That way! With this breeze, a little out of the north, we can reach them in two days' sail."

"Perhaps Kermorgan is right, master," said Lovi, shortly later. "With fresh water aboard, and livestock . . ."

"Once in port and paid off, we'll never get them out again. Besides, my purse is now so light I can hardly feel it. It's now—or never."

"Then it will be never," Lovi murmured angrily. Only Pierrette heard him. What did he mean? His recent behavior had puzzled her. For a while, after he had declared his intent to pursue her affections, he had been cheery and optimistic, but in the face of her undiminished stubbornness, he had become glum and surly, and had urged ibn Saul to give up this crisscrossing of the empty sea. Now his words had an ominous tone. He had sounded so sure of himself. How could that be, unless he planned to do something to make it happen—or not happen?

As the ship again plunged south and westward, retracing the course it had taken several times before, Pierrette kept an eye on Lovi, but saw nothing amiss. He spent most of his time peering out to sea at the clear, cloudless horizon. Nightfall brought high clouds with it, which obscured the stars and made of the crescent moon a hazy blur of cool light.

"Are we on course, master?" he asked ibn Saul. "Without any stars, shouldn't you make sure the helmsman hasn't turned us around—as he surely did before?"

"Fetch my lodestone and bowl, then, and a lamp," the scholar said. Pierrette's eyes followed Lovi aft, where their baggage was stowed. Why did he want ibn Saul to use the lodestone, if indeed he did not want his master to succeed?

Lovi unwrapped the brass bowl, the wooden disc, and the fragment of black rock. Then— why?—he pulled something from another sack and hid it at his waist. What was it? He dropped a bucket over the side, filled it with salt water, and poured some in the bowl. Returning, he laid the materials on the broad thwart by the mast, then sat down next to them. Ibn Saul carefully lowered the wooden disc onto the water, and placed the lodestone on it, with the disc's "north" mark pointing just aft the starboard beam, as it should be, if their course were correct. Then it swung around, past the ship's stern, and continued moving until it hovered just off the port beam. "You're right!" the scholar hissed. "We're not sailing south of west, but northeast! We're sailing back to Gesocribate! The treacherous pigs! Call that wretch Kermorgan over here!"

"Piers," said Lovi. "You do it. I want to keep my eye on the lodestone." Why? There was nothing to see. The stone was not going to move. Or . . . or would it? Then, as suddenly as if a light had been lit in a hitherto dark corner of her mind, Pierrette knew what Lovi was doing, and she knew what he had gotten from his sack. But she betrayed nothing.

She nodded, expressionless, and went to find the ship's master.

Ibn Saul confronted the captain with the evidence that they were actually sailing northwest. "You're mad," said Kermorgan indignantly. "I don't care where that thing is pointing—we have not changed course. I've had a log and line astern all this while, and it stretches straight aft, and has done so all day and night. We are heading a bit south of west, as you will see, when those clouds blow past."

"Bah! Turn the ship now. When the sun rises in the west, I'll apologize for doubting you, not before."

"When we see the Ar Men rocks off our bow for the second time in two days, I'll just keep sailing that way, right into port." The captain shouted orders, and soon the ship was a busy place as sailors hauled the sails about onto the new tack and braced them. But Pierrette was not watching the crew. She watched Lovi. Ibn Saul kept his eyes on the lodestone.

Lovi arose in a seemingly casual manner. He stretched, and shifted position aft. As the ship turned downwind and the yards were hauled amidships, he edged around further. As the sails refilled on the new tack, and the ship continued to turn, he moved slowly to the other side of the mast, and seated himself on the opposite side of ibn Saul's bowl, always keeping as close to it as he could.

From ibn Saul's viewpoint, the lodestone had obediently continued to point north as the ship turned completely around, but from Pierrette's perspective, the stone had followed . . . Lovi. Now she was sure of it. As the ship settled on the new heading, ibn Saul packed away lodestone and disc, poured out the water, and handed everything to Lovi. He then went astern, and for the rest of the night watched the line that stretched out over the ship's glassy wake. It was straight, in line with the keel, and if it shifted either way, he would see it, and would know that the ship was again changing course.

Pierrette sidled up to Lovi as he squatted and wrapped the lodestone and its accessories. "What are you looking at?" he snapped.

"I'm just watching," she replied. "Does that bother you?"

"*You* bother me!" he said, and turned away. But by that time Pierrette had edged quite close to him, and her hand darted inside his tunic. She grasped something cold and hard, pulled it free, and then backed away. "Give that back!" Lovi hissed.

Pierrette shook her head. She hefted the horseshoe, then threw it over the side. The sound of water slipping around the hull masked the faint splash. "Why?" she asked. "Why have you been toying with your master, making the lodestone follow your horseshoe instead of pointing north? All this time, we've been sailing in wrong directions, haven't we?"

Lovi turned away, leaned on the rail, and covered his face with his hands. "I want to go home, can't you understand that? Nothing is right anymore. Gregorius is gone. You will have nothing to do with me. My master is obsessed with finding those miserable islands, and I don't want to spend the rest of my life in this cold, forbidding land, chasing something that doesn't exist."

"How cruel you are! How selfish." Pierrette's indignation was genuine—even though Lovi's trickery had played right to her own desires; ibn Saul had not found the Fortunate Isles, and now he would not.

"If you were less cruel, I wouldn't have done it."

"That's not fair. It's not my fault."

"Just go away." Then: "Are you going to tell him?"

"Why? He'd just be more miserable than he will be, when he realizes where we're going." She went forward, and spent the last hours of the night snuggled up against Gustave.

At dawn, the sun rose in a glowing western sky. "Impossible!" yowled ibn Saul.

The shipmaster smiled smugly. "Since we have been sailing north of east all night, and are now halfway home, I intend to remain on this course as long as the wind holds. If you wish to follow your silly device all over the trackless sea, you must find another ship." Ibn Saul's vehement protests did not sway him. "You have not been watching my crew the way I have," the captain said. "You haven't heard how they curse you at mealtimes, when the worms in their moldy bread prove the best part of the meal. You haven't listened to the whispers whenever two or three of them gather to coil a rope one could coil. Another day of this aimlessness and you might find yourself overboard with a marlinespike pushed up behind your eyeballs. Be grateful for my caution."

Ibn Saul accepted the inevitable then, and spent the remainder of the voyage home sullenly alone.

❖   ❖   ❖

With shifts in the wind, and allowing for the tides, it was two days before they slid up to Gesocribate's wharf. "Where are you going, boy?" ibn Saul called out to Lovi. "Help us offload these sacks."

"I'm going to look for Gregorius. He may be here still, waiting for us."

"Bah! He is long gone. When the baggage is stowed in our lodgings, you may seek where you will. But you'll waste your time." Lovi reluctantly helped Pierrette lash the sacks to two poles, and the poles to Gustave.

The aroma of crisp lamb fat filled the inn, and as soon as possible they sat to enjoy their first decent meal since the last of the ship's pigs and chickens had been slaughtered. But despite good cider and fine, tender meat, it was a gloomy gathering. "Have you made further plans, Master ibn Saul?" asked Pierrette.

"I have seen vessels like that fat, single-masted one, the third from the end of the wharf, in my voyages along the Wendish coast, which is beyond the Viking lands. Unless I miss my guess, it will be homeward bound soon—and we will be aboard it."

"But master—I thought we'd be going home!" Lovi had seen the light of reason (and had smelled the lamb cooking) and had postponed his search for Gregorius.

"We shall—by the eastern river route to the Euxine Sea, Byzantium, Greece . . . why slog over dull, familiar ground when we can see new sights, and visit the fountainheads of true civilization, instead?" Lovi, Pierrette observed, had entirely lost his appetite, upon hearing that, but she herself was elated. "I will arrange passage for the three of us," the scholar continued, "And . . ."

"For the two of you, master," Pierrette said. "Our agreement was for me to accompany you in search of the Fortunate Isles. Though I would someday like to see Byzantium, I must postpone it. I have much unfinished work at home in Citharista." That was true, but misleading. It would remain unfinished a while longer. Through the material of her pouch, Pierrette squeezed the hard shape of the cylinder-seal the Hibernian boy had given her. The scholar accepted her pronouncement easily enough, but Lovi's silence seemed icier than ever. "I'm going up to our room, now," Pierrette said. "Try not to wake me when you come in." She swung her legs over the bench and departed.

Actually, her purpose was not immediate sleep, but a quick sponge bath. Aboard the ship, it had been difficult enough to find privacy for essential bodily functions, let alone cleanliness. As on most vessels of any size, there had been buckets for well-paying passengers to relieve themselves, and a wooden trapeze slung over the rail aft for crew (who of course urinated whenever and wherever they wished, as long as it was over the lee rail). Now Pierrette noted that the door to their room had a wooden latch on the inside that could be lifted by a string threaded through a hole, from the outside. Once in the room, she pulled the string back through. Anyone trying to get in would make noise, and she would have time to cover herself before they thought to stick a knife blade between door and jamb to lift the latch.

She tossed her filthy clothes in a corner, and laid out her only change of clothing—a worn tunic and trousers. The sun was setting, but she did not yet light the wick in the lamp-bowl. She poured water from a crock into the washbasin, and wetted a scrap of cloth, then wrung it out.

She scrubbed her bare skin until it glowed pink—or would have, if it had not become quite dark by the time she finished. Fumbling for the lamp, she uttered words she had not spoken for some time—her firemaking spell—and a brilliant spark leaped from her fingertips to the wick. Warm light filled the room.

She heard a sharp, hissing sound, as of someone drawing a sudden breath, and she spun toward its source. There, head and shoulders above the balcony rail, was Lovi, his eyes wide, and his mouth agape. "Ah . . . ah . . . I . . . you . . ." he gasped incoherently.

Pierrette's long masquerade was over. Even if she rushed for her clothing now, it was too late. Lovi could see that her chest, freed of its binding, was not a boy's smooth rib cage, and that no appendage projected from the dark shadow where her thighs met. When she turned away to pick up her *bracae*, he could also observe that her hips were wider than any boy's, her waist narrower, her buttocks fuller. "You . . . you . . . you're a . . ."

"A girl. Yes." She pulled the trousers on. "Now do you understand why I could not be your lover?" She slipped into her tunic, and laced it. "Since you are attracted to men, and I am a girl . . ."

"But that's . . . if I had known, that—then—then everything would have been different."

"You may as well come in. I wouldn't want you to fall to the street. Sit on the bed. You look like you're going to faint."

He sat. "All this time!" he murmured. His eyes glistened. "All this time, I believed you were . . . that I was . . ."

"I'm sorry to disappoint you yet again. I had no intention of . . ."

"It's all your fault! You! If it wasn't for you . . ." He looked as if he could not decide between anger and tears.

Pierrette was confused. "I don't understand. What have I done?"

"When you first came to my master's house, I . . . I fell in love with you."

"You hated me. You were cold and mean to me."

"I hated you because you were . . . a boy. Because that meant I was . . . I was . . . what I have become." He covered his face with his hands, and began to weep.

Pierrette's sat next to him, and put an arm around his shoulders. He shrugged it off. "If you had been a girl then—I mean, if I had known . . ." Again, he broke into spasms of weeping. With a sinking heart, Pierrette realize what he was trying to say—what, indeed, she had done. Lovi had not—always—been attracted to men. He had desired Pierrette. He had believed the boy Piers had rebuffed him because Piers was not . . . like that. But that couldn't be! Lovi was Lovi. She had not made him what he was. It was not her fault. He looked up at her, his eyes red and swollen. She felt so sorry for him, for his torment.

"I only went with Gregorius," he said, "because

I knew you would not have me. It wasn't what I really wanted . . . at first."

"If that is so," Pierrette murmured, taking his hand, "then it isn't too late for you to change."

His eyes held hers, while his hand crept under her loose tunic, and found her breast. She felt her nipple harden, pressed between his fingers. His eyes remained on hers, unblinking, while he caressed her with his clumsy, calloused hand.

Then he pulled his hand away and, averting his eyes, shook his head. "It really is too late. You are as foreign to me as . . . as a fish. I felt nothing at all. I have dreamed of touching you. I have laid awake, imagining a lie, and an impossibility, and now I am only . . . disappointed."

Pierrette knew nothing about such desires as his. Had he once indeed been an ordinary boy, with ordinary cravings? Or had he wanted her because she was—or so he had believed—a boy? She had no answers, and thus did not know whether to feel guilty, or only sorry for him.

"I'll find another place to sleep tonight," she said, sighing.

"It isn't necessary. This will be the first time— the only time—when we share a bed, even with my master snoring between us, when I will not feel the torment of desire for you." He did not have to say what he would feel. She believed she knew . . .

The wind had been off the land, not the warm sea, that long-ago day, and little Pierrette had shivered, even though her exertion on the steep upward trail should have warmed her. Ghosts of memories arose with each step.

Here had wound the glitter-scaled dragon, which was a winding line of townsfolk with torches. They had hunted her mother to her death. *There* was the cave where she and Marie had hidden from them. Beyond was the barren cape, plunging on either side to the sea, narrowing to a natural stone span that led outward . . . to the dark wooden doorway of the mage Anselm's keep.

She had hesitated near an odd willowlike bush. The upper surfaces of its leaves were rich green, their undersides pale and silvery. She stared as if the very force of her gaze would penetrate its illusion. Gradually, limned with light and shadow, she saw . . . a child. No, not exactly . . . The creature that appeared where the bush had been had great violet eyes, a rare color only seen in sunset, or dappling the sandy bottom of a cove. Those eyes were old, not young. His silken shirt shimmered like moonbeams and his baggy trousers were the green of young leaves in springtime. Tiny silver bells jingled on the toes of his soft, pointed shoes.

"Ha, child!" said Guihen the Orphan. He wiggled his overlarge ears. "That didn't take you long. Are you growing stronger, as well as more lovely? Or am I losing my touch? But then, you always saw through my illusion."

Pierrette wasn't sure what he meant about growing stronger. And more lovely? She was a small, bony-kneed child of seven. "What are you doing here?" she asked.

"I came to warn you."

"Of what?" Wisps of fine hair at the back of her neck stiffened. "You're only a willow bush, and I'll push you aside." She was angry. She wanted her mother.

Guihen sighed. "Elen is not here, child. She lives in a green and lovely vale."

"She's not in heaven. P'er Otho said so."

"No, her place is of this earth, but you won't find it on the Eagle's Beak. But there, beyond that gate, is the *magus* Anselm . . . and a terrible fate for a little girl."

"Mother said to seek out the mage."

"She was distraught. She didn't think. Go back to your father and sister."

"Don't try to stop me!"

"If you knock on that gate, you won't return to Citharista unchanged." Guihen's ears flapped, as if agitated. "Would you deny yourself an ordinary life: a husband, children, a place to call home?"

Pierrette hesitated. When the wood sprite next spoke, his voice no longer tinkled like the bells on his shoes. It echoed hollowly like wind in the door of an abandoned sepulcher. It was as harsh as the creaking of rusty hinges, as dry as old bones: "*Go back, or be doomed to make your bed in strange places. Go back, lest time itself bend about you, and you not find what you seek for a hundred hundreds of years!*" Little Pierrette did not comprehend what Guihen had meant, but the dire threat in his voice was clear, and she knew that a terrible choice was before her: go forward, and suffer, go back and . . . and what?

Pierrette was too young—then—to value the prospect of a husband and children. And her own bed was not the secure place it had seemed before that terrible night—the night Elen had been killed.

That time, she did as she was told, and made her way back to the village. But Citharista, her father and sister, her lonely, motherless house and bed, gave her heart no ease. She knew then that she was not like other children, and that she would not be like the others even when she grew up. She would indeed deny herself an ordinary life— husband, children, and a place to call home. Guihen's words echoed in her head: "Go back, or be doomed to make your bed in strange places. Go back, lest time itself bend about you, and you not find what you seek for a hundred hundreds of years!" But she had, at last, years later, gone forward.

Yes, Pierrette knew what it was like to be an outcast, to be denied—and herself to deny—all the simple pleasures of ordinary, conventional life. "I am so sorry for you," she said at last. "We are not as different as we seem."

"You had a choice," he replied, without heat or apparent resentment.

Did I? she wondered. Could I have chosen otherwise? She did not believe she would ever answer that. What was done was done, life went on, and everyone had to snatch what fleeting joy they could, what they were given.

Part Three ∾ Dawn

Pierette's Journal

I can safely conclude that the shadowy apparitions that have disgusted, distressed, and even terrified me are not unrelated to the answer I seek. They are palpable expressions of the principle of the Law of the Conservation of Good and Evil. I am forced to conclude that the balance they seek to restore with their westward migration is the one that Minho's spell upset.

That they are so evident in Armorica, but not in Provence, suggests that there is still time to accomplish my task, because the disturbance of balance they embody is still localized. Further, the shadows are by definition Otherworldly, and can perhaps best be described not as objects but as bare phenomena: voids in the veil between the worlds. But it is a terrifying Otherworld those tiny portals open upon: that realm of greasy blackness and crimson light might well be what Christian visionaries see, that they call Hell. It is frightening to consider that the nearer I approach Minho's private vision of heaven, the deeper must I plunge through its opposite to get there.

I have surmised another phenomenon, not directly observable: just as the world, perhaps the universe, expands as man seeks its limits, so the past becomes more remote—and the future also—as scholars contemplate the infinite. Snorri and Brendan's voyages implied the former, and it is reassuring to believe that explorers will never run out of new places to discover, and ibn Saul will never lack for new mysteries to debunk and destroy. It is also reassuring to consider that the very nature of the Black Time may be to recede, not to arrive.

If my hypothesis is correct, then the original end points, the original break in the Wheel of Time, are no longer the ends of it, for new eras and eons are being formed in future and past alike. Thus the proximate cause of the break—the terrible, destructive spell gone awry that caused it—will not be found at the beginning, but somewhere along the way; not at the end, but centuries, even millennia before those ever-receding moments.

Chapter 24 ∾ The Long Voyage Ends

Ibn Saul and Lovi departed at the peak of the tide, without additional parting words except conventional well wishes. Even when their vessel went hull-down in the distance, Pierrette lingered on the wharf as the water slowly receded, wet and dark.

When the tide went out, the foot of the stone wharf abutted an expanse of shiny, dark mud. Pierrette scooped a handful of sediment and kneaded it, squeezing it between her fingers until it had the consistency of potter's clay, then pressed it flat on a worn stone bollard. Brushing drying flakes from her hand, she worked two fingers into the neck of her pouch, and pulled forth the little gold cylinder. She set it at the leftmost edge of the flattened sediment, pressed it firmly in place, and then rolled it across the smooth surface. As it moved from left to right its impressed patterns remained in the soft material. First appeared the octopus, its tentacles now stretching leftward, two of them splayed upward, one down, and the rest reaching out toward two hitherto unnoticed dolphins now leaping from a wavy sea.

Pierrette rolled the seal until the pattern began to repeat itself, then replaced the glittering bauble in her pouch. She pondered what lay before her: Minho's engraved invitation to her, and her alone. A larger dolphin, with a star for its eye, lay left of the other two, and above them. A line traced between the three would form half a right angle with the bottom of the impression. Several other scattered stars completed the image of the telltale constellation that she recognized.

At the base of the image was a wavy line broken by upward-pointing teeth, and on the flattened top of the central tooth was a tiny rectangle, faced with three not-quite-semicylindrical marks, and surmounted by a large star. To Pierrette, the shape of those marks resembled the black-and-vermilion columns of the entrance to Anselm's keep—and the columns of Minho's palace.

Across the top of the impressed image were ten raised half-circles that she interpreted, knowing the engraver's intent, as waning moons. There before her was not just a picture, but a map, a simple star chart, and a rudimentary calendar. Tonight, she knew, was not only the tenth half-moon, but the autumnal equinox as well. Had Minho foreseen even that?

There before her was the route she must take to meet her dream lover in the real world, to step from a boat onto the solid ground of . . . the Fortunate Isles.

She scraped the mud from the worn stone, kneaded it into a ball, and then tossed it onto the tidal flat, where it immediately merged with the silt, the stranded seaweed, and the scattering of empty mussel shells.

Boats were plentiful in Gesocribate. Refugees— villagers and fishermen from the length of the coast beyond the gullet—had trickled in over several years, fleeing Viking raids on vulnerable coastal villages. For most of them, the craft they had arrived in were not necessities of their livelihood thereafter.

Pierrette bought one such idle craft for two silver denarii. Perhaps, she suspected, she only bought the right to provision it and sail it away, because the master of the little wooden wharf where it was tied alongside many others was clearly not a boatman himself, and she doubted he had clear title to any of them. He asked a high price for a gilded galley of six oars that leaned on keel and rotted bilge ashore, and placed low values on workaday vessels in the water, half sunken, sloshing with green duckweed. Those craft, their seams swollen tight, were better off than the pretty, rich man's toy ashore, whose planks had wracked and spread in dry air and sunlight.

Bailed dry, her boat stayed dry. She provisioned it with four kegs of water, a tight cedar box that held her few possessions, a dense, dry wheel of cheese, several flat salted fish, and a sack of crisp, unleavened black wheat biscuits. She wedged a clay pot of honey and a little cask of fresh cider by the boat's stem.

The boat's woolen spritsail, rolled on its yard, was striped with black mold and could not be trusted. She negotiated for a better one—as it happened, a bright red sail from the seam-sprung galley. Dry air, unkind to watercraft, was friendlier to cloth.

She paid the innkeeper's son to care for Gustave. "My little boat is no place for a donkey," she whispered to the beast, stroking his nose. "The boy has promised to give you a handful of grain every day, as well as your fodder. You would be wise not to kick or bite him." Gustave snorted his disdain.

When Pierrette approached her boat, there was her beast, his tether bitten through and dragging on the wharf. "Oh, no! Did the boy say something about 'work' to you? A small boat is no place for a donkey." The stableboy arrived, panting. Gustave glanced at him, and stepped nimbly into the boat, and planted all four hooves against the spread of the bow planks, as if pegged and joined in place as firmly as the timbers.

Pierrette sighed, and proffered the boy a coin. "How soon can you bring the fodder and grain you sold me to the dock? Clearly, he intends to go with me." The boy eyed her as skeptically as Gustave might have, had the situation been reversed. "An hour," he said.

Pierrette pushed away from the dock at dawn, two days after her companions had departed from the main wharf. Would their paths ever cross again? The sunny streets of Massalia, the great market above the Roman decumanus, and the little tavern opposite ibn Saul's doorway might as well have been in another world entirely. Another . . . an other . . . an

Otherworld. The last thing Pierrette had seen, as she rowed out of the shore's wind shadow, was a cluster of dark, formless shapes huddling at the end of the dock, as if yearning to follow her. . . .

She searched her craft from stem to sternpost for the slightest hint of an unnatural shadow lurking behind keg, crate, or coil of line, remembering her guide on Sena, crumpling in a rattle of dry bones. She did not wish to be responsible for transporting such a thing to Minho's fair land, where everything evil or even unsightly had been banished on that long-ago day when he had wrested his kingdom from the world of time's passage.

She sailed outward beyond the gullet into a sea unmarked by other sails. On long, time-consuming tacks against the westerly wind (now shifting northerly as winter approached apace), she had many uneventful hours to ponder. She was now sure that for the small evils wending ever westward, Sena had been only a stepping-stone on the way to their true destination, the focus of their yearning. If she drew lines on a map, westward from the Liger's mouth, southwestward from Gesocribate, they would converge precisely at the patch of sea where she and her companions aboard *Shore Bird* had seen unmoving clouds hovering about the peak of an unseen island, which was surely a ring of black volcanic crags . . . The shadows' destination, one and all, the focus of their mindless craving, was the Fortunate Isles.

She now understood what her true mission was to be. The goddess *Ma* was mistaken—for Minho's kingdom to recede into the mists of unprovable legend was no solution. Moridunnon's master, the

Eater of Gods, was also in error, whether he wanted Pierrette to succeed or fail. In one sense, if she did as *Ma* wished, there would be no counterbalance to his growing power, no single realm where evil did not exist. He would consume ever more of what remained, and the Black Time would come, when at last he was sated. But in another sense, his dominion would remain forever incomplete.

Minho, also, was a victim of flawed reasoning . . . but she did not dare to dwell on that. When at last she confronted him in the flesh, would the love he professed for her be strong enough to overwhelm the disastrous news she would bring him?

Pierrette leaned against the mast of her little boat. The steering oar was lashed in place, and she had nothing to do. A firm, steady breeze filled the little crimson sail, and she squinted past it, into the newly risen sun. Her last tack had been a long one, heeled over hard, sailing much closer to the wind's eye than a square-sailed craft could have done. Now she approached the stationary wisps of feathery cloud from the west, propelled not just by wind, but by rolling swells as high as her vessel's stubby mast, swells that first lifted her craft's stern, then raised the entire vessel enough so she could see for many miles. Several times, at the glossy crests of such waves, she believed she had seen a dark speck—a peak, jutting above the horizon?—at the base of those trailing clouds.

At last, finally, Pierrette was alone. Was she lonely? Many times, she had been lonely, even in crowded cities and marketplaces. She had not been close to Gregorius, and Lovi's assumptions and expectations had been an insurmountable barrier between them, but she thought with affection upon ibn Saul, and she missed the steady, quiet companionship of Yan Oors. Her mentor Anselm was a thousand miles away. Yes, she was alone, but she did not think she was really lonely.

Besides, there were distinct advantages to being alone. Grasping a wooden water cup firmly, she reached over the lee rail and filled it with salt water. She murmured soft words, an ancient spell from one of Anselm's books, then raised the cup to her lips; the water tasted as pure and sweet as if she had dipped it fresh from the Mother's own sacred spring. She would not have dared utter those words (or afterward, sip that water) in the presence of others, except perhaps Yan Oors or the sprite Guihen. But then, they were themselves magical beings and ordinary folk did not even see them unless they wished to be seen.

Alone, she was free to behave as she wished. Alone, there was no one to doubt her magic. Of course, that was a double-edged sword: without impartial observers, how could she say that what she did, and the results of the spells she uttered, were not simply illusion or even delusion? Alone, she existed entirely in a subjective universe where whatever she chose to believe was not liable to contradiction. When the tall, rolling swells lifted her small boat high, she could now distinctly see the black, jagged cliffs that rose from their encompassing bank of concealing fog. Had there been others present, would they have seen them also? Would she herself have seen them? Who could say?

Gustave could not speak, and at any rate showed no interest in scenery. His feed was stowed beneath the sternmost thwart, and he remained in the bow. His eyes, consequently, were most frequently fixed aftwards.

Pierrette saw them, however, and she knew what they were: fragments of the ancient caldera, the barrier islands that sheltered the inner bays, harbors, and wharves of the Fortunate Isles. As those black cliffs rose higher and higher before her, she adjusted the steering oar and let the sheet out just a trifle, because the gentle breeze that bore her forward had swung entirely aft. Even when her vessel nosed into the obscuring fog and she could not see to steer, she was confident that her boat would make no leeway, and would reemerge unharmed by rocks, reefs, or shoals.

And so it was. In the space of a single breath, her boat's prow slid out of the fog in the middle of a broad channel between cliffs so high and steep they seemed to lean inward, as if the strip of sky visible above was narrower than the channel through which she glided, below. Hardly any sunlight penetrated that gouge in the monstrous crater's rim, but ahead it sparkled on the water and illuminated warm, green tree-clad slopes, brown, fresh-turned fields, springtime-green ones whose crops were just pushing up from below, and others where golden-yellow grain waved in a mellow breeze, mature and ready to harvest. Now she was sure—only in the Fortunate Isles were crops planted year round, with seedlings, fruiting stalks, and stubble abiding in adjacent fields.

Now ahead, lesser craters' rims were broken in

places by channels that led further inward, toward the very center of the Fortunate Isles. Despite the craggy terrain on all sides, the breeze that filled her sail remained exactly aft, and she made no leeway to one side or the other. She adjusted the steering oar again, to bring her bow directly in line with one of those channels. On either side, the cliffs fell away, and she could see great waterways that diminished with distance and their own curvature. Those, she knew, were the concentric circular waterways of which Plato had written, in the land that he had named Atlantis. The Atlantis of legend was many times the extent of the Fortunate Isles—because the unit of measure in Plato's time, the *stadion*, could be either one eighth of a mile or a multiple of that, and deciding which measurement to use was a matter of context. Writing of such a fantastic, marvelous land, Plato, and later his readers, of course, assumed the larger, more fantastic, more marvelous measure.

But even one hundredth the size of legendary Atlantis, this place was fantastic enough. Buildings of white and golden stone dotted the slopes that ran down to the waterfront, where broad wharves stood clean-swept and empty; once, many centuries ago, those wharves would have bustled with carts, wagons, and laboring stevedores, because the kings of this land had controlled all the commerce on the Mediterranean Sea, and all ships docked here, for their cargoes to be inspected and taxed.

Here and there, dark upon the water, Pierrette saw fishing boats, oared, without sails. The appearance of anything larger, she knew, would have been a rare and momentous event on these quiet waters, for that was the way Minho, ruler of these Isles, wished it to be. Had he not wished her to be here, she was sure the friendly breeze that bore her inward would instead have beaten against her boat's prow and driven her back, the fog that wreathed the outer beaches would have obscured every channel, and she would have run up on jagged rocks, or would have found herself, confused, back at sea and heading away from the Fortunate Isles.

Here she was—and it was real, not a dream, not a vision. The cliffs were solid black stone, the trees at their feet were genuine, and their leaves shimmered in the palpable breeze that pushed also against her sail. She was here, and the long voyage she had—really—begun as a small child in Citharista, when first she dreamed of the sorcerer-king with the golden bull's-head helm, was soon to end. . . .

Chapter 25 ∾ An Inauspicious Welcome

She heard the singing before she rounded the last headland. A hundred voices, or two, or three, floated across the water and reverberated from the black cliffs above. There! Trickles of smoke rose from braziers atop fat columns, at the end of a projecting wharf. Even from her distance, Pierrette could see the undulating movement of a white-clad crowd that covered the wharf and the shore beyond. She could smell the smoke.

An important ceremonial occasion was in process—from her many visions, she knew that white, Egyptian-style garments were worn on formal occasions and in the presence of the islands' king. She deftly adjusted her steering oar, let out the sheet, and altered course toward another wharf; it would not do to sail disruptively into the middle of some solemn ritual.

High above the main wharf, at the end of what

appeared to be a processional road flanked by more
gleaming green stone columns, stood the portico
of Minho's palace. A chill ran up her ribs and down
her spine: it was real—vermilion-and-black pillars,
and beyond it, the windowed, multistory edifice
itself.

She edged up against the mossy stone wharf and,
slacking her sail, leaped ashore with a line in hand.
Methodically, with the force of long habit, she
secured the bow and stern to stone bollards. Only
then did she pause to look around.

What now? Closer than ever before to her goal,
the site of her childhood fantasies, she had never
felt farther away. There was a road at the foot of
the wharf that surely connected with the site of the
white-clad gathering, but how could she tread it?
Was she to shoulder her way through the crowd,
or find someone in charge and demand to be taken
to the palace? She glanced down at her frayed tunic
and cracked leather *bracae*—the gulf between this
moment and her vision of herself on a gold-and-
ivory throne had never seemed vaster. If only she
could just *be* there, and not have to *get* there. If
only she could float down into the palace on a
cloud or on seagull's wings and transform herself
in a poof of vapor into a visiting princess clad in
silk and fine wool . . .

A clatter of unshod hooves on stone paving
shattered her fantasy. Gustave! "Come back!" she
called after the beast, who was already at the
landward end of the pier. Gustave ignored her and
edged into the brush with fresh, green leaves
already dangling from between his mobile lips. Ah,
well. He would not stray far. She could retrieve

him later. Now, she had to make the best of her inauspicious arrival.

Climbing back aboard, she cracked open her small trunk, from which wafted the aroma of cedar. Careful not to let its contents drag in the boat's sloppy bilge, she shook out tightly folded blue cloth: a long, sleeveless dress. It was wrinkled, of course, but it was fine wool and would soon smooth in this sweet, moist air. With an armful of clothing, she returned to the wharf, and quickly slipped out of her tunic and into the soft blue dress.

She cinched her waist with a tan leather belt set with round gold *phalerae*. Two gold fibulae connected by a fine-wrought chain secured her soft Gallic *sagus*, a white wool cloak with a hood. When Pierrette admired the fibulae from the side, they were rampant stags with coral antlers. When she viewed them from a different angle, they were gnomish faces with inlaid coral hair—shifting, curvilinear patterns difficult to focus on. She looked for Gustave, but the donkey had retreated into the brush. Just as well. No one would try to steal him.

From the corner of her eye, she caught a glimmer of white beyond the tamarisk brush along the road linking the many wharves. Someone was coming her way. She hefted her leather pouch. It would hardly compliment her nice clothes, and there was little likelihood that she would need flints to light a fire, or coins. She emptied its contents on a flattopped stone bollard, and quickly sorted out coins, flints, and oddments from her travels—including the gold cylinder seal. She no longer needed that; its purpose had been served, getting her here. The remainder of the contents she returned to the pouch, which she hanged around her neck and tucked beneath the bloused front of her dress. She reached back to unbind her long, black hair, shook it out, and ran her fingers through it. Now she felt like a woman, if not like visiting royalty.

At first she thought the figure limping hurriedly toward her was an old woman with long gray hair straggling almost to her waist, but the harsh voice demonstrated otherwise. "Why did you do this?" the ugly little man snapped. "You've ruined everything! I told the king you'd be nothing but trouble, and now you've proven that—trouble for me! I now look a fool in people's eyes."

"I . . . what are you talking about?" Pierrette spoke in the staccato syllables of the Minoans' Asian language. "I only just arrived. I have done nothing at all."

"This is the wrong wharf! You should not be here."

"I'm sorry. Are you the harbormaster? Just direct me to the proper landing, and I'll move my boat there."

"Harbormaster indeed! I am Hatiphas, chief adviser to immortal Minho, and keeper of the palace."

"Adviser to Minho? Where is he? I must see him." Hearing her dream lover's name uttered, for the first time, by living human lips, made her heart pound with excitement.

"Why didn't you land over there?" Hatiphas snarled. His eyes were huge and dark, entirely ringed with kohl. His nose was sharp as a knife blade, and his teeth were gapped and stained. Pierrette immediately disliked him.

"There? Where all those people are gathered? Why would I do that? I didn't want to disrupt the ceremony or celebration."

"The celebration is for you, you fool! The king is there, expecting you! Everyone has waited all day, since first your sail was seen beyond the sea-gates! But now you've ruined everything!"

"For . . . for me? Why would anyone go to all that effort for me?"

"Hasn't he mooned and moaned about you for thousands of years? Haven't I had to listen? How could he not know?"

"I haven't lived eighteen years, let alone thousands."

"Didn't he meet you once, in a painted cave at Sormiou, and didn't you hunt a deer together? Wasn't he with you on the Plain of Stones, where the druid Cunotar sought your destruction, and didn't he save your miserable life? Didn't you cuddle with him beside the hot, fuming pools at Entremont, in the Roman camp? Have you forgotten all that?"

"You must be mad. That wasn't Minho." Pierrette's mind raced. She had hunted with the golden Aam in an ancient time when elephants and rhinoceri—the fabled unicorns—grazed on the green hills near Massalia, millennia before the city arose. But Aam had been tall and yellow-haired, and Minho was dark. And on the Plain of Stones, her almost-lover had been Alkides, a Greek trader in cattle, and their meeting had transpired seven hundred years before the Christian era began, when the great cities of Gaul were but villages, and Roma was a collection of mud hovels on two of its seven hills. At Entremont, she had dallied with the Roman consul Calvinus, and had supped with the historian Polybius, but Minho? No. Hatiphas was wrong. She shook her head.

"You little idiot! It was the spell *Mondradd in Mon*! Did you think you could use it to part the Veil of Years, to voyage through the Otherworld to those long-past times, without its echoes being felt the world around? Of course Minho was there, gazing from behind the eyes of your stone-age hunter, touching you with the calloused hands of that uncouth Greek cowhand, and growing hot and faint when you shamelessly pressed your breasts against that Roman's hairy chest! Bah! And didn't I have to endure his tantrums every time, when he begged you to come to him, and you slipped away instead?"

Minho! He had been there, riding as an unnoticed passenger in the minds of the men she had loved. That revelation did not please her as once it might have. Instead, she felt violated, as if the urchin Cletus had spied on her while she bathed, or as if she had startled a stranger prowling in her bedroom. And that was the third—or the fourth— time this mean-spirited little man had called her fool, or idiot . . .

"What are you doing?" Hatiphas snarled as she untied the springline that secured her boat.

"I'm leaving. You were to welcome me—with great ceremony, I surmise—and you've done nothing but insult me, and . . ."

"No! Please stay. Minho will . . ."

"Will have your head on a platter? Will have you horsewhipped? I shouldn't doubt it."

With visible effort, Hatiphas quelled his warring emotions—his exasperation with her and his anger at her insults to him. "Please. Allow me to escort you. My master eagerly awaits . . ."

"It is there a back way in? I don't want to push through a crowd of strangers."

"But . . . yes. There is a path up the mountainside. I will take you that way." Pierrette knew that she had won this encounter, but she also understood, from the majordomo's sullen glare, that she had made an enemy of him, and that the sweet, placid Fortunate Isles of her visions were indeed a fantasy that did not exist in this, the real world.

Considering the circumstances, Gustave would have to fend for himself awhile.

Chapter 26 ∾ The Sorcerer-King

The path Hatiphas chose proceeded by lengths of short, almost imperceptible slopes interrupted by polished malachite-and-jasper stairways. Each path was smoothly graveled with blue stones too tiny and angular to turn an ankle. Flowering thyme and blue bugleweed clumped beside the path, but no single weed or plant had the effrontery to push up between the stones.

The green-and-russet stairs gleamed, scuff-free and unswayed by wear. Even the occasional scattering of leaves fallen from nearby trees gave the impression of deliberate floral arrangements, compositions that elevated the mason's craft and the sweeper's lapses to an air of studied disarray.

As they ascended—and the alternations of stair and easy path precluded even the thought of breathlessness—Pierrette observed that the fruiting bushes and trees nestling in mossy pockets amid the rocks were themselves elements in the artist's composition, drawing the eye from azure stones to cerulean blossoms to the celestine arch of a clear, cloudless sky. Those were exactly complemented by the ocher and vermilion of pine bark, intensified by the umber of oak branches, brightened by a hundred shades of green—malachite stair treads, the springtime hue of young maple leaves, the silvery verdigris of olives, the deep, relaxing shade of broadleaf oaks.

Now this, she reflected, was her vision of the Isles—every element as if designed by a sensitive goddess to please the eye and mind from every aspect or vantage. Even the white palace walls and the bronze gate—cast in a single mold, lovingly burnished—were foreshadowed by shifting vegetal hues as white alyssum and brazen-flowered spurge appeared first intermittently, then predominantly, then in entirety, as the walker progressed. Reaching the palace wall and postern, Pierrette perceived them as floating effortlessly over a billowy sea of white blossoms. The path was now dazzling white marble, and beyond and above the palace roofs, select cumulus clouds puffed up in studied repetition of the themes and colors expressed in the blooms below.

Yes, this was that kingdom she had anticipated, that she had longed for. The clash with Hatiphas now forgotten, she pushed open the bronze door. The tinkle of water from bronze dolphins' mouths, falling into a stone basin, harmonized with the sweet tones of a lyre unseen. Grass like new-tied carpet cushioned her feet. She recognized this

courtyard—and the door at its far end. Relief
washed over her as she dismissed a fear she had
not previously admitted to consciousness: that the
real palace would not to be identical with the
rooms, corridors, and courtyards of her dreams. But
they were. Vindicated, she strode confidently ahead.

"Wait!" Hatiphas murmured, in the low tones of
a servant. "My master is still below, awaiting you."

"I know the way to his chambers," Pierrette said
with a bright, false, girlish smile. "I'll wait for him
on the bench just inside the doorway, and when he
removes his golden bulls-head helm, and seeks to
set it in its accustomed place he'll discover . . . me."
The artificial nature of her smile was easily
explained: *this* Minho was not the man of her
dreams. Her Minho would have known already that
she was here, and would have been on hand to greet
her—wouldn't he?

Hatiphas was also discomfited. He was perplexed.
Being used to an environment where everything was
predictable to a man of influence and stature, and
was thus controllable, he was also angry—again.
This pert, unpredictable sprig of a girl had upset
his most careful plans, and continued to demonstrate that he could not fit her spontaneous flit-
ting into any kind of sensible arrangement at all.

He did not follow her into Minho's private
chambers—what harm could she do there?—
because he wanted to find his master immediately,
and to warn him that he must not take anything
she uttered or did at face value. Her influence was
disruptive of the peaceful fabric of their placid lives,
and might, he feared, even be . . . dangerous.

✧   ✧   ✧

Pierrette, had she been privy to his considerations, might have agreed with him. As soon as the door had shut behind her, a further reality struck her with almost physical force: there, when she raised her eyes, was the very spot where she had lit, where her seagull's webbed feet had spread on the blue cap tiles of the parapet wall. "Find the Isles and their king, and then . . . you must destroy his kingdom, and he must die."

She knew *what* could destroy the Fortunate Isles. As yet, she had no idea of just how to bring that destruction about. And, as yet, she intended as firmly as ever to find a different solution to her dilemma, one in which her visions—now demonstrated to have been accurate in the small details—would be entirely fulfilled, in which she would indeed marry Minho, and sit upon that gold-and-ivory throne that even now awaited, she was sure, where the last great black promontory projected into the endless western ocean.

But solutions and decisions must wait—she heard a clipping of leather soles on the tesselations of the corridor, and knew that her brief respite for musing was at an end. She composed herself gracefully on the bench, and shook her dress out so that it fell in soft folds from her knees to the floor, its wrinkles entirely gone now.

The door swung wide. The figure emergent in its marble frame was taller than a man should be, and its head was not human: great horns sprung from it. From its nostrils gouted puffs of white, herb-scented smoke. Then Minho, sorcerer-king of the Fortunate Isles, reached up with altogether human hands and lifted his heavy headpiece from his shoulders—and as he turned to set it in its accustomed place, he gasped. "I was sure you had come. I felt a tremor in the earth when your feet touched my shore. But then, when you did not arrive among the welcomers . . ."

Pierrette smiled. Minho's aquiline features, his coiled ringlets of dark hair, contrasted with his present expression of boyish petulance. "Should I apologize for upsetting your plans? I won't. You could have warned me, somehow. I was in no condition, after a long sail, for a ceremonial occasion."

Petulant became crestfallen. "If you knew how difficult it was even to send you that star-map, you wouldn't berate me. Events beyond my shores have become mysteries to me, and clouds of uncertainty obscured your passage even along my own waterways. Why, even now . . ."

"We've only just met," Pierrette interrupted, "and we're bickering like my father and his wife." She imitated Gilles the fisherman: "Granna, my dear, I waited all morning in the olive grove!" And then: "Gilles, your memory's gone the way of your teeth. You were to meet me at my market stall."

Minho laughed. "In truth," he mused, resting his bull's-head helm on the floor and slipping in the same motion onto the bench beside her, "we are just such an old couple, and have known each other far longer than those two." He put his hand on her knee.

She lifted it away. Hatiphas's revelation of Minho's vicarious lovemaking rankled. "You know me because you've hidden behind the eyes of others whom I've loved—but for me, you are a vision seen in the Otherworld, a child's dream. Give me the time I need to know you in this world." She had not been offended by his touch, but she was confused by her own reaction to it. "Where were you when I was trudging the waste and forests of Armorica?" she asked silently. She had labored, struggled, and risked everything at the hands of Vikings and the *Gallicenae*, and had spent months on the rivers Rhodanus and Liger to get here. His casual possessiveness rankled. Where, indeed, had he been, and what travails had he endured, for this moment to come about?

He smiled broadly. "You are indeed a fresh breeze in this, my ancient land. It's hard to remember that once I did not get anything I wanted merely by lifting an eyebrow. But now, come—there is fresh fruit laid out on the terrace above."

Following him, she noted his easy grace, his broad shoulders, and wasp-fine dancer's waist, and imagined him vaulting over the horns of a bull—but she did not imagine herself held in his arms, her hands on that waist. Why? What was so different, now, from when she had been here in the Otherworld?

Just as she saw details of architecture and design that she had not remarked *then*, there was complexity in a real relationship that eluded a dreamer. She now perceived Minho not as a misty ideal, but as a person who, like all persons, had flaws. He had admitted one. What others were there? Those other times, she feared reality had adjusted itself to the needs of her vision. Her own memories of Anselm's keep, a lesser replica of this palace, had perhaps supplied her mind with what detail she thought she had observed in fact. When a moment became more intense than she could bear—as when Minho had kissed her—she had fled in a flutter of feathers on magpie's wings. Now, having stepped ashore on solid stone without dreamlike flexibility, she must deal with the equally indurate reality of Minho himself, with complexities unknown to her, as she would with any new-met stranger, because this was no dream, and she did not think she could flee in any form but her own, with all its limitations.

She was, she decided, not the callow child she had been when Minho courted her ephemeral Otherworld self with sweet words, meaningful gazes, and the promise of immortality. He would have to court her still.

"How lovely!" she exclaimed when she saw the silver, gold, and electrum platters laden with peeled, sliced fruit, many varieties entirely unknown to her. She chose a slice of apple—then hesitated, and murmured soft words.

Minho's brow wrinkled as if she had insulted him. "Why did you do that?" he asked. "You don't need such spells, here."

Caught—the spell she uttered was supposed to prevent a guest from incurring obligation to a host with each bite she took—Pierrette decided to brazen it out. She smiled mischievously. "Really? Then are all your promises as vapid? A girl might hope no detail would be too small to consider— if a man really wanted her . . ."

His smile took long, glacial moments to form. Then: "You warned me, once, didn't you? You said your presence here would upset every balance, would shake my palace . . ."

She laughed. "Of course! And I am no liar. I will do that. Can you bear it?"

"For you . . . I could bear anything at all."

Could he? She kept smiling. What, she wondered, would he do if she required him to come with her into the world of mankind, forsaking this splendor? What if . . . she had to concentrate to maintain her smile . . . she asked him to let down the great spells that preserved his land in this eternal moment, and become . . . mortal?

He clapped his hands, and musicians emerged from an alcove with flutes, lyres, and tambours. They struck up an airy tune. Most of the entertainers were men, wearing only the Cretan kilt, but several were women . . . Pierrette blushed. All were bare-breasted. That, she reminded herself, was the Minoan style. But though she knew that, and though the musicians were unembarrassed by their exposure, Pierrette was not. One tambourist's mature breasts swayed heavily with the motion of her upraised arms; a lyrist's small, pointed adornments seemed almost to brush the strings of her instrument. A young flautist's chest, hardly swollen at all, inflated and deflated regularly with the trills and warbles she produced.

Pierrette pulled her eyes away, and focused on Minho. "I see no meat on your table, King of the Fortunate Isles. Have you no taste for it?"

"You're baiting me. Can meat be eaten without tasting the death throes of kine or fowl? Fresh, foamy milk I can furnish, or aged cheeses of every flavor. There are boiled eggs and pickled ones, if you crave animal food. Try one of those with a pinch of salt . . ."

She shook her head. "Yes, I was baiting you. I know you banished everything painful or ugly from your domain, long ago—and though I enjoy a well-roasted haunch, or a crispy pullet sprinkled with rosemary, I can forgo such treats, if I must."

What was the expression that passed so quickly across his face? For a moment, had the sorcerer-king regretted the inclusiveness of his spells? Had he, just for the blink of an eye, remembered some favorite dish he had not tasted these two thousand years?

Quickly, she changed the subject. "In the keep of my master Anselm—once your student Ansulim—the sun always stands at high noon. Is it so here also?"

Minho laughed indulgently. "My erstwhile student's skills are rudimentary. How would olives know when to bloom, in eternal daylight? Wouldn't the pansies exhaust themselves? And the helio-tropes? Would their stalks stiffen, if their flowers always faced zenith? No. Here, the sun traverses the sky, but like your master's little enclave, no time passes in the world outside, unless I wish it to, and no one within ever ages a single day."

"Will you show me the spells that make it so?" she asked. "I've spent ages in Anselm's library, learning the nature of magics, and how spells mutate as the premises that underlay them are forgotten or reinterpreted. What a joy it would be to study yours—masterful spells uncorrupted by the flow of years, the rise and fall of peoples and their changing tongues . . ."

"With all my lovely land to explore, you want to bury your face in dusty archives instead? You'll have all eternity for that. Tomorrow I'll begin to show you . . ." She allowed him to describe the wonders of his island kingdom, but her mind strayed elsewhere. Did these apples really taste flat, those pears insipid, and that pomegranate sweet, but without savor?

Indeed the sun moved across the sky, though not as quickly as she might have wished. At last, when its ruddy glow painted half the heavens with rich mauves and ochers, with incarnadine flames edged with lemony yellow, she rubbed her eyes. "I haven't slept the night through for ever so long," she said apologetically. "On a boat, one must always remain alert for a changing wind or a coming storm."

"Of course," said the king. "Tonight, you shall sleep on a bed of cloud, with a coverlet as light as a child's dream." Again he clapped. A lovely girl of indeterminate age responded to his summons. Despite her Cretan dress, which left her breasts bare, Pierrette could not decide if she were child or woman.

"I'll settle for a straw pallet that doesn't rock with the waves," Pierrette said to Minho, resisting the girl's delicate tugging, "and plain wool or feathers will suffice to cover me."

"Whatever you want," he replied offhandedly. "Neheresta will see that you have just the thing. Until morning, then—though I shan't sleep a wink, just knowing you are at last here, and so near my own bed . . ."

Pierrette yielded to the girl, Neheresta, and allowed herself to be led through several fine rooms of marble and polychrome stone, painted between their pilasters with brilliant scenes of fishermen at sea, of oliviers in their groves. Neheresta pushed open a door, then waited while Pierrette entered. She smiled when Pierrette exclaimed how amazing it was—to the last detail a replica of her chamber in Anselm's keep, even to the heavy curtains at the window, that at home would have kept the perpetual noonday sun at bay.

When Pierrette sniffed and crinkled her mattress, it gave off the sweet aroma of fresh, soft straw, and the coverlet was the same indigo wool as her own. A tray displayed vials of oils and unguents identical to the ones that occupied the little table against the wall of her own room. She found a bronze chamberpot in an alcove. It was shiny and unblemished, as if it had never been used. Oddly, though hours had passed since she had used the wooden bucket aboard her boat, she felt no need at this time. Perhaps Neheresta's presence inhibited her.

When Pierrette loosened her cincture, Neheresta essayed to help her undress. "I don't need help," Pierrette said, not ungently. "You may go now." Neheresta's eyes abruptly filled with tears. "Must I?" she asked, her inflections only superficially childlike. "I wish to stay here, with you."

"There is only the one bed. Won't you need to sleep too?"

"I won't thrash about, or make noises in my sleep," she said. "Perhaps you'll allow me to rub the aches from your back and shoulders."

Pierrette had often shared a bed with far larger and more obtrusive companions, and this bed was—as she noticed now—considerably wider than her own narrow one. But when she was disrobed, Neheresta produced no shift or other sleeping garment for her. She just turned back the coverlet, and waited expectantly for Pierrette to get in. Then she slipped out of her own kilt and sandals, and slid gracefully beneath the soft, light wool.

Pierrette was not accustomed to being taken care of by another person, let alone a naked one, but when Neheresta's small hands urged her to roll over onto her stomach, and began massaging her shoulders and upper arms, it was not difficult to succumb to the delight. Neheresta's skilful fingers found aches Pierrette had not known existed, and kneaded them away.

Once Pierrette had relaxed under her ministrations, the girl smoothly swung one leg up over the small of her back, straddling her. The unfamiliar sensation of that small, smooth body intimately pressing against her created whole constellations of new tensions. Those in turn Neheresta labored to dispel. Soon enough, such was her fatigue, Pierrette began to doze.

She awakened abruptly to a different kind of sensation: a warm, rich, heady glow that radiated from the depths of her body. She gasped, and reached to pull away Neheresta's hand—but the arm she grasped was as rigid as iron, and would not be moved, and the fingers curved at her neck were no less unyielding.

"Be at ease," her companion's voice whispered, almost in her ear. "*This* ache is greater than any other. Soon, it will be gone, and you will sleep as never before." Neheresta continued her attentions, and despite herself, Pierrette succumbed as inevitably as the rocks of the shore succumb to the waves and the rising tide.

Later, pushing aside the veils of sleep, Pierrette rose on one elbow and looked at her bedmate, sprawled innocently beside her. As if her gaze was as solid as a touch, Neheresta opened her eyes. "Is this what children learn, here, in the Fortunate Isles?" asked Pierrette.

"Does a child look out from your eyes, that spent a century poring over your master's manuscripts, while your friends and your father aged not a day on the outside? I was a woman grown sixteen centuries before the apprentice Ansulim departed here on his ill-fated mission. In all those years, and in the centuries since, you are the first new person I have loved. Would you begrudge me that, because of my child's face and my girl's body?

Looking into her lovely eyes, as unworldly in their violet depths as those of a woodland nymph, Pierrette saw that her words were true. She saw also the vast desolation of all those years, in which the child Neheresta had never grown to the true adulthood she craved. But Neheresta saw more than pity in Pierrette's own eyes, and she smiled . . .

When morning sunlight sprawled across her coverlet, Pierrette awakened alone. She wondered how and where she would break her fast.

Neheresta had left no reminders of her presence, not even a scent on the bedding, and Pierrette was abruptly unsure that what she remembered had actually occurred, or if she had dreamed it—but when she saw Neheresta again, she decided she would know merely by looking in her eyes.

Neheresta had folded her blue dress and white wrap, and had laid out fresh clothing for her.

Pierrette picked up the stiff, crisp black skirt, and held it against herself. When she matched its constricting waist against her own slenderness . . . she giggled uneasily, and snatched it away. It was a Minoan dress, flared above the tightly tailored cincture, and then—then nothing. Even thinking about wearing that, Pierrette blushed. Her blush, had anyone been watching her, spread from her face downward, all the way to her feet.

No, she could not wear that. She laid it back down, but her eyes kept straying back to it. Wearing her own clothing, she would look conspicuous and foreign. Wearing the other, wouldn't she look . . . ordinary? Again, she giggled. She would certainly not feel ordinary. It would not hurt to try it on, she decided.

The garment could have been made to her exact measure. It fit smoothly around her waist and hugged her ribs. She felt less clothed than before she had put it on, now acutely aware of the soft air brushing her nipples when she moved. Perhaps if she wore her sagus over it . . . But no, that would look incongruous. Besides, she observed, an intricate gold necklace went with it, a confection with coral beads on long strings that dangled. It was designed to be worn against skin, not over a bulky garment.

Pierrette had almost decided to dare wearing the dress, just because the jewelry was so lovely. Would she ever again have the chance to wear anything so rich? Then she considered her pouch. She could not wear that around her neck with the gold and coral. Now that she had come so far in her determination, she did not want to be denied the chance.

She tried slipping it beneath the tight cloth over her ribs, to no avail. It was a painful and conspicuous lump. There was no way to fasten it beneath the flared skirt, unless she could obtain pins. She looked around the room. Could she hide the pouch somewhere?

As she surveyed the room, she felt an odd sensation, a prickling that centered in the palm of her hand: the pouch's mouth was agape, and the serpent's egg lay exposed against her skin. "What is this place?" demanded a cold, harsh voice. Cunotar. His brief exposure had already allowed him to sense how different were the Fortunate Isles from any other milieu. What else had he sensed?

"You don't really want to know," replied Pierrette. "The sorcerer who rules this land owns skills that surpass your most grandiose dreams, and he tolerates no others. Go back to sleep, before he senses your trespass."

"Sleep? How can I sleep, when I am never truly awake, in this durance. This is a strange place, an unnatural place. I feel no strife; no one's blood surges or sings. It is a land of sheep, not men.

"Your perspectives are distorted. King Minho long ago banned war and strife—and warriors as well, whether or not they are masters of evil magic, like yours."

"Evil? What is that? Try to define it, and it slips away like an eel through the bullrushes of the Camargue."

"I know it when I smell it, and the air is ripe with that stink, right now."

"I am not its source. Release me, and together we can seek it out, and expunge it."

"Ha! No chance of that. Besides—have you forgotten?—your death-wound still awaits you."

"Some things are worse than death. The body may die, and the *fantôme* that drives it, but the soul? The soul . . ."

"Have you become a Pythagorean philosopher, to speak of souls? Yours must remain pent within my egg. You must accept that."

"There will come a time when you'll regret your obstinance. Release me. We shall then see how powerful your sorcerer-king really is."

"I'm not that mad. I'll keep you where you are." She pushed the crystal egg back into the darkness and obscurity of the leather pouch and tightened the drawstring. Her hands trembled. The pouch felt greasy and foul, perhaps from her own sweat. Where could she put it?

Where had she hidden things at home? There was the replica of her bed, again looking no wider than the original. She lifted the straw tick and thrust her arm underneath, then withdrew it, empty now. No one would find the small sack there.

Cunotar's words troubled her more than she had let on. Of course, his idea of Evil and hers were not the same, but he had seemed so confident. What, exactly, had he been able to sense about this place, from his brief exposure? His talk of souls also troubled her. The Gauls of Cunotar's day—and centuries thereafter—had assumed that man's nature was tripartite: body, *fantôme* or ghost, and soul. Body was mortal, and *fantôme* motivated it. *Fantôme* was love and lust, fear and pleasure, rage and joy, and it might survive Body a while after death, to haunt a murderer or follow yearningly after a beloved child now orphaned, but as Body decomposed, and rejoined the elements, *fantôme* also dissipated. Soul alone remained, passed on, and sought new embodiment in a babe not yet born.

Pierrette did not know how correct that view of things might be. Perhaps the Christians had the right of it, that good souls ascended to a sweet place without strife or pain. The Christian heaven, by its definition, seemed much like this place, this kingdom—though there seemed to be no gods at all here, let alone an omniscient and omnipotent One.

She reflected that the common thread among all the religions she was familiar with was the existence of soul, of some essence that survived death. Thus, according to an essential principle, Soul was an irreducible phenomenon and an axiom. By confining Cunotar so he did not die, had she denied his soul's natural progression? She sighed, and pushed her concerns aside. Cunotar was far too dangerous to be released, even here. Perhaps especially here. She had no idea what terrible things he might do, in the scant minutes before his lifeblood drained away, and his soul fled.

She lifted the heavy gold-and-coral ornament over her head, and let its heavy, intricately strung links settle on her shoulders. The strands poured liquidly over the tops of her small breasts, parting like streams of water between and around them on either side. Abruptly, she felt more clothed than before. Now, where would she find something to eat? She pushed open the door, and began to retrace her steps of the night before.

❖   ❖   ❖

Hatiphas the vizier withdrew his eye from the peephole. What had that been about? Who had the interfering vixen been talking to? He had seen no one, only the orange glow that had, for a moment, lit her face. Where had it emanated from?

He scurried to the door of the hidden room he occupied, and peered into the hallway just as the girl turned the far corner. He slipped out, went directly to the bed, and groped under it. Then he stood and, loosening the drawstring of the worn leather pouch, reached inside with two fingers and withdrew a bauble of clear glass veined with red and blue like the breast of a fair-skinned maiden.

No vermilion light issued from Cunotar's prison, and no harsh, ugly voice, but Hatiphas was sure this object was what he sought. Enclosing it in his palm, he cast about the room. There. He snatched up a tiny round vial of scented oil from the tablette, and pushed it into the pouch, filling it with similar bulk and weight as before. Then he replaced it beneath the tick.

Cunotar remained silent. Had he a heart, it would have pounded in his chest—had he a chest. As it was, his eagerness had no outlet or expression at all. He did not dare speak, and risk frightening the one who clutched his glassy prison so hard he feared—and hoped—it might break. He must listen, and find out more about his new captor—find out just what words would convince him to free the druid at long last . . . and at just what crucial moment.

The terrace was much as it had been, the night before . . . She looked up as Hatiphas arrived. "Ah, there you are," he exclaimed. His tone was syrupy, and he seemed out of breath.

"Hatiphas!" she exclaimed. "Is your master about?"

"Not any more. He waited for you, reading dispatches from his village chiefs and headmen, but when you did not awaken, he went down to the archives, where he must daily maintain the magics that preserve us." His tone was dismissive. The king had vital tasks, and had wasted enough time on her. Who was she even to inquire? Hatiphas hated her. That was clear. Did he fear she would usurp his place in Minho's favor? But she had no political goals, no taste for palace intrigue. What she wanted most, right then, was breakfast.

The tables were well supplied with baskets of flat bread, fresh and stewed fruit, and a large pot of mixed-grain porridge that steamed on a brazier. Pierrette ate, at first enthusiastically, then desultorily, as resentment built up inside. Had she come all this way simply to be ignored? The food had little taste.

"When will I see him?" She straightened up from the table, and the movement made her aware of three things: the heavy gold that she wore, the tightness of the garment that constricted her ribs, and the cool air on her bare bosom.

"I couldn't say. I am a vizier, not a king." Then Hatiphas noticed her garb. "At least you look less the barbarian today," he said with a disdainful sniff. "When my master returns, I am sure he will approve."

Pierrette then realized that Minho's opinion had not factored into her choice of dress at all. It had been the challenge, no more. "I could not care less for his approval." Had Hatiphas himself not been so coldly analytical, she might not have spoken. Obviously, he did not find her breasts attractive. She did not know he had been a eunuch since boyhood, but even so, he might have been nicer about it.

Pierrette leaned forward and took a bite from a plump peach. "Where is Neheresta?" she asked Hatiphas, with her mouth full. His expression bordered on disgust as he watched her chew.

"Who?"

"The girl who . . . who waited upon me, last night."

"I didn't notice who it was. There are a hundred servants here. Do you think I know all their names?" Of course he did know, but he would not tell the interloper anything. Neheresta had not obeyed him precisely enough. She had seduced the girl (he knew, because he had watched everything) but she had entirely forgotten the drugged wine! The bullish male slave who had waited with him, rank with the scent of his own arousal, had to be sent back to his chamber unsated. Hatiphas had already had . . . words . . . with Neheresta. She now felt a proper regret for her oversight.

Pierrette strode angrily to the balustrade, and stared outward. The view, she had to admit, was magnificent. Facing west, the successively lower roofs of the palace complex stepped down the steep slopes to the inland waterway—one of the circular canals the Egyptians had described, that Plato had misunderstood, thinking them works of man, not of natural cataclysm. Beyond was a long, curved island covered in small fields in every color from raw soil to mature grain. A jagged ridge backed it, and beyond were other islands, even more steeply ridged to seaward, and a third rank whose tall peaks reached almost to the scattered clouds.

Some islands were linked by what appeared to be bridges or causeways. In a gap between two of the furthest ones, she glimpsed the open sea, dotted with white-spumed rocks and shoals. Beyond those lay nothing (according to the scholars of her age), or else lands perhaps more vast than all the known world (if the Irish and Viking tales were true).

Across one of the outermost islands sprawled a riot of colors, like gambler's dice painted every possible hue, strewn not quite randomly. Trickles of smoke rose here and there. It was a city. It was a grand city, with innumerable market squares and a thousand streets; its bright-painted tendrils stretched like clusters of beads up the mountain slopes and out of sight in the valleys. But it was a strange city, because no monumental works towered over the multitudes of flat-roofed houses. No pillared temples gleamed, no golden domes, no red-tiled basilicas.

Though it was too far away for details to stand out, Pierrette imagined a street scene identical to every other street, where what variety and pleasure met the eye were small and subtle: the curve of a garden wall, a gate festooned with bronze birds or dolphins, a cluster of tall flowers in a niche or in the angle of two walls, where no one trod.

For a moment, the lack of impressive vistas furnished for the denizens of those houses, those streets, troubled her. Then, pulling her eyes away from distant subjects, she looked around herself at the single magnificent focus of all eyes in this island kingdom: she walked from one side of the terrace to the other, and took in everything, from the outermost shoal to the very balustrade she leaned her elbows on. Everyone in the almost-circular archipelago could also see . . . this palace.

Minho's palace—black, white, vermilion, and scarlet, gleaming with highlights of polished bronze and gold—was the sole monument, the unique glory, the crowning beauty of this kingdom. Of course there were no temples to a dozen or a hundred gods, no monumental tombs of generations of emperors. There were no hippodromes, amphitheaters, or arenas where men and animals provided mincing dramas, deadly races, or blood sport. This was not Roma in its latter days, or even Massalia in the present. This was Minho's perfect kingdom, and all such imitations and imperfections had been banished from it long ago, when even Roma was an undreamed millennium in the future.

"Is there a more lovely prospect, anywhere?" Minho had arrived unnoticed. Now he stood beside her at the balustrade, his gaze sweeping the intricate vista of islands, channels, roads, and bridges.

"I've seen nothing to equal it," Pierrette replied. "The panegyrists of Greece and Rome did not describe anything as lovely." She turned. "I'm glad you're here. I have so many things I must ask you . . ."

"Is that all?" He mimicked disappointment with a stylized moue. "I am, you know, more than just a walking library."

"Of course you are. You are the greatest sorcerer of all time, and you have dust on your kilt." She brushed a cobweb away. Light and linty, it floated over the balustrade, was caught by an updraft, and drifted fitfully out of sight into the sun's eye.

"Dust!" He laughed as if in self-deprecation. "Of all the evils I banished when I wrested this land from fiery death, the one I forgot was . . . dust."

"Evil? I wouldn't consider so small a flaw evil. It is an annoyance at worst, when I'm in the aftermost cart of a dozen on the road, or when I lift a long-undisturbed volume from a shelf, and I sneeze." She felt an undefined tension. Evil? She imagined a film of dust on a polished table, and from it arising a darker shadow, that slipped over the edge and crept away—westward, or a bit north or south of that, depending on just what city she imagined the table to exist in.

"What of dung?" she essayed. "When a donkey defiles your cobblestones, what do you do?" She felt a pang of guilt. What of Gustave, left alone? But he was resourceful. He wouldn't starve on this island rich with greenery.

"Again you're baiting me! Would you believe that I don't know? Perhaps it dries and blows away, or people collect it and spread it on their fields."

"When you cast your great spell, didn't you have to consider such details, at least once?"

"You call it a great spell. That hardly means it must be complex or cumbersome. It was an elegant spell, only a few simple words, and everything you see before you proceeded from that. Such a spell needs no detail, because it is art, not mechanics. One does not build a spell like an edifice, laying

one lump atop another. One creates it, a child of
mind and spirit." Pierrette was inwardly dismayed,
but did not let it show. Minho's high-flown words
were like the air atop a mountain, offering little
sustenance. Spells were not inspiration and spirit.
Every last aspect of a spell was inherent in its
premise, and followed logically from it.

Pierrette's heart sank in her chest. She felt no
closer to the answers she had sought since first she
realized as a child new to Anselm's tutelage that
all magic proceeded from sets of initial postulates,
and were thenceforth as subject to logic as were
theorems of geometry.

In fact, her introduction to geometric theorems
had provided the initial insight into the dilemma
that had, by many circuitous byways, led her to this
moment and this place: when people's beliefs
changed, ancient postulates shifted their meanings,
and a spell that had once given warm fire resulted
instead in a cool, brilliant Christian light—or a
sullen crimson glow with the stench of oily death.
"I am fire," said an ancient god. "I give warmth
and light, yet I sometimes rage unchained and
destroy everything I touch." A later god, in earthly
manifestation, said, "I am the Light and the
Life . . ." and a postulate, a single line at the
beginning of Pierrette's fire-making spell, was
changed.

Minho's mellow voice recalled her from her
racing thoughts. "Where did you go? I felt you
depart."

"I'm sorry. Your words transported me. Show me
your great spell. Let me study it and understand
what makes great—and elegant—magic."

Once again he laughed indulgently. Again Pierrette reflected how different this experience was, in the flesh, from her visions. Once Minho's indulgent tone had seemed affectionate, doting. Here and now, Pierrette resented it, because it was condescending. "Dare I write it down, for you to peruse at your leisure? It exists here alone." He touched his forehead. "Every day, I must revise it in subtle ways, as I have done since your Christianity arose, and the old gods began to die." His mercurial face became charged with anger and frustration. "I have become a tinkerer, a musician ever tuning his lyre and never playing it! If only Anselm had been up to his task, and had quenched that religion's first spark!"

"It wasn't his fault," Pierrette objected, ever loyal to her mentor. "He brought you the Hermit, who first spread Jesus' words among the gentiles, and you subverted him. Is he still here, somewhere, living perhaps in luxury, ever regretting that he had abandoned his Cause?"

"He is here, but Anselm failed to subvert the one who arose in his stead: the one born Saul of Tarsus, who wrapped his master's simple precepts in chains of mystery, symbols, and Greek logic— with magic almost as strong as mine. Now the Christian emblem itself sickens me; I have forbidden it, in all its forms. But how can I prevent two twigs from falling upon the ground, one over the other? How can I order two shadows not to make a cross on a sun-washed wall?"

Almost as strong? thought Pierrette, though she did not dare say it aloud. The Christian domain had now spread to the furthest known lands, and every crossroads shrine now bore a crucifix or a Chi-Rho sign scratched in a stone. Every ancient sacred pool but one was now a Christian font, and the holiness of one saint or another emanated from its waters—usurpers, to be sure, who often partook of the aspects of the earlier gods and goddesses that they had supplanted, but firmly in control of the sacred places and the people who visited them. Almost? The religion of Saint Paul grew, now spreading among the Saxon tribes and—as she had seen, on that remote skerry only a few days' sail away—among the Norsemen, the most savage pagans of all.

The Hermit was still here. Like his successor, Saul of Tarsus, he was a weaver of words and concepts that shaped the very fabric of reality. Was he, perhaps, a key already thrust into the lock, but not yet turned? A key to the destruction of Minho's kingdom not by violence or competing magics, but by . . . conversion? Somehow, she felt, she must get free of the king and his palace, and must find the Hermit.

That thought led to others: she must find poor Gustave, too, before some woodcutter or mason caught him and put him to work carrying bundles of fagots or heavy stones. Gustave was spoiled, stubborn, and independent, and she could not endure imagining him bruised and beaten by a harsh new master who did not tolerate his ways.

There were other reasons to find a way out of Minho's direct purview also. Just as the Hermit might provide a way for her to obey the letter of the goddess's command without supporting the spirit of it, there might be other solutions as well, ones she could not imagine until she knew more, and they presented themselves.

But she was not finished here, not yet. . . . "Hatiphas said you were down in your archives, working. Will you show me? May I watch you work?"

"No one has gone where I go. Do I dare show you my most secret retreat?"

"Did you call me here to condescend and deny? Though I was attracted to you as the subject of my childhood fantasies, I hardly know Minho the man, and Minho the sorcerer not at all. Could I stay here and marry you, without becoming jealous of your other mistress, hidden away, never knowing her?"

He sighed. "I must blindfold you."

"You trust me so little?"

"I would trust my wife, my queen, with all my secrets."

It was Pierrette's turn to sigh. "Then I will endure momentary blindness. As for the future, I cannot see it. It must unwind in its own time."

Minho clapped, and Hatiphas appeared almost instantly. Had he heard all they had said? Hearing his master's desire, he then rushed off, returning moments later with a strip of jet-black, heavy silk. Minho gently—and carefully, and snugly—wrapped Pierrette's eyes. Not a glimmer of light got through.

"Come," the king said, placing her hand on his forearm as if she were a crippled crone. He led her inside the palace—the changing echoes of his sandals and hers told her that. First came a short passageway, then a long one where the returning sound of footsteps was ever so slightly delayed. At each intersection (and perhaps other times as well) the king put hands on her shoulders and turned her several times, to disorient her. Still, some sense not blocked by the blindfold allowed her to believe they had gone in the direction of Minho's quarters, and when she heard the sigh of a heavy door opening on well-oiled hinges, she believed it was his own chamber they entered. But she could not be sure.

He muttered soft words, too softly for Pierrette to understand, but the cadence of his speech seemed oddly familiar to her, as if she should recognize what he had said. "What was that?" she asked. There was, abruptly, a chill in the air, as if a cloud obscured the sun or a cellar door was opened, releasing the dampness.

"It was nothing," he said offhandedly. "Stand here a moment. I must . . ." She heard the dull sound of something heavy being pulled or pushed across the floor tiles. "Now step carefully," he said. "A staircase lies ahead."

"Down or up?"

"Why, down."

Pierrette cautiously extended one foot, and did not place her weight upon it until it was firmly planted on the first tread. With one hand again on Minho's arm, she felt rough stone brush her shoulder, and she understood that the stairway was narrow, or the king would have moved over to give her more room. She counted each step as they descended, and when they reached the end of them, memorized the number. The rough, irregular floor underfoot now felt like plain stone, not tile, and grit rasped under her soles. Again, Minho spun her around, then led her forward. In places the floor was slick, in others gritty, like the drying stone of a tide-washed sea cave.

Again, Minho bade her stand alone. She heard a rasp and swish as of heavy cloth being shaken out. She smelled the oily odor of a just-snuffed lamp wick. But why would Minho put out a lamp? Entering a room, it was more usual to light lamps, not extinguish them. She tracked his footfalls back and forth several times, and at last felt his hands behind her head, loosening the blindfold.

She blinked. One dim lamp flickered on a worn table. A single backless stool stood close by. Something large and round-topped stood beside the table, draped in dark cloth. Was that what Minho had covered with cloth, to hide it? If so, she wanted to see it. All she could tell was that it resembled a round-bottomed pot, upended and resting on its rim.

The single lamp's glow only illuminated the near wall. She then understood Minho's actions: had more lamps been lit, she would have seen farther, and might have observed . . . she did not know what, except that there were things the king did not want her to see. What she did see were banks of shelves packed with round objects—the ends of hundreds of scrolls, most without wooden shafts or handles, or tags to identify them. "This is it?" she asked, dismayed. What was so special about this ugly, gloomy place? But there was something . . . it was a diffuse, tingling sensation not exactly unfamiliar. What was it? When had she felt it before?

It was the aura of magical power. She had felt something like it in Moridunnon's lair, and on other occasions as well: in a Gallic fane where a hot spring bubbled up from bedrock crevices into a pool, and . . . with the goddess *Ma*. Was it Minho's power she felt? Then why wouldn't she have sensed it before? No, it was the power not of a person, even of a great sorcerer, but of this place itself. This place, and specifically . . . there.

The ancient rough-hewn stones were almost outside the lamp's range. A moment or two earlier, before her eyes had adapted, they had been so. Now she sidled toward them. She placed both palms on the waist-high rim of what appeared to be an ancient well. Of course. This cavern was not only a magical place. Like the grove outside Citharista, it was also a sacred one—or once it had been. Minho had not created this place. At most, he had rediscovered it. No Minoan had hewn those ancient stones. No metal tools had ground them like that, irregular, but fitting seamlessly. They were far older than metalworking. They enclosed a basin just large enough for a small person to bathe in, had that been their purpose. But they were neither a Roman bath built over a sacred spring, nor a natural pool. She could not see far into the well, but she sensed that it went down, and down.

"Come away from there!" Minho had noticed her leaning over the well. "Be careful. That hole is deep—and dangerous."

"Where does it go?" She did not move away, but continued to peer downward. A waft of warm air brushed her face. Its acrid odor made the inside of her nose tingle, and reminded her of a forge, of glowing charcoal and hot metal.

"Come." Minho grasped her arm, firmly enough

to hurt. "It's nothing important. Just a hole." She would learn nothing more from him, so she allowed herself to be guided away from the well. She knew enough. It was very deep, threading its way into the very roots of this island. And the heat, the odor? Was that a relic, a remnant of the ancient volcano that had—in the world of Time—destroyed everything of the Minoan kingdom except what Minho's spell had saved? Did molten rock still seethe at the core of his realm?

"This is a frightening place," she said. "I can feel its magic."

"The real magic of my isles is not in this place," Minho said. "It is all here." He tapped his forehead. Pierrette was sure he believed that—or wanted to.

"But Hatiphas said you must work to maintain your kingdom," she protested. "You yourself complained of being a tinkerer. Where are the tools of your trade? If this is your workshop, then show me your work."

"It is not glamorous," he replied, pulling the stool out, and sitting on it. "I sit here, like this, and cast my vision outward, into the darkness, and I see before me . . . my kingdom. I look here, and there"—he demonstrated, moving his head from side to side—"and when I see something amiss, I reach out and . . . and I repair it. If I see a woodcarver making something lovely that pleases me, I reward him with good thoughts, and he basks in the glow of my affection. If a weaver has begun a cloak of black-and-yellow threads that disturbs my eye, I chastise him. That is all."

"I do not understand how you do that. Do you

go upstairs and find Hatiphas, and order the one man given gold, and the other one whipped?"

"Of course not! Didn't I explain? I reach out into my . . . my vision . . . and I touch the one who has pleased me, and he feels my pleasure. The other feels my distress."

"That's all?" Pierrette did not feel that he was lying, not exactly, but she was even surer that he was not telling all the truth.

His expression said nothing at all. "Being ordinary people, they cannot readily encompass my emotions, and their joy or suffering is intense. It is reward and punishment enough."

Pierrette's dismay was undiminished. Was that all there was to it? Was the great spell that had created, and now maintained, the Fortunate Isles so intuitive, so lacking in structure that she with her postulates, premises, axioms, and rules of logic could not possibly learn it? Her mind rejected that. If it were so, then nothing made sense, and there was no hope. Then indeed the Black Time would come, for nothing could stand against it except the intellect, spirit, and élan of a great sorcerer—of whom, besides Minho, there were none.

Still she persisted. "And if you see something less abstract than poorly chosen threads—an instability that threatens your kingdom? I cannot imagine what it might be, but surely your labors are not all for causes as trivial as carved wood and woven cloth. What, when something serious happens, do you do about it?"

His expression was smug. "In those scrolls, that vast collection of spells, there is one for every contingency. I simply reach for the one I desire, and . . ."

"But how? There are no labels, no order to them. Have you memorized the stains and flyspecks on each one, that you can grasp the right one without opening it and seeing what it contains?"

He was smug indeed. "I feel them," he said. "It is a talent. My hands go immediately to the proper scroll. My eyes immediately fall upon the exact words I must utter. It's simple—for me."

Simple, Pierrette reflected, for an innate talent, for someone with two thousand years to hone instincts entirely undistracted by logic or common sense. Was there nothing she could learn from Minho except the fact that she was incapable of learning anything at all?

He surely saw the dejected slump of her shoulders, for he arose, and put his arm around them. "Don't be discouraged," he said softly. "I will take care of you. You need never fear anything. Marry me, and you will have no need to struggle for mastery you cannot attain."

That was not what Pierrette wished to hear, but she steeled herself not to snarl at him. "I've seen enough here," she said. "Take me back now. I yearn for the warmth of sunlight on my face. Later, perhaps, we can discuss things magical again."

He was happy to accommodate her. Of course, he apologetically said, she would have to be blindfolded again. Again, she tried to figure out where he led her, but with no more success than before. When he removed the blindfold, she found herself again on the terrace.

"If I stay with you, I want to be your helpmate and partner," she said. "If you cannot show me how you do things, in a way that I can understand, then how can I learn your magic?" She sighed softly, "If I cannot do that, then how could I possibly bear to stay?"

"Can't you just enjoy it? Else you will have to wander my islands, road by road, crossing every bridge and causeway until you have learned every detail of what I have wrought, and then work backward from that to the essential nature of my spell." He shook his head. "Come now. Even if my spell cannot be shared, much else can. I still hope to persuade you, and there is something you must see."

Chapter 27 ✤ An Imperfect Vision

The narrow path led northward. It reminded Pierrette of the causeway across the red rocks of Eagle Cape, which led to Anselm's sanctuary. On either side, a single misstep would mean tumbling to destruction on the jagged rocks far below. Pierrette followed Minho as if in a dream—for only in dreams were such symbols accreted, jumbled, and juxtaposed.

The path broadened between an olive and a lemon tree, both heavy with fruit and flowers—surely a dreamlike manifestation, because olives and lemons did not bloom simultaneously, and neither bore bud, flower, and ripe fruit all at once. But this was no dream. This was the reality that had engendered her visions—for there, on a verdant promontory draped with moss, stood . . . two thrones.

"Mine," said Minho, pointing, grinning broadly. "And the other one is . . . yours!"

Pierrette gasped. Thus, then, were dream, vision, and otherworldly flight made real: this was the time and circumstance she had longed for since she had been small. The throne was as she remembered it . . . And yet it was not. It was stone, ivory, and gold, but she remembered no sinuous band of lapis lazuli and garnet about its base, nor the face of an open-mouthed god with hair full of eels and fishes that adorned its back.

The inexactitudes troubled her but, true to the script she had learned, she smiled and, twirling her skirt, seated herself, and placed her hands on the throne's carven ivory arms. "Join me, King of the Isles," she bade him, batting her long, dark eyelashes shamelessly. "Stretch out your arm and tell me the names of those islands, that city . . ."

Minho sat. His strong, slender hand covered hers—the thrones were quite close, though she had not noticed it before. "The first island," he said, "is called 'Pierrette's footstool,' because it lies at your feet."

"Stop that!" His facetiousness annoyed her—but this was the culmination of her dream, and she should not be annoyed. "What do the farmers who till its fields call it? What would the olivier who attends his gray-leaved groves say, if I asked *him* its name?"

"He'd say 'This is Pierrette's Island,' and would direct you to its most ancient wharf, where your name was carved in the mossy stones so long ago it is almost worn away. It has been so named since first I knew you would come to me."

Pierrette believed him. Now, in retrospect, she could imagine his eyes hiding behind those of her lovers past—Aam the hunter, who shared her kill, in the hills above Sormiou, who had shouldered the gutted doe, her sacrifice, the other self that she had slain to feed the people. Minho had peered out from Alkides's eyes on the Plain of Stones, when that cattleman (who would later be named Herakles) had taught her how to defy the will of the gods without disobeying their commands, by loving him without losing the maidenhood that the goddess required she keep.

Had Minho truly lurked behind the dark Roman eyes of Caius Sextius Calvinus, consul and general, when she dallied with him in his *praetorium* by the sacred hot springs below Entremont, on the eve of the battle that opened Gaul to the legions, and the world to Rome's might? Those three encounters—the totality of her romantic life—had all taken place in the long-ago past, made accessible through the Otherworld by the spell *Mondradd in Mon*. She had visited Entremont in the one hundred and twenty-fourth year before the Christian era, had dallied with Alkides six centuries before that, and had hunted with Aam in a past so remote that no memory of it remained. Yes, Minho could claim to have known her for a thousand—or fourteen thousand—years.

Resenting Minho's sorcerous meddling in her private moments *then*, Pierrette's brow wrinkled into a frown, *now*. What right had he to know her intimate moods without having labored to woo and seduce her? What claim had he on the recollection of her cries of delight, her struggles to release the lovely heat her lovers' hands, lips, and loins had engendered? Then she thought of . . . Neheresta.

That had been—because of its very nature—more intimate, more private even than the other times. Had Minho been there? The other times she could forgive: they had been men, as Minho was, and she almost felt sorry for him, unable to venture out in the great world on his own. But last night—even if it had been only a dream—had been different. There was no place for a man, any man, in it; male eyes and male mind could not comprehend it, and male lust could not parallel it. Such an intrusion would be . . . unforgivable

She lifted her eyes from the vista of islands and gleaming sea, and her gaze locked with Minho's— his, doting and smug, hers, resentful, angry, and cold. She forced a smile. "Are you sure you are ready for me?" she asked. "Can these sweet, peaceful isles withstand the wind of my breath when I cry out, or my laughter, that will shake your mountains free of every loose stone and cause ripe and unripe fruit alike to tumble from your unnatural trees? Are you sure you want me, King of Hy Brasil, ruler of Thera, brother of Minos of Knossos?" Even as she uttered those scornful words, they shocked her, because they were not sweet or flirtatious, as in her dream. Her challenge was not playful, as she had once believed it would be.

But Minho smiled indulgently, thinking her charming, her questions a coquette's ploy, her anger a child's petulance or a whore's pretension. "Shake my mountains with the waves of your lashing hips when we join as one, queen of my islands," he crooned. "What fruit would I not sacrifice for a taste of yours, when I peel away your innocence?"

She saw how his kilt had risen with the strength

of his anticipation, and she imagined not the slender gold-framed member of Aam, or a Roman consul's stiff pride projecting from curly darkness, or the great, swinging bullishness of Alkides, but instead she envisioned . . . the hot, red shaft of Cernunnos, the forest god, his form and semblance now only a vestment worn by the Eater of Gods.

That terrified her. That was not her vision. This scene was right, and the words, but her rage, her fear, her disgust, were not! In desperation, she raised her hand and uttered the words she had spoken before, when this moment had been lovely and flirtatious, when she had called up the storm . . .

Then a child, she had not known what she knew now. Then, she had thought of magic as Minho now appeared to: a vast puissance that welled from the soul of the magician, a talent, an art. Now she knew otherwise: at the foundation of every magical utterance was a principle that could not be proved or denied. Combined and juxtaposed with lesser axioms, words became a spell that influenced what was—and here, in this kingdom wrested from time's grasp, no Christian axioms had written over the existence of ancient gods. The essence of the spell she formulated was something like this: Taranis is. His lower half is a squid, but his head is a man's and thus has ears. He is a storm god. Storm gods command the elements. Like men, gods are capricious and jealous. . . . She did not need to state such concepts aloud. The spell framed a reality in which, when she cried out Taranis's name . . .

She whispered words of great power, and upon the western horizon grew great clouds, first as wisps, then billows that turned dark and flashed ominously with bloody light. "Come, Taranis," she murmured between clenched teeth. Those clouds reached like eager arms, arching across the sky toward the island kingdom. The leaves of willows, olives, and lemon trees trembled with their approach, and darkened as the clouds blotted out the sun. The storm winds whipped leaves from the trees as they came ashore and mounted the cliffs. They swept Pierrette's long dark hair slapping and streaming across the back of her throne. "Come, god of thunder," she said (the wind drowned her voice, and she might as well have whispered), "and show this little king your might."

She saw his lips moving and knew he was reacting almost instinctively, intuitively, wrestling from his millennial memory one spell after another that might mute the power that lashed his kingdom. There were axioms that could nullify his spell: the Christians stated that all power stemmed from one God, one Creator, and appealed (as it were) over the heads of lesser deities. But Minho did not analyze. He only reacted, and his wild, undisciplined spells had no effect. . . .

She raised her hand, and sparks crackled at her fingertips, ebbing and surging with the lightning that leaped between the oncoming clouds. Out of the corner of her eye she saw her host, his face distorted into a grimace by the battering wind, his hair lashing his eyes. Squinting, Minho grated out words between clenched teeth: "Enough! Send it away!"

For a long moment Pierrette hesitated. What if she did not do so? What if she changed the script learned in childish visions by simply not saying the words that would quell this tempest? Would the storm winds sweep every living thing away, leaving only bare, black rocks? Was this the moment the goddess awaited? Would Taranis's wind pluck Minho himself from his throne and fling him into the sea? But no, she could not allow that. Minho was petulant, condescending—but he was not evil.

She waved a hand as if dismissing a servant. The wind abated. Out of the corner of her eye she saw Minho slump against the back of his throne, and she knew she could have destroyed him. She could have changed what was written, what she remembered—and she would have been swept away herself on those terrible winds. But now the sky lightened, and the clouds dissolved wisp by wisp, first gray, then white, reversing the order in which they had appeared. Anon, the horizon was again clear, the waters unroiled and blue. "There!" she said, remembering to say the words she remembered saying before. "Now your Fortunate Isles are again at peace. See what a terrible disruption I would be?"

Minho responded exactly according to the script in her mind: "Better storms with you than sunshine without. Marry me. Rule with me." His words, she thought, sounded hollow—empty bravado, the words a king would have to say—but he had seen her power now, and he knew she was no simple girl to be overwhelmed by pretty, shallow words.

The script ended here. She had no further dreams to guide her. Beyond this moment all was new, uncharted territory, and the pretty visions she had cherished were gone. She sighed, and turned to face Minho.

"Now you've seen what I tried to tell you," she said, not ungently. "An eon of thinking men have struggled to define the principles of logic and magic, and philosophy, and all that time you have been here, in this timeless place. Pythagoras, Aristotle, Saint Augustine . . . they all have something to say. Won't you listen to them? To me? No? Then show me your spells, King. Give me a glimpse of the power you wield, that you would share with your bride."

His eyes were hard and unloving, his smile brittle and false—but his words continued the charade. "I'll give you seventeen days in my villages and fields, seventeen nights beneath my stars. Go among my people. See what gifts I have given even the least of them. I'd not scant my bride by giving her but seventeen times more. Besides, if you would know my spell, you must know its subject. Go."

Pierrette shook her head. "Are you trying to get rid of me, now? Are you having second thoughts?"

"I think you are. You're angry with me, and I don't know why. Take the time I offer you." He sighed. "Go. When you come back, if you still wish it, I'll show you the way to my hidden chamber, where I labor day and night to preserve all that I have wrought."

Was that a promise? Pierrette asked herself. Was it enough of one? She sensed that she would not get more, and she had her own agenda, that required she get out of the palace. . . . "Very well," she said. "I'll tread your roads a while, and sup with merchants, shepherds, and fishermen, and hear what they have to say. The day is still early—which way should I go?"

Minho seemed pleased that she did not intend to postpone. "You can use your boat if you wish, though all the islands are joined by bridges and causeways. However, you'll surely see more afoot. Incidentally, the Hermit lives in the city you saw from the balcony. Perhaps you'll want to visit him."

Pierrette arose from the throne. Minho drew breath as if to say something else, but thought better of it. Pierrette left him with his eyes fixed on the placid horizon where her great storm had formed.

In the seclusion of his narrow room, with a heavy cloak over the only window, Hatiphas's face was lit only by the dull glow of the foreign witch's crystal orb. It had not spoken to him, but he had heard her one-sided conversation with it, and he did not believe her mad. Thus, sooner or later, it would acknowledge him, and he would find out what it was.

"I am Hatiphas," he murmured over the bauble. "I am vizier to Minho, king of the Fortunate Isles. I will tell you things of great interest, and when you have heard enough, or are curious enough, I hope you will respond, and I will hear you speak." For an hour, then two hours, then three, Hatiphas persisted, murmuring at the inert glass. Its glow neither waxed nor waned, and the vizier's throat became coarse and parched. At last, when he was about to get up and pour himself wine, Cunotar the Druid spoke. . . .

Gustave the donkey eyed the succulent watercress with great anticipation—and great skepticism.

Ordinarily, watercress was a treat, a delight. The tiny, crisp leaves and stems were sweet and peppery, tingling his innards and making him feel spry as a colt. But ever since putting hoof to solid ground here, he had experienced only disappointments. Here, he wondered, would even watercress be without spice and savor?

He leaned over the cold, small spring, front legs splayed, and buried his muzzle in the water. With nose-flaps closed and jaw agape, he swirled up a great bite of the tender cress, then lifted his head, and chewed. Again, as so many times before, his skepticism was warranted; the leaves had no piquancy. He took bite after bite, each time hoping the next would be better than the last . . .

Chapter 28 ∾ Black Metal and Bronze

Once again dressed in her comfortable shipboard garb, Pierrette kicked her little vessel away from the mossy wharf. Now, at last, she understood. What had the goddess *Ma* told her over and over, from the time she was small? "Nothing is what it seems. Nothing is as it first appears. Nothing."

How could a little girl have known the feelings her older counterpart would feel? How could she help but color her vision with little-girl sweetness? When a prince, a king, begged her to marry him, what girl-child could imagine refusing? And all those years, while growing up, what young woman would know when to brush off the illusions she had created and examine the perceived event itself with cooler, more mature eyes?

How sad. All those years she had loved a Minho she had created. Sorcerer-king he was, with the knowledge and power to maintain this land in timeless beauty, but was his magic any better than her own? She now knew the flaw in his masterpiece—that even he did not. If indeed he must needs spend his hours tinkering with his spell, maintaining it against the continuing onslaught of changing premises brought about in the religious and intellectual ferment of the mainland, the breaking of ancient rules and the creation of new ones, then she alone understood why it was unstable.

Seventeen days? Perhaps. Or seven, or seventy. Where would she go first? She knew the answer, even as she asked her question: the city. Minho had said the Hermit was there.

Two hours sail saw her beyond the inner island ring, and in two more she reached a bridge between a pair of larger islands. By then, the sun had dropped below the peaks, and the city's lights and fires speckled the broad apron of land beneath them. She drifted into a creek mouth, clear and pristine even though it issued from among the city's streets. Befouled water, in the lexicon of the king of the Fortunate Isles, was surely an evil, and was not allowed . . .

The hair on the back of her neck stood up, prickling, and she felt a chill. What waste was not foul? She sniffed, and smelled only the aromas of spices and flowers. Where were the jakes, the cesspools, and the middens? Minho, she remembered, did not know. Or did he?

Another key to the puzzle eased into place. She reviewed her time on the terrace with him. At the time, she had been seeing so many new things she had not noticed the important ones, such as: had Minho actually eaten any of the lovely, tasteless fruit from the platters?

She had no particular need to relieve herself, having had use of the wooden bucket aboard the boat, but nonetheless she squatted in the shadows of the creek bank, because she did not know when next she would have the chance. In the spirit of true inquiry, she considered waiting nearby for a while to see if anything . . . odd . . . transpired there—but she would have confirmation soon enough, if her hypotheses were valid.

It was now night. She was neither sleepy nor hungry, but if she could find an inn or a roadhouse, she would be able to begin her observations. She felt a bit like a spy or an unannounced inspector in a military camp: she would record everything she saw (though not in writing) and weigh it, and eventually judge. "You must destroy his kingdom, and he must die." She had not made any decision about that. She had passed up one chance already. She began to hope that had been the right choice. Now she was almost sure there was another way, not a direct confrontation with Minho, that she might or might not win, and not a Pyrrhic victory that destroyed her as well, and . . . She had almost all the information she needed to do it. She only had to decide one way or the other.

She found no inn, instead spending the hours of darkness in a smith's open shed, leaning against his furnace, which retained much heat in its stones and clay mortar. She slept with her back warm, her sagus draped over her knees and shoulders.

"What have we here?" asked a cheery voice, awakening her. Pierrette squinted against the clear, fresh morning light. The smith had returned.

"I had no place to sleep," she explained, rubbing her eyes.

Had this been any other land, he might have been angry to find her there, but this was no ordinary country—thieves had been banished from its inception, and the smith was only curious that she had no bed of her own. Travellers were unknown to him: why would anyone wander about, when everything a man needed was always close at hand? He laid a fire in his furnace, and lit it. He loaded a round-bottomed crucible with broken bronze knife blades and other fragments.

"Someone must bring you fresh bronze, from time to time," she reflected, "And someone must carry away the new tools you make. Someone must mine that copper and tin, and bring it here. Not everyone can stay at home all the time."

He eyed her oddly. "When a tool breaks, its owner tosses it in my basket, by the entrance, there," he said. "I melt it down, and cast a new one for him. No one—neither he nor I—need venture so far from his bed that he must sleep on the ground." He dribbled charcoal from a basket on top of the now-blazing wood.

"You mean you only make replacements for what is broken? You don't make anything new?"

"Why? What would I make? Who would want it? If I made a hammer with bronze from two knife blades and a scissors, what would the tools' owners do? Share the hammer? Would the olive grower bludgeon the fruit from his trees, the woodcarver beat designs into his wood, and the tailor hammer bolts of cloth into garments?"

The charcoal glowed brightly now. The smith nestled his crucible among the coals, and compressed his bellows-bag with one foot. Sparks flew up and red coals turned yellow. No conversation was possible while he labored to maintain that high heat, forcing air onto the coals, then tugging and pulling on the leather bag to reinflate it. Pierrette considered that process cumbersome. On the mainland, a smith mounted his bellows-bag between a fixed plank and one attached to a springpole. He could both inflate and deflate the bellows with one foot on the movable plank, leaving both hands free for other tasks.

"Why would I do that—and what other work do I have to do while the bronze melts? Besides, I'm sure such things must be forbidden. Someone would tell the vizier's watchers, and I would be whipped through the streets." He eyed his crucible. "Now why isn't it melting?" he murmured.

Pierrette pondered his words. He replaced old tools with new, broken with sound, but made nothing except exact replacements. He had no motivation to improve his processes, no materials to do so with, and Minho actively suppressed independent thinking and change. That furthered her budding conviction that something was very wrong here, but she could not see, just yet, what it was.

"It isn't melting!" the smith exclaimed. Pierrette peered into his crucible, where the scraps remained inert and solid. She felt something warm near her hip, and moved away from the hot furnace stones, slapping at her skirt. But there was no burn mark on the blue cloth. The heat that she still felt was within the folds of her garment. It was emanating from . . . her pouch.

Her first thought was that her crystal "serpent's egg"—the blue-and-red-veined glass bauble that held the captive soul of Cunotar, the Gaulish druid— had broken, and that the spirit of the angry mage might at any moment emerge from its ruin. But nothing happened.

"Why won't the bronze melt?" cried the smith. "Why is it still black?"

"Are you sure it is bronze?" asked Pierrette, trying to be helpful. "Did you instead fill your crucible with iron scraps? Iron demands more heat than bronze."

"*Nisi? Ensi?* What does that mean?" For want of a Minoan word, Pierrette had used the ancient "*nsi*," which was "black metal." The smith had never heard of that. Or rather . . . "It is good bronze! It should not suck heat from the coals without melting." He lifted the crucible with a bent twig of wet willow, and dumped its contents on the slate floor. "It is bronze!" he exclaimed, his hand hovering over a broken cloak pin. "But it's not even warm!"

Pierrette's pouch, however, was all too warm. It felt as if it would burst into flame. She edged away from the furnace, into the street, then out of sight around a corner. She lifted her pouch and shook it. The "serpent's egg," the gold chain and cross from father Otho, and most of her gold, bronze, and copper coins remained inside. A few small coins gleamed against the dark pavement.

The little iron ring that had been her mother's

glowed dully red. It was the source of the heat: iron—cold iron that sucked the heat from coals, the life from ancient souls. Wood sprites and tree spirits shunned it. The elusive folk of the oldest breed fled from it. Pierrette's mother, of that ancient Ligurian stock, had only been able to possess it because she knew a spell to contain its greed for heat and for helpless spirits. Pierrette, a half-breed, had never suffered from iron's ancient malevolence, nor did anyone of Gaulish or Roman blood. But here, in this ancient land removed from the progress of history, there was no iron at all, except . . . except one small, thin ring, that had stolen the heat from the smith's bronze.

She daintily touched the ring. The dew-damp pavement had cooled it somewhat; it was not too hot to touch. She heard the jangle of bronze as the smith returned his innocent metal to its crucible, then heard the wheeze of his bellows forcing air through the tuyere and onto the coals. Clutching her ring, she quickly put distance between herself and the smith's shed.

The Hermit was not hard to find. Everyone seemed to know the eccentric fellow, and Pierrette followed the pointing fingers of one person after another through the tortuous, winding streets. They were, of course, no more crooked than the streets of any town not laid out with Roman precision. When she found him, she was shocked and aghast. His domicile was no gilt-and-ivory mansion, a king's bribe, but a hovel of sticks and rags, furnished only with a worn pallet of coarse cloth stuffed ungenerously with straw mostly gone to powder.

The Hermit, she decided, had obviously had second thoughts following his betrayal of his Christian fellows, and had declared his own penance. Surely Minho had not forced him to live like this.

He himself was little better off than his surroundings. His iron gray hair straggled unbound down the sides of his face, and mingled with a disheveled beard. Dry leaves and grass seeds clung in both hair and beard. His cheeks were hollow, his eyes deep set and dull with fatigue, hunger, or apathy. Yet he welcomed her kindly, and offered her a seat on the worn curbstone beside his hut.

He seemed amazed that anyone from the world outside remembered him. "After all," he said in a voice gone harsh from disuse, that nonetheless resonated from nearby walls and tiles, "it has been a thousand years or thereabouts, and I betrayed my Master's cause before I had hardly begun to preach it."

"That is so," Pierrette agreed matter-of-factly. "Those who remember you can be counted on the fingers of one hand, leaving enough free to play a three-stringed lyre. In that sense, Minho's plot to nip your religion in the bud succeeded."

"I feared as much!" he wailed. "But I beg you, tell me all is not lost, that my Master's apostles and their successors have not gone down false paths, worshipping carpenters' hammers and preaching His Word from the backs of wagons wrought with the tools of his carpenter's trade?"

Pierrette shook her head. "No one wields hammers, chisels, adzes or awls in the name of the Carpenter of Nazareth, but you have been forgotten, as if you never preached in Jerusalem, Rome, Athens, or amid the ruins of Babylon."

He covered his face with both hands. "Then all is lost, my betrayal is total, and the Black Time will engulf the world—and only I will remain a living Christian, here in this unChristian kingdom." He wept great silent sobs that shook his gangling frame.

Pierrette let him weep a while, because she did not approve of traitors, and thought he deserved to wallow in his despair. Then, in a while, she relented. "I did not say your Master's cause is forgotten, only that you are, and the words you once preached."

"How can that be?" He raised his tear-streaked face.

"Great spells—great concepts, if you will—have weight and substance of their own. If you pushed a rock off a cliff, would you need to jump after it, and continue pushing lest it stop falling? Even though you abase yourself, you still have too much pride. Another Apostle took up where you left off. He did not pick up the Master's hammer and tools, but the cross upon which he hanged, and this . . ." She reached into her pouch with two fingers, pushing aside the shapes of coins and the roundness of the serpent's egg, and withdrew Father Otho's tiny gold cross on its chain. " . . . this is the emblem of the Church Saul of Tarsus founded, in your stead."

The Hermit eyed the little symbol with something approaching horror. "But that is a cross! It is a symbol of shame and death! At least the hammer stood for labor at God's tasks."

"Don't remonstrate with me. I am no Christian, though I respect many Christian principles, when they are applied with sincerity. What cause do you have to complain? You were not there. You were here."

Chastened, he hung his heavy, overlarge head. "You are correct," he admitted. "I will meditate on this tiny cross—I am a traitor and apostate, and I dare not pray. Perhaps I will come to understand how this . . . distasteful symbol has become meritorious. May I . . . may I touch it?" He extended a tremorous hand.

Pierrette hesitated. What had Minho said about crossed twigs and shadows? He did not allow such symbols here, and if he had known what was in her pouch, he would surely have ordered it destroyed. But who was he to command her, or to deny this poor old traitor the meager solace of a little gold bangle? She sighed, and dropped it, chain and all, into his outstretched palm.

He gasped, and picked it up between thumb and forefinger, holding the tiny cross upright. Stray flecks of bright sunlight reflected in his moist eyes. "Keep it," Pierrette said softly. "For me, it is only a bauble, the gift of a friend. For you . . ."

"For me," said the Hermit, rising to his feet (he now seemed much taller than before, and when Pierrette also arose, he towered over her), "this day has become the one when I made my erring choice. I am once again young, and my mission is yet ahead. This time, I will not betray it. I will speak in the squares and marketplaces, on the beaches where fishermen draw up their boats and tie their nets, and this cross will be my warrant, my emblem and . . . when once I understand its import, my guide."

His eyes strayed over Pierrette's head, and he strode toward the center of the plaza, where several women were drawing water from a raised pool. He mounted the several steps and addressed his happenstance audience in a rich, mellow voice that no longer hinted at impending failure.

Pierrette was more than a little annoyed. He had spoken of the Black Time. Was that only a chance expression? She was not going to find out now. Should she wait around until he ran down, or the women threw water on him, or departed hooting and catcalling? She looked again. They stared raptly up at him, and several others had now joined them. Were they just curious, or had the prophet now found not only his voice and his message, but the beginnings of a following? It was impossible to tell. She would have to wait and see. Perhaps she could return here one more time before her seventeen days were up, and find out.

She made her way along the streets, somewhat remembering the way she had come, but to a certain extent merely keeping the westering sun at her back or over her right shoulder. She should emerge not far from where her boat was moored, in a reasonable time.

Chapter 29 ∾ The Attraction of Opposites

Not twenty-four hours had elapsed since Pierrette had begun her tour of Minho's kingdom, but already she suspected she knew what she needed to know. Still, she had seventeen days before Minho would receive her again. What now?

A delicious aroma swirled past her nostrils. Somewhere nearby, someone was baking bread. She turned first one way, and the scent lessened, then another and it became stronger. She began walking, tracking it toward its source. There: a small shop stood open to the street, and in front of it was a huge basket heaped with brown loaves. A slender woman clad only in a short wrap was removing steaming ovoids from a brick oven with a thin wooden paddle. She placed the hot bread on woven willow shelves to cool.

As Pierrette entered the shop, she saw that the loaves in the basket by the entry were all broken.

She tapped one with her fingertip. It was hard and stale. "Your bread smells wonderful," she said.

"Doesn't it, though?" replied to the baker, smiling. "Here take this and break it." She handed Pierrette a hefty loaf, still quite warm.

Pierrette tore a chunk loose, and chewed it appreciatively. "Delicious," she said, not at all clearly, because her mouth was full. Actually, the rich-smelling bread had no flavor at all, but she couldn't say that, could she?

The woman was eying her strangely. "What are you doing?"

"Why . . . I am eating your bread, and . . ." What did the baker mean? Pierrette was standing, she was breathing, and she was definitely wondering what she had done wrong.

"I see. But why are you doing it? I've never seen anyone do that before. What will become of the bread that is inside you?"

"I don't understand," Pierrette said, confused. "What should I do with it, if not eat it?" If all the woman's bread smelled so good, and tasted like dusting rags, perhaps it was solely intended to be enjoyed with the nose. She did not, however, express that ridiculous thought.

"You must be from some far island," the baker said, "where customs are different. I can't imagine why you put my bread in your mouth. How will you return it to the basket, now?"

"Return it to . . . to that basket?" Pierrette indicated the container full of stale loaves.

At that moment, a new arrival interrupted them, a man wearing a leather apron with wood chisel handles projecting from a dozen small pockets.

"That was fine bread, Aphrosta," he said, tossing two broken loaves atop the others in the basket. "We enjoyed both of them."

"Then here, have two more," the baker said.

"Thank you. My wife will warm them, and we'll break them at dusk, and cut ripe apples to go with them. There's nothing better than the aroma of fresh-cut apples and a newly broken loaf."

"It's one of life's genuine pleasures," the baker agreed. The woodworker departed with his fresh bread.

"Ah . . . what should I do with this?" Pierrette asked, holding the remains of her loaf.

"Just put it in the basket, of course. Can you also return the morsel you put in your mouth?"

"I've . . . no. I'm sorry. I ate it. But here . . ." She felt in her pouch for a coin. "Take this instead."

"But it is metal. What can I do with that? I would prefer to have my bread back. I can't crush metal with the stale crusts and bake fresh loaves from it."

Pierrette backed away. This was all too strange. It defied reason. Did she understand what she had heard, or had the dialect of Minho's folk diverged from the classical Minoan she had learned from Anselm, so that she had misunderstood everything? "I must go," she said.

"Well, if my morsel falls out of you, put it in the basket. Still, I suppose no one will miss such a little bit, when it will be divided among all of the loaves I make tomorrow." She returned to her task, lifting loaves from the oven.

Though Pierrette had seen little enough of Minho's city, it felt like too much. If every encounter with its denizens were as troubling as those she had experienced, she would soon be begging someone to awaken her from this mad dream. Unfortunately, it was no dream, and her escape from it would not be so easy. She made her way back to the boat. Once afloat, things would hopefully return to normal, and she still had real food aboard, that did not taste like sawdust.

But something was wrong: the moist green moss and clumps of soft grass around her landing place were gone. The soil lay exposed, bare and black, as if fire had consumed everything. The bare patch was almost circular, and it centered upon the dead, dry branches of . . . of the bush beneath which she had relieved herself. That bush had been heavy with succulent green leaves, before.

She tiptoed gingerly across the ugly, barren ground, and waded into the creek to cleanse the soles of her sandals before climbing over the boat's rail, pushing off at the same time. When she hoisted the lugsail's spar, an offshore breeze filled the sail and the clean, sparkling gap between her and the infected shore widened.

Looking back, she wondered if the circle of devastation had grown larger. As she stared, she became conscious of movement at its edge, something dark, nebulous, shadowy and unclear, that crept along the boundary between green and black, consuming moss, leaves, and tender grass, leaving behind only dead, dry dust. She knew what it was. She had seen its like many times, more times than she wished to remember, but . . . this time it was not scurrying westward, seeking some distant goal. It had reached its destination: the destination its

horrid fellow-shadows all sought, and it
was . . . eating.

Horror-struck, Pierrette stared, but what she
saw were images within her mind: a greasy shadow
emerging from the mouth of a villager along with
his infected tooth; another, wriggling free of a
dead rat, a rabbit too long in the snare, a heap
of dung in the road. She remembered Sena,
another magical place, and a woman's dry bones
crumbling away even as she watched, until nothing
remained. They were all the small evils of the
world, oozing free from the stink and corruption
that engendered them, rushing away toward their
opposite, toward . . . the Fortunate Isles, the land
where no evil was allowed. Now she had released
just such a creature here, despite her precautions,
and even alone it was striving to right the balance that Minho had upset two thousand and
some years before.

She tugged on the sheet and secured it, braced
the gaff, then adjusted the steering oar. Her little
craft pushed ahead vigorously, its small bow wave
chuckling like a cheery mountain rivulet, a con-
tented sound. But Pierrette was far from content.
How much sweet, green grass, how much life and
goodness, would the shadow consume before it was
sated, or before it simply evaporated, nullified and
canceled out by its opposite substance?

Should she sail back to warn Minho, so he could
destroy the bridges and causeways that linked that
island to the others, and thus save at least a portion of his kingdom? She shook her head. The small
heap she had left behind that bush could not
encompass the destruction of an entire city, and

Minho had been quite clear: seventeen days. Only one had elapsed.

It was her fault. She was a plague carrier, a curse upon this lovely land, bringing death, and black destruction. These people were not concerned with the disposal of their wastes because there were none. Broken bronze was melted, and made into new tools. Broken bread was not eaten. Its aroma was savored, and then the tasteless stuff was crushed and baked again into fresh loaves. But she could not subsist upon the sweet, yeasty smell of bread. She craved its substance. She knew now that when she had eaten the flat, insipid fruit from Minho's table, the king had eaten none. What had he thought, watching her push slice after slice into her mouth, watching her throat ripple as she swallowed it? No wonder he had, despite his protestations, been eager to get rid of her even for a fortnight and a few more days.

She knew enough, now, to destroy this kingdom, to fulfill the goddess's command. A few ships full of ugly little shadows gathered from the rocks of the Armorica coast would be enough—but could she do that? Even if she could get a ship past Minho's protective spells, spells he had let down to allow her passage, could she bear to do it? Could she cause the very devastation she had just witnessed, on a grand scale encompassing not only grass, leaves, and moss but the smith whose bronze would not melt, the baker whose morsel she had eaten, and thousands upon thousands of others, all as innocent and inoffensive?

She eyed the rising shore of a smallish island connected by two soaring bridges to larger landmasses of the outer and the middle rings. The gray-green foliage of lush old olive trees dotted its grassy slopes. No, she had not seen enough of this land to consider destroying it. That would be like burning a scroll unread, because the color of the ribbon that bound it offended her. She had to see it all for herself, and besides, though she now had one answer she did not have the other: how could she *not* destroy the Fortunate Isles, but save them, and yet not disobey the one who had sent her? One solution was not enough. Just as the shadows of worldly evil nullified unworldly goodness, she needed not only the spell but also a counterspell. Now, she was no longer sure that seventeen days would be enough.

Pierrette passed the following day and night at sea, but whether she did so from caution concerning what she had seen, or merely to have time to ponder the twists and turns of events, was not clear, even to her. Then, by morning's slanting rays, as she rounded another small island, driven by an easy breeze astern, she observed a patch of bare, dark soil much like the one she had left behind on the city's margin. The wind and current did not favor a landing, or even a close approach, so she reluctantly sailed onward. It may have simply been newly turned soil, ready for sowing, she told herself. One couldn't discount that explanation, here where there was no fixed season for each agricultural activity.

Then, with the sun high overhead at noon, she spotted still another blackness. This time, she was able to ease her craft close in, though she could not moor among the blocky volcanic boulders that lined the shore, where there was neither beach nor quiet backwater.

Yes, she saw, it was much like the previous devastation, but with differences: tendrils of green ivy reached inward from the margin of destruction, and tiny seedlings had taken root where the breeze had blown them. How long ago had the causative event occurred? That depended on several things: the fertility of the bare soil, the heaviness of the morning dew (there had been no rain, in fact no clouds at all). Could it have been only two or three days? She wondered this because, if her budding hypothesis had merit, only the impingement of someone from outside Minho's enchanted realm could have caused it, and she had never set foot on that island, or the one before. But perhaps Gustave had.

She envisioned her errant donkey wandering from island to island, keeping to thickets and ravines when people were about, crossing bridges and causeways at night (because Gustave was inherently cautious, and skeptical of all humans). Munching tender shoots here, succulent leaves there, and fat sunflower heads laden with oily seeds elsewhere, he would sooner or later find the need to lighten his internal burden, and . . .

She almost laughed. Would Minho be busier than ever, in the coming days, pulling scroll after scroll from his shelves as he searched for an adjunct to his great spell that specifically countered . . . donkey dung? And Gustave? Did he find the luscious island vegetation all flat and insipid, as Minho's lovely sliced fruit had been to her? Would he eat less— and thus destroy less—because his meals had no savor, or would his sampling be ever more eclectic and more frequent, as each lovely scent led him along to one and another patch of disappointingly flavorless fodder?

Could she follow his dark, intermittent trail, and perhaps coax him back aboard her small vessel with grain brought from the outside world, whose ordinary aroma might by now hold extraordinary promise, in his deprivation?

Elsewhere, in a curtained room where no lamps burned, a chamber illuminated only by the vermilion glow of a red-and-blue-veined glass bauble that resembled a tiny beating heart, the vizier Hatiphas and the druid Cunotar continued their conversation.

In yet another place, a secret chamber in the bowels of the great palace, but separate from it in a manner not clearly defined, King Minho labored at a task that had little to do with the preservation of his seminal spell (for he was no longer able to maintain it to his satisfaction, and his efforts were now directed toward a different solution, one he believed would prove final and complete, requiring no further tinkering, ever). His success with that task would determine the ultimate fate of his kingdom—and, as well, the fate of his intended and long-anticipated bride.

Chapter 30 ᴥ The Not-So-Fortunate Isles

The days and nights that ensued on those islands and among them were for Pierrette a concatenation of events and encounters superficially different, but monotonously similar when viewed according to the principles they illustrated. She observed an olive grower dumping baskets of shriveled olives beneath his trees, then watched him fill those baskets with plump, fragrant black fruit from the branches above. She followed him to a shed where he pressed some between flat stones, and she smelled the rich oil they produced. When he departed, carrying a clay amphora of old oil on his shoulder (to be poured out on the ground, she was sure, to feed the roots of the trees) she stole a handful of his fruits and ate them. For all their aroma, they were without savor, but they allayed her hunger and seemed to sustain her.

She caught no glimpse of the donkey Gustave,

but she observed the evidence of his passage: patches of bare soil, sometimes dotted with the stumps of saplings, mostly consumed, sometimes entirely dead, but often exhibiting traces of fresh growth. That was reassuring to her. The dung of a single donkey, at least, was not so strongly defined as "evil" in Minho's spell that its effects continued unchecked.

In her mind, Pierrette created a map of such places, and she attempted to rank them by their apparent age or freshness. This was made difficult because the meandering course of her travels did not take her back across old routes often, and she had few opportunities to observe the same spot twice or three times, to establish the stages and sequence of recovery of the vegetation, from tendril and seed-leaf, vinelet and sprig, to leafy vine and small bush or clump of grass.

With no fixed itinerary, she was free to experiment, to attempt to predict where, from the limited evidence, a fresher patch of devastation might mean she was hot upon her four-legged companion's trail. Thus far, she had encountered rather more barren spots with ungerminated or freshly rooted seeds than chance might account for, but she had not attained success, which would be to find Gustave himself.

As for her own private functions, she limited them to appointments with the wooden bucket beneath the center thwart of her boat, and emptied it only when she was well offshore, with equal distances of all-absorbing salt water in every direction. This she did more from the desire to leave the evidence of Gustave's passing unmuddled than

from any consideration for her royal host, whose
labors were surely, she believed, made more difficult by such things.

On one island, she watched a weaver's husband
unravel old, worn garments and untwist every
thread. A flock of children then carded the wool,
and spun it, and the weaver worked the new
yarn on her loom into cloth ready for the tailor's
cutting. While Pierrette watched, several people
deposited old garments in a basket by the door
then chose new ones displayed on tables. When
she did the same, leaving her old, worn tunic
and choosing another, no one paid particular
attention to her. But a few minutes later, as she
watched from across the street, the thread-picking
husband found the tunic she had left, gasped,
and turned it over and over in his hands. "Wife!"
he cried, "What cloth is this?" Together they
examined its crisscross Gallic plaid, the faded
pattern of colors unlike anything the wife might
weave. "Take it to the Watcher," said the wife.
"It is not right."

"I dare not. The Watcher will think we made it,
and we'll be punished."

"Then unravel it, before someone comes, and
sees it." They dithered, unsure how to treat the
nonconforming garment, and at last decided to bury
it beneath the rest in the basket, and not think
about that complex cloth, the contemplation of
which they feared would drive them mad.

"Where is the Watcher?" she asked a peddler of
bronze needles and pins, squatting with his polished
wooden box of small, shiny wares.

"I have nothing of interest to him," the peddler

replied without addressing her question. "My pins are all much alike, one to another, and all are proper pins, though hardly exceptional."

"Where might I find the Watcher?" she asked a vendor of dried fish, who sat between two baskets of equal capacity. As it was early in the day (as she would realize later) the basket on his left was full of whole, flat fillets encrusted with salt, while the one on his right contained a scattering of cut, broken, and even soft, stewed morsels, but none chewed, none eaten.

"In the usual place," was the reply. "I have no need to go there. My fish are neither exceptionally odorous nor lacking in fishy aroma." Then why, Pierrette wondered, had he averted his eyes, as if afraid. Was everyone secretly terrified of King Minho and his unseen, perhaps immaterial, spies? Was his pleasure perhaps expressed less often than his pain? And did that signify an imbalance, even in this perfect realm between the substandard and the exceptional, and did fear of singular accomplishment in either direction incline everyone to conscientious mediocrity?

When she found the Watcher it was by accident, straying into a small square where three streets met. There, between two parallel marble walls seemingly purpose-built, was a statue of Minho himself. But what a strange statue! Approached from the left, Minho smiled and held out both hands in the manner of one receiving a gift. From the opposite end of the walled passage, which was hardly wider than the king's shoulders, his brow appeared furrowed, his nose wrinkled as if someone had eaten spicy food, then broken wind nearby. His eyes seemed narrowed in anger. His palms were raised as it to fend off something unpleasant.

Pierrette went back and forth between both viewing positions several times, but she could not tell if the statue turned, and changed expressions, every time she walked around to the other side, or if it had been carved with two faces, two welcoming arms and two that rejected. She tried to crawl through, between the statue's legs, but could not fit. Peering up between its legs, she could see no evidence of a second face at the back of the head.

Did Minho peer from the statue's stone eyes, then reach out with an ephemeral hand to bless visitors from the east, or chastise approachers from the west? Or did each visitor's own convictions about the quality of his goods govern his choice of entrances, and did his predispositions themselves generate whatever feelings of pride, pleasure, dismay, or despair he experienced, without burdening the overworked king with trivial rewards and punishments?

In villages and ports across the islands, she would find other Watchers, all much the same, but would find no immediate clarification of their exact functioning.

One evening, Pierrette sat at the feet of a poet, in a tavern where men sniffed wine, but did not drink. She did, but the wine tasted like pond water, and failed to raise her spirits at all. The others seemed to progress toward drunkenness as they sniffed and raised their cups. The tavern master collected goblets already sniffed, and poured their contents into a tun. When that vessel was filled, his strapping son took it away for aging, and brought another, fresh and cool from the cave.

The poet sang of glories past, of the ancient Sea Kings who mapped and explored, and circumnavigated the world. Of course Pierrette knew that the earth was a sphere, or nearly so. Anyone who had read the Ionian Greeks knew that, and understood the means of calculating its size. It was vast, and she felt it would be wasted if that sphere were mostly ocean. Lands surrounded the Middle Sea: surely the great ocean that lapped these island shores must also be ringed with undiscovered continents, however far away those lands might be. The irony of her thoughts was not lost on Pierrette. She had found the Fortunate Isles, the ultimate destination of explorers everywhere, and already her mind reached out for more distant unknown strands.

The climax of the poet's narration was the story of Minho himself. He had shared his mother's womb with a twin, whom his father named Minos after himself. It was the traditional appellation of the kings of Knossos and Thera. When the elder Minos stuck out his thumb, his little namesake had sucked it most greedily, and yowled his disapproval when it gave no milk. Little Minho, however, only eyed his father with his great, dark, baby eyes.

Only one son could become king, in his appointed time, and aggressive little Minos was the obvious candidate. But the doting father did not scant his gentler son. "I will divide my kingdom," he decided. "Minos, who commands and demands, will be king, but not high priest, as is customary. Instead, sweet Minho will rule my spiritual realm."

Thus it transpired. Minho, not required to learn the art of war, the science of control, the mathematics of taxation, instead studied the accumulated wisdom of the scholars, the natures of the gods, and, of course, magic. Chief among the tools of his trade was the Great Orb, which the poet called a "water-sphere." In its clear depths the universe existed in simulacrum, as clouds and shadows that sometimes coalesced into images, and at other times merely obscured. Because the poet described it as mounted on a bronze ring and three legs, Pierrette suspected it was not water but crystal or glass, like her little "serpent's egg."

In his sphere, Minho saw fire within the earth, fire that gathered beneath the rocky bed of the island where he lived and studied. He foresaw a great devastation. Fields, orchards, and cities would be destroyed, and such a pall of gray ash would fall, even on lands far beyond the realm of the Sea Kings, that many nations would collapse when crops, roads, and seaports were buried. Minho foresaw barbarians in armor of strange black metal laughing around campfires in the ruins of Minos's palace at Knossos. He foresaw distant Egypt convulsed in revolution, so entire subject peoples would pack up their querns and looms, and flee into the desert.

Minho sent couriers throughout his brother's kingdom with promises of gold and steady work, and gathered the best of every trade—potters, bronze, silver, and goldsmiths, masons, farmers, poets, and dancers. All others—warriors, taxmen, and trolls who made black weapons from red rocks, he turned away, and all lesser scholars and magicians also. When the fires below would no longer remain pent within the rock, he uttered a great spell.

Plunging his hand into his magical sphere, he plucked his chosen land—this very kingdom—from the face of the earth, and floated it in a pool left behind by the receding tide. When the cataclysm was past he returned it to its place, but its ties to the bed of the sea were broken, and thereafter, with a nudge of his finger, he could move it first here, then there, at his will.

"And so it is today," concluded the poet. "Here, all is perfect, for all that is evil was left behind.

"Sing praise to Minho," he cried, "who preserves us always in our perfection." Voices arose, as one, in a song all knew well. Pierrette remained silent, for she knew neither the words nor the tune, and she was not as impressed as they were with Minho's great feat, or indeed with their own complaisant perfection.

She slipped away from the gathering. Because she often ate the lovely but tasteless fruits of their labor, which they merely sniffed and admired, her requirements differed from theirs. Because her boat and the cedar bucket were not nearby, she performed her necessities in a secluded willow copse. When she looked back, from afar and above, the copse was already leafless amid a spreading circle of black devastation. Was this, she wondered unhappily, the means by which she would destroy

Minho's kingdom—bit by bit, insidiously, without shouting or the clash of arms?

Seventeen days. Six had passed. Eleven remained, and already she was tired of tasteless pap and innocuous people. She missed ibn Saul's snappishness, Lovi's petulance, Gregorius's elaborate lies, and Yan Oors's dark ugliness. She missed the stinks of offal and wet ashes and the raucous cries of crows, all long banished from these islands. She even missed bruising rocks beneath her hip and shoulder when she slept on the ground—because here, wherever she lay down became as soft as a bed of flower petals and smelled as sweet.

But her patience had rewarded her; she had learned several important things. Minho's tale, as recorded in Anselm's scrolls, had made no mention of a magic sphere that contained a universe in miniature, that could be manipulated at the sorcerer-king's will. Now she knew what Minho had concealed beneath the drape of dark cloth. She knew also that he had lied: was the "water-sphere" a device of his own conception and creation, or was it an artifact of an age earlier still, a creation of some mind that surely understood, as Minho did not, the logical basis for all things magical? And almost hidden in the poet's tale were other nuggets: iron was forbidden here—but she had her mother's ring, which sucked the heat from Minho's forges. And what did Minho fear, that he had banned all other practitioners of his sorcerous art? Yet against her thigh (or so she believed) was a crystal egg that held the soul of Cunotar the druid, his malevolent spirit bound for almost a thousand years in reticulations of blue-and-crimson glass.

Here, people sacrificed the pleasures of food and drink lest their indulgence conjure elements at odds with insipid perfection. But Pierrette did not. Here, Neheresta, old and jaded, remained forever trapped in the body of the sweet child she had been, on that momentous day when Minho had uttered his spell.

Thinking of children, the recollection of another vision swam before her eyes. The vision itself was simple and straightforward, of two young people standing amid a multitude, the man's left hand and the woman's right resting on the shoulders of a smiling boy of perhaps seven years' age. The significance of that vision requires exposition of events that transpired a year or so in Pierrette's immediate past.

Even in Anselm's ensorcelled keep, the histories written by Diodorus Siculus and Titus Livius had begun to fade from the mage's books. All the events more than 126 years before the birth of the Christian savior were disappearing from the pages—and soon would fade from the memories of men. Somewhere in the past, Pierrette understood, something had been changed, and the course of events that led to her age—and to her existence—would no longer come about. She, and everything she knew of the world, would cease to exist. What new history would replace them? Desperately seeking a solution, Pierrette discovered that one event, only one, was causing the devastation: a battle fought in her world, her history, that now remained unfought, circumvented by the Eater of Gods—and everything that had happened thereafter was changing. Voyaging through the Otherworld of the spell

Mondradd in Mon, she had meddled with that historic crux: if the Roman consul Calvinus stormed Entremont, the citadel of the Gauls, and vanquished Teutomalos, their king, then Marius would drive off the Teutons a few generations later, and Julius Caesar would make all Gaul a Roman province. If Calvinus dithered and procrastinated, Teutomalos would become strong enough to defeat him, and where Imperial Rome might have been would be a vast Celtic and Germanic state, an evil empire in which even gods themselves were slaves to that entity Father Otho did not dare name.

Pierrette had succeeded in goading Calvinus to battle, and the resultant historic outcome was not much different from what she had known before. Even the tales people told, centuries later, were the same. One such legend recounted how the centaur Belugorix had fled the slaughter at Entremont with his lover Aurinia on his back and had, after long journeying, attained the Fortunate Isles. Belugorix, whom Pierrette had known as Bellagos, had been indeed a *kentor*, a captain of one hundred Gaulish cavalryman, and at Pierrette's urging had fled with bright Aurinia, already carrying their unborn son in her womb. When the dust and smoke of battle were centuries gone, and Pierrette had returned to her own—almost her own—era, she had again quested through the Otherworld and had seen the loving couple in a crowd outside Minho's palace. Their son Kraton looked to be seven or eight years old, and by that she knew their quest had been a hard one, and seven years long.

Where were Aurinia and Bellagos now? What

had become of young Kraton? When Pierrette got
up from her makeshift bed in a grassy hollow—
no dew clung to her cloak, which was still white
and clean—she knew how she would occupy the
final days of her exile from the palace.

"The enemy of my enemy is my friend." It was
an old adage, generally useful, and Hatiphas considered it applicable to present circumstance. The
druid Cunotar more than hated the girl Pierrette.
He loathed her, despised her. His voice dripped
venom and sour bile at the most oblique reference
to her.

Cunotar was also—though loath to admit it—very
much afraid of her. She had trapped him in his
present state, body and spirit alike compressed into
the glassy orb that now rested on Hatiphas's table.
The vizier hardly dared contemplate Cunotar's rage,
after so many centuries without food, drink, savor,
or challenge, afforded only brief and tantalizing
glimpses of a world that had evolved in a direction he would not have allowed, had he been free
to influence it.

But "friend," as Hatiphas defined it, had strict
limitations. There might come an appropriate time
to shatter Cunotar's crystal prison, and thus per-
form what the druid would consider a friendly act,
but that time was not yet at hand. Hatiphas's master
had expressed strong feelings about the presence
of other sorcerers in his realm. Though Cunotar's
desire to eliminate the troublesome young witch
felt genuine, and coincided with Hatiphas's own,
King Minho, blind with that madness that afflicted
all males unaltered as Hatiphas was (to their

detriment, and the detriment of clear thinking) had not yet abandoned his ambition, which was to tame her and possess her.

Thus Hatiphas would not—yet—free the druid. If all else failed, and the king's present efforts bore no fruit, then was soon enough.

Cunotar also pondered. He could not see much of this Minho's unlikely realm, but because Hatiphas was less careful than Pierrette, and did not store the egg in leather wrappings, or seal it in a wooden box, Cunotar was able to sense many things. One was that the gullible vizier accepted him as he portrayed himself. He also sensed changes occurring in this changeless land. Some he felt only as the righting of ancient imbalances, and they did not trouble him. Others were more sinister, and were the efforts of a sorcerer as powerful as himself. They did not have the fresh piquancy of the girl Pierrette's spells, so they could only be emanating from one source: Minho.

Cunotar reflected that Hatiphas also sensed something going very wrong, but he had not been able to define it. He erroneously blamed it on the girl. What would he do when he found out that his benevolent master was behind it?

Minho's task, had anyone been in a position to observe him work, gave him the semblance of a large, dark spider weaving a web of great complexity. In actuality, he wove nothing; the web's gossamer strands had been woven by processes entirely natural, and beyond the capability of any sorcerer to shape or alter in their least, most insignificant detail—except for one.

At the moment the king had first uttered his great spell, there had been no threads. The moment after, they had existed, and ever since had lengthened, had woven in and out amidst each other.

Each strand originated not in a place, but in the idea of a place: the emptiness where Minho's kingdom had been, when he had uttered his fateful words. Each one terminated in a person, an individual who had been saved from fiery death at that moment. Each soul in Minho's realm was thus not entirely free of its mortal origin, but remained linked to it by one tenuous thread.

In the centuries upon centuries since, the orb that men call "the world" had spun about itself three hundred sixty-odd times each year, twisting those threads. It had swung ponderously around its luminary a hundred times each century, and created great looping skeins of soul-stuff. And upon the face of Minho's island kingdom, men and women had danced by moonlight in intricate patterns, and by day had trudged this road and that, had sailed hither and thither, like tatting weights on a lacemaker's board, creating of their strands that intricate weave Minho now studied.

Could he untangle them?

Could he trace each lone thread through its convolutions and unweave it from the rest? Or was the only solution to cut them all at once, as Alexander had done to the famous and unfortunate Gordian knot? Minho knew of Alexander only by rumor. He had been a thousand years yet unborn when Minho had performed his magic, and the sorceror-king could not remember Alexander's fate.

For now, he would continue to unweave the cloth of centuries, and would do nothing rash. He had given his bride-to-be seventeen days to make her decision. If her choice favored him—or if not—then he would decide.

Chapter 31 ～ The Ancient Child

Sailing from one creek mouth or harbor to the next, the Fortunate Isles seemed a small kingdom of fourteen significant islands and a few score tiny ones out on the barrier reefs that protected it from the world beyond. Once ashore, it seemed much larger, and she often hiked for days across an island she could sail around between a single sunrise and sunset. Afoot, the kingdom seemed larger than Francia and Iberia combined, its people as numerous as all Roma in its heyday. "Bellagos," she repeated at every inn and crossroad. "His wife's name is Aurinia, and their son Kraton looks to be seven years old."

"Kraton?" replied a shoemaker. "Does he deal in leather? I know someone of that name, but he is about my age, though less well preserved." He laughed. After two thousand years, everyone was, of course, "about his age," give or take an inconsequential lifetime or so.

"I knew a Kraton, once," said a farmer resting behind his plow. The grain he had harvested seasons ago now lay thick in his furrows where he had returned it as golden flour, hulled, winnowed, ground, and sifted, but never baked with water, salt, and oil into bread. "It seems to me," he continued, "that he was a maker of bows, instruments for killing, and was left behind."

So it went, until the fifteenth day of Pierrette's sojourn. "Of course I know them," the cheery, bright-eyed washerwoman said. Perhaps, Pierrette thought, she was cheery because alone of all the tradespeople and laborers, her task was entirely genuine—dirty clothes went into her wooden vat, which steamed with sweet herbs, and clean ones came out to be dried on tree branches in the perfect sunshine, where clouds were always "over there," and never between her and the golden orb. "The parents live right above me, in the village, and their golden-haired son—so like his mother— entertains his friends in that country house whose roof you can just see over the ridge."

Thus directed, Pierrette began the last leg of her quest, down the hill to the sprawling mansion where she would find young Kraton, playing at ball or pick-up-sticks with his little friends. What use, she wondered as she approached the magnificent dwelling, did a child have for a palace? How many rooms could he fill with toys? In how many courtyards could he toss and kick a leather ball? There was, she reflected uneasily, something terribly amiss.

"Kraton? Of course," said a tall, effete Minoan lolling by the gate. "Come. You're new here, aren't you? Imagine the looks on their faces when I introduce you. We've seen no new face since Kraton himself arrived—and that was, oh, centuries ago."

Indeed, Pierrette caused a stir. Men and women—all young, all lovely—crowded around, eagerly absorbing her unfamiliarity. "I saw her first," one tall youth stated. "Come with me," he urged her. "Imagine—breasts untouched by anyone I know, myself included. Thighs unparted by . . . You wouldn't, by some lucky chance, be a virgin, would you? That would be novelty indeed." Pierrette turned away from him, ashamed and disgusted. Where were Kraton and his friends? What were these jaded and debauched people doing here?

Kraton. At last. The blond boy sat at the center of an interior courtyard, in the arms of a marble statue of some god or hero of old. Around him danced men and women entirely naked but for golden spikes, pins, and chains that penetrated their bodies, some emerging from natural openings, others from slits and punctures in every fold, crevice, and protuberance of limb, trunk, and face. Kraton himself, she saw, with growing horror, wore a delicate chain that originated at his eyeball—an orb of gold, not blue like his other one. The chain snaked down his cheek, entered his mouth, and— Pierrette shuddered uncontrollably—seemed to be identical to one that emerged from beneath his buttocks, and terminated in a matching golden eyeball that he swung back and forth in front of his face.

"You can't be the one my parents spoke of!" he complained, his face twisted in a petulant frown, his voice high and immature. "You look ordinary! My parents said you were a goddess, but you are not. Come here." Hesitantly, she approached his perch.

He reached out and squeezed her breasts painfully. She drew back, hurt and shocked. "At least you're real," he squealed. "At least you're new. No, wait! Don't go! I want to play with you."

At that moment, Pierrette understood what evil she had wrought, all those hundreds of years before, a thousand miles away. As the battle for Entremont had drawn near, she had asked Bellagos, "Would you rather see Aurinia a slave in Rome, drawing water for some senator's herb garden, and going afterward to his bed?" Instead, she should have said, "Stay here and die with your sweetheart, for long life is an evil far worse than death."

How had it been for young Kraton, when his family finally achieved these shores? Had Aurinia set him to play with other children—children like Neheresta, perhaps, already ancient except in body—who had made of him their novelty, their toy? Or had he just become bored with the passage of years, then centuries, during which his body remained impotent and manhood never arrived? Now she looked upon the travesty, the monstrosity, she had unwittingly created, and . . . her last meal—olives, an apple, and gruel she had made of steeped, uncooked grains—rose in her throat, and spewed over the grinning Kraton.

He continued to grin, wiped his face with an extended finger, and asked, "What is this? What new thing have you done?" Then, as he examined his finger, it began to change. First, it faded to the unhealthy hue of sour milk, then darkened through chestnut to ashy black. As Kraton stared, uncomprehending, his flesh turned to powder and crumbled away. A twig of black bone remained.

Pierrette saw—as he did not—that his nose and his cheekbones were also changing, darkening, and soon Kraton also realized that what he had seen happen to his finger was occurring everywhere that Pierrette's vomitus had come to rest. But he seemed to feel no pain—or else pain, like everything else, was so prosaic, so boring that it no longer moved him. He smiled, even as his ravaged face began to crumble. "When at first I cried that my little dogcart was no longer fun to ride in, Mother said 'Pray to the goddess, that someday you will again find pleasure in something new.' I have not prayed for a long time, and you were a long time coming . . ." His lips were now stiff and brittle, and Pierrette had to lean quite close, in order to hear his last words: " . . . but you heard me . . ." He crumbled to the gleaming pavement, that had never before been soiled.

"I am not the goddess," she whispered. "I am less than her fingernails, or the breath from her mouth, but I now know she heard you. Fare well in your new adventure, child. You have long lived in the beginning, and now find the end. Perhaps in the Otherworld you'll live out the middle, which I denied you."

Someone jarred her shoulder and pushed her aside. Another figure, blurred by her tears, came between her and the darkening heap on the shining tiles. In no time at all Pierrette was edged away as the occupants of Kraton's house crowded around his remains to witness, for the first time, something entirely new. She fled, retracing her route, and did not stop running until she topped the ridge. Then she wiped her eyes on her skirt, and watched the villa roof collapse inward in a cloud of black dust. A vagrant breeze plucked at the roiling mass, and scattered it eastward across the island's spine.

She heard no one approach her vantage, so when something soft, warm and velvety nudged the back of her neck, she leaped up. "Gustave!" she squealed. The donkey, cautiously assuming her sudden move as rejection, skittered away, then turned his back on her as if insulted—but nonetheless rolled one large, brown eye in her direction, on principle. When she knelt and encircled his neck with her arms, kissed his forehead and scratched his ears, he relented slightly, and his nuzzling almost pushed her over.

"How did you find me?" she asked. Of course, he might not have told her, even if he had suddenly acquired the gift of speech. Donkeys had few advantages over people—else they would hold reins and ride, and people would bear donkeys' burdens for them—so those few tricks of their equine trade were best left unmentioned.

Even without halter or lead (Gustave had rid himself of those early on) she had no difficulty getting him to follow her to the boat, or to climb awkwardly aboard, where he stood expectantly by the sternmost thwart, beneath which were his bags of tender, sweet, and flavorful grain.

By the time Pierrette reached her boat—several hours after the terrible events of the day, or so it felt—a vast swath of ashy darkness lay across several hills and fields. By the time she had raised sail and pushed off, it seemed no larger. In truth it was not, for there had not been much evil in her even by King Minho's severe definition, except the blind pride she had exhibited when she instructed Bellagos to seek not a mythic death, but a long life, in the Fortunate Isles.

Part Four ~ A New Day

Pierette's Journal

Now I have most of the answers I need to decide, and to act. I cannot discover the others except through the consequences of my action. The clues were there all along. Minho pulled his kingdom out of the stream of time, but not (entirely) from the realm of causality, of consequence, and as long as the Isles remain accessible from and to the mundane realm, they cannot be entirely free of its constraints. Thus Minho's strict prohibitions against change, innovation, and above all, consumption, are not results of his spell—they are the spell, or are at least an essential axiom within it.

I only require to discover just what those constraints are. What are the bonds Minho has been afraid to break, that keep his kingdom from drifting entirely away, but also threaten to pull it back to its point of origin, and its destruction—at the very moment it was saved. This much I now understand: every change, as when I ate the baker's bread or defecated beneath a bush, has weakened Minho's spell. How has he dared allow me the freedom of his kingdom? Surely he has felt the ripples and snags I have caused in the fabric of his creation. There can be only one conclusion: that while I have been dawdling about, temporizing, unable to decide, he has been working to make final and complete the separation of his kingdom—while I am still in it.

Once entirely outside the frame of reality that encompasses both worlds I know and have experienced, Minho's spell will be unrestrained by consequences: consumption and change, defecation and innovation, will not affect it. Minho's power will be absolute, and mine, based in an Otherworld no longer accessible to me, will be gone. I will be bride or slave, at his wish, but the consequence to me will be as nothing when weighed against the suffering the world has endured, and will forever endure.

The terrible initial spell that caused the Black Time did not truly break the Wheel. It weakened it, and made the route from past to future along its rim impassible, but the Wheel of Time is not broken. It has stretched. Just as the universe expands to fill the ken of questing eyes and hearts, so time stretches backward and forward to the limits of speculation, for the circle unbroken is not, as the ancients had it, infinitely recursive, a constraint upon time, but is infinite.

I surmised that the event that caused the Black Time would not be found within its devastation, but I underestimated the stretching of the wheel. No primitive shaman of the hunter Aam's era uttered that spell, for Aam's remote past did not yet exist. The originator of that cold and final Hell is here, in these so-called Fortunate Isles, and his name is . . . Minho.

Chapter 32 ∾ The Fall of the Kingdom

Pierrette carefully wrapped her journal in oiled cloth and returned it to her small watertight chest. She was a day short of her exile's end, but there was nothing left for her to see. The central island lay ahead, and she was approaching it opposite her original landing place. Was there somewhere she could go ashore unseen?

She could not dismiss that last sight of Kraton's island, that vision of black despair. Horrified, she realized that she had seen it before, repeatedly, beginning the first time she had eaten a red amanita mushroom and a pinch of nightshade beside the sacred pool. It was the Black Time, the end of the world and the beginning, which she had long foreseen. Like the universe in Minho's water-sphere, it was a microcosm, a miniature, but not a false beginning or end. Viewing it, she at last understood the full enormity of Minho's crime.

He was the sorcerer whose spell had warped and distorted the ever-turning Wheel of Time. He was the usurper who had taken goodness from the world and hoarded it, upsetting the balance and giving rise to the Eater of Gods—whose advantage was ever so slight, but which made him unstoppable. Minho's magic, his overweening pride and self-importance, had caused the distortion of all magics, had destroyed the pristine beauty of the sacred groves, the elusive beauty of nymphs and dryads, the wisdom of centaurs and small sylvan godlets. His twin was not the only greedy one. Just as Minos had sucked the material wealth of his kingdom, so Minho had done with the awe and wonder, the mysteries, the elusive joy of discovery. Love him? Pierrette was surprised, upon reflection, to realize that her feeling for him fell short of outright hatred. Now the puzzle was solved. She knew what she must do, to obey the goddess *Ma*, and she felt no qualms about doing it. No qualms at all.

Once again wearing her rough-and-simple boy's clothing, Pierrette steered her boat close along the shore of the palace island. There had to be a sea entrance to Minho's archives, because in the bard's tale the king had rested the miniature simulacrum of his land in a tidal pool. There were many niches in the rock, with overhangs that blocked the bright moonlight. The darknesses looked like the entrances of caves, but on close inspection, all turned out to be only shadows.

The night was half gone. Pierrette had no time to waste. She had hoped to find another entrance, because she had no idea what kind of reception she would get at the palace, a day early. With a sigh of resignation, she tugged on the steering oar and, shortly, felt her boat's prow grind against rock beneath an overhang that would conceal it from sight except from the sea. "Stay aboard and wait for me," she commanded Gustave. Then she began the long climb to the palace. There was no obvious trail, so she tramped over the lovely blossoms that turned their tiny white faces toward the moon. It was a long climb. She was out of breath when she reached the top.

Edging around to the portico and the entrance, she pushed on the great door, which swung wide on silent hinges. Only then did she hear the clipping of hard hooves on the tiles. Gustave had not obeyed. She sighed. "Very well then, you may come with me, but if you leave turds on the carpets or eat the lace from the draperies, blame only yourself if someone beats you." No one was about. She made her way toward Minho's chambers; the secret stairway to his archives would not be anywhere distant or inconvenient for him. She listened at the door. There was no sound—but then, she hadn't expected there to be: surely, fastidious Minho's great spell precluded such prosaic and annoying trivia as snores. She couldn't imagine him snoring as her father did, or ibn Saul.

That door also opened easily. A single lamp glowed warmly upon the wall. Minho's great bed, with a coverlet of white fur, was empty. Truly, the task he had set himself must be an arduous one, if he found no time to sleep at night. She examined the walls for any hint of a crack or a protrusion that might hide a secret latch, but she found nothing. She pulled back a rug, hoping to find a trapdoor in the floor, but saw only smooth, unbroken tiles.

At the far end of the chamber was another door. Heavy bronze brackets were mounted to its casing, and a thick oaken bar stood next to it, but it, too, opened easily at her touch. She gasped, amazed. This was no man's room; the white marble walls were streaked with palest rose, like a hint of sunrise on a clear morning. The translucent floor was shot with glimmering gold. Pierrette suspected it was not marble, but hard, fine quartzite—and that the gold was real.

Looking for a second exit from the room, Pierrette found another chamber, hung with women's clothing in the Cretan style—skirts and dresses designed to leave the breasts bare, and sheer capes that would neither warm nor conceal. Pierrette, in her leather trousers, felt like an invader in that place.

The bed, centerpiece of the frilly chamber, was large enough for several people to sleep comfortably—or for two to frolic in. Curtains of sheerest diaphane were drawn back from a window . . . but no, it was not a window at all! It was hard, flat, and painted with a scene of sheep grazing on a hillside of impossible pink flowers. Though this room was not at all to her taste (which was simple), she knew that it was intended for her. It was more than a bedroom; with its false window, it was a prison. She was sure that the clothing in the small room—nothing she would dream of wearing—would all fit her to perfection.

She heard a noise from beyond the door. The skin on her arms and back tightened, and goosebumps formed. Now that she understood what the room was, she was afraid that she might be caught in it. Someone could shut the door and place the bar in its cradles. Her fear of discovery was drowned in her terror of being trapped. She exited into Minho's own room.

The noisemaker was Hatiphas. "You again! You aren't supposed to return until dawn. What are you doing here? Snooping? What are you looking for?" Thankfully, Gustave was not within his line of vision.

"Where is Minho? Where is his secret door?"

"If I knew, would I tell you? The king is engaged upon a vital task. Why would I allow you to disturb him? You, of all people?"

"Why not me? Is it because his task concerns me? Is it because I've given him sixteen days to prepare himself to confront me? Let Minho decide for himself. Where?"

Hatiphas laughed snidely. "Look all you wish. You cannot get there from here. You will not find him until he is ready to be found—until he is ready to put you in your proper place, which is . . . there." He nodded toward the pink-and-white prison, then departed.

Pierrette looked around herself. The entrance to Minho's secret place had to be here, in the palace, in Minho's own suite. The fibrous, linty dust on his kilt, that day on the balcony, would not still have clung to him if he had traveled any great distance outside where there had been a breeze. Dust. Lint-laden dust. Pierrette threw back the coverlet on Minho's great bed. Had the scraping sound she had heard, blindfolded, been the noise of the bed being pulled aside? On her knees and elbows, she peered underneath. Was there a faint shadow on the tiles, there? There was plenty of dust.

She tried to push the huge bed aside. It would not budge. Disheartened, she looked toward the door. Hatiphas *knew* where the secret entrance was. Would anyone else know? A servant? The dust under the bed was not so thick that it had never been swept. But who would have swept it? Not Minho himself.

The image of a delicate, youthful face arose before her eyes: Neheresta would know. With all her years, she would know everyone in the palace and, likely, whose chore it was to tidy the king's chamber. Where would she be? Pierrette reviewed what she knew of the palace. She did not think there was an understory beneath her feet. Where would servants live?

The levels of the palace were successively lower, following the slope. Surely the kitchens were adjacent to the large hall, and the cooks' rooms not much further away. The quarters for domestics would also be close to their work. She looked both ways down the hall outside Minho's door. One led past the room where she had slept, and the hallway seemed to continue for a long distance. The corridor to her right was shorter, turning a corner only a few doors past where she stood. That way: ordinary residents could expect to wait for a servant to trudge the long hall, bringing an extra pillow, but it would not do for

Minho to have to wait for anything. The domestics quarters would be close at hand.

Just around the corner, dozens of small, unimpressive wooden doors lined the hallway. She had no time to examine each room. She shrugged. What did she care whom she disturbed? "Neheresta!" she cried out. "Neheresta!" From several doorways she heard grumbles and the tossing of bedclothes. Some distance down the hall, she saw the ancient girl emerge.

"What is it? Why are you calling me?" Neheresta, Pierrette observed, did not look well. Her hair was tangled, her hands trembled, and . . . were those the marks of a whip, on her shoulders? She offered no explanation, so Pierrette did not pursue that.

"Neheresta, you must help me. I must find Minho. Who here knows the way to his hidden archives?"

"Who would dare tell you? Who would risk being banished to a salt mine or a desolate orchard on the slopes of an outermost island?"

"You do know, don't you? Please, tell me."

"Hatiphas will punish me."

"How can you speak of punishment? Isn't your every day punishment enough? How long can you endure your own life, such as it is?" Then Pierrette had an idea. There was a word in the Minoan tongue for what the Celts and Romans called *anima*. Soul. Where a word existed in a language, a concept did also. "Do you have a soul, Neheresta? Do you believe that you do?"

"Of course I do. Doesn't everyone? What does that have to do with anything?"

"*That* is your only escape from the endless

torment of your pointless life. It is the only way you will ever grow up, to know the joys of adulthood."

"Do I understand what you are saying? That the only way I will ever be free is to die? To be reborn, somewhere else, some other time, and not remember who I am? How will I know I might be better off?"

"You can't. In the real world, no one ever can. But if you don't help me, Minho's kingdom will endure exactly as it is, forever. Never again will you see a new face like mine—he will break the last ties that hold these islands in this world. Never again will you know a visitor from the outside, and your last chance for freedom will be gone."

What was Neheresta thinking? Was she remembering the terrible indignities Hatiphas had inflicted upon her, and contemplating a thousand additional lifetimes of such insults to her body, her dignity, her very . . . soul? Was she considering the risk not of risking all for a matter of philosophy, but of failing to do so?

Pierrette stood silent, almost seeing the thoughts that rushed through Neheresta's mind. At last, the girl spoke. "You can't get there from here," she said.

"That's what Hatiphas said. What does it mean?"

"I don't know. That is what the king says also."

"Minho said that? Now I think I understand. . . ." Pierrette turned back the way she had come. Now she knew why she had felt a chill the last time she had entered Minho's sanctum. Now she also knew what his muttered words on that occasion had been.

"Let me come with you," said Neheresta.

Pierrette slowly shook her head. "I'm sorry.

Minho was right. *You* can't get there from here. But I can get there from . . . *there*." Not from this palace, but through . . . the Otherworld. "Thank you. You have told me what I need to know. There isn't much time, but I might yet prevail."

Softly, Pierrette murmured the words of the great, ancient spell. "*Mondradd in Mon* . . ." Then she looked around herself; nothing seemed to change. It was the same plain, unadorned hallway as before.

"What strange words are those?"

The unfamiliar voice sounded harsh and old. She spun around. There stood an ancient hag with thin, bedraggled hair and yellowed eyes. Her wrinkled breasts hung like empty sacks upon her bony chest. But that dress she wore was . . . Neheresta's. And what was that thin, hazy line, like a jellyfish's tendril, that stretched from her brow and away into the murk of the hallway? Where had she seen something like that before?

Then Pierrette remembered: when first she had used the spell *Mondradd in Mon*, such a tendril had linked her wandering soul to the inert body that rested beside the spring in the sacred grove. Later, more experienced with magic, she had learned how to voyage in the Otherworld without leaving her body behind, but never without a certain anxiety that should she be trapped there, her stiff, cold corpse would be found where she had left it, on the cold, foggy hillside of Sainte Baume, or on a marble floor in the ancient Roman baths of Aquae Sextiae.

The tendril linked Neheresta—for indeed, the hag was none other—to her own origins in the remote past, to the devastating eruption of Thera that had put an end to the great age of the Minoan Sea Kings. What would occur if Minho succeeded in tearing his land entirely away from the world of Time? Without the link to her faraway origins, would Neheresta be no longer an ancient girl, but . . . an immortal hag, forever locked into the ancient, hideous body that Pierrette saw, there in the Otherworld?

Suddenly, Pierrette was sure of it. In the Otherworld, things were as they were, not as they might seem. No deception was possible, and the inhabitants of Minho's realm would forever, day and night, be forced to endure themselves not as his spell had made them seem, but as they really were: warped, wizened, corrupted ancients bearing all the scars and ugliness that were part and parcel of their unnatural estate. What choice, given one, would they make? Would they choose as Neheresta had done, to take their chances, as all mortals did, that indeed what lay beyond this life was at least no worse than what they faced here? But they would have no choice. They had had none when Minho had brought them to this pass, and they would have none now. Either she would stop Minho, or he would defeat her. The rest would suffer one fate or the other, and there was no help for it.

"Wait here. Don't try to follow me," she said, looking away, afraid that Neheresta would see the revulsion in her eyes. She turned back the way she had come.

Busy Hatiphas pattered down the hallway toward her. Pierrette stepped into the shadow of an ornate doorway, and the vizier rushed by, trailing a milky, elusive tendril. The brief glimpse Pierrette had of his face showed that he too was raddled, wrinkled, and ancient—far more so than before. Then, to her horror, she saw his thread snap. The broken ends recoiled, one toward Hatiphas, and the other away, twisting and coiling, returning to its origin. Hatiphas turned the corner, and Pierrette was not able to ascertain more.

In Minho's bedchamber, she looked around. Where was the entrance? It had to be here, in this room. She had a brief vision of herself, a small child, crawling out of the dark space between the planks of the floor and the bedrock underlying her father's house, where he had stored her mother's powders and potions—and where she went to play, and secretly to experiment with them. She imagined herself emerging with dust clinging to her clothing, linty dust just like that which had clung to Minho—dust that had sifted between the boards of the floor, or between the similar boards that supported Minho's thick, soft mattress . . .

She rushed to the bed, and began to push. Minho had broken Hatiphas from his past, his roots and origin. That was how he intended to accomplish his end: he would break all his people away, every thread and tendril, and there would be nothing left to hold them here. Desperately, she shoved at the heavy bed. Neheresta's link had been intact. Minho must be choosing first those people closest to him. Did that mean she still had time to stop him?

"Gustave, come here!" She tied two corners of a silky coverlet together, and dropped the circlet over a bedpost. She lowered the remaining bight around Gustave's neck, and held it against his chest. "Now pull!" she commanded. The cloth tautened across the donkey's breast, and his sharp hooves scraped and scrabbled on the floor tiles.

Pierrette leaned against the other bedpost and pushed again. The bed moved. Once moving, it slid across the slick marble floor, revealing the darkness of a rough stone staircase that had not been apparent before, when Pierrette had peered at the dust beneath the bed. She stepped down the first riser and then the next . . .

The rough stone walls on either side were irregular. This was a native cleft in the rock, not a carved passageway. This, she realized, was the entrance to a sanctum already ancient long before the first rude shrine had risen on the site of Minho's palace. She reached the bottom of the stairs. She felt Gustave's warm breath against her hand. She feared she was leading him into danger unnecessarily—but what security was there for him anywhere in this unnatural land? Would he choose to be the only immortal donkey in a world where even the nicest treats tasted like sand? He was just as well off with her as elsewhere.

Three passages loomed darkly ahead of her, in the failing light from above. Wasn't there less dust on the stony floor to the left? She turned into the darkness, feeling her way ahead with her toes. The floor was gritty, as it had been before. As she progressed, the darkness remained incomplete; ahead was a sickly light . . . and ahead was Minho. He hunched over a globe that glowed like fungi in a cave or the phosphorescence of a ship's wake at night. It was the crystalline microcosm that contained the sorcerer-king's realm. Along one rough-hewn wall were the sagging shelves lined with scrolls. Before them stood a heavy table, old and battered, with green mold staining the lower portions of its legs, with more scrolls scattered across its surface. On a wall above the table, no longer obscured by darkness, hung a massive, double-bladed bronze axe—the *labrys*, emblem of the Minoan kings, stolen from the even more ancient rulers of the land, who had first occupied these subterranean chambers and worshipped here—and who were women. Women. And did they worship a god? Of course not. This had been a goddess's sanctuary.

Without a sound, she crept forward. Between her and the king was a rough stone construction, the low wall of the ancient well. Somewhere deep within her was a small child, crying, not wanting to give up her dreams. She wanted Minho to say something, do something, to relieve her from making a choice. Again she crept forward. Minho, concentrating on his task, seemed unaware of her approach. Almost leaning over his shoulder, Pierrette observed what he was doing. His hands were within the glowing sphere. Through some trick, some crystalline distortion of perspectives, his forearms seemed to diminish in girth, to stretch and elongate until the tiny hands at the ends of them seemed miles and miles away, reaching downward into his miniature kingdom.

What was he doing? She crept closer. Absorbed in his task, he remained unaware of her presence. As she peered over his shoulder, into the microcosm, she felt a wave of giddy nausea, a disorientation, as her perspectives shifted from without to within the tiny scene. She now saw where she "was." Her vantage was a gull's, or a magpie's, hovering unseen over the city where she had met the Hermit. And there he was: he was not speaking with a few women at the fountain. He stood atop a two-story building that fronted on a broad public square, and the crowd he addressed surely numbered in the thousands. Pierrette could not hear his words, but the multitude surely did. Every eye in the plaza was upon him as he spoke—and as he raised a gleaming object high over his head.

It was a cross, a golden cross, like the one she had given him, but much larger, as tall as a seven-year-old boy. Was it the same cross, expanded by a trick of distorted perspective, or a replica in wood, leaved in thin gold? Who could say? As the Hermit raised it, she heard an angry grunt. Minho also had seen what she saw. What was to her a muffled sound must have resonated like the rumble of thunder within the microcosm, because the rapt faces of the crowd—and the Hermit's own eyes—lifted upward, to what was, from their low vantage, still a clear blue, cloudless sky.

Minho's hand clenched into a fist, a fist raised as if to crush an insect. What did the crowd below see? They saw something: many fell to their knees, their faces tight masks of terror; others covered their eyes, or looked to the Hermit to save them. The Hermit also saw. He raised the cross again, holding it up over his head. His defiant eyes seemed to look right at her—or at Minho.

"No!" She reached within the tiny scene. Her

hand seemed to attenuate as if with distance, and she grasped Minho's wrist. "Stop!"

He gasped, and turned. He saw her. "What are you . . . how did you . . ." His hand and hers both lifted from the water-sphere, and became ordinary, though she still grasped his wrist.

"You were going to kill him," she spat. "You would have crushed them all!"

"He betrayed me! Didn't you see it? A cross! A gold, Christian cross! He dared!"

"You can't destroy him for that, or a thousand of your own people, just for listening to him."

"My own people? No longer. They have become Christians. Traitors. I'll not have them in my kingdom."

"Then you'd better crush me first. Where do you think he got that cross? How did he know to abandon his useless hammer, a forgotten symbol, and pick up the emblem of Christianity today? I gave him that cross."

"Then you've sealed their fate yourself. They will all die."

"Why? Must everyone worship you? You're not a god."

His expression turned sly and mean. How had she ever thought him otherwise? "I will be," he said.

"What do you mean?" He was so confident. Pierrette felt sick with terror.

"You interrupted me. You were supposed to stay away another day. I would have been finished, then. But I forgive you. Now you can watch as I sever the last ties that bind my kingdom to the world. We'll drift alone in a universe of my own."

He laughed harshly. "Already I have the powers of a god. Life? Death? Mine, to decide. In a universe where there are no kingdoms but mine, no rulers but me—I will indeed be not just a god, but God. And I will have no son. The Hermit and his foolish followers will have none other to worship."

"You're mad! Don't you understand that you've already unbalanced everything? You banished age, death, and pain from your realm, and gave the Eater of Gods a pretext to exist, and gave him an undefeatable advantage in the world outside. You can't just sail away, now, and leave everything else to him! You must return to the world, to set things right."

"I'll hardly do that. When I and my kingdom are gone, what will I care what happens there? It won't happen in *my* universe."

"No! You can't do that!"

"Will you stop me? Here. I'll show you . . ." Again, his hands reached within the sphere. Again, they attenuated, and stretched, reaching for . . . for a thread. The roof of the miniature palace was as immaterial as vapor, no barrier to sight or to Minho's hands. With a twist of distorted wrists, the sorcerer-king broke the tendril that linked a tiny harpist to his origins. Then he reached for another, a small figure still standing in the gloomy hallway where Pierrette had left her. Neheresta.

Why her? Why had Minho chosen her? She was a servant, unimportant, insignificant. Hatiphas hadn't even known her name. At that precise moment, Pierrette's last doubt fell away. Minho chose Neheresta because he knew. He had been there, a parasite in her old, jaded mind, using her—and using Pierrette.

"No!" Pierrette gasped. Minho's shoulders stiffened, and he turned. His handsome face was ugly now, twisted with the selfish destruction he had wrought upon those who trusted him, who were doomed to follow him, to serve him and his egotism forever. This was no longer the dark, charming king who had wooed her with sweet words and smiles. Anger twisted his features.

Someone gasped. The king turned toward the sound. His hands withdrew from the water-sphere, and Neheresta was safe, for the moment. There stood Hatiphas. Pierrette recognized him by his clothing, but little else was the same, except his knife-sharp nose. His face sagged and wrinkled as if he were truly ancient, as old as all the years he had lived. His skin hung in folds on his skeletal frame, raddled with angry red sores, mottled yellow, white, and brown. His hands were bony claws, his fingernails yellow, and almost as long as his fingers, like the nails of a corpse, that had continued to grow after death, in its sepulcher.

"You did this to me," he croaked. "You made me like this!"

"I did? No, you fool. You did it yourself, by choosing to live, when you could have died. I did not do that to you. Time did it."

"You're lying! I was not . . . like this . . . until now. It's your fault—what you're doing here."

"You dare blame me? Better you get on your knees and thank me for the two thousand years I've labored, and struggled, to maintain your illusion of youth and vitality, while in truth you aged and shriveled, and wasted away. Now you see what you truly are—and have been all along. You blame me for that?"

"It's true? This is . . . me?" Hatiphas held one hideously clawed, contorted hand in front of his face. "Then he was right! I argued with him, because I didn't want to believe him, but he was right. He was telling the truth."

"Who is this that you're babbling about?" snarled Minho.

Hatiphas's rheumy, ancient eyes became evasive and cunning. His claw reached to his neck, and lifted a thong over his head. On the thin leather dangled . . .

"My egg!" Pierrette gasped. Her own hand crept to her pouch, squeezing it, and something shattered within it. Her hand came away wet and slippery with oil, and the reek of distilled flowers filled her nostrils. It was not a crystal serpent's egg that had shattered.

"This is who," grated Hatiphas, as he swung the glowing serpent's egg by its thong and threw it against the stone wall. It shattered noisily, as if it had been much larger than it seemed, and made of brittle glass.

Minho's eyes strayed to the wall, where greasy black smoke now arose, shot through with an evil reddish light. Something even darker than the smoke loomed up, inflating like a pig's-bladder football, taking form—human form. Cunotar the Druid stepped forth. He wore the branching antlers and fur-covered deerskins of Cernunnos, the horned god, and he held his long, bloodied Gallic sword in his hand. His eyes met Pierrette's.

"Now it's up to you," he said. "Only you can free my soul to wander." He clutched his side. Blood trickled between his fingers.

"Me? What must I do? What can I do?" Behind Cunotar, Pierrette saw something move—something dove-brown and white, with large ears. But it was only Gustave, who had followed her down the long, dark stairs.

"You've done enough!" spat Minho. "Did you bring *him* too? Who—and what—is he?"

"He is the druid Cunotar," she said with a tremor in her voice.

Minho's eyes now filled with panicky brightness. "Have you gone mad? Or were you sent here to destroy me? How did you know, to do that?"

"To do what?" Pierrette asked, feigning innocence.

"A sorcerer! You brought another sorcerer here! There can be but one of us. And that Christian cross! Do you mean to destroy my spell?"

"Can I do that? What else must I do to bring that about? Tell me, and I will do it."

His eyes gleamed with mad and angry light. "Your goddess sent you, didn't she? But she failed to tell you everything you must know—that a foreign sorcerer alone is not enough."

"She did not need to tell me. I kept the druid Cunotar entrapped in my jewel because I had no other way to confine him, and I dared not let him loose upon the world, or leave him where some innocent might accidentally free him from his prison. But I don't believe in coincidence: something greater than gods, goddesses, or sorcerer-kings made it inevitable that I would carry Cunotar here . . ."

"Something greater? I think not, because it is not enough. I will destroy him."

Cunotar grinned broadly and raised his sword. "Then let's have at it, king. I've blood enough in me to last a while." His gaze fell on Pierrette. "Now's the time, little masc. Do what you must."

"I don't know what to do!" she cried out. Did everyone know but her?

"You had three things in your pouch, with your flints and coins," said Cunotar. "Three. I spent enough time in there with the other two."

"Three things?" What was he talking about? Why wouldn't he say? Of course—he didn't want Minho to know, because . . . because he could still stop her? Then she knew what it was. There were three things Minho had forbidden: other sorcerers, anything Christian, and . . . and iron. She groped in her oily pouch among the shards of the broken vial, and felt the heaviness of her mother's ring. Now what was she to do with it?

Hatiphas had edged away from Cunotar, and now stood near Pierrette. "Give it to me," he whispered. "I know what to do." Could she trust him? His sense of betrayal by Minho seemed genuine enough. She had little choice. She unobtrusively slipped the ring into his clawed hand. He edged away, and toward . . . of course! The well. The entrance to a realm more ancient than this one, where beat the fiery heart of a deity Minho had not yet banished—a female deity, indeed, whose volcanic shrine this had been, long before the sorcerer-king had usurped it. Despite his crippled and hunched condition, Hatiphas made good time, and from the lip of the well he cast her a smile—

in fact, an ugly grimace, marred by gaps between his eroded yellow teeth.

Minho had not seen the exchange, but he sensed something, and now lunged toward Hatiphas. The vizier's smile encompassed his erstwhile master now, and he held the ring over the well, tauntingly. Then, just as Minho would reach him, and knock him aside, he dropped the ring. Even over the sounds of the scuffle, Pierrette heard the clink and tinkle as it tumbled downward, bouncing off the hard, ancient lava of the well shaft.

Then several things happened all at once, and Pierrette had no clear image of any of them. Cunotar was coming for Minho, Hatiphas was scuttling away from him, and Gustave, panicked by all the sudden action, lashed out with his hooves, catching the king in the thigh. Minho staggered aside, and fell against the pedestal holding his water-sphere. The orb teetered, then fell sideways toward the floor. The entire cavern shook! Stone fell from the ceiling's darkness above with resounding crashes. The lamp flickered and went out, but a new glow illuminated everything: the fiery light of hot lava bubbling up from the well, and oozing over its edge. The cavern floor tilted, and Pierrette fell sideways, which had become down. Scrolls poured from the shelves as the wall that held them became a ceiling. The enormous bronze axe, the *labrys*, tumbled through the air. Minho snatched it up.

"You!" he snarled, raising it high. Pierrette tried desperately to scramble away. "You did this!"

A shadow interposed itself between her and the king: Cunotar. The druid warrior's sword caught the axe haft and hung there. "Now let's fight, king!" he bellowed, laughing. "Let's trade a few blows before my soul flees this body and the opportunity's lost. Who knows whether I'll be a warrior in my next life?"

Even as he leaped back and wrenched his sword free, he said to Pierrette: "Flee, little witch. Leave before it's too late."

Too late?

"Come," said Hatiphas. "There's a way out, a tunnel. There's not much time." She hesitated. "Look there," he said, pointing. There: the water-sphere lay on the floor, upright again—and the floor of the cavern was again down, and no longer trembled. Within the sphere, she saw the tiny kingdom as a whole, its rings of islands. From the central island, the very isle beneath which lay this cavern, rose a great column of smoke, and tiny sparks of glowing white, yellow, and crimson that flung themselves outward from the black billows. On all the other islands, smaller columns of smoke also rose, as fires swept away forests, fields, and villages.

"It has begun," cried Hatiphas. "You must go."

"What has begun?"

"The end. The eruption that will destroy us."

Then she understood. She understood many things, but she could not put them all together, not then. She glanced again at the microcosm. There, atop the central island where Minho's palace had stood only minutes before, rose a great black cone of ash and glowing melted rock. From its peak spewed roiling clouds of black and sickly yellow smoke, shot through with flying chunks of glowing red lava, with white-hot gobbets that flew outward and away, and started fires wherever they landed.

She heard the clank and clatter of weapons, and saw that Minho and Cunotar fought on. Neither seemed to have the advantage. Could the dying druid hold out long enough, until it was too late for Minho to save anything? She could only hope so. She had seen what Minho could do, when he reached inside his water-sphere, and feared he might yet be able to quench the flames. She felt Hatiphas tugging at her arm. "Gustave!" she cried, and was rewarded with an alarmed bray. "He's already ahead of us," said Hatiphas. "Hurry!" He pulled her through a passage she had not seen before, hidden in shadows, a tunnel whose stone walls glowed dull red. Along the floor behind them flowed a sluggish mass, lava, its surface cracked and black, but glowing from within with deadly heat.

Acrid smoke swirled around her. The earth itself groaned and heaved, above and below. She intermittently heard the clatter of Gustave's hooves ahead, and the fall of rocks from above. She staggered on, Hatiphas half dragging her. With her eyes blurred with tears, Pierrette hardly noticed when they emerged in the light of day, on the rocky, wave-lapped shore, not more than two hundred paces from her boat.

Pierrette wiped her eyes. What great, dark clouds were those, looming in the gaps beyond the outer ring of islands? Pierrette rushed to her boat; if a storm were rising, she might not be able to get away in time. She scrambled down the sharp rocks, and tumbled into her little craft. The once-smooth water rose and fell rhythmically, and the boat's masthead thumped and scraped against the over-hang. Gustave already stood braced in the bow, his brown eyes wide, the whites of them yellow in the glow of lava from above.

"Hatiphas," Pierrette shouted over the rumble and roar. The vizier still stood on the shore. "Get aboard!"

He shook his head. "I'm already lost. Minho has trapped me here with him. Cunotar's soul can still fly free—wherever it will end up, and so will the others. Perhaps the new-made Christians' souls will find their Heaven as well . . . but mine? The cord has been cut. I am what I am—what you see. So will I remain.

"But . . ."

"It must be. Minho was right. I chose, long ago. I chose long life, and this hideous form is what I got. I chose to serve Minho, and I'll still serve him, in whatever Hell remains of his kingdom. But you must be beyond the furthest islet before all is lost. Hurry!"

"Good-bye!" she shouted over the crash of rocks, the roar of the fiery spume. But Hatiphas was already gone—back into the tunnel, or crushed by a bolt of flaming lava. She would never know. Likely, it would be the same, one way or another, in the end.

In the trough of one wave she pushed desper-ately against the rock, and the boat edged outward, only to be pushed back on the next crest. The mast flexed ominously between solid rock above, the buoyancy of the sea below. Again, she pushed, and on the next crest the masthead slipped from beneath the rock.

The contrary wind blew first from one quarter and then from another. Pierrette raised the yard and sail with little hope that the fickle air would favor her. She unshipped the heavy steering oar and used it like a paddle. Slowly, the clumsy boat moved away from the sharp, black rocks of the shore.

On the high ground above, where the walls of the cavern had fallen away down the slope, amid the growing thunder of the eruption, she heard bellows and shouts of rage. By some trick of the heat-distorted air, she saw Minho raising the great axe, and there, facing him, was Cunotar, wielding the sword that had pierced his guts and was still killing him. He showed no sign of being weakened by his ancient wound. He parried the broad, swinging blows of the *labrys*, and the serpent tongue of his sword darted in and out. Was that blood from Minho's injuries or his own, that spattered the rocks, or was it molten lava? Pierrette could not tell. Neither apparition seemed to have the advantage of the other.

Pierrette did not dare linger. Now out of the wind shadow of the shore, her sail filled. She remounted the steering oar and set her course toward the gap between two inner islands. It would not be easy to get away in time; the route to the open sea was circuitous, and already glowing chunks of pyroclastic rock were screaming down from above, splashing into the sea around her, raising billows of steam. If one of those struck her boat, it would shatter it.

The wind held steady. In a while, Pierrette dared to look back. There was Minho, a giant astride the ruins of his palace, and there was Cunotar, fallen upon his knees, his sword a broken stub. The great battle-axe swung down in a sweeping arc, and buried itself in Cunotar's head. Its weight and momentum carried it through the druid's body, and it only came to rest halfway down his chest. Slowly, the two halves of his upper body sagging to either side, he tumbled over, out of Pierrette's sight.

Had Minho won? What would happen now? Was he really as huge as he seemed? The Otherworld, Pierrette knew, distorted such things—and she had not yet uttered the spell that would bring her back from it. Could he stride across the channels between his islands, and confront the Hermit, step on him and crush him like an ant beneath his foot? Could he still be victorious—and drag Pierrette with him into some impossible netherland, where she would never again see Anselm, or Father Otho, or even Magister ibn Saul?

But the great black clouds billowed ever larger above their growing peak. The heavy, sulfurous yellow smoke drifted ever more thickly down the flanks of the island, and spread like a heavy blanket across the water. Surely Minho could not prevail against that with a battle-axe.

Either way, there was nothing Pierrette could do. Silently urging the winds to cooperate, to push her ahead and away, she trimmed her sail as she rounded the first headland and emerged in the outer channel. Fiery projectiles still fell all around, undiminished by her greater distance. Now, when she looked back, the black conical peak jutted high above where Minho's palace had stood. Of the sorcerer-king, there was no sign.

One desperate hour passed thus amid the hail

of fire, and then another. A rain of glowing gobbets splashed into the bilge, sizzling, burrowing into the moist wood. Pierrette slopped salt water on them from her cedar bucket. Some fiery morsels exploded when the cold water touched them, pelting her with jagged, stinging bits. She threw bucket after bucket of water on the sail, which was already riddled with black-edged holes. If the wind strengthened, the weakened cloth would be torn to shreds.

At last, Pierrette could see the gleam of the open sea ahead. Amazed, she saw what she had thought from a distance were black storm clouds; they were much more solid. Rising up from the sea were great cliffs, cliffs that were not a part of the Fortunate Isles. Furthermore, they were familiar precipices; she had sailed past them, and had even stood upon them, at Raz Point: the cliffs of the Armorican shore.

When the water-sphere and Minho's miniature kingdom had fallen from its pedestal to the floor (and when the cavern below the palace had turned topsy-turvy) the entire kingdom had been moved. Just as Minho had once lifted his kingdom from the microcosm and floated it in a tidal pool to protect it from the cataclysms that destroyed ancient Thera, so the fall to the cavern floor had nudged Minho's floating realm toward the shore.

Now she stared in horror. The beaches nestled between the cliffs were not warm and sandy any more: they were black, and they pulsed with a horrid semblance of life. All of the shadows, all the stinks, corruptions, aches, pains, and annoyances of the world beyond, declared evil by Minho and banished from his kingdom, awaited their moment of return. Now Pierrette knew for sure that the sorcerer-king was truly defeated. Now she knew that she indeed had won—but she knew also how much she had lost: the dream that had sustained her through her childhood and youth, the promise that someday she would be queen of the most wondrous realm of all, the Fortunate Isles, and would sit beside the king her lover and laugh, and tease him by calling up a storm.

Her eyes filled with tears—selfish, self-pitying tears—and for long moments she did not realize what would soon happen: the gap between the Fortunate Isles and the shore of Armorica grew ever narrower, and soon the two lands would come together in a clashing and gnashing of rocks only slightly less tumultuous than the spitting, spewing, smoke-and-lava-belching eruption behind her. She, in her tiny boat, could not survive that.

With the strength of desperation, she pulled the sail around and hauled on the steering oar. Evil black clouds scudded across the sky overhead. There was no sun to show her direction, but if the Armorican shore was on her left, and the doomed Isles on her right, then she was headed south— and that was the only direction of possible salvation. South of Raz Point were hundreds of miles of open sea without a reef or skerry.

Pierrette pulled the sheet as tight as she dared, and the little boat jumped ahead. The mast leaned far over, and racing water streamed by scant inches below the wooden rail. Pierrette heard a great roar like the gnashing of demons' teeth or an immense landslide. She hardly dared look back. One glimpse was enough: the Fortunate Isles had come home. The opposing shores had come together with a great crash and rumble, shattering cliffs and promontories into rubble and gravel as they met.

The water caught between them now rose in an enormous wave that made the treacherous tidal bore seem no more than a ripple. Tossing and turning on its great crest were timbers and whole trees torn up and shattered in the cataclysm. Still several miles away, the wave seemed to Pierrette to tower above her mast, to block out half the sky. It seemed to grow even as she watched, coming nearer, travelling much faster than her little boat. She clung to the steering oar and the sheet, gritting her teeth.

It was not a wave like any other wave. As it approached, it did not suck water from ahead and beneath to add to its height and momentum. It was as if it were pouring out of some immense jar—which, in a sense, it was: there was no room for it between the landmasses, so it was pouring southward like slops dumped in the gutter. It had no long, easy leading slope that would lift a boat before it and carry it over its crest unharmed. Instead, it would crash down upon Pierrette's vessel, bludgeoning and shattering it, grinding the fragments apart between the huge thrashing logs and tree trunks it carried.

The roar of its approach was deafening, but Pierrette could not let go to cover her ears. In that final moment, almost too late, when the darkness of its shadow flung itself across the water ahead, she realized what she had forgotten: this was still the Otherworld, and if she died here, she had not the slightest idea of what her ultimate fate—and that of her immortal soul—would be. Desperately, unable to hear her own words over the all-consuming roar, she repeated the spell:

> Mondradd in Mon,
> Borabd orá perdó.
> Merdrabd or vern,
> Arfaht ará camdó.

The tumbling water struck her frail craft with immense force, tearing away the sail and shattering the mast. With a hoarse squeal, Gustave was swept overboard by the flailing sail. The steering oar jerked from Pierrette's hand and spun away. The boat broke apart beneath her, and she was thrust deep under the salty water. Something struck her chest, hard, and she instinctively wrapped her arms around it, clutching it to herself. The impact of the rushing water drove the breath from her lungs, but even as she tumbled deeper and deeper, she stubbornly resisted the urge to fill them.

The silence of the deep was as deafening as the thunder of the wave above. She could hear the tumult recede into the distance. Then suddenly she found herself thrust to the surface, and she drew in a gasp of cold, salty air. She heard a roar, then another, but the brilliant flash of lightning that preceded the second sound told her it was not another wave, but that she had emerged within a storm.

The object she still clung to was her little cedarwood chest. But for its buoyancy she would never have risen to the surface in time, with her lungs empty of air. She was exhausted, and several times opened her eyes suddenly, realizing that she had lost consciousness or had dozed, but she never let go of the box. Though the water was so cold that she could not feel anything below her waist or beyond her shoulders, the sharp, uncomfortable edges of the wood against her breasts assured her that she still held it.

Chapter 33 ～ The Way Home

She slipped between awareness and deathlike sleep. When she heard voices, she tried to wake up, because that was surely a dream, but she continued to hear them. One, deep, booming and male, she recognized. Another was sharper, harsher, but no less familiar. "Pull her up, you great ox!" cried the latter.

"She won't let go of the box," said the other. "I'm afraid I'll break her fingers trying to pry it loose."

"Then bring it aboard," said the harsh, accented voice of Muhammad abd' Ullah ibn Saul.

Pierrette felt strong arms lift her from the water, and at last relinquished her hold on the chest, which fell to the deck, its thump inaudible over the noise of the storm. She opened her mouth to the sweet, pounding raindrops that fell on her face. "She's thirsty! Lovi! Bring fresh water immediately."

"Master ibn Saul?" Pierrette whispered weakly. "And Lovi? What are they doing here?"

"Hush now," said the first voice, the deep one. "You're safe now, and there will be plenty of time for questions when you have recovered."

Yes. Pierrette knew she was now safe. "Gustave!" she muttered.

"He's aboard. With all his braying, we found him long before we found you." Then Pierrette allowed herself to slip into exhausted sleep in the iron-hard arms of Yan Oors.

She awakened to the gentle motion of a large ship quartering the swells on an easy tack. The close, muffled sounds of the water, the creaking of timbers, told her she was belowdecks. The rustle beneath her and the woolly scratchiness above informed her she was in a bunk. She opened her eyes. "Master ibn Saul?" she asked when she saw who sat beside her bed, "what are you doing here?"

"You thought you had me fooled, didn't you?" he replied with a good-natured grin. Pierrette tugged the wooly blanket up to her chin. When they had pulled her from the water, she had been wearing her boy's garb, but someone had removed the wet clothing. Someone now knew she was no boy.

The scholar chuckled. "You are prettier as a girl," he said, "even soaking wet."

"You must have known I was not a boy. Surely Lovi told you, even before we all left Gesocribate."

"Lovi? He still doesn't know. He didn't get close when we pulled you aboard. All he saw was your nose, sticking out of a roll of blankets."

"But . . . I don't understand." Of course Lovi knew she was a girl. "Then what did you mean, that I'd fooled you?"

"You knew all along where those pesky islands were. When you thought Lovi and I had gone, what did you do but buy a boat, and set off in search of our goal? I suspected you would do as much, so as soon as we were out of sight around the headland, I bade the captain put into a little estuary, and sent Lovi back into town to spy on you. The big ugly fellow was there, also, seeking you, but Lovi—quick-thinking lad—threw a grain sack over his head and arms, and subdued him. Later, when he was also sure you were gone, he came with us willingly enough. When you set sail, we followed you at a distance."

"I would have seen you!" Pierrette protested. "The horizon was clear."

Ibn Saul shook his head. "The greater height of our mast allowed our lookout to keep you in sight without your spotting us whenever you looked behind."

Pierrette pondered that for several long moments. "But where were you when I was ashore?" she asked at last. "Did you sail back and forth out there for eighteen days?"

"Ashore? Are you still asleep, and dreaming? You did not go ashore anywhere. When I saw those great volcanic peaks looming up from the empty ocean, where none should be, I knew what they were, but when you sailed into that fog bank, our captain refused to follow you, not knowing what treacherous rocks and shoals they concealed. We did sail back and forth, awaiting your return, but it was only a half day, a morning, really, and there you came again, sailing madly close to the wind with your rail awash, as if a sea serpent or a shipful of pirates were in close pursuit.

"When the storm came up, we lost sight of you, but as luck would have it, we spotted your red sail and broken mast, and hove to on the spot, sending every man aloft to look for you. And we found you, didn't we? For here you are."

"Let me see if I have heard you aright," she said. "You only lost sight of me for a matter of hours? It seemed much longer to me." Seventeen days longer, in fact, though she did not say that.

"From shortly after dawn," he affirmed, "until just into the noonday watch."

Of course, Pierrette realized then: like Anselm's keep, the Fortunate Isles were—had been—outside the stream of time, and all that transpired while she was within the influence of Minho's spell had occurred in a single moment from the perspective of someone outside.

But surely ibn Saul could not have missed seeing the rending clash of Minho's kingdom against the Armorican cliffs. And what of the great wave? Then she remembered: that had occurred not in this world, but in another. Only at the last moment had she remembered to utter her spell. So what had happened to Minho and his kingdom? Were they truly gone, destroyed in the final cataclysm of the eruption, shattered against phantasmic Armorican rocks that remained unbroken here and now? Or, in their final moments, had all those tight-stretched threads and tendrils drawn the Isles back to their origin—and into the midst of the original eruption that by all rights should have destroyed them two thousand years before?

A chill took her. "Shall I get you another blanket?" asked ibn Saul.

"That would be kind," she replied, not because she was cold, but to gain a moment alone to think. If there had been no cataclysm in this world, it could only be because the lattermost case was true: in this one, Minho had never cast his great, arrogant spell. He had not cast it, and thus Thera had not been saved, and the Fortunate Isles had never existed—in this world.

Again, she shuddered. What else was not as she knew it to be? What else was different?

Ibn Saul returned, shook out another blanket, and spread it over her.

"Yan Oors is here, isn't he? I remember him pulling me from the water. I remember his voice."

"He has not left your door since then."

"I wish to speak with him. Bid him come in." Yan Oors needed no bidding. His great shadow filled the doorway, and with a cock of his head he dismissed the scholar. Obviously, Pierrette realized, he no longer pretended to a servant's meekness in the presence of the other man, and did not fear the power of the scholar's spells. That had changed.

"Tell me what happened to the shadows that plagued us all through Armorica," she demanded immediately, when they were alone.

"What shadows are those?"

Then Pierrette knew that the course of history as she knew it had truly changed. "You don't remember the small, ugly wraiths that scurried away under our feet, always going westward?"

Now it was Yan Oors turn to wonder if Pierrette's suffering had affected her mind. "I think you need more rest, before we talk further," he decided. "Your thoughts will be clearer, then."

Pierrette knew otherwise, but there was no point in arguing about it. If the Fortunate Isles had returned to their origin, and were destroyed just as if Minho had never uttered the great spell that broke the ever-turning Wheel of Time and divided the world into separate realms—his, where no evil existed, and the other, where it could not but prevail—then of course there had never been any small shadowy evils rushing westward in search of a long-lost balance. That balance had never been lost.

Pierrette waved Yan Oors away and closed her eyes, pretending to doze. What would this world be like, if evil were truly evenly matched with good? Would either one exist, or would they nullify each other? She had no idea at all what she would find, when this vessel at last put ashore.

Pierrette did not feel well enough to be up and around until the following morning. Then, after breaking her fast with bread baked on the ship's tiny brick hearth, she joined ibn Saul, who was leaning over the rail forward. "I can see we're sailing southward," she remarked. "We must be well past the mouth of the Liger by now—so what is our destination?"

"Ultimately, we are going home—me, to Massalia, and you . . . to Citharista, I presume. I plan to sail up the Garumna as far as possible, then rent a smaller craft, or travel overland on the Via Domitia. Does that coincide with your own desires?"

It did, indeed—but she did not seem as happy about it as ibn Saul thought she should. "I wonder how Master Anselm is doing," she mused, seemingly pensively, but unable to keep a certain amount of tension from her voice.

"Anselm? Unless he's finished the last of that fine Tuscan wine I brought him on my last visit, I'm sure he is making no more complaints than is usual for him."

Pierrette sighed, tremendously relieved—but she would not explain just what, in the scholar's seemingly ordinary remark, had pleased her so much. It was this: Yan Oors did not remember the dark, fleeting shadows, the small evils, because they had never existed. And Anselm was equally a product of the Fortunate Isles—Minho's apprentice, sent out into the world centuries before, but still tied by chains of causality to his place of origin . . . or so she had feared. Yet ibn Saul clearly remembered him, and thus he had not vanished, even the last memory of him. She could only conclude that because the spell that preserved him was separate from Minho's, and because within his keep he was not ever really in this world or the other, his existence was no longer tied to an origin at all. Just as Pierrette's memories of everything that had transpired during her seventeen-day sojourn in Minho's nonexistent kingdom still remained, because she had not been in this world at the time of the destruction, so Anselm himself remained, one last embodied memory of that mythical land, ensuring that its legend, at least, would not perish.

"What will you do next, Master ibn Saul? Have you had enough of disappearing islands for a while?"

"I am not a poor man," he replied, "but having

hired a ship twice now, and having nothing to show for it but a glimpse of peaks rising above a bank of fog, I intend to confine my researches to more accessible places. I have still not seen the lands across the Indus, or followed the Silk Road to its far terminus, and I can travel with other people's caravans without having to finance them in their entirety."

"I don't think Lovi will be eager to leave on another voyage so soon. He hopes he will be able to find Gregorius again, in Burdigala or even Massalia."

"Who? Gregorius?"

"Master ibn Saul, were you daydreaming? Did you hear anything I . . ."

"I heard. But who is Gregorius?"

Pierrette felt a sudden chill. She chose her next words very carefully. "Didn't we meet him in Arelate, where we camped aboard the galley?"

"What are you talking about? We didn't stop at Arelate. We kept rowing, because the moon was full and the sky clear."

"I'm sure you're right, Master ibn Saul. I am sure everything will be clearer to me when I have fully recovered. But now I must see to Gustave's feeding. I'm so happy that you recovered him too."

"You can thank Lovi for that. He's the one who got kicked, hauling him aboard."

"I'll do that."

Now Pierrette's thoughts took an entirely new turn. Of course they had stopped in Arelate. They had spoken with Bishop Arrianus, who had foisted the vagrant priest Gregorius upon them. "Of course" there had been evil and shadows as well—

but not in this world. In this history, Minho's kingdom had not survived the eruption of Thera, Lovi had not been anyone's lover, and . . .

Gustave would have to wait. She questioned ibn Saul further while saying very little herself. What she learned was this: indeed they had been seeking a legendary island off the coast of Armorica, but it was the *Insula Pomorum* they sought, the burial place of the ancient Britannic kings—Avalon, not the Fortunate Isles. Now Pierrette's head swirled with conflicting memories: it was going to take years of study, in the eternal daylight of Anselm's library, to establish just how different the world was, without Minho in it. But that would be later. Now, she realized she had the opportunity to recover a treasure she had thought forever lost. . . .

"Why are we doing this? What is down here?" Lovi complained as he followed Pierrette into the darkness of the ship's hold. "What great secret is hidden here, among these bales of smelly wool? I can't see anything."

"Stop complaining. We don't dare bring a lamp down here. A fire among these bales . . ."

"I know. I know."

Pierrette wriggled between two bales, and emerged in a small open place. She reached back and grasped Lovi's hand. "You're almost there now. Come in."

"What is this place?"

"My secret nest. I have feathered it with my cloak."

"It's hot down here."

"Take off your tunic. We'll be here a while."

"How will I find it again in the darkness?"

"I'll make a light, later. Now do as I say." She heard his muffled grumbles as he struggled out of his garment. Then she stretched out her arms, and drew him to her. Her own clothing lay in a heap nearby. The springy hairs on his chest made her bared nipples tingle.

"You're not . . . you are not a . . ."

Pierrette giggled, and ran her hand across the front of his *bracae*. "Not a boy? Indeed not—but you surely are."

Even in that dark and stuffy place, a vagrant current of fresh air found its way to them, cooling the sweat that slicked Lovi's arms and shoulders, that pooled in the small of Pierrette's back as she sprawled on top of him. "What are you trying to do?" she murmured as he wriggled about.

"I want to see you! I can feel you, but I won't believe until I can . . ."

"Is that all? Stop thrashing, then. Here. I'll make a light." She whispered the words of the first spell she had learned as a small child. Just above her upraised fingertips appeared a faint glow, like sunlight through the haze of a summer morning, warm and welcoming yet without the heat that would come as the day unfolded. As it brightened, it gave her skin an olive cast, a lovely contrast against Lovi's pale, sun-bathed bronze, and it caused his hair to shimmer as she ran her fingers through it.

"Now do you believe?" she murmured. He did not reply, only cupped her small breasts in his hands, then stretched to kiss them.

Later still: "We must go soon, or ibn Saul will think we've fallen overboard."

"I don't want to go. When next I see you in your boy's clothing, I'll think this was a dream, and that you are only Piers."

"Would you care? Aren't you attracted to boys?"

He feigned a slap that became a caress. "I am attracted to *you*. Was I blind, before, or had you ensorcelled me? You were so cruel. I almost believed that I was . . . that I . . ."

"Never mind," she whispered. "I was cruel to you, but I suffered also. When first I deceived you, I knew no better. The goddess said I must remain virgin, or I would fail, and would become . . . ordinary."

"Never that," Lovi murmured.

"I did not dare let my feelings for you show, because I knew where that would lead. I was not wise enough to understand that there is a considerable space to wiggle in, between the words of a goddess's command, and what she really intends. A very wise man taught me that."

"I am grateful to him."

Pierrette glanced around herself, as if someone were watching them, there in that tiny secluded nest. Was it Aam, peering through the Veil of Years, feeling her heat and her happiness? Was it the Roman Calvinus, or Alkides, or all three of them? One thing was sure: it was not Minho, King of the Fortunate Isles.

"Welcome, my dear friends," she whispered. "Thank you for this gift."

"What did you say?"

"I was just wondering if you were content,

even though we did not . . . consummate . . . our union?"

Lovi laughed. "I won't complain. You must obey your goddess, and . . . and at least you're not really Piers, and a boy."

"There is that," she said as she laced her tunic and made ready for the climb back into the light of day.

The next day they moored at Burdigala, where ibn Saul hired a galley, and they made good time upstream over the next several days. Eager to be home, the scholar did not hesitate to hire a well-sprung Gallic carriage for the eastward leg of their journey on the Via Domitia.

Less than a month after Pierrette had been plucked from the sea, she found herself, again alone except for Gustave, on the heights above Citharista, just beyond the dragon's bones. At the last, a few miles back, even Yan Oors had left her, pleading that he had seen—and smelled—enough of cities on this one voyage to last him another lifetime as long as his own. She had parted from Lovi outside Massalia's Roman gate; even love—if that was what indeed they shared—had limits, and there was no place for her in ibn Saul's household, just as there was no place for another apprentice in Anselm's.

Far away and below, on the knifelike scarp called the Eagle's Beak, stood Anselm's fortress, unharmed and unchanged. East of the scarps, enclosed within crumbling walls, the red tile roofs of Citharista were like garnets set in the lid of a reliquary box. Had anything changed? It did not seem so.

That was no idle concern. Once before, when she had parted the Veil of Years, Pierrette had returned home, and a little boy named Cletus, whom only she remembered, had never been born. Soon—when she turned onto the trail that led to the beech grove, she would pass the foundation of an old house, abandoned when its Roman owners departed, and never reoccupied. In another history, one only she remembered, they had never left, and their descendant, little Cletus, had lived there, in a room never torn down for its stones. How often had she walked him home at dusk, because—in that world—the road had not been safe for a child, beyond the town's protecting walls?

Now Cletus was not, and never had been, and again, Pierrette had changed what was and what might have been. Did the vagrant Father Gregorius still regale Bishop Arrianus's subordinates in Arelate? Or had he turned north or west on some road leading elsewhere, and ended up in another town instead? Or had he never been born, his tall tales of life among the Vikings never told?

Her anxiety intensified as she descended from the heights and turned onto the northeastward trail. There stood two ancient olive trees, the remains of a grove planted by Greeks, two trees that had felt the heat of a thousand summers, whose roots had sipped of a thousand winters' rains. But the last time she had passed this intersection of paths, this crossroad where a small unnamed god presided over the choices men made of which way to go, there had been only one surviving tree and a gnarled stump—hadn't there?

A mile beyond that turning, swathed in brushy oaks whose leaves were no larger than her father Gilles's thumbnail, were the remains of the Roman fountain whose waters had once splashed into a man-made pool. The Romans had diverted waters from the sacred grove to fill that fountain, but now the trickle had regained its earlier course, and the fountain was dry. . . .

Now more anxious than ever, Pierrette quickened her pace, even as the slope steepened and the defile became narrower. Her thigh muscles burned with that effort. Her mind burned with another effort entirely: the sacred pool and the goddess would not be changed, she told herself. They had existed long before Minho had uttered (and now had never uttered) his terrible spell. They would not be changed.

When she clambered over the last blocky boulders that delineated the boundary between damp and cool, sere and dry, between tiny-leaved scrub oaks and moisture-loving beeches and maples, she was—slightly—reassured, because the air was indeed sweeter here, and the sun's rays were broken into small, dappled patterns that fell not upon dry gravels, but upon green, lush moss . . .

"Whatever for are you hurrying so?"

Pierrette spun around at the sound of the familiar old voice. She had not yet eaten a red mushroom or taken a pinch of the dried blue-and-yellow flowers from her pouch, but here, before her, in the same homespun skirt, patched and frayed, the color of old dried leaves . . .

"You don't need the spell any more," said the goddess *Ma*. "The barrier is gone. You need no mushrooms to deceive your mind, no deadly flowers to fool your body, before you can see me."

And so it was. Of those long hours until dusk dimmed the reflection of beech leaves upon the smooth waters of the pool, Pierrette has never spoken, so what was said there and then cannot be written down.

Perhaps she berated the goddess of the pool for tricking her, because the choice to save or destroy the mad king's realm had never really been hers. She had cast no great counterspell; she herself had been the goddess's weapon, and had brought the three things that destroyed Minho: the sorcerer Cunotar, the iron ring, and Father Otho's gift to her, a tiny golden cross.

Was the hand of the goddess at work when Father Otho gave it? He was no longer the good Christian he had once been (he knew better than to deny the existences of powers he could not understand) but Christian he remained, and preferred to think otherwise, and write only that Pierrette was a catalyst, and that whatever the ultimate causes, she brought what was needed, when it was needed.

Perhaps she was disappointed that her prowess as a sorceress was not tested, but it was better that way, because she harbored no guilt. She did not destroy the enchanted kingdom, or send all those ancient souls to whatever fate awaited them. As a Christian, of course, her chronicler chose to believe that the thousands who heard the Hermit's words gained access to a proper Christian Heaven, and that a forgiving deity gave Pierrette credit for that, pagan though she was. But only God can say.

When she at last returned the way she had come, it was the moon, not the sun, which cast a shadow ahead of her. She passed through the east gate of Citharista unnoticed, and slipped shadowlike through cobbled streets, passing her father's house, where warm lamplight spilled from beneath the door—but she did not stop there. Her father Gilles was within, unchanged, she was sure, and she would let him wait a while longer before announcing her return. Morning was soon enough to greet him, once Pierrette had ascertained just how new this new world really was, from the books in Anselm's library.

Were there still *Gallicenae* on Sena, or were they now lost in the mists of forgotten history, never written down? Were the accounts of Titus Livius, the tales of Homer and Virgil as she remembered them? After all, the destruction of "Atlantis" had spawned many legends and the lost Fortunate Isles many more. Perhaps the former tales were still told, at least. She would have to see if Plato's *Critias* still described that mythical land.

If that research took her an hour or a week, a month, a year, or a decade, it would make no difference. After all, Pierrette was already very, very old—though not yet eighteen—and only she and the mage Anselm would notice that time had passed, and would wonder how long it had really been.

Epilogue

The land is no less vast and no less ancient, and the loss of a kingdom here, a city there, cannot change it much. I, of course, cannot know the true scope of the changes Pierrette has wrought, for I am part of them, changed along with all the rest. But sometimes I awaken in the night, my bedclothes damp with icy sweat, having dreamed that hard cloven hooves were clattering on the floor of my chamber, with the reek of the demon's sulfurous breath swirling in my sleep-dulled mind, if not in my nostrils.

At times like those I am most grateful the world is a different place, because those dreams are not of this world at all. Perhaps I (though no sorcerer, and unable to part the veil and step through into the underworld at will) was not quite "here" at the critical moment when what was real became unreal, and the world took the shape it bears today. Perhaps in such dreams I am remembering how things once were. In this world, the Black Time is far, far away, and may never arrive, and Satan's name may be spoken aloud without trepidation.

But all is not again as it once was, before the Wheel of Time was broken. As if it were yesterday I recall a very small Pierrette who considered it unfair that the past should be an open book accessible through scrolls and dusty tomes, inscriptions on stones, and the contemplation of ruins, while the future remained remote and unknowable. That remains unchanged. The spell *Mondradd in Mon* still allows no single glimpse of the future. Neither mage, scholar, nor masc can penetrate *that* veil with spells, researches in libraries, or contemplation among the ruins of towering fortresses yet unbuilt. Only if some seer not yet born should look back upon this era and deign to speak might we be given a glimpse in that direction.

Still, sometimes, when I turn a corner or step from the gloom of a darkling wood, or open my eyes in the middle of an afternoon doze, I find myself in a magical place, where I spend an hour or two. Sometimes I meet a philosopher there, a saint, or even a pretty girl with no clothing but the luxurious fur God has given her kind, and a charming scut of a tail, like a doe's.

Pierrette tells me that was not always so. The Otherworld was not easily visited when a harsh and heavy cynicism bore down upon everyone and everything. But now—and don't ask me how I know—even if Pierrette's vision of a world dominated by great machines without souls comes to pass, I am convinced that there will still be corners to be turned, and naps to awaken from, and magical patches of sunny woodland where furry, uninhibited girls—and boys, as Pierrette insists—await us.

Otho, Bishop of Nemausus
The Sorceress's Tale

Afterword

I have already discussed the changing nature of myths, the mutation of names, and the sacred landscapes in the notes for two earlier books, *The Sacred Pool* and *The Veil of Years*, so I'll confine myself here to a few specifics of *The Isle Beyond Time*. See the earlier books for a comprehensive bibliography of sources for the three stories.

Place Names

I have used the Roman names for places, when I could, thus "Burdigala," not "Bordeaux." I am sure that by Merovingian or Carolingian times the transition was already well under way, but whether it was pronounced as "Bordala," "Burgala," or in some other intermediate manner is nowhere recorded. I have simply assumed that educated people might still be constrained by the older form, as written in sources available to them, if not to us today.

In other cases, such as the Ar Men Rocks out beyond Sena (modern Sein Island), I have chosen the modern Breton name, which sounds appropriate, whether its Celtic ring descends from the early Continental Celts or the much later "Briton" immigrants.

More or less

The Proto-Indo-European syllable *mor* had two meanings in Celtic languages. One meant roughly, "great," and the other "sea." Thus Morgana (mor + ganna, seeress) might mean either "great seeress" or "sea witch." Bishop Morgan (mor + geni, "sea-born"), Saint Augustine's opponent, latinized his name as Pelagius, while remaining mor + gan, "Great Seer" among his own Celtic adherents. The Celts were masters of double entendre.

The noun "merlin," which is a pigeon hawk, was given to Welsh Myrddin in the French-language versions of the Arthurian tales because "Myrddin" sounded too much like French *merde*. The old shaman and sorcerer might not have minded being called "Shit," but a noble lady of the court of Eleanor of Aquitaine wouldn't have gotten the joke, that compost, like Merlin, is indeed the product of sun god father and earth mother. After all, the *Morte d'Arthur* was Plantagenet propaganda, written to legitimize that Johnny-come-lately family's pretensions. Myrddin may derive from "Moridunnon" (mor + dunnum), which can mean sea-fortress, great fortress, or great strength, and his name is thus not unrelated to Bishop Pelagius as well.

The Tarasque

Pierrette's Christian tale about the monster of
Tarascon is the local tradition. The pagan tale is
my synthesis of a known element—that the Rhone
River (Rhodanus Flumen) contains the name of the
goddess Danu (as do the Danube, Dnieper,
Dniester, Don, Eridanus, and a score of other
rivers), and my speculation that the similarity of
"Taranis," a Gaulish god, and "Tarasque" is no
coincidence. The Ligurian or Celtic word ending
"asco" (also *asca*, *asci*, etc.) means roughly "of," thus
Taran-asco, Tarasque. The final tale comes cour-
tesy of my friend Alain Bonifaci, an architect from
Aix-en-Provence.

Taking Liberties

The cylinder seal Minho gives Pierrette is stylis-
tically Minoan, but the superposition of a star chart,
a calendar, and a map of the Breton Coast is, of
course, fantasy—though the idea that the Minoans
may have been better navigators and mapmakers
than anyone else up to the nineteenth century is
hardly new. Needless to say, Pierrette's ability to
determine latitude from the North Star requires a
bit of magic as well as good eyes.

For the convenience of my readers I have used
our modern convention of placing north at the top
of maps. Map makers of earlier ages more often
oriented their charts, that is, read them with east

at the upper edge. The same motive led me to presume a "year" beginning at the winter solstice, roughly our New Year, so the "tenth moon" on the seal would fall in October.

The settlement of Iceland is conventionally dated to the latter part of the ninth century, its conversion to Christianity considerably later, but there are hints (Diciul's A.D. 825 tract, for one) of an earlier Irish hermetic or monastic presence. My "Thule" is not Iceland, not exactly, nor is it the first Thule recounted by Pytheas of Massilia in the fifth century B.C., but it partakes of the spirit of such remote places, where strange bedfellows might make common cause against a hostile land and an inimicable sea.

I combined several historic shrines (at Gennes, Behuard, and Pil de Mars) on the Loire (Liger) into one place, for the story's sake, and may have nudged some villages, streams, and islands a few miles from where they might turn up on a current map. But of course Pierrette's world is not ours, not exactly, and who's to say?

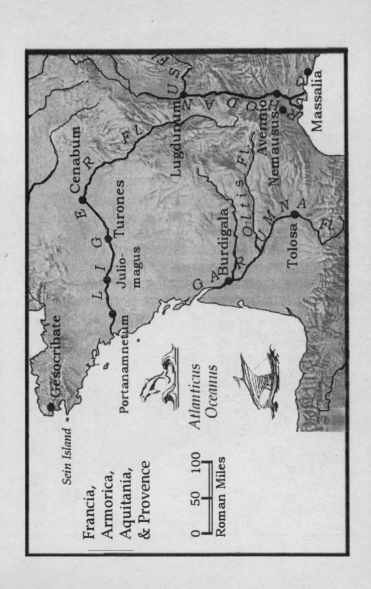

Francia,
Armorica,
Aquitania,
& Provence

Sein Island • Gesocribate •

Portanamnetum

Atlanticus Oceanus

0   50   100
Roman Miles

Cenabum

L I G E R

Turones
Julio-
magus

F L.

Lugdunum

Burdigala

O L T I S   F L.

G A R U M N A

Tolosa

Avennio
Nemausus

Massalia

F L.

TIME SCOUTS CAN DO

In the early part of the 21st century disaster struck—an experiment went wrong, bad wrong. The Accident almost destroyed the universe, and ripples in time washed over the Earth. Soon, the people of the depopulated post-disaster Earth learned that things were going to be a little different.... They'd be able to travel into the past, utilizing remnant time strings. It took brave pioneers to map the time gates: you can zap yourself out of existence with a careless jump, to say nothing of getting killed by some rowdy downtimer who doesn't like people who can't speak his language. So elaborate rules are evolved and Time Travel stations become big business.

But wild and wooly pioneers aren't the most likely people to follow rules... Which makes for great adventures as Time Scouts Kit Carson, Skeeter Jackson, and Margo Carson explore Jack the Ripper's London, the Wild West of the '49 Gold Rush, Edo Japan, the Roman Empire and more.

The Time Scout series
by Robert Asprin & Linda Evans

Time Scout	87698-8	$5.99	___
Wagers of Sin	87730-5	$5.99	___
Ripping Time	57867-7	$6.99	___
The House that Jack Built	31965-5	$6.99	___
For King & Country (HC)	7434-3539-7	$24.00	___

THE SHIP WHO SANG IS NOT ALONE!

Anne McCaffrey, with Mercedes Lackey, S.M. Stirling, and Jody Lynn Nye, explores the universe she created with her ground-breaking novel, The Ship Who Sang.

THE SHIP WHO SEARCHED
by Anne McCaffrey & Mercedes Lackey

Tia, a bright and spunky seven-year-old accompanying her exo-archaeologist parents on a dig, is afflicted by a paralyzing alien virus. Tia won't be satisfied to glide through life like a ghost in a machine. Like her predecessor Helva, *The Ship Who Sang*, she would rather strap on a spaceship!

THE CITY WHO FOUGHT
by Anne McCaffrey & S.M. Stirling

Simeon was the "brain" running a peaceful space station—but when the invaders arrived, his only hope of protecting his crew and himself was to become *The City Who Fought*.

THE SHIP WHO WON
by Anne McCaffrey & Jody Lynn Nye

"The brainship Carialle and her brawn, Keff, find a habitable planet inhabited by an apparent mix of races and cultures and dominated by an elite of apparent magicians. Appearances are deceiving, however . . . a brisk, well-told often amusing tale. . . . Fans of either author, or both, will have fun with this book."
                                                                —*Booklist*

Got questions? We've got answers at

BAEN'S BAR!

Here's what some of our members have to say:

"Ever wanted to get involved in a newsgroup but were frightened off by rude know-it-alls? Stop by Baen's Bar. Our know-it-alls are the friendly, helpful type—and some write the hottest SF around."
> —**Melody L** *melodyl@ccnmail.com*

"Baen's Bar . . . where you just might find people who understand what you are talking about!"
> —**Tom Perry** *perry@airswitch.net*

"Lots of gentle teasing and numerous puns, mixed with various recipes for food and fun."
> —**Ginger Tansey** *makautz@prodigy.net*

"Join the fun at Baen's Bar, where you can discuss the latest in books, Treecat Sign Language, ramifications of cloning, how military uniforms have changed, help an author do research, fuss about differences between American and European measurements—and top it off with being able to talk to the people who write and publish what you love."
> —**Sun Shadow** *sun2shadow@hotmail.com*

"Thanks for a lovely first year at the Bar, where the only thing that's been intoxicating is conversation."
> —**Al Jorgensen** *awjorgen@wolf.co.net*